ALSO BY CHARLES GAINES
Stay Hungry
Pumping Iron (with photographs by George Butler)

Dangler

By

Charles Gaines

Simon and Schuster • New York

Designed by Martin S. Moskof
Manufactured in the United States of America

1   2   3   4   5   6   7   8   9   10

Library of Congress Cataloging in Publication Data

Gaines, Charles.
Dangler

I.   Title.
PZ4.G138Dan   [PS3557.A352]   813′.54   79-29744

ISBN 0-671-25281-X

This book is dedicated to my parents,

Margaret Shook Gaines
and
Charles Latham Gaines, Jr.

Three things are necessary for the salvation of man:
to know what he ought to believe; to know what he ought
to desire; and to know what he ought to do.

—St. Thomas Aquinas

Become first a good animal.

—Ralph Waldo Emerson

·

ONE

·

Back to Back

I

_____

For five years before he went away to prep school Kenneth Dangler marched with the Knickerbocker Grays, and the experience had affected him as permanently as polio.

Though Cobb hadn't known him at the time, he had a clear image of his best friend in the white trousers, gray tunic and plumed cap, armed with rifle and sword, marching down Park Avenue in the annual Church Parade alongside one hundred ninety-nine other fancy little soldiers: Rockefellers, Harrimans, Fishes, Vanderbilts. A spring Sunday, the lilt of "St. Julien," flags and guidons snapping —and all along the avenue, from Sixty-sixth Street to St. Bartholomew's Episcopal Church, murky potato-eaters gape at the precision, the far-apart eyes, high foreheads and sharp noses of these miniature empire builders. That was how Dangler learned to walk, under scrutiny of the rabble, and by the time he got to Andover his fourteen-year-old step (even from the dorm room he shared with Cobb to the john) was permanently arrogant.

Like most things about him, the walk had set up early and stayed the same, Cobb noted as he followed Dangler and Erica out of the marsh. His own walk, pushed to keep up with the long-legged Danglers, felt a little shaky. He had arrived at the camp late the night before and had proceeded to eat and drink too much to sleep well. And on top of that, there had been the disorienting duck hunt this morning.

They had come into the marsh by Land Rover a couple of hours earlier, just before dawn. Dangler and Erica had taken two of the guides up to the north end of a small pond near the center of the marsh, leaving Cobb and his guide at the south end. While the guide moved the gear into a blind, Cobb had stood outside in the foggy predawn silence. Watching the decoys begin to take shape on the dark water, he had filled his head with the smell of the cranberry bog and tried to remember everything he knew about duck hunting. For a number of seasons he had shot at wood ducks along the Contoocook River, and at one time he had read everything he could find on the sport. Woodies, he figured, were probably the only ducks that used this pond. But there might also be some blacks. He had seen black ducks occasionally, flying above the Contoocook, but had never taken a shot at one. Thinking about them while he watched the decoys made Cobb feel suddenly wide-awake and excited.

A few minutes later, all he had felt was mystified. Swaddled in camouflage clothing, he lay flat on his back atop some sort of padded table that seemed to the creepings of his right hand to be covered with naugahyde. Hanspeter Gruenig, his guide, had motioned him onto the table as soon as Cobb crawled into the blind, and though Cobb hadn't much wanted to, he had mounted it.

"How am I supposed to shoot at anything lying on a table?" he had asked after a few seconds of prostrate silence.

"Couch," said Gruenig from behind him. "A Gruenig Shooting Couch. And I vill put you in position. All you haff to do is pull the trigger, sport. You know vair the trigger iss?"

The first ducks were wood ducks and they came in at 6:50, exactly when Dangler had said they would. A couple of minutes before, Cobb had been turned abruptly, with a nasty hydraulic sound from the couch, to face south. He had decided not to speak to the ill-tempered guide again unless absolutely necessary, so he said nothing, assumed he was meant to pot anything within the dome of his vision, and only wondered what shooting from his back might do to the vertebrae.

He heard the ducks coming, whistling like tree frogs, apparently at the same time Gruenig did, for just as he lifted the gun, the upper half of the couch shot up forty-five degrees and locked. Suddenly Cobb found himself reclining as if on a chaise, in perfect position to the flock of eight or nine ducks, and being swung from right to left along the path of their flight. Despite his surprise, shooting from this position was so natural and effortless that it seemed automatic, like another function of the couch. Turning evenly with the ducks, he picked one near the middle and fired. As that one fell, the last bird flared, flashing its white belly, and climbed over Cobb's head. Instinctively he tracked it with the gun and was thrilled to feel the top section of the couch tilt smoothly back with the bird's flight. It fell two feet from the blind.

"Not bad," said Gruenig.

"God. You . . . that was wonderful," Cobb said, struggling to sit up. "This couch thing is just wonderful. Where the hell did it, uh . . ." Really seeing Gruenig for the first time was an unsettling experience. His whole face seemed to drain toward the middle down the peasant slope of his cheeks. His hair, and a sort of mustache that was shorter than his upper lip, were skimpy and fox-colored and his eyes were narrow and silver, like slivers of mirror, and absolutely empty. ". . . come from?" Cobb finished, and lay back down on the couch. Gruenig had been looking back at him as if he weren't all that crazy about what he saw either.

"I invented it. Next time vait to shoot until the dox are further over the pond. You sent two of them back. The Danklers got only five below."

They stopped shooting at 8:10. By then the pond was littered with ducks, and aside from the woodies, Cobb had never seen any of the species before; he had never even heard of two of them. Each flock had come in ten minutes after the one before it. After Cobb had shot a duck or two out of a flock, he would stop firing and ask the guide what he had just killed. Gruenig would check his watch and identify the bird with a grunt.

At 8:10 nothing happened.

Seconds later Cobb heard Gruenig snap his fingers and curse, and seconds after that Dangler's voice floated imperiously down the pond.

"Yaaah?" answered Gruenig.

"Where the hell are the ruddy ducks, Hanspeter?"

"I forgot to tell you," Gruenig shouted. "Ve are out of them."

"*Out* of them?" said Cobb.

Gruenig flipped up the couch. "You can get up now, sport," he said. "That's all she wrote."

While Gruenig and the other two guides gathered up the ducks from canoes, Cobb had stood with Dangler and Erica outside their blind. The fog had burned off, leaving a delicate and perfect morning. Sun sifted down through the evergreens to the pond and the air was cool and warm at the same time.

"Did you enjoy yourself, Andy?" asked Erica.

"It was wonderful. I do have one question, though—small thing."

"Shoot," said Dangler.

"How do you do it? Even you. I didn't know there were this many ducks in the state."

Dangler seemed pleased. "We order them from all over the country. They're released from a tower about a mile south of here at ten-minute intervals and fly to the pond because they are fed here every day. We try different ones every month or so."

"But I thought you meant a real hunt," Cobb said. "I even bought a license."

"We like to make it *seem* authentic—shooting at dawn and all. But there isn't any duck hunting in this part of New Hampshire. The season isn't even open. Gruenig usually spoils it by telling people. How did you two get along, by the way?"

"He seemed a little rude as a matter of—"

A trumpet had interrupted him. It was playing Reveille. Though the sound was distant, every one of the maniacally cheerful notes was separate and clear. The three of them listened without moving or speaking. Erica stood by Cobb with her hands on her hips, her long hair pulled back and tied, her face and throat flushed to the second button of her chamois shirt. A slight breeze stirred. The morning was fully achieved, every shape as clarified as the phrases from the trumpet . . . but everything looked wrong to Cobb. The strong light and cool air had him suddenly exhilarated and dizzy, and in the brightness everything seemed grotesquely unreal: ducks flying out of a tower? Reveille in the middle of a *marsh*? He looked around for some reality to test.

As Reveille died around them, Dangler murmured, "Whether it's at work or play, find a challenge every day."

"Excuse me?"

"That's our motto here," said Erica.

"There's no need to chew on sticks, Andrew," Dangler had said then, clapping Cobb smartly on the shoulder. "We'll get you some breakfast and then show you the rest of the camp. You haven't seen anything yet."

Yards behind Erica and Dangler now, Cobb scrambled up a steep bank and into a spacious piny wood where all the trees seemed to be the same size and placed at the same comfortable distance from each other. It was resinous and shadowy in the woods. Dangler marched jauntily over the brown needles, whistling as he walked, in as fine fettle as Cobb had ever seen him. Cobb himself felt distant. The combination of little sleep the night before and the eccentric hunt seemed to be coating the landscape: everything he saw had a sort of crazy sheen to it.

A hundred yards or so into the woods they passed a cottage. Built of stone and cedar, it blended expensively into the trees. "Hare's Den," said Dangler, waving at it. "The de Fauriers." A moment later they passed another one. "Grouse House," he said.

There was a middle-aged couple coming out of Grouse House. Dressed alike in chinos, red flannel shirts and hiking boots, they stopped on the porch and blinked at the sunny September morning. Dangler gave three liquid yelps and a hoo.

"Good morning, good morning," boomed the man.

"Good morning, Chief . . . Erica," said the woman, and tried a timid little yodel of her own.

Dangler waved without turning. "The Watermans," he told Cobb. "Solid campers."

They came out of the woods within sight of the house by a pruned hedge that ran along either side of the mile-long gravel driveway. As they turned up the hedge, a bell rang.

"That's the breakfast bell," Dangler said. "We're on the nose."

"It's too loud," said Erica. "I've told you that bell is too loud."

Dangler kept walking. "Has to be, love. These people are used to sleeping right through . . ."

"It's too *loud*, Kenneth. It drives every animal in the state up a *wall*."

Dangler looked at her. "OK, darling. I'll quiet it down."

"*Now*, please," she demanded.

"I'll take care of it after breakfast." Dangler took three military strides to his wife's side and put an arm around her, but she shivered him off and stalked up the hedge.

"Just needs a little exercise," said Dangler cheerfully. "She gets antsy without exercise."

"Right," said Cobb, massaging his eyes. "Right, right . . ."

Erica waited for them on the flagstone steps to the house. Sitting on the top step between two marble dogs, she watched them come across the wide gravel turn-around in front of the house. In the center of the circle was a fountain in which green marble fish stood on their tails spitting. Cobb, feeling her gaze, tried to keep the fish between himself and her for as long as he could. He had discovered that it made people nervous to be stared at by Erica Dangler.

She was an inch or two over six feet and proportioned so precisely that she seemed to have been engineered. Her face was delicately planed but heroic, with an emotional mouth, a square jaw, and green eyes that were calculating and unafraid as a shark's. On neither of their two previous meetings had Cobb been able to look at her for very long without his mouth beginning to sag. She seemed to fetch and threaten at the same time, like some snowy mountain peak.

"Excuse my manners, Andy," she said as they came up the steps. There were campers coming out of the woods on both sides of the drive, looking scrubbed and bright. The Watermans passed them on the steps, nodding. Then a man and another couple. Erica stood up and gave Dangler a quick funny look. "Can we eat upstairs? I'd really rather."

"Sure," he said. "Tell the kitchen and go on up. Andrew and I will be along in a minute." He took Cobb's arm. "You get to assist the matinals."

"I'd rather eat."

"Earn it," said Dangler, and led him through the brass-bound door and the cavernous entrance hall, where he picked a newspaper from a silver tray, down a long central hallway to the dining room. Like the rest of the house, the room was arch and Arthurian. Light entered in solemn diagonal lances from high clerestory windows. On the dark paneled walls hung heraldic shields and crossed swords, along with the dusty heads of collared peccary, mountain goat and bison. Pewter gleamed in stout oak cupboards, and the floor was stone. Dangler stood in the oval entrance, tapping the newspaper against his trousers until all the campers were seated at the twenty-foot mahogany table. Twelve smiling, affluent faces beamed up at him. In front of each was a slice of cantaloupe, a linen napkin in a pewter ring and a glass of milk.

"There will be no afternoon hike today," said Dangler when the room was quiet. "The men are improving the trail. For those of you who will be with us into the winter, Hanspeter will be starting cold-weather classes this afternoon at four-thirty in the lake cottage." He looked around the table, smiling paternally. "I won't be eating with you this morning, but have a challenging day." Then he raised his hand and bowed his head. "Lord . . ." he said conversationally.

"Lord . . ." repeated the campers.

"Bless this food to our use," they went on together, "that we may bring renewed enthusiasm to the enjoyment of Thy gifts. Help us today to find and meet new challenges, to struggle and to triumph, and to continue with cheerfulness and bravery to fight the good fight. We ask this in Christ Jesus' name. Amen."

"That prayer . . ." Cobb said on the way upstairs.

"Mine. Just about covers it all, doesn't it?"

"What good fight are you fighting, exactly?"

"You'll find out," Dangler told him.

Erica was reading *Vogue* in a lounge chair on the porch off the bedroom, surrounded by potted plants. Breakfast stood on a warming oven, and a table was set near her chair. She had changed into a pale flowing gown that exposed large areas of tanned chest and shoulders. Her hair was untied and her face was flushed.

"How do you feel?" Dangler asked as he came onto the porch trailing Cobb.

"Better. Hungry, Andy?"

"Starved. Aren't you cold like that?"

"Feed him, Kenneth. There's some of that new ham."

"You'd better put on a sweater," said Dangler.

"I'm getting some sun. Have you asked him yet?"

"Not yet." He handed her a cup of coffee and poured for himself and Cobb.

"Asked me what?"

"In good time, Andrew. Come over here a minute." He was standing at the balcony looking eastward. At the far edge of five or six acres of clipped lawn was a pond with a brook running out of its north end. Beyond the pond were light woods and then immense Lake Webster, its surface gleaming in the sun.

"I don't remember the pond," said Cobb.

"It's new. I had it put in last month for fishing. We can skate and curl on it in the winter. The brook, incidentally, is full of those little spotty trout you like." He pointed north to a small domed building. "Bubble tennis court over there. Beyond that's a new pigeon range."

"You've done a lot since June."

Dangler smiled. "Wait until you see the mountain. I've cut two downhill trails and put in a special lift. Built an approved thirty-meter ski jump, a cresta run . . ." He trailed off and leaned over the balcony.

"And he did it all in six days," said Erica. "Now, how about getting some food on the table, hot shot?"

After three buckwheat cakes Cobb felt better. Things were beginning to appear normal again, and he chose to ignore a developing sense that all was still not right with Erica. She remained in the lounge chair as he and Dangler ate, thumbing her magazine, sipping coffee and speaking infrequently, but seeming to Cobb somehow to swell. Then Dangler mentioned that he wanted to take Cobb up to the mountain the next day to show him the machinery.

"Afraid not," Cobb said. "I'll have to get back this afternoon."

Dangler sighed and shook his yellow head. "Ah, we grow older, Andrew. Affections and loyalties wane . . ."

"Come on, Kenneth," said Erica. "For Christ's sweet sake."

"I'd like to, but I'm working on a divorce case," Cobb said. "I have to prepare a trial brief."

"What matter old friends, tested and true in their devotion? Divorce cases are where life really is." Dangler held up his hand. "No, no. I understand. Doubtless it's your fascination with these things that has kept you from so much as one lousy visit in four months."

"Three. I was up here for the camp's opening."

"And that caused you to leave early on my birthday . . ."

"Leave him *alone*, Kenneth. Can't you leave him alone?" Erica shrilled.

"All right," said Cobb, fearing trouble. "What can I do for you?"

Dangler leaned to him with great dignity. "Do for *me?* Listen, buddy, Dangler's International Adventure Camps represent probably the most significant human experiment in the second half of this century. Ask what the hell I can do for *you.*"

"Camps? I thought there was only one."

"There'll be others. Four in this country, one in each corner. Three in Europe, and one on each of the other continents. This thing is going to be more popular than money." He took Cobb's plate. "Have another piece of pig. It's cured with rum."

Out of the corner of his eye Cobb saw Erica jerk and sit up. "OK," he said amiably, "what can you do for me?"

"Just stick around until tomorrow. Let me show you what we're doing up here."

"What *are* you doing up here? Besides shooting tame ducks."

"Things of great pith and moment. And that's my point —you don't know. That hurts me more than I can say."

"I get your literature," Cobb said. "It all sounds pretty strange, to tell the truth."

Dangler looked at him, chewing a tip of his mustache. When he wanted something, he had a way of looking at people that made them feel compliance was the same thing as self-improvement. Unblinking, unnervingly assured, his blue eyes would fix the subject. You will be a better human being, they seemed to promise, if only you do what is being asked of you. Cobb messed with his ham. "I would like to know how it works," he admitted. "I guess I can stay until tomorrow morning."

Erica slammed her magazine to the tiles and flew off the couch, her thick hair whirling. "Bastard," she screamed at Dangler. "You manipulative bastard . . ."

Before she had made three steps across the porch, Dangler caught her around the waist and held her. She struggled for a minute and then went limp. Dangler led her to his chair and eased her into it. "Your best friend," she sobbed, "and he's a *lawyer* and all, and has things to *do* for people." She looked around with unfocused eyes, then snatched up Dangler's coffee cup and clamped it to her mouth.

"Fine," said Dangler. "That's fine now." He winked at Cobb and disappeared through the glass door into the bedroom.

Cobb looked at Erica pressing the porcelain to her mouth as though to stop a bleeding, her eyes frantic and vague, and wondered if all this might seem more intelligible if he had slept better the night before. He was on the point of asking Erica if there was something he could do when Dangler reappeared at the door holding a gleaming double-barreled shotgun.

Cobb leaped to his feet and backed against the balcony. "Please put down the gun, Kenneth," he said quietly as Dangler raised the shotgun neatly, squinted down the barrel, took a practice swing, and fired. Two feet to Erica's left a pot of geraniums exploded brightly, raining petals, dirt and shards of clay across the porch.

The cup didn't even tremble in Erica's hand. Cobb realized that he had been staring at her face ever since Dangler appeared with the gun, unable even to blink. Now he watched her eyes close, softly, as if in a drowse. When she opened them again, they were focused and clear, returned to their preternatural calm.

"Sweetheart?" she said, putting down the coffee cup, "I don't think I'll join the tour this morning." She uncoiled lazily from the chair, tossed her dark head and drifted over to Dangler on the gauzy billows of her gown. She laid her arms across his shoulders and tilted backward slightly at the waist. "I'm a little tired from the hunt this morning. I think if you and Andy will excuse me, I'll take a nap before lunch."

"Fine, darling," said Dangler.

They were both smiling, mingled in each other. Dangler pulled her waist to him and bent along her curve, brushing her nose with his. Then he kissed her slowly and gently, as if they had just finished a long quiet talk. Their position was so classical, their attentions so lost in one another, that they seemed briefly to Cobb to disappear from the porch, to separate from the morning and float back into some sepia print of Victorian love.

II

————

Cobb had never heard the place referred to as anything but a summer cottage, a term that had always seemed to him to drip with decadance. Even before Dangler started fussing with it, the property included eleven thousand acres, seven lakes, an entire river system, part of a mountain range, twelve miles of paved roads, numerous outbuildings, and Wildwood—the seventy-four-room main house. Constructed of cedar and stone quarried on the property, the house contained between stout castellated towers a museum collection of armor, a three-thousand-volume library of sporting books and a hundred and sixty mounted heads—all of it collected by Dangler's great-grandfather, who had had the place built near the end of the last century as a base for his lumber interests and then retired to it for the last five years of his life to drink Scotch whiskey and hunt, undisturbed.

Killing animals had been the central passion of the old man's waning years. To insure himself of an accessible variety, he placed a thousand-acre corner of the estate behind a ten-foot fence and filled it with Russian boar, aoudad, sika deer, Asian ibex, Corsican rams and blackbuck antelope. By the time he died at eighty-nine, much of the fence had been destroyed by falling trees and poachers; there were 300-pound snaggle-tooth Russian boar rooting all over the northern third of the state, and many a backwoods family had dined on hoofed ruminant mammals they didn't know the names of.

There were still plenty of boar around, coming and going like pet pigs through the property when Cobb first visited Wildwood in the summer of his fifth-form year at Andover. Largely because of them his strongest memory of the place was a hair-raising sense that this was as far up as civilization would stretch—that beyond this was where the lions were, off to the north in the blue haze and building storms of the White Mountains.

He and Dangler stood on the back veranda looking over the polo field to the river, lying haphazard and bright as a ribbon at the base of Mount Webster. Above the mountain a red-tailed hawk hung motionless in the sky, the air around it glittering with wildness. Between the house and the river Dangler had cut down thousands of first-growth fir and pine, creating a huge perky meadow of unlikely-looking playing surfaces. He had reduced acres of coniferous fastness behind the house to the trivial-looking organization of a summer camp, and Cobb found himself wondering idly if that weren't dangerous somehow, this far up in the woods.

Dangler pointed riverward with a black briar walking stick. "We'll end up down there. There's a show I want you to catch at eleven-thirty."

He had changed into a tan bush jacket and leather boots that laced to his knees. A pair of binoculars hung around his neck. He had said nothing about the scene with Erica, and Cobb, whose sense of propriety was always larger than his curiosity, hoped that he wouldn't.

Dangler took his arm. "We'll start with the hockey field I built for the girls. It makes them feel like they're back at Emma Willard." He paused, squeezing Cobb's arm. "Actually, we have a wonderful life together. Erica's a wonderful girl and we have a wonderful life together. The thing at breakfast didn't mean diddly-squat."

"Fine, fine," said Cobb, looking energetically around the porch.

After the hockey field Dangler took him to a raised asphalt oval. Guy-wired to it was a powder-blue helicopter with "Adventure Camp Wildwood" stenciled on its side.

"I've got another one ordered," Dangler told him. "Ask about ice."

"How about ice?"

"There are heating pipes installed under the asphalt to keep it off," he said, moving on.

Walking east behind the house, they looked at the croquet lawn, the spanking-new gray-green Apsite bubble housing two Acrylex tennis courts, and six outdoor Laykold courts with Devoe glare-baffled lighting, the boccie-ball alley, and the horseshoe pits. Cobb inspected it all in silence, nodded to Dangler's enthusiastic descriptions of pitch, sun compensation and surface life, watched a skinny male camper in knickers play two lonely wickets of croquet, and three others, each on a separate Laykold court, bat at balls being thrown across the nets to them by machines. He was led next across a lime-lined softball diamond to the front of the house, then south through an orderly woods that seemed identical to the one they had come through earlier that morning, and out onto a service road that ran east and west from the driveway to the lake.

"You're puffing." Dangler had made the road a good fifty yards ahead of Cobb and was studying a squirrel's nest with the binoculars when Cobb emerged, red-faced, stripping off a sweater.

"I just don't see the point."

"In what?"

"In *any* of this. Specifically in hurtling through these goddamn woods."

"We are hickory-tough up here, Andrew, keep that in mind—you who so recently were a mediocre stroke for Dartmouth. We don't spend our days going to pot in a law office in Concord." Dangler eyed him sharply, adding, "Exhaustion makes cowards of us all."

"Screw you. I shouldn't have come. That insane opening of yours in June should have been enough to—"

"Just *snap back*. We haven't even begun."

Cobb batted furiously at a pod of burrs on his corduroys. "But what are you doing? What's the *point* here? A bunch of middle-aged people playing campers. I mean, *God*, Kenneth—all these games . . . the waste of money."

"You'll get the bottom line, boy. You'll get the master plan." Dangler waved the stick down the road at a group of rectangular buildings with mansard roofs shingled in pale new cedar and strode toward them. After briefly reviewing the options, Cobb followed. "That's the nerve center of the operation—maintenance, machine and cabinet shops, generators, pumps, sewage treatment, warehouse . . . everything you need to run a town the size of Roanoke, Virginia, in there."

Just beyond the nerve center, at the top of a knoll where the road began to dip toward the lake, a huge saffron building bloomed from the pines. "I had that thing built for the staff," Dangler went on. "We have twenty-two full-time people now. Since you were here last, we added the chopper pilot, three more recreation assistants, a barber-hairdresser and a nurse. Knowing your curiosity about such things, their salaries plus operating expenses total out to around seventy thousand per month. But at four thousand dollars per guest, twelve guests per session and two sessions per month we're grossing almost a hundred in the same period, so—amortizing the land taxes and not counting capital expenses—we're not losing much. Is this boring you?"

"These people pay two thousand dollars a *week* here?"

"They get their money's worth. It gives them, how should I say . . . a grip on the rest of their year. I am sensing a nasty reluctance of real interest on your part."

They had stopped within sight of the lake. Off to their left was the stable, a place Cobb remembered. It was one of the estate's original buildings, built of whole cedar logs and set picturesquely into the woods at the end of a gravel path. Behind it was a riding ring and beside that a fenced pasture where five or six Morgan horses grazed, necks bowed, hides rippling. Cobb stood in the warm road nodding, resting his eyes on the quiet plausibility of the scene, his temper improving.

"I *am* interested," he said. "You know I'm interested in everything you do. But you've had projects like this before."

"Not like this one."

"The Luxury Safaris . . . ?"

"Not thought out; no commitment."

"The hotel in Nepal?"

"Absentee management. Question of commitment again. This is different. I have drawn a line in the dust with my boot. I am thirty-five years old: the Adventure Camps and I will stand or fall together."

Watching him speak, Cobb was moved for the second or third time that morning by a new quality in Dangler's face, something he had seen somewhere else but couldn't place. The old playful irresolution of his features, the charming aristocratic look of going in four directions at once, seemed to be gone. His face looked reduced and re-fined somehow, as though it had been run through a filter. Something, it appeared, had changed with Dangler.

"OK," he said. "You have my complete attention."

The cool vaulted boathouse smelled of varnish and punky logs. From overhead beams hung thick winching chains and hooks. Floating in separate bumpered slips were two twenty-foot lake boats, a Boston Whaler skiff, three canoes and a Sailfish. Fifty yards out in the bright purling lake a couple in matching red Windbreakers secured a din-ghy to the moorings of a blue-and-white Star and helped each other aboard, their arms full of puffing yellow sail.

"Erica actually came up with this thing in Rye, but it wasn't until we came to New Hampshire that we really got our hands around it. There were all these people up here, retired executives, artists, people who inherited something, all of them able to do what they want, who had moved here to live like Cree, you know—close to the land. But they were coming apart—drinking themselves into comas, di-vorcing, shooting themselves. It was even worse than in Rye. And why? The *woods*, Andrew. The wild. We studied it. They start off well enough. They take walks, paddle a canoe, listen to loons. But their legs can't take it. Or it's too cold, or the blackflies are out, or they get lost. They find out the woods are something they don't deal in anymore; pretty soon they stop getting near them, and then all those trees turn into negative space. People quit seeing them. The woods become just what's between you and Boston—and that, my friend, is when you're in trouble. There's nothing *up* here, you say. There's nothing *out* there, Edna—no good Camembert, no Wyborowa vodka, no Henri Bendel's. Frenzy sets in then, you see."

They walked north from the boathouse along a man-made beach ribbed with rock jetties to protect it from wash-out. A quarter of a mile offshore was Dangler Island, at whose center, Cobb remembered, was an ancient Louisiana gazebo, all its lacy trellised woodwork intact, that Dangler's grandfather had found in New Orleans, dismantled and shipped to New Hampshire for use as a picnic cottage.

At the end of the beach they turned into the woods on a path that led shortly to the pond Cobb had seen from Dangler's balcony at breakfast. It was fiddle-shaped, with sloping grassy banks. Separated from it by a succession of aerated pools was a low concrete building. In each pool was a different population of salmonoid fish: Kamloops, cut-throat and golden trout, coho and chinook salmon. Inside the hatchery building was a maze of bubbling tanks, feed bins, oxygenators.

"Here's the way I make it," Dangler went on. "Up until, say, a hundred years ago, everybody had to scratch just to stay alive—just for shelter and food and whatnot. Living was combat, you see—moving rocks out of your cornfield, building fences, chopping wood. That's the history of the race, and the impulse to struggle is as much a part of our evolved equipment as the opposable thumb. Then, presto, all at once in the magic of history there's nothing *real* left to struggle against. We reach the other shore. Everybody's rich and insured and fat, and there's nothing left to fight. So what happens then, Andrew? . . . We turn on *ourselves* is what happens."

A stream ran from the north end of the pond, its flow controlled by gates. They followed it, past slatted casting piers that jutted into the current above each pool, past a cage with a black bear in it, for nearly a mile to the loud south bank of the Monnussuc River.

"And the wild . . ." said Dangler, "the wild is both the problem and the solution."

It was 11:15. The river was fifteen yards across where they stopped, broadening from the mountain's east slope where it pincered down through clefts of limestone strata into a thick concentrated glide. Just below, it was splayed by a field of boulders into distracted rushes and foot-high waves. A goshawk circled downstream above a dead beech. The tracks of a hunting coon left a stand of fir, followed the bank, and disappeared into a raspberry thicket.

"What we're doing is giving people real but harmless things to struggle with. Surrogates, like old Hugo back there. We're giving them *natural* confrontations, and ones they can win. We're putting them back in touch with a nature they can deal with, Andrew."

(Hugo—eight years old, brindle to sable, four hundred pounds, born in Maine and trained by a circus trainer in Boston—had been sitting in his ample cage picking at his chest with declawed paws. The cage, made of iron bars and concrete, lay astride the path by the stream. One end was enclosed to form a hutch, the other sloped down the bank and five feet into the water, providng the bear with a fishing-wading area. Blue Styrofoam mats covered the central floor of the cage; it was on one of them that Hugo sat picking at his chest. Cobb had seen the creature before on the weekend of the camp's opening, thinking then that he was only there for the occasion, for something like scenic effect. Now he learned that Hugo was meant to be wrestled with; was, in fact, a professional human wrestler who had never won a match or caused an opponent so much as a bitten ear. "An artist," Dangler called him. "Even with the muzzle on, he growls it up. There's one camper from Hartford who wrestles him every afternoon. When Hugo feels the fellow tiring out, he rolls over and flops his head on the mat. That means he gives up.")

Dangler checked his watch and squatted on the riverbank facing upstream, one surprisingly muscled hand fiddling with his walking stick. Just downwind, Cobb caught the smell of witch hazel, a lotion Dangler used so persistently that its odor seemed a permanent part of him. His long yellow hair and mustache were afloat in sunlight. His face inclined to the river, throwing off glare. Cobb, squinting to look at him, thought: Custer. It was the same seized, blond unambivalence that charged out of an old daguerreotype portrait Cobb owned of George Armstrong Custer at twenty-five.

"See, it's really a business we're in. We're selling top-quality revitalization, and these people don't even notice the two grand a week they pay for it. They'd pay five, because we produce. We do what we advertise, and what we advertise, humbly put, is the best leisure-time package ever marketed." From a pocket of his bush jacket he produced a small expensively printed brochure and handed it to Cobb. "Second page, please."

" 'What Adventure Camp Wildwood Offers You,' " Cobb read at the top. " '1. A self-sufficient resort community, open from June 1–January 31, providing luxury accommodations, gourmet dining and morning stock quotes in a controlled wilderness setting.

" '2. A 4-season world of supervised sport and adventure, including: golf, trail-riding, fishing, bird-watching, polo, all-weather tennis, sailing, softball, field hockey, archery, petanque, canoeing, boccie, hiking, four types of shooting, swimming, croquet, rock-climbing, bear-wrestling, mountaineering, big-game hunting, skiing, curling, dog-sledding, cresta, and more.

" '3. Individual activity programs hand-tailored to your interests, abilities and medical profile, and supervised by a personable recreation staff. First-run movies, lectures, chamber music, bingo, and other activities to enliven your evenings.

" '4. A vitalizing daily intimacy with our great natural heritage of water and forest, mountain and marsh, that will write out a new lease on your passionate inner nature.

" '5. Revived senses and slimmer, healthier bodies, effortlessly achieved by the robust, carefree life here.

" '6. Our specialty: controlled natural challenges that allow you to prove over and over again to yourself the supremacy of man, and to taste the keen exhilaration of physical adventure.

" '7. A healthier, saner, more confident you. You will return home better able to cope with the stresses of life outside the camp and with a greatly reduced will toward conflict.' "

"All it is," said Dangler proudly, "is what the whole world is looking for."

"It's certainly imaginative," said Cobb.

"Is that your final word? How about humane, no-ble . . ." Dangler was interrupted by a turmoil of sound coming from upstream. He held up a hand. "Now, watch the faces here. The faces are the thing."

The noise hastened at them—a yipping, a moan, a re-signed male bleating—materialized at the first upstream bend, riding the current in an eighteen-foot birch-bark canoe. There were four people in the canoe, a man in the bow, another in the stern and two gunwale-clutching women on the floor between them. Coming out of the bend, the canoe picked up speed and hurtled down the long fast glide in front of Cobb and Dangler. The men made desper-ate tossing motions with their heads and worked their pad-dles furiously, flailing more air than water. The one in the stern kept hunching oddly to port as though to body-en-glish the canoe ashore. As they sped by, one of the women spotted Dangler lolling on his haunches. Her eyes gathered themselves, sprang from the boat and coiled around him. "Chieeeeeef . . ." she wailed, her arms open.

"Yodelahee-oo," said Dangler without much feeling. At the head of the rapids the canoe hung for a moment and then plunged among the rocks.

"They're all going to be killed, of course," said Cobb mildly. "I can only hope you have sufficient counsel."

"I don't. That's precisely the point, but we'll get to that in a moment. Just keep watching."

The canoe shuddered through the first rip into an eddy near the far bank, slewed back into the current inches above a piano-sized boulder and shot miraculously through a gap between two smaller ones on a white plume of water. The man in the stern had gone rigid and was clutching his paddle in front of him at present-arms. The other whipped his back and forth across the bow without changing grips, making frenzied punches at the water that seemed to man-age, somehow, to keep the canoe on a clean course through the rocks.

Cobb felt casual enough to whistle as he waited—for the splintering crash, the cartwheeling canoe, the water full of bobbing bodies. But the boat shot on, lurching through haystacks, cutting crosscurrent and once even *up*stream to clear a half-submerged tree. And then it was gone—

through the entire rapids without a scrape and out of sight around a bend to the left, trailing one thin female scream. After a moment it was quiet again except for the rustle of the river. Cobb waited awhile before he spoke, conscious of being at the apex of some Dangler-designed momentum, paused at the peak of a swing.

"Well?"

"Well what?"

"Why the hell aren't they dead?"

"The canoe is on a track. There are ball-bearing wheels connected to a fixed plate between the bow and the center thwart that have locked articulation with a four-rail underwater track. Allows the boat to pitch without yawing. It's Gruenig's design. And of course the campers are strapped into place. It's all very safe. It took six men three months just to lay a mile and a half of track."

"But how do you keep them from knowing? I mean, all that yelling. . . . Don't they *know?*"

"Of course they know. It's like a roller-coaster ride— the mind knows you're safe but the body doesn't." Dangler looked at him warmly. "Do you know the word *accidie?*"

"No."

"Late Latin. It means spiritual torpor. Condition of numbed inertia. It's what's killing off our class of people. And *that,* Andrew, is what we're after. We're in the business of destroying it wherever we find it and however we can." He walked a few steps down the bank and turned around. "Frankly, we need you on the team."

"Excuse me?"

"You know how to dream. We need that. We want you to sign on as full-time attorney in residence for the rest of the season. We'll be back to back again . . . and I'll give you a thousand a week plus room and board."

III

———

The next morning Cobb drove to Concord in a pelting rain. Somewhere around Bristol his Volkswagen developed a steering problem that made it drift like a gum wrapper over the wet road. When he finally floated up in front of his office, he pulled up the hand brake, lit his pipe and watched the wipers for a moment. Then he got out, leaving the car running in the middle of Centre Street.

All the buildings on that street were rickety little colonial homes restored into law offices. Cobb's was called Farrow, Perch and Oldham, and after eight years he still had to check the sign sometimes to make sure which of the red-brick, double-chimneyed, white-shuttered buildings it was. This morning there was a doleful drip of water falling from the beak of the American eagle over the sign.

Grace Hurd, his secretary, had a runny nose of her own. She was holding a lavender Kleenex to it with one hand and working an adding machine with the other when Cobb came in. His office was on the street side of the building and consisted of two tiny crooked rooms with hand-stenciled wallpaper, a chandelier and a view of the gold Capitol dome across the street. Grace liked the office, Cobb did not. But he stayed, backing into filing cabinets for her pleasure in the view of the dome.

In that way and others Grace Hurd controlled most of the spaces of his life. She had done so convincingly for a couple of years now, ever since a weekend in March shortly after she began working for him, when Cobb succumbed to a number of carnal curiosities about her—the way she licked her lips when she talked, the smell of her tweed suits, her hiker's legs—and, at her suggestion, took her off to the Trapp Family Lodge at Stowe, Vermont.

"I am a lot of woman," she told him simply on the drive up. "I will probably ski you into the ground up here. And if this works out, I'm going to redecorate your house."

She had been redecorating it ever since. She also bought his groceries, washed his clothes, paid his bills and read his mail.

"Welcome home, Pooh," she said through the tissue. "How was that crazy friend of yours? The Costello brief is on your desk, and a new divorce libel. Your father called yesterday. . . . And, hey, I ordered a Hoosier cabinet for the kitchen. Oh, Perch says not to forget your squash game at noon." She blew her nose, threw the Kleenex away and smiled at him. "God have I got a bitch this time."

"Look, I can't stay. I have to take the car to the garage."

"No you don't. It was serviced two weeks ago."

"It's *broken,* Grace. The steering doesn't work."

He picked up the new libel from his desk and looked at the first page. Elizabeth Sward, of 42 Taylor Terrace, Webster, N.H., was suing Robert Sward, of the same address, praying for a decree of divorce from the libelee, permanent custody of three minor children to this marriage, and for an order of support for herself and said minor children.

"Hook's office sent it over," said Grace, licking her lips. "He's representing the wife himself, so it has to be a shakedown."

Cobb sat on the edge of his desk and scanned the papers, looking for something of the man he was supposed to counsel. Halfway down the page he read:

> Your libelant testifies that she has always behaved as a
> dutiful wife, yet alleges that the libelee, heedless of his
> marriage vows, is and has been guilty of extreme cruelty to
> your libelant at various and diverse times in said Webster, so

as to seriously injure her health and endanger her reason, to wit: on the evening of July 17, 1978, the libelee did strike the libelant in the face with an Antonio Zoli Model #14 muzzle-loaded rifle, causing her a fractured nose and doing extensive damage to her lower jaw. . . .

"I don't want it," said Cobb, tossing the libel back on Grace's desk.

"Nobody does. Perch sent it down to you." Grace stood at the shuttered window looking out through the gray drizzle at the gold dome, her powerful legs planted wide. She poured a cup of coffee and sniffled.

"Well, send it back anyway, goddammit. I won't take it. Besides, I'm thinking about going . . ."

"Hey!" Grace said. "Hey, Pooh. Chambers is out there writing up your car, I hope you know. I hope you know that. You *can't* just go around leaving your car in the middle of Centre Street."

"I have asked you not to call me that," said Cobb. Walking stiffly to the window, he found himself wondering what Dangler's campers did when it rained.

"It's not every day," Erica Dangler had told him the night before, "that you get a chance to do something for the world and for your best friend at the same time." She said it a little haughtily, Cobb thought, her jaws locked into the slight Massachusetts malocclusion that made her look to be clenching something in her teeth as she spoke. Being a little tight, he had laughed.

They were in the library, where she had taken him just before dinner and closed the carved oak doors, turning after a second to face him, her hands resting on the twin brass doorknobs at the small of her back in a posture so emotionally accurate that she made it look original. She was sheathed in a floor-length black dress, a single strand of pearls at her throat. Her rich hair galloped around her face and shoulders.

Cobb, in a blazer and sport shirt, had just learned that everyone at the camp was expected to dress for dinner; he had decided that there was no way he could do what Dangler wanted him to do; and he felt now, alone with Erica, who lingered on the door, staring at him across the Aubusson carpet, like someone picked off the street to play a scene with Greta Garbo. He sucked at his third bourbon and soda as Erica let his opening laugh hang and dwindle on the air between them.

"There's some more of that stuff behind you," she said, waving disdainfully at a bar in the rear of the library.

"I'm fine."

"You are, aren't you? All set up down there in Concord with your goat and your farmhouse and your squash games and your skiing. Like a bug in a rug."

"Drink?" said Cobb, making for the bar.

"Kenneth and I have one Jack Rose cocktail before dinner. It is served in ten minutes."

"You don't mind if I . . ."

"I simply wonder what your fluids have to say about all that poison. Have you ever listened to your fluids on the subject? But the point is, you're not going to do it, are you?"

"I have a practice, Erica. People who depend on me."

"Have you told him yet?"

"No. I tried, but he asked me to sleep on it."

"Has he ever turned you down when you needed him?"

"He doesn't need me. He can put any lawyer in the state on the retainer to do what he wants."

"But he wants *you*. And he wants you here. Can't you *see* anything . . . how involved he is in this? How much he needs people around who love him and understand what he's trying to do? What could you *possibly* be doing that's more important than showing love and support for Kenneth?"

Later—after a Currituck duck dinner with the campers and some of the staff, who stared at him as though he might be a sanitation inspector staying over for a meal, and after the bourbon, one Jack Rose cocktail, four glasses of wine and two snifters of cognac—Cobb took himself for an unsteady walk around the grounds to try to sort things out.

He stood on the flagstone lip of the fountain and watched the illuminated marble fish. He walked down the drive, his loafers slipping on the gravel, feeling emotional as he always did when he drank, sighing and talking to himself. The three-quarter moon had a pearl-gray nimbus around it, boding rain. It was still rising, a faceless, ungenerous moon arcing out of the south, and it caused Cobb as he shuffled up the road to muse on longitudes and coincidences: on the dark azimuthal curve of continent connecting this place that great-grandfather Dangler had invented out of northern wilderness, to Jacksonville, Florida, where Cobb had grown up and where the same great-grandfather had first begun hacking, down one coast and up the other, the railroad that opened up the state and made his name as common there as Ponce de León's. The phrase "sidereal time" occurred to him.

"The kingdom and the power . . ." he muttered to the moon, imagining as he said it the Dangler name, each letter spelled out in giant lightbulbs, forming an enormous rainbow-curved marquee down the East Coast—the D situated in the sky right above Wildwood, the N blazing over Baltimore, the L over Cape Fear, and the final brilliant R marking the exact sandy spot outside Jacksonville where the first Dangler obsession had begun. ". . . with God on your side, who needs a divorce lawyer?" he wondered aloud.

The thought made him feel a good bit better—it made things seem easier.

At the top of a small rise about a half-mile from the house Cobb stumbled to a halt, thinking he heard music. He listened, turning his head like a dog in the pine-fragrant air; then he moved a few steps down the road and listened again. The sound was coming straight out of the woods to his right. He stalked it, creeping through the hedge and around trees until he was close enough to recognize it. It was a country-music song, a song he knew every deep-South country word of.

> . . . *shake it loosh and let it fall*
> . . . *lyin' soft against your skin—*
> *like the shadows on the wawwl . . .*

" 'Come and lay down by ma side,' " Cobb murmured along, " 'till the early mawhahawnin light . . .'

"Oh, my God," he said quietly. Somewhere out in those dark Yankee woods Sammi Smith was singing "Help Me

Make It Through the Night." Her voice was thin with distance, lost and out of place as a sweetgum tree among the pines, but she was out there, by God. Foggy and sentimental, Cobb sank to his butt in the pine straw and listened.

From where he sat he could see through the trees the lights and outline of Wildwood, and behind it the vast looming hulk of Mount Webster. Against the mountain the enormous house looked temporary and insignificant as a stage set. As he listened to Sammi, awash in the loneliness of the song and drunk as a coot in the moonlit woods, a couple of things ran together in his mind and Cobb began to sob—softly at first and then in great throaty gasps.

"We're all so small," he choked. "Kenneth's not any different . . . we're all just *human,* for God's sake, and we all need friends. Ahhh, God, Andrew, can't you *see* how much we all need help from each other?"

". . . let the devil take tomorrow," the song went on, planing to him through the dark. ". . . for tonight I *neeed* a frennn . . ."

"Sing it, Sammi," Cobb had shouted into the still trees, his voice breaking. "Tell em how it *is,* honey."

Bob Perch sat on a bench in the locker room of the Concord YMCA, holding his squash racket by the throat. Perch was five years older than Cobb, a full partner in the firm and casually expert at law, his marriage, friendship, and almost any sport you could name. Cobb liked him fine. Perch was the closest thing to Dangler he had found since college.

"You'll need at least five points a game today," he told Cobb. "I've already hit with Neal, and I'm dynamite."

Cobb yawned and opened his locker. "OK," he said. "I'll take them."

Even with the points he lost three games in a row, though Perch played lazily, hogging the middle of the court, chewing gum and using his reach instead of running. Cobb, who could usually play him almost even by chasing down every point, lost his concentration early and quit trying. Sometime during the second game he developed a nearly desperate claustrophobia.

Then midway through the fourth game, down nine to three and preparing to serve, Cobb glanced over at Perch. He was settling himself into the swaying semicrouch of professional tennis players that it pleased him to assume while receiving service. Crouching at the center line, his left hand supporting the neck of the racket, he stared at the back wall and swayed musically back and forth from the ankles. Cobb turned around to face him, dangling his racket at his side. He had seen Perch do this hundreds of times before without being offended, but this time the motion seemed so fatuous and studied, so hopelessly familiar and trite, that Cobb could have screamed. Staring at Perch, he realized how badly he needed a change.

It was a full thirty seconds before Perch interrupted his swaying to look over at Cobb.

"What the hell . . ."

"Hey, Bob, you know that libel you sent down about the nut with the muzzle-loader?"

"*Serve,* goddammit."

"Well, you've got it back. I'm going to go have some fun for a change," Cobb said, tossing him the ball and heading for the door.

He called Wildwood from the Red Blazer, where he and Perch went to lunch. Cobb was lightheaded with pleasure by then, realizing that he was doing what he had wanted to do all along. And Perch, after some initial kidding, had said he would help work things out at the firm.

A male voice, thick with accent, answered the phone.

"Yah," it said.

"This is Andrew Cobb. Is Mr. Dangler there?"

"No."

"How about Mrs. Dangler?"

" . . ."

"I said, how about Mrs. Dangler?"

"Who is this, please?"

"This is Andrew Cobb, Hanspeter. Look, would you give Mr. Dangler a message for me? Tell him I've changed my mind, I'm coming up."

"Does Mr. Dankler know you?"

"This is Mr. *Cobb.* I shot ducks with you yesterday."

" . . ."

"Would you give Mr. Dangler my message, please?"

"You are the von in my blind yesterday?"

"Yes. Tell him I'll be up in about a week."

Gruenig made a liquid chuckle into the phone.

"Maybe I should call back," Cobb said, his pleasure in the call disappearing. "You know, rudeness never made a dime, buddy."

"Are you afraid of bears, Mr. Copp?" Gruenig's voice now was high and teasing. "You know ve haff bears up here. Und big pikks. . . . Maybe you saw von of them las' night, yah? Maybe that's vhy you vas out screamink and cryink in the voods . . . ?"

IV

———

Sitting at his desk in the basement of Wildwood, Hanspeter Gruenig cleaned his nails with a penknife and chuckled for nearly five minutes after he talked to Cobb. When the conversation no longer seemed amusing to him, he dictated an order to Sacramento Waterfowl, Inc., for two dozen pintail ducks, looked over the job application of a pastry cook, phoned in an order to Curly Labeau's Sport Shop in Colby, and wrote a memo to the electrician about quieting the meal bells. Then he went to look for Dangler.

It had stopped raining. Clear weather was riding down from the north on a fresh breeze, and as Gruenig walked over the softball field, behind the fish hatchery through the woods to the lake, the Canadian air stirred him. It had a taste to it of winter, his favorite season. He felt light, savage and happy.

In the boathouse he untied one of the twenty-foot lake canoes and paddled out toward Dangler Island, whistling "Okie from Muskogie" and enjoying the strength of his wrists against the chop.

As he neared the south end of the island he could make out the mast of the Sailfish in the cove where Dangler hid it on the frequent visits that he and Erica made here alone. Gruenig had discovered the practice one morning while water-skiing a camper and since then he had spied on it regularly, more or less equally for the views it provided of Erica and for its anecdotal value back in town if he ever figured out what was going on. So far, he was stumped; he had no idea what to make of the crazy games and wild talk that transpired out here between the Danglers—though he sensed that they were really just an ornate form of something simple, like the shed at the center of the island. And because he didn't understand what was happening, or how to feel about it, he couldn't be sure yet how to represent it to Curly Labeau and Tom Clover and the rest of the boys in town. He wanted to save the story until he could tell it with authority, so he waited, crouching once or twice a week among the evergreens that skirted the gazebo, in a humid quandary of lust, disdain and curiosity.

This afternoon he beached the canoe and moved into his usual position behind a hemlock tree on the mainland side of the island, within thirty yards of the gazebo. The little octagonal building sat fancily on a knoll, separated from the open lake by a grassy slope that gave onto a sand beach. At the top of the slope Kenneth and Erica Dangler, dressed in matching white shorts and blue sweaters, lay on their stomachs, facing the lake and talking.

Kneeling noiselessly behind the tree, Gruenig caught a thread of the strange cool scent that followed Dangler everywhere and felt the hair at the back of his neck rise. Gloating on the keenness of his senses and on his perfect stealth, he peered out from behind the tree to discover that the line of his sight ran directly between Erica's long coppery legs.

"Remember buying the almonds in paper cups on the beach?" she was saying. "And that white dust up in the hills?"

Dangler didn't answer her.

"All right, do you or do you not remember the festival in Mandouki—walking around with that huge bottle of ouzo that Doak bought the baby carriage for?"

"Bottom line," said Dangler.

"Wait a minute. Let me do the drive down to Sounion."

Erica shifted onto her side, changing Gruenig's view to a shining slope of thigh and hip. As she talked, she picked up and let fall the thick blond hair on the back of Dangler's head—just picked it up and let it float back in a lazy, winnowing motion that affected Gruenig strongly in the loins. Hunkering closer to the mossy earth, he unzipped his fly and, watching Erica, tried as hard as he could to imagine that her passionate talk, about pistachio nuts and salt flats and whales, had something to do with him.

"Not bad," said Dangler when she finished. "But we're not leaving New Hampshire now for all the pistachio nuts in the world. Besides, the Greeks are oily and revolutionary."

"A long vacation, then."

"Maybe next year. During the break."

"Kenneth, it's about these people here. I mean, I know it was my idea, and I love your perseverance, but I can't find you sometimes . . . and there are all these *grundges* around from Lake Forest and Canaan."

"That's the clientele."

"But why us?" Erica came up suddenly to her knees, wringing her hands, her voice rising. "Why should we be the ones sacrificed? We don't *need* this."

Spent, chewing on a pine straw, Gruenig felt an unaccountable inclination to run. What the fok? he asked himself.

"Yes we do," said Dangler. "Do some push-ups."

"It's not *fun* anymore, with you always off somewhere, checking something. I neeeed you, Kenneth. You said we'd do everything together."

"Most things."

"But you said *everything*. You *promised*." Erica sprang to her feet and looked wildly around, the panic in her eyes freezing Gruenig. "Oh, God, I might as well be a fruit fly!" she screamed directly at his tree; then she clamped both hands to her open mouth. What happened next remained in Gruenig's memory as a crazy blur, hectic and inaccessible as a dog fight.

"I am going to *burst*," wailed Erica through her fingers, and then she was on the ground and she and Dangler were wrestling each other, grunting and churning up the earth beside the gazebo. For a few seconds they fought evenly;

then Dangler seemed to gather her up. With his legs and arms he locked her to himself and rolled around with her until she stopped struggling. For a long time they lay together, Dangler on top, without moving but whispering and crooning oddly to each other. Finally Dangler lifted his head and looked at her. Moving slowly, he freed a hand, picked a damp strand of hair from her face and kissed her.

It was the way people kissed in movies, Gruenig noted. He heard Erica moan, and with a dizzying rush of excitement thought: he's going to plug her right there on the damn grass. Anticipation and mystery cut him like a wind, and he shivered slightly against the tree.

"I want to be your skin," Erica said. Her face was tilted up, her eyes closed. Gruenig could see the shine of her lips and a small vein pulsing at her temple. "I want to be so close to you that I can hear your blood."

Propped above her, Dangler dipped a hand and traced each of her features, describing it with his forefinger, then bent to kiss it.

"You *are*. . . ." He held her face, cupping it in his hands, and touched his tongue to her nose, her cheeks, to each eyelid. "You are my life—my heart and my mind. I love you more than anything on earth."

My God, thought Gruenig. In his glands he felt the moment rise and hover near some loud, Cinemascopic consummation, and as he waited he realized that this was it, this was why he squatted out here day after day. He *had* to see this happen.

Erica opened her eyes and stared at Dangler. Then she pulled his head to her chest and held it there, stroking his hair.

"Couldn't we . . ." she said. There was a strange silence. "I adore what you're doing. No one could do it but you."

"*Do* it," Gruenig pleaded.

"I'm sorry I nerved out on you . . . and on a tea party." She began to cry.

"It's all right," said Dangler. "Everything's going to be fine. I love you more than life—it's as simple as that. And as soon as we get things moving here, it will be just like before, but even better. Then we can go to Greece for a while, or anywhere you want to go."

"I'm fine. I'm fine now . . . but I love you more."

There was another silence. Then Dangler sat up, grinning.

"What we need is a little proof. I'll race you to the north end of the island and back."

Scuttling over the loose rocks toward the canoe, nearly blind with frustration and hampered by a second erection in less than fifteen minutes, Gruenig was in a killing frame of mind. As he neared the water, he looked around for a lizard or something to stomp. And then, all at once, his anger disappeared and he began to laugh. Gushing mysteriously, the laughter grew on itself, seizing him so completely that after he had pushed off the canoe and back-paddled fifty yards from shore to make it look as though he were just coming in, after he had yodeled three or four times and Erica Dangler appeared on the rocks to demand what he was doing out there, Gruenig was barely able to speak.

"Tell the chief," he shouted to her, his voice warbling hysterically, "the dox are ordered, the bells are beenk fixed, and that crybaby who vas yesterday in my blind—he says he is comink here."

Andrew Cobb studied the hill of exotic equipment piled on his lawn. It had taken him a week to buy and borrow it all, and this was the first time he had seen it together.

"I may have to rent a trailer," he said to Grace Hurd.

"Why don't you just buy one? Your fancy friend wouldn't think twice about just buying one."

She sat on his terrace, dressed in her gardening clothes, dipping early-turned maple leaves into a pan of glycerin and water. Each fall she preserved enough leaves this way to dress a full-grown tree. Then she stuck them in vases all over Cobb's house. Like canning her own vegetables, saving grocery bags and making all of Cobb's Christmas-tree ornaments, the leaf preserving was part of a pinchpenny Yankee frugality that Grace referred to as "making do."

"If you don't have an oil well, you have to make do to live in the country," she would say.

"Waste not, want not." She would also say that, and

had, in fact, just a few minutes before, as Cobb tore into the cardboard box containing a new pair of Galibier Superguide mountaineering boots. "That is a perfectly good box."

She had been sniping at him all week, for his decision to go to Wildwood, for his choice of friends and, particularly, for the prodigious amount of money he was spending. Cobb was tired of it.

"Look," he had told her, "I come from a generous part of the country where people do not hoard things like squirrels against the winter. I am a grown goddamn man who pays his own way and I will waste precisely anything I want to waste."

Now, as he looked at the heap of stuff, trying mentally to stuff it all into his Volkswagen, he wasn't so sure about the grown-man part. What lay on the ground in front of him looked very much like a thousand dollars' worth of toys.

The list of things he was supposed to bring with him to the camp had reached Cobb a little over a week ago by telegram. It was the sort of communication Dangler loved, glinting with brand names and specifications. For years Cobb had received similar messages from all over the world, cataloging his friend's pursuits since Harvard. Once, from Prague, Marseilles and then Cologne, Dangler had sent him a series of war correspondences, one a week for two months, in the form of fat, energetic cables that bristled with troop strengths and deployment, artillery capacity and topographic information, concerning a small but elegant ground war created by Dangler solely for the sake of the correspondence.

Before "the war" his lists had come from places like Yucatán, East Africa and Brazil, and were mostly straightforward inventories of the equipment and hazards involved in an imaginative variety of physical adventures. But after it, his interests had swung to the abstract, focusing on individuals ranging from Hannibal to Cochise—"men of pith and moment," he called them—whose accomplishments moved him and whose legends he tracked, often into remote corners of the world, collecting facts and dispensing them to Cobb. In March of 1970, for example, Cobb had learned from Missolonghi, Greece, that Lord Byron on the day of his death there weighed less than eleven stone, that his last meal consisted of two spoonfuls of arrowroot, and that his parting words were, "I want to go to sleep now."

Shortly after Missolonghi, Dangler left for Ireland in pursuit of Cuchulainn of the Red Branch but discovered Erica instead, and the letters had stopped. That was seven years ago, and Cobb had found that he missed the lists—or, more precisely, the sense they had afforded him of being involved in beautifully crafted purposes, however eccentric; of participating, even if vicariously, in the massive, meticulous assaults that Dangler mounted on life.

What he really missed was Dangler, Cobb realized as he stood on his lawn staring into the pile of expensive new gadgets and feeling in his chest the same incipient excitement he had felt all week. In Dangler's company he had always felt a little charmed—as if anything could be done, and as if anything that could be done would have to turn out well. More than anything else, he missed that feeling in his life right now.

He closed his eyes, and an image formed behind them. He and Erica and Dangler were in a canoe, at the head of a long rapids that any sheep could tell was wicked. The water below sounded like a high wind. Erica sat on the floor of the canoe, looking vexed. Cobb grinned at her from the bow, and then at Dangler, who winked at him, looking like Custer around the eyes, and said, "That, boy, is important water." Still grinning, Cobb slid to his knees, bracing his thighs against the sides of the canoe, reached for a stroke and yelled out over the roar of the water. . . .

"Are you asleep out there or what, Pooh?" asked Grace Hurd.

She was standing on the edge of the terrace staring out at him, her hands on her hips, her head wagging in a long-suffering tilt.

"I'd better come out there and help, or you never are going to get this thing off cock."

"Let 'er rip, goddammit!" Cobb shouted at her.

V

His first week at Adventure Camp Wildwood left Cobb feeling like a gunslinger who had ridden from Dodge to Tucson to back a friend's play, only to find that he had misread the note.

Before leaving Concord he had convinced himself, if not Grace, that Dangler was in trouble—that his request for Cobb to "join the team" was really a face-saving plea for help. To support this conviction he had formed an image of the camp as hopelessly snarled in a web of unworkable ideas, peopled with rebellious, litigation-minded campers, and of his best friend—recently reduced to shooting flowerpots—as fending for his life with a bent sword.

"OK, where do we start?" he asked on his arrival, expecting a kind of war council. "I want you to know I'm here for the distance." He threw an arm over Dangler's shoulders.

Dangler had just helped him move his stuff from a U-Haul-It trailer to a suite upstairs in the main house. They were standing in a large, high-ceilinged sitting room. Connected to it were a bath and an even larger bedroom.

"Teddy Roosevelt stayed in these rooms whenever he came here boar hunting. It is my hope that you will occupy them with as much verve as he did."

"Right. I brought along three boxes of verve, as a matter of fact. Now, where do you want me to begin?"

"I think by unpacking," Dangler said. He looked around at Cobb's things. "Where are the snowshoes?"

"Somewhere in there. I meant on our . . . legal situation."

"Oh," said Dangler. "Don't worry about that. Begin anywhere you want."

Except at meals he saw very little of Dangler over the next few days, but he did see plenty of Erica. After breakfast on his first morning he carried his books and files down to the basement office he'd been given next to Gruenig's, and had just begun to wonder how to occupy himself when she appeared, wearing jodhpurs, and announced that they would begin with a trail ride.

"I have to work."

"At what?" she asked him. "The fact is, you won't really know what to do until you've poked around a little."

For the rest of the week, for two hours every morning and every afternoon, during the camp's "Activity Periods," she had him sailing, riding, playing tennis, hiking, bicycling, water-skiing—all of which she did passionately and tirelessly, and with such infectious pleasure that despite Cobb's suspicion that Dangler had detailed her to get him into shape, he enjoyed himself. Between athletics she led him around the camp introducing him to guests and staff, showing him through the kitchen, the shop, the greenhouse, explaining equipment and procedures—doing all this intimately and a little shyly, as if the place were an unusual game that she and Dangler had made up and she was teaching him to play it.

She was relaxed and gentle in a way Cobb hadn't imagined she could be. She was playful, pliant and funny. She hung on his reactions, watching him with defused eyes, and everything he said seemed to delight her. Charmed nearly witless, he followed her around, loudly approving the pig yard, the garbage-removal system, the infirmary.

And after a day or two of observing the camp, his skin began to tingle. It began to tingle in response to a small hum, like the sound of a vacuum cleaner in a far-off room. The hum had nothing to do with Erica. He had heard it before—once while eating crabmeat in the dining room of the Homestead Hotel in Virginia, and for an hour one late afternoon drinking sherry and reading about Jess Willard in the library of the New York Racquet Club, and for several days straight returning from England on board the *Mauretania* with his mother. He knew what it was. It was the sound of things being done right, of the right service being provided at the right time—of people being made comfortable and happy according to some exact, perfectly correct rhythm.

Dangler's taste and talent for luxury were everywhere: in the dozens of cut flowers arranged throughout the house each day, in the beds made every morning with fresh Irish linen monogrammed with the family crest; from the hand-squeezed juice and sterling-silver pots of coffee and copies of the New York *Times* delivered to each cabin on a tray at Reveille, to the hot-water bottle placed in the foot of each camper's turned-down bed at night. All day the huge staff glided through the house emptying ashtrays, polishing silver and brass, replacing coffee-table copies of *Town & Country, Barrons,* and *English Country Life,* and filling orders from the campers for Mt. Gay rum and Dr. Laszlo soap, while outside the service road swarmed with trucks and cars delivering fresh seafood and fruit from Boston and wine and Cuban cigars from Montreal, bringing to work maintenance men and gardeners and bonzai-tree experts from New York, and string quartets or hypnotists or lecturers for the evening's entertainment.

This flow of goods and services through the camp, massive and constant as it was, was so well organized that it was barely noticeable except by its results. The day-to-day life of the place seemed to float above it all like a partying Caribbean windjammer on a late night current.

Impressed, Cobb asked Erica how they had managed to pull everything together so neatly in only four months with no experience.

"It's Kenneth. He's possessed," she said without smiling.

Another surprise was the campers themselves. In line with his other pessimisms, Cobb had expected, at best, a snooty contingent of mannish women with sailing tans and men in Lily pants on leave from Watch Hill; or, at worst, a bunch of braying oil tycoons with fat wives. What he found was an energetic group of large, smiling, childlike people. He discovered that he liked most of them. They put him in mind of Polynesians.

"Who are these people?" he asked. "What do they do in real life?"

"Own the country, mostly," said Erica, and led him to a calf-bound ledger in which Dangler listed and classified every camper who came to Wildwood. Quite a few, Cobb noticed, had stayed for two and even three two-week sessions, and one couple, a Mr. and Mrs. Peter Bigelow from Avon, Connecticut, had been there ever since the camp opened. Among the names were Morgans, Drexels, Astors, Pierponts, Gores, Lowells, Vanderbilts.

"I see," said Cobb. "You stacked the place."

"Not at all. Anyone can come. They just happen to like it here."

"I don't see a Rockefeller. No Mellon . . ."

"We had a Mellon. All he wanted to do was shoot woodchucks. Kenneth had to put him in with the D's."

D stood for "Doubtful or deficient characters." Along with the E's ("Egregious in the extreme"), they were listed in the back of the book. The names in front were classified by a letter printed beside them in red—a C for "Common camper, welcome, neither especially advantageous nor disadvantageous"; a B for "Better than average, some distinguishing talent or trait"; or an A, for "Advanced camper, admirably suited to the aims of the camp."

"We took the system from the Lake Placid Club," Erica said. "D's and E's don't come back, and C's aren't encouraged to. We're aiming at a small, regular group of A's and B's."

What surprised Cobb most about the two A's, five B's, three C's and two D's presently at Wildwood was how intensely they believed in the place. Here were twelve certified members of America's ruling class, their eyes and talk brimming with camp spirit, singing songs and jingles, and engaging all day in a schedule of activities that seemed to Cobb like something a berserk scoutmaster might have invented.

A sheet called "Your Camp Day" was posted throughout the main house and in the cabins. It read:

8:30 A.M.	Reveille
9–10 A.M.	Breakfast
10–12 noon	Morning Activities
12–1 P.M.	Bouillon Hour
1–2 P.M.	Lunch
2–4 P.M.	Afternoon Activities
4–5 P.M.	Classes
5–7 P.M.	Free Time
7–7:30 P.M.	Cocktails
7:30–8:30 P.M.	Dinner
8:30–10:30 P.M.	Evening Entertainment
11 P.M.	Taps

Activities were divided into Group A, "Sports and
Games," and Group B, "Adventures and Confrontations."
Each camper was encouraged to balance his schedule between the two groups, and to vary it daily. On a Monday
morning, for instance, he might choose an hour of archery
from Group A and a ride on the tracked canoe from B.
That afternoon he might play a game of petanque (A), then
take a hike (B) in the heavy woods east of the house, on
which, if he chose, he could become separated from his
guide and "lost" until dinnertime. On Tuesday he might
wrestle Hugo the bear, play a round of golf, fish for salmon
and take a late-afternoon ride on one of the trained "runaway" horses.

The combinations were often so bizarre that just hearing how someone had spent the day could produce in Cobb
a sensation close to motion sickness. Yet, improbable as it
seemed to him, he could detect no self-consciousness whatever in the campers—only a bushy-tailed enthusiasm to try
anything suggested to them.

He accused Erica of putting something in their soup.

"Why?" she said. "All sorts of people go to places like
Main Chance and eat celery all day. I think people will do
anything and adore it if it gets them what they want. Don't
you?"

Cobb said he didn't know, but he was hedging. Right up until Saturday night, his sixth at Wildwood, he refused to accept the possibility that grown people could take the things they did here seriously.

Saturday was the last night of a two-week session, a "campfire night" for the six campers who were not staying over. At sunset all the campers, Dangler and Erica, some of the staff and Cobb gathered around a small fire by the river. They all sat on blankets in a circle, except for Dangler, who stood at the center of the circle by the fire, wearing a Cherokee war bonnet. Six canoe paddles lay beside him on the ground.

He began the ceremony with a longish speech on the relationship of man to nature. Then he addressed the departing campers in turn, citing their individual achievements. As he called their names, they rose one by one, joined him by the fire, and accepted their paddles with solemn faces.

When all the paddles had been given out and the campers were seated again, Dangler sang in a quiet vibrato: "We are climbing higher, higher . . ." The others joined him. "We are climbing higher, *higher*. We are *climbing* higher, *high*er . . . Soldiers of the Cross."

Cobb had started out incredulous, even suspecting for a few minutes that the ceremony was being staged for his benefit, as a kind of practical joke. Then, as it became apparent that no one was kidding, he had felt uncomfortably embarrassed for the campers. But halfway through the song, with no warning, the gathering dusk and popping fire, the campers dressed in suits and evening dresses, their mouths moving sincerely, clutching their knees and staring into the flames with dilated eyes, even Dangler in his get-up, fused for him and became suddenly believable—even moving—and Cobb found himself singing along with the last refrain of the song.

Feeling unsettled, he walked around outside for a while after the ceremony. Then he went back to the house, poured himself a drink in the study and wandered into the living room. Only two small lamps were on, and the vast center of the room, full of wicker rocking chairs, oak card tables and velvet ottomans, was a jumble of shadows. The

Jupiter Symphony was playing quietly on the stereo system, and feeling soothed by the music and the shadows, Cobb sat down. It was a couple of minutes before he noticed that he was not alone. Sitting in a corner by the fireplace was Dr. Noble Whitney Swann, one of the campers who had just received a paddle. Dr. Swann was a stooped, dignified man in his eighties who for forty years before his retirement had been the official White House gynecologist. He was leaving the camp, Cobb had heard, because of deteriorating health. The old man sat in an armchair, his head resting on a lace antimacassar, his bony aristocratic face pointed at the ceiling, and Cobb thought he might be asleep until he suddenly rose and shuffled over to the big picture window overlooking the river and the mountain. Standing before the window, he flipped a switch, illuminating the back lawn all the way to the edge of the polo field; then he made his way over to the stereo system and leafed through a pile of records stacked beside it. Choosing one, he took off the Mozart and put the new record on. Then he fiddled with some knobs on a panel that Cobb knew had to do with the public-address system. When he turned back toward the window, he seemed distinctly sprier.

A terrifying howl filled the room, freezing Cobb to his chair. Emanating from two hundred speakers on the grounds and in the woods around Wildwood, the howl seemed to encircle the house. It was answered by a longer howl that broke into a spine-chilling series of watery yelps, and then the whole out-of-doors seemed to erupt into a mad, terrible cacophony of howling, yipping and barking.

"We know you're out there!" cried Dr. Swann. He stood in front of the window and shook his fists at the bright lawn, his feet planted firmly, his old back straight as a sapling amid the recorded frenzy of hunting wolves. "Come on," he shouted at the lawn—this Whitney on his mother's side, this nationally revered figure who had personally tinkered with the plumbing of Eleanor Roosevelt—"Come on and make your play, you yellow-bellied bastards!"

VI

────────

"What's going on up there?" asked Grace Hurd the next day.

"It's hard to describe over the phone," said Cobb. "How are things at the shop?"

"Fine. Williamson, that little schmuck clerk, is using your office, and Bob and Harold have taken over your cases. *I* still belong to you."

"What else?"

"I bought a Jotul stove for the kitchen and six cords of wood. It'll save on our oil bill."

"Let me speak to Perch."

"What's the matter?"

"I didn't want a Jotul stove."

"Do you miss me?"

"Some. Let me speak to Perch."

"I dreamed about your body last night," Grace said in a throaty whisper. "Do you want to know what I dreamed?"

"Yeah, what?"

"That you were getting white hairs on your chest."

As he waited for Perch, Cobb looked over the one piece of work he had managed to get done since his arrival. It was a general-release form, designed to protect Dangler from the dozens of liabilities the operation of the camp left him open to. It was an awkward document but a comprehensive one, and Cobb was pleased with it.

"They won't sign it," said Perch after Cobb read it to him over the phone. "Not a chance."

"Why not?"

"Because those people are millionaires. Millionaires won't even sign a check without an attorney. I wouldn't sign it myself. You know what it is? It's too broad. And that means that even if they do sign it, which they won't, you'll have to get about ten million dollars' worth of insurance to cover some heir claiming it void as against public policy on the grounds that it's too broad and therefore unconscionable."

"They'll sign," said Cobb. He hadn't thought about the insurance.

As he was putting down the receiver, he heard Grace's voice.

"Pooh?"

"Call some insurance companies for me."

"I heard. Who loves you? Even when you forget the insurance."

"I didn't forget it—I just didn't want to do it. Now I do. . . . Please don't listen to my conversations, Grace."

"I can't help it, I'm horny," Grace said, and hung up.

He put twelve copies of the release in his briefcase and went outside. It was a little after noon, so he walked around the house to the back terrace where the bar was set up for bouillon hour.

There were half a dozen campers on the terrace, grouped around one of the big wrought-iron tables. Cobb was happy to see that none of the new people scheduled to arrive that day was among them. He wanted to start with the ones he knew. He made himself a Bloody Mary and was standing with it on the terrace, enjoying the bright early-October sun on his face and pondering how best to bring up the releases, when someone lifted the glass from his hand. Cobb turned to see a blond man in a pink cableknit sweater tasting his drink.

The man made a face.

"This is shameful, Rebel. I watched you build it—you failed to really make an effort."

"Ames Cravens," sighed Cobb. He had not seen Cravens since prep school, but the face was unmistakable.

Cravens led him back to the bar, dumped the drink and rinsed the glass. "I *learned* this way of handling a Mary from some people in Hobe Sound. Your problem is that you never cared about the right things."

At Andover Cravens had had a way of emphasizing certain words that irritated Cobb. Other things were his cutesy Philadelphia expressions (he would leave a group at night with the words "nighty-noodles"), his haughty beautiful face, and his doglike devotion to Dangler.

"You haven't changed."

"Don't even speak," said Cravens. "Just watch."

He poured the glass half full of Sacramento tomato juice, ground in some pepper, added the juice of half a lime, dashes of Tabasco and Worcestershire, and a shake of celery salt. He worked on the drink slowly, his blue eyes squinting with the measurements, his high, elegant forehead wrinkled with concentration. Looking at him, Cobb remembered how spiffy he looked in a bow tie. Then he remembered how Mr. Walters, one of a number of Andover masters who loathed Cravens, had told him one night at supper in front of seven other boys including Cobb and Dangler that he, Cravens, looked just like the Arrow-collar man. Used to compliments, Cravens thanked him and asked him who that was.

Mr. Walters said the Arrow-collar man was a man with a pretty face who used to be in ads. It was a face, he said, that symbolized a decade—pretty and empty. "Pretty and empty," Mr. Walters had repeated. "Exactly like yours, Cravens." There was a silence at the table, during which Cravens turned red with embarrassment. Then Dangler had cleared his throat and said icily: "How about mine? Do mine next, Mr. Walters, since you're such an expert on faces. Then you can do Cobb's, and Jemison's over there, and Tull's. . . ."

"Curry," said Cravens, "is the secret." He stirred a teaspoonful of curry powder into the drink, added vodka and ice and turned to Cobb with the drink, his face beaming. "Kenny *told* me you'd be here—actually I'm delighted. Wonderful idea, this place, don't you think?"

"Are you here as a camper?" Cobb asked.

"Committed—I may stay into the winter."

"I need to show all of you something. Would you mind if we joined those others at the table?"

"Not at all," said Cravens. "*Nice* people here, niiice people. I didn't really know what to expect."

The campers at the table were watching something. They were passing around a large pair of binoculars, and as Cravens and Cobb sat down, Peter Bigelow handed them to Cobb.

"It's Rocque," he said in a whisper. "He's in a little hot water up on Revelation."

Revelation Cliff was what a Pleistocene glacier had left of the southeast slope of Mount Webster—a nearly perpendicular granite face, a thousand feet high and a quarter of a mile across, rising directly from the far bank of the river. Because of its size and its awesome appearance, the cliff had been a landmark in the state for over a century. Cobb had read descriptions of it in the journals of Nathaniel Hawthorne and Daniel Webster, and he knew that Thoreau was supposed to have hiked to its rim by way of the mountain's east ridge and spent a day and a night there listening to the crash of the Monnussuc River as it reverberated up the rock. For as long as Danglers had owned the mountain they had allowed public access to the cliff, and over the past fifty years it had become famous as the place where more good rock and ice climbers were killed each year than any other in America. A total of twenty-four men had died trying the wall, including two college friends of Cobb's. Cobb had done some rock climbing himself at Dartmouth, and he had heard all about the terrible exposure on Revelation, about the scarcity of protection and the grinding length and technical difficulties of its routes. But he had never needed that information to keep him off the cliff. The first time he saw the vast expanse of rock, and every time after that, he knew without thinking about it that he would just as soon climb onto the back of a rabid dog.

He focused the binoculars on the jumble of scree and granite boulders at the bottom of the cliff and brought them up along the green wedges of stunted spruce and fir that dwindled upward for a hundred feet and then disappeared into the homicidal face itself, where the rock was smooth and gray and striped with wavy intrusions of darker gray. About two hundred feet from the top, Cobb spotted the man.

"He's been in that one spot for twenty minutes," said Peter Bigelow. "We think he's about to make a move."

The man on the cliff made Cobb think of a wood-pecker. He wore a bright red balaclava cap and he clung to the rock quietly, moving his head from side to side and up and down as a bird will. His death seemed so foregone in that place that Cobb felt less concern for him than regret at not having prepared the releases sooner.

Ames Cravens tapped him on the shoulder, his eyes bright with excitement. "Look at him, Rebel—up where the eagles soar. Why don't we give that a try after lunch?"

"No thanks," said Cobb, "I think I'll leave that to the paying guests."

Though he had spoken quietly, Weezy Bigelow looked at him over her drink and laughed, her big eyes squinting. "You might as well try to get into the spirit of things up here, Andy."

"Adventure is the name of the game here," said Cabot Waterman. "You'll have to get your feet wet."

"I guess I'm just not the adventurous type," Cobb said.

"None of us was before we got here," said Peter Bige-low. "Not really, I mean. Weezy and I certainly weren't, and we'll try anything now."

"And win at it, too," Cabot Waterman added reso-nantly.

Weezy Bigelow laughed again. "Well, you might as well forget losing here. Kenneth simply won't *let* anybody lose."

"He makes you know you can 'do it,' is what Weezy means," Peter Bigelow told Cobb. "A lot of us aren't used to knowing that nowadays, what with one thing and an-other."

"Do . . . ?"

"*Any*thing," Ruth Waterman said, rattling the ice cubes in her glass for emphasis.

"Anything you make up your mind to do," said her husband, Cabot.

Cobb knew what they were talking about. Dangler had always had a major talent for making people believe in themselves. It was one of the things Cobb loved and ad-mired most about his friend, and if Dangler was using that talent now to make these campers believe they could stand off wolf packs and climb impossible cliffs . . . well, fine, he decided; more power to them. Looking around the table at the group of handsome people, he found he no longer felt so ironical about them and what they were doing here as he had all week.

"Do you remember the Exeter game our senior year?" he asked Cravens.

"Fourth and goal!" said Cravens with delight, leaning into the table. "I'm an offensive guard, right? Cobb is the tackle on the other side of the line, and Kenny is fullback —All State, All New England, everything. Last game of the season and we're undefeated, but Exeter is ahead seventeen to fourteen. We're on their five and it's fourth and goal. Eleven seconds on the clock. Now, what do we do? Do we kick for the tie . . . ?"

"Hell no. You go for it," said Cabot Waterman.

"Well, but we're hurting, see? We've worn the grass down to gravel at the end of the field, and the gravel is all in our hip pads and shoes. Kenny is the worst—he's limping and his hips are bleeding. So Marston, this *slightly* prissy quarterback we have, calls a pass."

"He called a sweep first and changed it to a pass," corrected Cobb, grinning.

"So Kenny—now listen to this—Kenny says, 'There's nothing *fancy* about fourth and goal, Marston. Just give me the ball and everybody block.' But Marston starts arguing about how they're looking for off-tackle, and how everybody in the line is hurt. So Kenny looks at me and he looks at Rebel here, and Tull the other tackle, and Carlson the center, and he says, 'You hurt, Ames? You hurt, Andrew? You hurt, Bob?' and everybody says, 'No, no, no.' Then he says, 'Sounds like nobody's hurt but you, Marston, so you better give me the ball. I'm going over Cobb's tackle. And if you don't call that play, I'm going to throw you down on the fifty-yard line when this game is over and hump you like a dog in heat—' "

"He's moving," shouted Weezy Bigelow, and pointed at the cliff. "Rocque's moving."

" '—and everybody out here is going to *think you're queer!*' " whooped Cravens. "Kenny had a hole big enough to run to Massachusetts."

"Come on, Roquefort," whispered Madelaine de Faurier, the climber's wife, who had not spoken or taken her eyes off the cliff since Cobb sat down. She banged her little fists on her knees.

Cobb had passed on the binoculars, but even without them he could see the man's right hand explore the rock above his head, as though feeling for a light switch, and settle on something. Then his right foot crabbed outward, the toe of his boot making little circles across the rock, until it found a hold. There was mild applause at the table. The man rested for a moment, arranged like a capital K against the cliff.

"Oh, *no*," said Madelaine de Faurier. "He's going to do it."

They all watched the figure coil, and then, with a sudden thrust of the right leg, shoot upward, claw impossibly at the crack two feet above him—and fall.

"Damn," said Ruth Waterman.

"That's that," said Cabot Waterman.

"Well, it's his own fault," Madelaine de Faurier said with pure disgust. "Two hundred times they've told him: climb, don't jump."

"In Rocque's defense, that move with the right foot was anything but shabby," said Peter Bigelow, waving his swizzle stick at Revelation Cliff. "You just don't know until you've been there."

Rocque de Faurier was obviously annoyed. Seated in a sort of harness of straps clipped to a steel cable that ran from the top of the cliff, he kicked at the rock. A moment later he leaned backward in the harness and shouted something at the top. Though the cliff was a good half-mile away from the terrace where Cobb and the others sat, they could hear his voice.

"He's packing it in," Madelaine sighed. "First he jumps, then he gets angry and makes them winch him up. Every day, the same thing." She lit a cigarette, waved the smoke away from her face, and watched as her husband made a couple of impatient circles with his right hand. The cable holding him jerked once; then, smoothly and briskly, Rocque de Faurier, Houston drilling-bit millionaire, was lifted to the top.

"What I wonder," said Madelaine after a long silence at the table, "is how he ever made out in the Cordillera Blanca without a winch."

Dangler did not come to lunch, and it took Cobb half the afternoon to find him. By the time he did, his anger had faded and he was feeling only despondent. None of the campers had been willing to sign the release, though the ones at the table had seemed on the verge of doing so until de Faurier joined them.

Cobb had handed him a copy of the form as soon as he sat down. "I have a little something here I'd like to show you, Rocque," he began.

"Do I know you?" asked de Faurier coldly. He had replaced the red stocking cap with a large white Stetson. A little hammer hung from a holster at his hip, and slung over his shoulders like bandoliers were nylon straps holding an assortment of metal clips and pins.

"Of *course* you know me—I've been here for over a week."

"This is Mr. *Cobb*, Rocque," said Weezy Bigelow, "Chief's lawyer friend."

"Sweety," said Madelaine de Faurier, smiling icily at her husband, "we were all wondering something. I think it was Ruth, actually, who put it into words—how on *earth* did you make out in the Cordillera Blanca without a winch?"

"It's just a simple release of responsibility," Cobb told de Faurier quickly, and read from the form: " 'designed to remise, release and forever discharge Dangler's International Adventure Camps of Colby, New Hampshire, of and from any and all manner of action or actions, cause and causes of action, suits or claims . . .' "

"Wait just a minute here," said de Faurier.

" . . . should you suffer, or be made to suffer, either death, injury, maiming, the loss of sight in one eye or both . . ."

"*Stop*, goddammit." De Faurier clenched his teeth, making muscles pop in his long Gallic jaw. "That list is unpleasant in the extreme. We are all quite satisfied that nothing along those lines could happen, otherwise we wouldn't be here. We are not daredevils, Cox, only people to whom the ordinary challenges of life are insufficient." He stood up, his hardware jangling. The others stood up with him. "Now, I believe it is time for lunch," he said.

"Not one of them would sign it," Cobb told Dangler. "Not even Cravens. I saw the other new ones at lunch."

"It doesn't matter," said Dangler.

Cobb had found him sitting under a maple tree near the edge of the fishing pond, surrounded by topographic maps, compasses, and half a dozen small camping stoves. Throughout Cobb's story he had tinkered with one of the stoves, turning a brass key backward and forward. Now he held it up.

"The Svea 123R. Seventeen ounces, self-cleaning. Six-ounce fuel capacity, boils water in six minutes and with the Optimus mini-pump is suitable for winter use. What do you think?"

"That unless you make signing the releases a pre-condition for coming here, there is nothing more I can do. I'm sorry, I feel I've let you down . . . I suppose I should resign."

"Don't be ridiculous." Dangler placed the little stove on the ground in front of him and poured a few drops of white gas out of an aluminum bottle into the burner head. "Getting the releases doesn't mean diddly-squat. You're doing fine." He put a match to the burner head, lighting the primer fuel, and stared at the orange flame licking around the base of the stove. He seemed to be finished with the conversation.

"I haven't done *anything*," said Cobb, "but eat your food, be exercised like a horse by your wife, and fail at the one thing I tried to do. Look, I apologize for taking your valuable time away from whatever this is you're doing, but let me just put a few things in perspective here. A: not even God could afford to operate this place without signed releases—the potential liability runs into the hundreds of millions. B: your campers refuse to sign the forms, or even discuss them without their lawyers. And C: even if they did sign, the releases would have to be insured. I talked to my secretary a half-hour ago and she informed me that not one of the seven companies she called will touch it. In short, we, that is, you, are in a desperate situation and I can do nothing to help you beyond advise that you quit playing with that little thing and instantly go make sure that no one is being hurt."

The flame at the base of the stove had gone out. Dangler turned the key and lit the pressurized gas that hissed from the burner head, producing a transparent blue flame that burned with a loud whooshing noise. Agitated as he was, Cobb couldn't help staring at the fierce little fire. After a moment Dangler turned the key again and the stove died with a pop.

"Just think," he said slowly, "what we could manage here on earth if all of us burned that way." He shook his head, loosing a waft of witch hazel. Then he stood up, suddenly animated. "Do you think I got you up here to make out *forms?* I don't care about the goddamn releases. I'm not running some chickenshit dude ranch, I *want* the responsibility for my people. We drive in the passing lane up here, Andrew—taking chances is what this place is all about." He took Cobb firmly by the shoulders, his eyes unnaturally bright. "We are working toward great things here. I have certain ideas brewing. I am very close to something big, and I cannot be distracted. I need durability around me, Andrew. Do you know that I can hardly stand to look at someone's face anymore? If I look, I want to ask, 'How durable are you—how much can you take?' Well . . . ?"

"Well what?" said Cobb, feeling vulnerable. "I am looking as durable as I can."

"You are the best friend I have in the world. I have loved you like a brother ever since our freshman year at Andover and I would happily lay down my life for you. Now I need your finger in the dike and you talk to me about forms and the ugly possibility of your resignation. Is that fair?"

His expression offered up an ocean of disappointment. Cobb shook his head.

"I need commitment, dammit. I need your help."

"But help with *what?* There's nothing here to help with."

"And you won't be alone much longer." Dangler flashed his famous grin. "I have reinforcements coming."

VII

When Divina Thayer, Erica's oldest friend, arrived at Wildwood the following week, Dangler threw a day-long party for her.

Among the three hundred people who came were Ambassador and Mrs. Bundy Phillips, the Iselin Robinsons, and Mrs. Codman Sears from Boston; from New York, the Locust Valley Hewitts, the Frick Vanderlips, and Feuile Gardner Gore; Mr. and Mrs. Marshall Van Courtlandt were there from Philadelphia, and old Mrs. Allen Pennington; the Legares Alstons came up from Baltimore, and the Morgan Van Rensselaer Copes from Fishers Island; the Duchess Gracie D'Artelli was there with her daughter Chessy, and the Wyatt Tilghmans from London, and Viscount du Pont Firestone Signy.

Except for a publicized senator and a beautiful actress-journalist who was taking pictures, Andrew Cobb had no idea who most of these people were, though it seemed that he should. It was Divina Thayer, leading him around and introducing him, who characterized them for him. Cobb had mentioned that they all seemed unpretentious and nice, despite their fancy names—meaning that, like the campers, they reminded him of big, cheerful, well-dressed children.

"Oh, these aren't *famous* people, lovey, like movie stars," Divina told him. "But if a bomb hit this place today, America would have to start all over."

Cobb had first met Divina Thayer at another Dangler extravaganza, the camp's opening four months earlier. That day had been hot and aswirl with excess: brass bands playing near the lake, a thousand anchored helium-filled ballons, a group of Portuguese trampolinists, a full-scale polo game, and twenty pigs roasting on spits. Trying to adjust to the scale, Cobb wandered over the bright lawns clutching a frosted mint julep, studying things. Only once had he run into Dangler, who, Porcellian tie pulled away from his throat, white suit rumpled, and looking poleaxed with pleasure, grabbed him passionately and yelped, "Jesus God, Andrew, it's wonderful to have you here."

Around noon, lonely, grouchy and nursing a head-ache, he had been sitting in a striped lawn chair near the patio when a positive-looking woman with graying hair and a cheerful face approached him.

"Hello," she said. "Erica sent me over to take care of you."

"That's nice of you," said Cobb.

"Shall we stroll in the woods? I'm a birder, are you?"

Over the next few hours she identified a pair of red-breasted nuthatches, a Canada jay, and three varieties of northern finches. Between sightings she talked nonstop, wearing down Cobb's headache and his bad mood. When she got into a 1960 Morris Minor to drive back to Boston, she left him feeling restored and gay, and he was not even slightly disappointed when he learned from Erica later that evening that she was not, as he had believed all afternoon, Ethel Kennedy.

"Who she is," Erica had told him, "is a Boston Thayer, the best field-hockey player who ever went to Bennington, and the only unselfish person alive."

Divina arrived at the camp early on the morning of her party, and Cobb ate breakfast with her and the Danglers upstairs on the porch where Dangler had shot the flower-pot. Erica was in a grand mood and made them "colonels" out of rum and grapefruit juice to toast with. For breakfast they had bluefish and broiled tomatoes, and after they ate, Dangler opened two bottles of champagne and they made more toasts, to each other, to the camp and, beginning at around eleven, to the steady flow of guests arriving in the courtyard below. It was a cool day. There were high thin clouds but a lot of sun and a bracing west wind, and when they walked to the other side of the porch they could look down on the huge lawn, leading to the river—where Dangler had dozens of games set up and Sousa marches playing over the public-address system and bunting flying from posts and yellow beach umbrellas and two hundred lawn chairs and thirty men in white coats to pass champagne punch and hors d'oeuvres, and the lunch when the caterers from Boston got there with it, the whole scene dappled in sunlight and shade from the high-flying clouds—and beyond to brilliant red and yellow stands of hardwoods, and beyond that to the massive gleaming of Lake Webster.

"Oh, Divina, look at your *day*," said Erica. She stood between Divina and Cobb, an arm around each of them. "I could just drink the lake, I'm so happy." She called to Dangler and he came over, carrying a new bottle of champagne. "Darling, hug us. Let's all hug." Dangler put his arms around Cobb and Divina, still holding the champagne, and Erica pulled the whole circle toward her and kissed each of them. "God, it's too perfect," she said. "We have to stay like this, the four of us, don't we, darling?" Dangler smiled at her, a little distantly thought Cobb, who was sure he had never seen anyone look as ravishing as Erica did that morning, dressed in black wool gaucho pants, tall green boots and a green cashmere sweater, her hair pulled back and pinned above her ears so that it rode her neck and back like a mane, her lovely face gay and vivid. "Isn't it wonderful that they're both here—that we're all here together?" she asked Dangler.

"Yes."

"We can do anything now, can't we?"

She unwrapped herself from Divina and Cobb and took Dangler's face in her hands. "Oh, God, I love you, Kenneth. Mary Baird says no one is really beautiful after you've been married to them for a year, but you and I have been married forever and you're the most beautiful person I've ever seen." She kissed him quickly and laughed, and Dangler, no longer distant or playful or anything other than intent, kissed her back. Erica pulled away, smiling, and looked out over the party, in full swing on the lawn, to the lake. "Wouldn't the island be wonderful today?" she asked Dangler. "Don't you think it would?"

Dangler grinned at her. "I think we should go out later and see," he said.

They finished the third bottle of champagne on the terrace, making more toasts and shouting to people on the lawn, and then they were whistling downstairs, with Dangler leading them, and outside; and the chatter and clinking glasses, the laughter and all the pleased healthy faces hit Cobb like a double whiskey after the champagne, and suddenly the day felt delicate and gorgeous to him as a piece of blown glass. The acres of velvety grass, the games and the perfumed people all seemed inexpressibly beautiful and fine.

Divina squeezed his arm. "Wasn't Erica marvelous up on the terrace—she was positively in heat."

He and Divina ate lunch with a big voluble group near the horseshoe pits. In a daze of good spirits Cobb ate lightly, sipped at a glass of white wine, watched Divina, and listened to Mrs. Alston Lowell tell how her aunt in Newport took luncheon guests out to the stables to watch the horses have "love affairs."

He heard Ames Cravens say: "You've got it all wrong, the cresta *is* only done in St. Moritz."

And Lolly Haas say: "I suspect they are rather like dogs, these people—they just sort of roll on the babies if they don't want them."

And Norris Fish IV, one of the new campers, say: "I don't care *what* they do for West Hartford; they are common, common, common."

And he listened to Mrs. Marshall Van Courtlandt when she turned to him and Divina, wiped her small mouth with a napkin, and said: "You're both interested in birds, so you know of course that he got rich by stealing the Audubon bird call from the Italians. He was over there for World War II and he saw how they put the little tube in the little tube, you know. Now every time you buy an Audubon bird call you put two dollars in that little snake's pocket."

"Yes indeed," said Cobb, grinning and nodding.

After lunch they walked along the riverbank, passing a long line of people who were waiting to ride the tracked canoe. Divina held Cobb's arm and chatted endlessly into his ear. She loved to talk. Her conversation was so constant that it seemed a physical part of her, like another facial feature, and she carried it on in a thrilled, chesty voice that made Cobb think of England and horses. She was a happy, compact, nut-brown woman with strong hands, wide gray eyes and cool, precise movements. Cobb enjoyed looking at her, and he enjoyed listening to her. Being with her gave him a satisfaction like the one he got from sitting at an antique Hepplewhite desk that Grace Hurd had bought for his house.

Later they visited Hugo at the trout stream, and checked in on a fishing derby at the pond in time to see Wyatt Tilghman land a forty-pound chinook salmon. They watched Tilghman tail his fish, drag it ashore, weigh it on a brass scales attached to the outside wall of the fish hatchery and write "Hen chinook. 40 pounds 4 ounces" under his name on a blackboard also attached to the building. Then he dumped the salmon into a large bin. He was wearing waders and a puffy fishing vest bristling with little devices.

"The British are running away with it," said Peter Bigelow. He was standing a few yards offshore from Cobb and Divina, casting with a small bamboo fly rod.

"I understand Wyatt is quite good with fish," Divina said.

"He certainly looks it," said Peter Bigelow.

Cobb wondered if he was being ironic. He liked Bigelow, a tall, stout man who drank heavily, who was good-humored but quiet and had a melancholy face that was aging quickly. He remembered hearing Madelaine de Faurier say one morning that every man she knew who had married a hundred million dollars had a face like Peter Bigelow's.

"How are you doing?" Cobb asked him.

"I took two rainbows and a nice brown on an Adams before everybody got here. Tilghman is taking all the good fish now with a sinking line. The others just keep throwing bigger and bigger dry flies, but the fish are down. At least nobody here will throw a pork chop out there."

He picked up his line with a roll cast, and Cobb noticed that there was no fly at the end of his leader. "You don't have a fly on," he told him.

"I used to fish the Allagash every summer with my father before they ruined it. I fished the Battenkill and the Au Sable before they ruined them. And the Snake before they ruined it."

"Before who ruined it?" asked Divina.

"Insurance salesmen," said Bigelow.

Just down the bank from them a lady in a jaunty Irish fishing hat lofted out a huge cream-colored fly that hit the water with a splat and lay there looking like a soda cracker.

Cobb decided it was time to go. "Have you seen Erica and Kenneth?" he asked.

Peter Bigelow made a false cast and shot an effortless sixty feet of line with the little rod. He looked natural and content, casting beautifully with no fly.

"One night at the Cabanas in Cozumel a group of us were trying to feed the tarpon. We were eating dinner on that patio, you know, and throwing down little pieces of bread, but the tarpon wouldn't touch them. They just lay near the underwater lights ignoring us. There was an insurance salesman from New Orleans at the table next to us, and he threw down a tomato. His wife threw part of an egg, and a whole fruit salad. Finally someone else at their table threw a pork chop to the tarpon. That's the sort of thing that happens all the time nowadays, everywhere but here."

"I'm afraid we have to run," said Cobb.

"The Danglers were here awhile ago. Erica got edgy and Chief took her off. To the island, I think he said. What's-his-name left too."

"Who's that?"

"That little foreign manager. He was the weighmaster here. He left at the same time Chief and Erica did." Peter Bigelow looked up from his casting and smiled at Cobb. "Now we all have to weigh our own fish."

"God, what a strange man," said Divina when they were clear of the pond. "Anyway, I'm glad Kenneth is staying with her."

"Why?"

"Because parties make her nervous. She can act terribly at parties."

"I think she's all right," said Cobb. "I've never seen her better than she was this morning."

They walked west from the pond into the evergreen woods in front of the house.

"A year or so ago," said Divina, "she and Kenneth had a seated, black-tie dinner in Rye for all those stuffy American Yacht Club people. At some point Erica decided that she absolutely couldn't stand anyone there, so she put Istin in the chocolate mousse. They had a walled garden in back, and everyone went out there for coffee, and that's where it hit them. She locked all the French doors."

"Where what hit them?"

"The Istin. It's a laxative for horses. She kept thoroughbreds in Rye, and they were always constipated."

"My God," said Cobb.

"Well, she wasn't happy there. They left Westchester right after that, and she's been much happier here. She *did* seem so wonderful this morning. Maybe Kenneth was wrong." She took Cobb's arm again and pulled herself close to him. "Anyway, I'm glad he asked me to come."

Cobb's mind was back in the walled garden, imagining the agonized guests clawing at the French doors.

Divina stopped walking and faced him. "Shall we go hawking? With this wind they should be moving. We could start in the marsh."

"Is there something . . . wrong with Erica?" Cobb disliked the sound of the question as soon as it was out.

Divina stared at him, chewing on her lower lip. "If your father had killed himself by drinking a whole bottle of lye, there might be something wrong with you too." She tossed her head. "Let's go look for an osprey, and I'll tell you about it."

For the next two hours they walked around the edges of the marsh near the duck-hunting pond, and Divina talked about Erica and looked for hawks, spotting two, a male osprey and a red-shouldered hawk, which she called a good sighting for October. The marsh was well into fall. The scarlet swamp maples ringing it were already beginning to drop their leaves, and the tangle of alder, poplar, cattails and broom grass near the center had lost its odor. It was very quiet in the marsh, and when the sun fell behind the west flank of Mount Webster, cold—though Divina didn't seem to notice it.

It was almost six o'clock when they started back. The wind had died. The sky was clear, a hard gray blue, darkening fast. They left the marsh at the south end and walked up a ridge in the general direction of the house, through evergreens and then birches. The air was still and cold in the woods, and Cobb shivered despite the uphill going. His earlier exhilaration had worn off. He felt tired and drained by the day, and badly disturbed by what Divina had told him.

"Do you mind if I comment on something I've noticed about you?" asked Divina halfway up the ridge.

Neither of them had spoken for a few minutes, and Cobb, almost out of breath, didn't want to now.

"No," he said.

"Well, you're very *formal* about things. You shouldn't be afraid to say what you're thinking—that's the one thing therapy taught me."

"I'm not."

"Yes you are. You're what my therapist calls tied-off. So am I—that's how I know."

"It might not hurt if more of us were a little tied-off," Cobb muttered, thinking of what he had just learned about Erica.

Divina stopped in front of him. She put her cool, leather-gloved, scented hands on his cheeks and kissed him quickly on the mouth. "You don't have to be afraid to say anything to *me,* is the point. I'm your very good friend from now on."

At the top of the ridge they came out on a dirt road. They turned east, and had walked only a few steps when they could hear Tammy Wynette singing "Take Me to Your World."

"Oh, no," Cobb said. He stiffened in the road.

Divina seemed pleased. "Is that coming from the party?"

"It's too close."

"Well, come on," she said.

As they walked, the music grew louder, the same song playing over and over. By the time they got to its source, they had heard "Take Me to Your World" two and a half times, and a strange anxiety had settled on Cobb like the cold.

"Keep walking," he said, "just keep walking."

But Divina had stopped in the road and was staring with delight into the woods. She grabbed his arm. "Will you *look* at this place," she shouted to him over the music, "it thinks it's Mount Vernon."

It was a trailer she was looking at, a thirty-one-foot Airstream, set off the road at the back of a small dirt clearing. The trailer was dark. A white wooden porch ran its entire length, the roof supported by four fluted wooden columns. On the porch were a couple of rocking chairs, a number of large metal barrels, a telescope on a tripod. A huge spiraling antenna stuck up from one end of the Airstream; at the other was a decorative concrete chimney painted to look like brick. In the clearing in front, carefully arranged over the hard dirt, were a concrete birdbath painted red, and a plaster flamingo, three plaster deer and a big silver ball on a pedestal. Pulled into the woods behind the ball was a pinstriped Chevrolet Blazer with a bumper sticker that read "Born to Die."

"Isn't it *won*derful," said Divina.

Cobb didn't think so. In fact, without knowing why, he was frightened by the place, the things in the yard particularly. They seemed to slant toward him out of his past, awash in Tammy's pleading voice—prodding him obliquely like a memory or a nightmare.

He put his mouth on Divina's ear and said: "I have to go now."

"Do you know who lives back there?" she asked him when they were well down the road from the trailer and could see the lights along the drive leading back to the house and the party.

"No," he said, and was not exactly sure why he lied.

The owner of the trailer thought briefly about shooting Cobb and Divina, or at least shooting at them, when they stopped in front of his place, and he might have if they had come off the road onto his dirt, or if he had felt good enough to get up. But they didn't and he didn't, so he just lay on his bed, his right hand tapping "Take Me to Your World" along the neck of a bottle of Rock and Rye, letting his ears make out what they were doing, thinking he sensed fear, almost thinking he knew who one of them was, without bothering to look out the window. And when, after less than a minute, they left, he groaned, pulled at the bottle, and went back to feeling like a gut-shot animal.

That afternoon Gruenig had gotten what he had wanted for weeks. Not only had he seen it all, he had *filmed* it, through the zoom lens of an Elmo Super-8 movie camera. But the getting of it had made him so sick that all he had been able to do since he returned from Dangler Island was lie on his bed and drink and listen to Tammy Wynette, and watch in his mind against the darkening back wall of his trailer the same humid scramble of images that was in the camera: of lovemaking that was more like fighting, performed on a black fur rug, of green and black clothing, and of a female body more lush than any he had ever imagined, or even seen in a magazine. Having finally gotten what he wanted, all Gruenig could do with it was lie on his bed drinking and aching, and knowing miserably that things would not get better until he could put himself in those images with Erica Dangler.

VIII

When Cobb was twelve years old his mother told him this: "You are a big strong boy with fine blood, good health and a sweet heart. So forget about yourself and just be as helpful as you can. Almost everybody else needs help."

Caroline Cobb was a Ph.D. in biochemistry who had always wanted to be a missionary, a full professor at Jacksonville University who wore white gloves and a double strand of pearls to her classes, and a Christian stoic who loved life and human beings, and who died ungrudgingly of stomach cancer when Cobb was in his sophomore year of college.

Almost everything Cobb knew about how to behave he had learned from watching and listening to her. She had been so central to his development and sense of himself that it sometimes seemed if he looked closely enough, on one of his ankles maybe, he could find her signature. He had her long nose, her lank auburn hair, her wide forehead, even her laugh. Before he could read, he had learned from her how to listen to people, never to take the first or the last biscuit, and to respect suffering; and by the time he turned thirteen he had adopted most of her values, particularly loyalty, optimism and a conscientious kindness toward other people, because he had seen with his own two eyes how well they worked for her—how sunny and intelligible they had made her life.

For a long time those values worked for him too. At prep school and college, amid hordes of rich Yankees, he was undistinguished except for them. He was average-looking, a fair athlete, a mediocre scholar. His family's circumstances, affluent by north Florida standards, were Appalachian in comparison to most of his classmates'. But Cobb knew what he believed in, and most of them did not. He believed in being genuinely nice, and he worked hard at it, and at Andover and later at Dartmouth he was one of the most popular boys in school for no better reason than that. People came to him for advice and support; he was relied upon and trusted. On through law school and for a long time afterward, living felt to Cobb like carving with a good knife. He felt organized, purposeful and whole, and he felt in his bones that he was being helpful.

Then, a few months ago, he had suddenly lost that feeling. One Sunday morning in April he woke up, smelled bacon being fried downstairs by Grace, and found that he no longer believed in himself. He locked the bedroom door. Lying in bed, he examined his life, noticing for the first time a startling assortment of loose ends—a diminished sense of purpose, a growing inability to act decisively, an overall . . . tentativeness. He noticed also that he was working at a job he did not really enjoy, living with a woman he wasn't sure he wanted to live with, and being of no demonstrable help to anyone. He felt ambushed and frantic. Scrambling for answers in the hot bed, he wondered if it were possible for ideals to turn to flab after thirty, the way stomachs did—wondered if his cultivated unselfishness could have somehow slid to diffidence, his eagerness to be kind to a timid willingness to let other people have their way.

Over the next few weeks he read the collected works of St. Thomas Aquinas and joined the Concord Youth Services Program as a financial adviser. Feeling guilty about his father and sister, whom he had seen fewer than half a dozen times in the fourteen years since his mother's death, he visited them in Jacksonville. His father had remarried for a second time, sold his real-estate business and moved to a condominium in Atlantic Beach. He wore loud Hawaiian shirts and Gucci loafers, kept poodles, and played tennis every afternoon. His sister had simply gotten fat. She spent her mornings by the pool of the Timuquana Country Club, where, massive and gleaming, she lay in the sun with pieces of damp cotton on her eyelids, talking to Cobb about her children. Sitting beside her one morning, Cobb realized something: that life tended to grow less specific as you went along. He looked at his sister and thought of her beautiful mezzo-soprano voice, the most significant thing about her as a girl. He looked at her plump, bronze throat and felt a tightening in his own. Get up and sing, he wanted to tell her. Go stand on the diving board and sing "House of the Rising Sun" and see if the pounds and the years don't just fall off.

When he went back to New Hampshire, he felt better. If nothing else, being with his father and sister had reminded him of how his mother had refused to let life happen to her, of how she had stayed in gear, using herself aggressively and precisely until the day she died. A tune got in his head on the Eastern jet between Jacksonville and Boston. He drank a Manhattan and hummed it until he remembered its title. It was "You Can't Be a Beacon if Yo' Light Don't Shine."

Three months after he returned from Florida, Cobb went to Wildwood, believing he was being invited there to help, and that the camp would provide an opportunity for him to become morally active again, to put his values and abilities back to work in the service of his best friend and possibly even a good cause. But when, two weeks and two days after he arrived, he finally learned what it was he was supposed to help with, his first impulse was only this: to run.

He and Divina were standing along the edge of a marsh and Divina had been talking for two hours about Erica. She had just finished by saying, "That's the irony, you see: the closer he gets to what she wants for him, the more it takes him away from her. She's on an absolute *rack*. . . . Kenneth says he doesn't know what she would do if you and I weren't here to help keep her in line."

Cobb considered the phrase. Tumblers seemed to fall in his mind and he heard a click. Of course: Dangler had gotten him up here to *help with Erica.* Two hours ago that knowledge would have been a surprise, even a mild disappointment, but it would not have had him wondering as it did now what emergency he could invent to get himself back to Concord. Two hours ago he had not known about Erica Dangler.

Born Erica Schuyler, only daughter and youngest child of one of the banking Schuylers of Boston and a Philadelphia Van Pelt; direct descendant of two patroons, Governor Wentworth, Alexander Hamilton . . . "Next to her," Divina had begun by saying, "*every*body is a Hottentot."

And that, she believed, was part of the problem. Everything had always been so . . . ultra for Erica. Her horses were the most expensive, her birthday parties the most elaborate, her parents' house the largest on Beacon Hill. And her parents: this admired, brilliant father, the youngest man ever elected president of the Somerset Club, this *story-*book father; and a gay, beautiful mother who was pale-skinned and dazzling, and who with her beauty and gaiety had made Erica's house seem the most exciting place in the world. It was all so *bigger than life.* Even the horrible thing. When Tom Schuyler killed himself, it made national television and all the wire services, *Time* magazine published rumors of problems with his family's bank and a South American diplomat's wife, Boston could talk about nothing else—and within two weeks of his death his widow sold the house in town and the huge white summer cottage in Manchester-by-the-Sea, and moved herself and Erica and the two boys to Bermuda. Just like that. Erica, said Divina, was simply in school one day and gone for good the next. She was twelve years old.

" 'Overwrought' is the word. Everything in Erica's childhood was overwrought." One image in particular, she said, was stuck in her mind, where it had the look and feel now of an old photograph. Erica is about eight years old. She is standing beside a boxwood hedge in the backyard of the house on Louisburg Square, looking somber and exquisite, like Lady Caroline Howard in the Joshua Reynolds portrait. It is afternoon, and probably spring or early fall, because she has on the light French camel-hair coat her mother bought her at Lord & Taylor. Standing behind her in a semicircle is a solemn crowd of about fifty people. Mr. and Mrs. Angier are there, and Erica's uncle Perry and the Gardner Popes, and Pearl, the Schuylers' cook. Divina is there with her parents. Everyone is dressed up—some of the men wear gray vests and black bow ties, and a number of women have on veils. The closest of the people to Erica is her beautiful mother, in a long black dress and a black pillbox hat, looking sad. Everyone looks sad. Erica is holding a box. In a moment she will kneel and put the box into a hole in the ground. Walter, the gardener, will throw dirt over it with a shovel and tamp the dirt down. Then Mr. Schuyler will come out of the crowd and read from a prayer book. Divina remembered him reading that the dead "shall rest from their labors," and remembered wondering what labors Theresa could possibly have had. Theresa is Erica's turtle, and it is Theresa who is in the box that she holds. After a while Mr. Schuyler will stop reading; there will be a moment of silence and then suddenly everyone will be inexplicably happy, chatting and laughing and milling around, and servants will be passing canapés and champagne on the lawn.

"It was a party," said Divina. "A thousand-dollar funeral party for a turtle. And Erica standing there with that box was the sort of centerpiece. 'Overwrought' is definitely the word. She never saw . . . she was never shown the polite limits of things."

And overwrought was what Erica herself was when her mother sent her off to Miss Porter's school in Farmington, Connecticut—too much so, and too remote to be popular at girl's school. And too noticeable: she was already five feet ten and reedy, and her big head drooped like a sunflower when she walked. She was lonely and bored; she wanted to be back in Somerset with her horses, so she began to pitch fits, and by the end of the year Miss Porter's wanted her back in Somerset too. That was how it began, Divina believed: Erica's peculiarity. Somehow the fits just grew on her.

Divina didn't see her during the next two years. She

went to a private school in Hamilton and had a tutor. She got mad about sports and took up swimming and track, and she began to fill out and to stand up straight. She was active and learning new things, and her disorder was mild enough during this time so that her mother and brothers could write it off as temperament; but when she left Bermuda next, for college, she left with it full-grown and imminent.

Divina encountered it first that fall, when her parents let her take a room with Erica at the Pierre Hotel for Thanksgiving weekend. Erica came up to New York from Hollins trailing a freckle-faced Washington and Lee junior named Charlton Downes and proceeded to try to kill him. She kept him out all night for three nights running, took him on dawn jogs through Central Park and midmorning swims at a Y in Brooklyn Heights and afternoon horseback rides around the reservoir. When he showed signs of tiring she would throw things at him and accuse him of trying to ruin her vacation, and Downes would apologize formally with a Maryland accent, wash his face with cold water, and stumble out again behind Erica to Ernie's or Nick's or the Village Vanguard.

Divina said, "I remember how puzzled he was. He just didn't know what had hit him. I didn't either, exactly, but it seemed inevitable to me, whatever it was. . . . He was the first one she bombed. She bombed quite a few after him. One named Horst actually died of exposure in the Pyrenees. And all of them, at least all the ones I met, were puzzled. None of them seemed to realize that he was accommodating a condition."

"Which is . . . what, exactly?" Cobb decided to ask.

Divina studied him. "No one has told you about this?"

"No."

"Well, I don't believe it has a name. After she was sent home from Hollins, her mother packed her around to Austin Riggs and Menninger's, and that place in Switzerland—everywhere. No one seemed to know what to call it, or what to do about it. What it amounts to is that Erica has this psychological craving for things to be dramatic or terrifying or exhausting. She just can't stand for life not to be thrilling all the time, and sometimes when it's not, she has these tantrums. She will be absolutely fine for a while and then she will get very bored or unhappy, or she won't get enough exercise, or someone will affect her in the wrong way, and she will go really a little off: break things, scream, attack people. Actually they are more like seizures than tantrums, because she can't control them. And she can be very dangerous when she's having one. She almost seems to give off steam."

"I know," said Cobb. "I've seen it. How long do they usually go on?"

"It depends. They *can* last for hours. If she exercises, they go away faster, and if she is frightened or startled, they sometimes disappear immediately, like the hiccups. When her brother Preston was traveling with her in Europe, he carried around a bag full of rubber snakes."

Cobb tried to smile casually at Divina. "How often does she have these . . . spells?"

"She doesn't have to have them at all. As long as there's someone sort of managing her, making sure she gets enough exercise and doesn't get bored and so on, she's fine. But that can be taxing. She went through quite a few paid 'companions' right after college. Her two brothers had her after that, and neither of them has done much since. Then she met Kenneth. Which had to happen, of course."

They met in Ireland. Erica was twenty-five. She was there with her brother Preston for some fox hunting. In the previous five months, ricocheting around Europe with him, she had become the first woman to dive off the Cliffs of Moher, practiced with the Italian bobsled team, ski-jumped in Austria, and steeplechased at Aintree. Dangler was twenty-six, combing the world for heroes. John Huston introduced them. He had just finished filming *The Bible,* and bringing Erica and Kenneth together, Divina reckoned, must have seemed to him at least as inspired as parting the Red Sea.

Very likely no one appreciated their meeting more than Preston, who stole off to England and spent the next month resting while Erica and Dangler ran each other ragged all over Ireland. At the end of the month they were married in a formal naval ceremony, arranged by Dangler, aboard an American destroyer in the middle of Bantry Bay.

Preston didn't come. But a great many other people did, including Divina; and after the wedding she joined the Danglers in London for a week.

"Erica seemed cured. She seemed complete. Both of them did. It was obvious that they sort of filled in each other's holes, and it was thrilling for me just to be around them. They just seemed to *float,* doing all these really criminally absurd things, and making them look wonderful." Divina stopped talking and chewed her bottom lip for a moment. "I had never seen that before—one of those relationships where two people can do anything, can crawl on their bellies like snakes, as long as they do it together, and make everyone envy them. It was very exhilarating for me. And for them as well. I asked them one night toward the end of the week what their plans were. Kenneth said they were going to travel for a while and then go back to Westchester where his family was and do something significant. 'We've decided to do only significant things,' is what Erica said."

Of course, Divina went on, when they finally did come back to Rye, it was a disaster. Kenneth tried one huge expensive venture after another, and each one just sputtered and died. Socially they were snooty and fed people horse laxative, and before long the town hated them as much as they did it. And Erica's condition came back. Dangler, said Divina, was patient and sweet and inventive about it, but it and the business setbacks wore him down. He got thin and nervous; Erica was hysterical a lot. They almost seemed to be disappearing right before your eyes. And then Erica saved them. Somehow she came up with the idea for the camp, and the two of them talked about it and realized that they had found what they were meant to do.

And that, Divina said, would probably have been that, except for one thing.

"Nobody knew how demanding of Kenneth this place was going to be, or how *fixed* on it he would get—he feels he has to make it into U.S. Steel. And Erica wants him to. But she needs him terribly; they need each other, and this camp thing is separating them. That's the irony, you see: the closer he gets to what she wants for him, the more it takes him away from her. She's on an absolute *rack.* . . . Kenneth says he doesn't know what she would do if you and I weren't here to help keep her in line."

Cobb's first reaction to learning the real reason for his being at Wildwood had been quite straightforward: he decided to go home. But walking out of the marsh, he had felt uncomfortable with himself, even before being told he was "tied-off." And a few minutes later, led by Tammy Wynette to what, mysteriously, he knew to be Gruenig's trailer, he had been seized by an unmanning and inexplicable fear. He had almost deserted Divina, and then he had lied to her about knowing who lived in the wretched place.

Now, trudging down the road toward the house, he considered his behavior over the past few hours and felt punier than he had ever felt before in his life—bottomed out and hopeless, as if he had pushed the wrong button and come out on some sleazy basement level in himself. When the road intersected with the driveway, he stopped and stood with his arms dangling, staring at a lilac bush.

"What are you thinking?" asked Divina. "You can tell me."

"She's just a person," he muttered. "God knows that's all any of us is."

He stood. And within seconds he was furious with himself—so furious that he had to bite his tongue to keep from baying at the evening. The anger felt cleansing and overdue.

"What I'm thinking," he said, "is that I appreciate your telling me about Erica, and I want to be as good a friend to her and Kenneth as you are. I'll be happy to help in any way I can. . . . And by the way, that trailer back there belongs to a man named Hanspeter Gruenig."

·

TWO

·

Pith and Moment

IX

The last ten days of October were splendid. The weather was clear and crisp, and what was left of the hardwood foliage was still brilliant. Invigorated by the weather and the season, and feeling at terms with his position at the camp, Cobb relaxed and began to enjoy himself. He slipped into a comfortable schedule. From nine o'clock each morning until the bouillon hour, and for an hour each afternoon, he sat at his desk in the basement creating work for himself from a carton of papers Dangler had given him. The rest of the day he spent outside, hiking or sailing or riding with Erica and Divina, or fly-fishing for brook trout with Peter Bigelow, or playing tennis with Ames Cravens.

Erica was not a problem. He and Divina walked or rode with her every day in the gaudy woods, and she was consistently calm and cheerful—though distant whenever they were not discussing Dangler. Dangler was the only subject that really interested her. She could talk about him in a variety of ways, but her favorite was to describe some small quality or habit of his in detail, and with an academic sort of reverence that irritated Cobb after a while. Dangler had not been much in evidence around the camp lately; his scarcity felt definitely high-handed to Cobb, and hearing him discussed over and over as if he were an Elgin Marble didn't help. But he wanted badly not to upset Erica, so he didn't say anything until one afternoon when, listening to her brag about Dangler's eyesight, he couldn't help himself.

With Divina they were walking down the service road toward the lake. The road was lined with huge sugar maples whose remaining leaves had turned a burnished copper color. Divina, who was encyclopedic in the woods, said that the color in a maple leaf appeared only when the leaf was dying, unlike the yellow in beech and birch leaves, which was present all year round but couldn't be seen until cold weather killed off enough of the competing chlorophyll.

"Kenneth could see it," Erica said. She had been looking at the sky, miles away, until then. "He has the best vision ever tested in the state of New York. He can see a woodcock on the ground at fifty yards."

"I'm sorry," said Cobb, "but no one can do that."

"He can. At three hundred yards he can tell you if a flying mallard is a drake or a hen."

"I doubt that, but I'm sure about the other. In my life I have only seen two woodcock on the ground, and both of them were less than fifteen feet away."

Erica stopped in the road and tilted her head. "What you can do has nothing to do with it. He can also read the numbers off a dollar bill at thirty feet."

"I'm really sorry, but I can't buy that either. Besides, if he could see that well, I would know about it."

"Now, listen, dearie . . ." said Divina brightly.

Erica's face began to cloud. "Kenneth's vision is one of the few things he's proud of, and he is proud of it because he has *worked* on it over the past year. If I were you I think I'd watch my attitude."

"Look," said Cobb, "I'm not trying to be argumentative. I have to doubt that anyone can read the numbers off a bill at even fifteen feet, let alone thirty, but I'd be happy to be proved wrong."

"A83723883B," said Dangler, peering at them over a book. "I'm occupied."

Standing in the doorway to the library, Cobb knew he was a good thirty feet away. He checked the bill.

"I apologize," he told Erica. "You were right and I was wrong. He's the true American eagle."

"I'm going to immortalize him," said Divina, and photographed him with the camera she carried with her everywhere.

"You should have believed her," Dangler told Cobb. "I hope you lost big money." He was seated at a long walnut table behind piles of books and maps. There were more books stacked on the floor beside his chair. He looked avid and impatient. "Hello, love," he said, and stuck up his hand. Erica walked over and took it—a bit nervously, it appeared to Cobb.

"I'm sorry to bother you," she said. "But your little friend was being a pain in the ass."

"No one's seen you in ages," said Divina.

"This place doesn't run itself." Dangler pulled Erica to him and kissed her briefly, then he turned her toward the door and patted her on the behind. "Andrew, as long as you're here I'd like to talk to you for a moment," he said, and went back to his reading.

The book was called *My Life with the Eskimos;* Cobb found to his chagrin that he had to move five feet inside the door to make out the title.

"You're disappointed in me—I know that pouty lower lip from way back," said Dangler when Erica and Divina were gone. "You think I'm being insufficiently attentive, am I right?"

"Don't be ridiculous. What do you think I am, a child?"

Dangler smiled at him. "I meant toward Erica."

"That's none of my business. Why didn't you tell me yourself what you really wanted me to do up here?"

Dangler got up explosively, pulling at his mustache. He marched to a window and looked out at the crisp blue sky.

"She's my soul is what she is. I'm going to take her off to Greece as soon as the camp lets out in February. But right now, and for the rest of the season, I have to be left alone—I have to be given some *slack.*" Leaning against the window casing, he looked tired and overwound, and watching him, Cobb was not surprised to feel a familiar urge to be on his side, wherever that was. "If I can't count on you," Dangler said, turning around, "who can I count on? I didn't tell you about Erica because I was afraid you wouldn't come." He paused. "I hoped that once you got to know her better . . ."

"Right. . . . Of course. Let me just say that I *am* enjoying myself here. And Erica is wonderful." Cobb felt suddenly expansive. "You know, for someone who's been through so much, she seems—"

"Goddammit, don't get personal," Dangler barked; then he strode around in majestic outrage for a minute or two.

Cobb waited until he stopped.

"Listen, Kenneth, I'm having a good time up here, and I like Erica. I'm happy to help out until the end of the season, whether you're around or not. But I'll be goddamned if I'll be yelled at."

Dangler came over and stood in front of him. "I've read forty-two books since Friday, and had only nine hours' sleep. Do you want to go hunting?"

"Why?"

"Why what?"

"Why have you read forty-two books in three days?"

Cobb went to the desk and looked at some of the volumes: *The Art of Survival* by C. C. Troebst, *How to Keep Warm, ABC of Avalanche Safety, Mountain Craft* by Geoffrey Winship Young, *Your Guide to the Weather, Wildwood Wisdom, Living off the Country* by Bradford Angier, *Knots for Mountaineering, Canoeing with the Cree* . . .

"What's going on?" he asked.

"We are almost ready to move into Phase Two. I can't afford to miss anything important." Dangler looked at his watch. "I have to take Cravens and this new fellow Fish out for a sika deer. Come with me and I'll tell you about it."

Down the hall in the gun room Cobb was given a Ruger .44 magnum revolver in an oxblood holster.

"What is this for?"

"Purely cosmetic," said Dangler, strapping one of the guns on himself. "Put simply, there's too much badminton and golf and croquet going on around here—the place is starting to feel like the Greenbrier Hotel. You don't find consequences on a croquet field. Where you find them is in the woods, and I'm not talking about pissing around playing wolf records on hikes and losing people for an hour or two. I'm talking about expeditions. Phase Two is Expeditions."

"Expeditions," repeated Cobb. He was watching Dangler, who was seated on a stool lacing a pair of knee-high boots. He was chipper and jaunty now, lacing his boots with the energetic relish he took in doing anything physical, even the smallest act. To Cobb it was the most characteristic and irresistible thing about him, this limitless, flexible, indiscriminate capacity for focused pleasure—the thing he thought of first when he thought of Dangler. When Dangler finished with the boots he put a whistle around his neck and an Australian bush hat on his head. Watching him, and feeling the weight of the holster around his waist, Cobb remembered an afternoon when he and Dangler, on spring vacation from prep school with Dangler's parents in Montana, bought water pistols, tied bandannas around their faces and ambushed forty shrieking children and a walleyed engineer aboard a miniature train outside of Virginia City.

"I have a core of capable campers now, Hanspeter has been giving survival classes for over two months, and I have read it *all*—everything from crevasse rescues to tsetse flies. We'll start simply, of course, with overnight trips, and then branch out to horse-packing in East Africa, trekking in Nepal, canoeing the Omo River ..." Dangler paced the room excitedly, looking like a bizarre guerrilla chief. Watching him and remembering the train stickup, Cobb grinned. They had demanded gold.

"I'm talking about full-scale expeditions, with major but controlled consequences. And the campers will handle them. We are making them competent again, Andrew. These people are descended from the families that built this country, and we are returning them to their birthright." He stopped pacing and examined Cobb. "You are amused?"

"Do you remember when we held up that train in Montana?"

"The 'Badlands Express.' Virginia City, 1960. We sallied forth."

"Exactly. Do you have another one of those hats?"

Ames Cravens and Norris Fish IV were waiting for them in front of Cravens' cabin. They looked irked.

"You're half an hour late," said Cravens.

"Couldn't be helped," said Dangler. "You men don't mind if Andrew comes along."

"Mmm," said Norris Fish. "We've got a job to do here." Fish was short and meaty. Dressed in a pair of leather knickers, a shooting coat and a velvet Tyrolean hat, he looked to Cobb like someone's idea of an elf. "We're losing light. I've heard these sika get spooky toward dusk."

"Plenty of time," said Dangler. He picked up Fish's gun and examined it. "You're overgunned."

"I take it along whenever I'm in new woods—you never know when you might want the stopping power."

"You see those knickers, Kenny?" said Ames Cravens. "Moose hide. From a Boone and Crockett bull Norris took at eleven paces on the Skeena River. I hardly think he needs advice."

It occurred to Cobb that the mean little set to Cravens' mouth probably had to do with Cobb's presence on the hunt.

"What are you shooting at 'em, Twist?" he asked.

"Don't call me that, please. No one has called me that in years." He showed Cobb his rifle. "She's a 7X57 Ferlach with a 1.5 to 6 variable Hensoldt Wetzlar scope. Let's just say I *generally* hit what I shoot at."

Dangler was standing a few feet away, sighting down the barrel of Fish's gun. "Say, Norris," he said heartily, "you've done a lot of hunting—what's the second most important thing you take into the woods?"

"Well," said Fish, "it would depend on where I am. . . ."

"How about you, Twist?"

"Listen, Kenny, no one has called me that in years."

"Toilet paper, my friends," boomed Dangler. "Toilet paper."

They walked west out of the neat woods where the cabins were, to a dirt road and then south along it under a towering sky. Though he had never been deer hunting before in his life, it seemed to Cobb that Merlin couldn't have conjured a better day for it. About a half-mile down the road they came to a seven-foot mesh wire fence with a large sign on the gate that read "Danger: Trespassers May Be Eaten."

"Load up," said Dangler when they were inside the fence.

"Are we standing or driving?" asked Norris Fish.

"We have to find them. You and Twist walk right behind me on either side, and don't pull on anything until I tell you to."

"What else is in here?" asked Cravens, looking around.

"Moose, elk, goat, aoudad sheep, turkey, a few bison, nilgai, Himalayan tahr."

"What about boar?" asked Fish.

"They're in a different area. Don't worry about the boar."

Fish dug at his crotch. "I wouldn't mind an elk too. How much do you get for an elk?"

"If you have to ask, you can't afford it," said Cravens, and winked at Cobb. He had relieved himself against a tree twice in the past five minutes, and Cobb noticed that he looked considerably nerved up around the eyes.

"You have to order the elk in advance." Dangler drew his .44, cocked it, let the hammer down with his thumb and tested the safety. "Keep your eyes open," he said. "They could be anywhere."

They walked west from the gate along a trail, with low white-spruce country on their left falling to a stream, and a series of ridges and hillsides on the right. Within a quarter of a mile Dangler turned off the trail and they followed him uphill, making a slight northerly curve through old sheep meadows overgrown with pine. They walked slowly, and after a while the hunt began to feel like a hike to Cobb. Fifteen or twenty yards behind the others, he listened for birds and practiced rolling off the balls of his feet going uphill the way Divina had taught him.

After exactly a half-hour of walking Dangler stopped at the edge of a small cliff overlooking a bowl of birch, evergreen and beech. Breathing raggedly, Fish and Cravens dropped to the ground behind him, legs splayed.

"What the hell is this?" demanded Fish. His face was pink and sweating and he seemed to be grinding his teeth.

"Are we hunting deer or mountain climbing? I haven't even seen a rabbit up here."

"I think we've gone far enough," said Dangler. "We'll just sit here and watch this little bowl for a minute." Crouching on the edge of the cliff, his right forearm lying across his left knee, the bush hat pushed back on his head, he squinted into the mat of trees below. A raven cawed over his left shoulder. The moment looked choreographed to Cobb. "Sometimes you can smell them this time of year," he said quietly. Fish and Cravens sniffed the bowl. After another minute or two Dangler pulled a long black piece of beef jerky from a bellows pocket of his pants, bit off a piece, and handed the rest to Fish. "You men had better take a little nourishment." He stood up. "There's only one other place they could be, and it's a little rough down there."

Cravens studied him. "Did you get those pants at Hunting World, Kenny?" he asked.

They came back to the trail almost exactly where they had left it, completing a forty-five-minute circle. It was nearly 4:30 and Dangler looked brisker and more business-like now. He indicated the spruce woods on the other side of the trail.

"You'll want to be a little quiet from now on," he said. Then he gave two sharp blasts on his whistle.

"What the . . ." barked Norris Fish.

"Abenaki Indian trick—the whistle stirs them up," said Dangler, and ducked into the woods.

They followed him down a path through the thick spruce for about a hundred yards, and emerged into a small clearing shaped like an amphitheater. A few feet to the left of where they stood was a bright pile of animal innards. Cobb could see two other piles on the opposite edge of the clearing.

Dangler took a breath and looked around. They seemed to have arrived.

"We've had good luck in here before," he said. "Norris, I'm going to leave you and Andrew here. Just stand behind this pine tree, keep quiet, and watch that opening over there between the birches. Twist, you come with me."

As he waited behind the tree, Cobb wondered about a

number of things. He wondered why Dangler had picked up on his unintentional use of a nickname they both knew Cravens hated (at sixteen, ordering his first drink in the Rough Rider Room of the Roosevelt Hotel in New York, Cravens had asked a waiter for a Budweiser with a twist). He also wondered if Fish and Cravens could really be taking this hunt seriously. But most of all, he wondered what was going to happen next. Given Dangler's inventiveness to this point, anything seemed possible. It was darkening fast in the heavy woods, and Cobb found that he had to concentrate to keep his imagination from overrevving. Deer with three sets of antlers? Giant deer, the size of rhinoceroses . . . deer on wheels? He could hardly wait. He looked over at Fish, who was breathing heavily through the mouth. Then there was a shot.

"Cravens," whispered Fish.

There was a second shot, then a third.

Fish turned around and stared at Cobb, his plump face puzzled and open as a baby's. "Three shots heap shit."

"I beg your pardon?"

"That's what we always say in East Africa." Fish was shaking slightly. "You know I take my kids hunting. This is the way you keep kids close to you—out of the house, away from the cocktail parties . . ."

Off to their right Cobb heard something that sounded like brush being cleared. He nudged the still-talking Fish. The noise was coming toward them, growing in volume and complexity, full of snappings and chuffings. Then it materialized in the exact spot where Cobb was looking, cracking through saplings along a lane in the trees, looking like a black cape being waved, and making whuffing hysterical swine noises as it came.

Cobb was delighted. A wild *boar*—and after saying there were none in here. Of course! He wondered if the thing was a robot, or possibly a trained pig made up to look like a boar. Whatever it was, it was thirty feet away and coming fast when Fish fired. His first shot kicked up dirt to the right of the animal; his second caught it flush in the snout, and it dropped in place, its left hind leg kicking, not twelve feet away.

Cobb felt like applauding.

"Attaboy," he said, turning to Fish. But Fish was somewhere else. All the blood seemed to be gone from his face, his mouth was open and he was smiling crookedly: he looked as if he were listening to music by earphones.

"Thassa wild goddamn *boar*," he said softly.

"Right. Let's go look at him," said Cobb, taking Fish by the arm. He was eager to see if he could tell how the thing was rigged.

As they approached the boar, Dangler stepped into the clearing, brandishing his pistol, followed by Cravens, and looking diversely harried as a stage manager.

"Nice work, Norris," he said. "It looks like a brother of the one Twist got. They must have come in through a break in the fence." He knelt and ran a forefinger experimentally in and out of the fist-size hole at the back of the boar's head, bringing out bits of bone. "Head's all broken up, but it won't hurt your mount. We'll have Divina take your picture with it tomorrow." He drew a knife from his belt and slit open the animal's belly.

"Incidentally, Kenny, that's enough of that Twist crap," said Cravens in a firm new voice. Cobb looked at him. His eyes were narrowed, his hands were bloody, and he was holding something that might have been a skinned rat.

Dangler looked up at Cravens; then he turned and smiled at Cobb. "You bet, Ames," he said. "Sorry, fella."

"I thought you only shot these things in a cage or something," said Fish loudly. He looked fuzzy and a little frantic. "These bastards'll rip you asshole from elbow." He noticed Cravens. "What's that you've got, Ames?"

Cravens studied him coolly. "The liver. Kenny cut out the liver for me. What's wrong with you, Norris?"

"I want my liver too," Fish said shrilly.

"Goddammit, Fish, get hold of yourself," said Cravens. "Act like a man."

Dangler looked up from gutting the boar. "Ames, why don't you ask Norris nicely to help you drag your boar back here. Then we can string them both up in a tree for the night."

When they were gone, he said, "I'm not too crazy about the way your man is reacting. I'm afraid he may turn out to be a D."

"Give him a chance," said Cobb. "After all, it was very

realistic." Bending over Dangler, he took a close look at the animal for the first time. He looked at the deep chest and narrow hindquarters, at the mean ruff of brindle hair around its neck and at the yellow scythelike tusks protruding five or six inches beyond its nose. "Let me get something straight," he said slowly, "this is a *real* wild boar?"

"Trapped yesterday off the old preserve. Wild as they come."

"But you shoot them here all the time—these other piles of intestines . . ."

"All deer."

"This is the first time?"

Dangler nodded. "And it went perfectly. Hanspeter brought the cages up and we released them onto the lanes just like the sika. They ran right for the clearings."

"Uh-huh."

Cobb watched Dangler work for a while and tried to stay calm by concentrating on the blue-gray coils of boar intestine. In a few seconds, though, his hands began to shake, so he put them in his pockets.

"Then what was the catch?"

"What do you mean?"

"What I mean is, how did you have it fixed so that this thing couldn't kill us if Fish missed?"

Dangler stood up, his hands dripping gore, looking uncommonly happy. "He did miss. So did Cravens. Twice. I shot Cravens' boar and Gruenig shot yours—that's how I had it fixed. Now, help me string this fellow up."

"Oh," said Cobb.

With night closing down the woods around them, he was willing to leave it at that and ignore a mysterious intimation, slight and indefinable as a rustle in the underbrush, that some real danger had just passed him close by.

X

At ten A.M. on Tuesday, the last day of October, Cobb stood on the brick terrace at the rear of the house, full of honeydew melon and poached eggs, sipping French-roast coffee from a hand-painted cup and looking around. The morning activity period was just commencing, and below him the thirty-acre wedge of playing fields and paths that lay in smoky sunlight between the river and the woods fronting the lake was busy with activity. On the far side of the trout stream a tiny figure in a Tyrolean hat appeared to be shooting skeet. Closer in, the Fairfax sisters, two new campers from Bryn Mawr, Pennsylvania, walked toward the bubble tennis court; Cabot and Ruth Waterman were stringing bows on the archery range; and a red Bronco crossed the river and turned left, as it did every morning, carrying Rocque de Faurier out to Revelation Cliff.

Cobb's view—of distant figures caught up variously in a sunny, ideal landscape—reminded him of the French painter Fragonard. It made him feel, as Fragonard's paintings often did, a well-fed, God's-in-his-heaven brand of contentment. In fact, he felt wonderful on this breezy Indian-summer morning. Yesterday he had discovered a monstrous mistake in the tax assessment of Wildwood, and in a few minutes he was going to drive into town to render his first valuable professional service to the camp by correcting it. In the meantime, he was pleased and content to stand here on the terrace, finishing his coffee and observing the smooth articulations of leisure below.

Humming "The Tennessee Waltz," he stuffed a pipe and was preparing to light it when a grimy red-and-blue tanker truck with "H. R. Clover Oil" written on its side crunched down the gravel service drive and stopped noisily in front of him, filling the landscape. A man in a stocking cap with an exceptionally stupid and dirty face leaned out the window, regarded Cobb primitively for a moment, then gunned the engine twice and roared off, scattering gravel.

Cobb sighed, lit the pipe and sat down, thinking that there was still the trip to town.

"Don't get too comfortable," said Erica. She was standing on the edge of the terrace, dressed in riding breeches, rapping a leather crop across her thigh. "You and I are going riding. I can't get Divina out of bed."

"I have to go to town," said Cobb.

"Fine. I'll drive you, then. There are some errands I can run."

She walked across the terrace to him, her mouth set in a high-pitched smile and her head carried oddly, tilted backward somehow, as if she were balancing something on it.

Oh, no, Cobb told himself. For confirmation he checked her eyes; then he picked up his briefcase and got to his feet, feeling condemned.

As he followed her down the driveway toward the garage, it occurred to him that he should probably try to precipitate whatever was going to happen before they were locked together inside an automobile. "Is there something wrong?" he asked. "You seem a little upset."

"Me?" Erica laughed theatrically. "*No,* no, sweetie. But I *am* wondering what you could possibly have done with Divina last night—she never sleeps this late."

He had taken Divina to Plymouth for dinner and a movie, and he told Erica that now, but she kept talking in a high, unnaturally bright voice about all the gay things they *probably* had done and the fun places they probably had been, so disconcerting him that he didn't notice until they arrived at it that they had come to the boathouse and not the garage.

"I have to go to town," he said again.

Erica was unlocking the oak door to the slips. "I *know* you have to go to town, dearie, and I'm going to take you there. Now, just trust Erica." Taking his hand, she led him into the boathouse and down a spongy wooden ramp to one of the lake boats. "Divina really has very little talent for fun," she said, "which is why it's so wonderful that you're taking her around to all these wonderful places."

Three movies, two dinners and the Franconia Fall Foliage Festival was, in fact, it, but Cobb was too concerned about his next fifteen minutes to care about correcting her. "Isn't she gorgeous?" Erica said, stepping into the boat.

It was a twenty-foot Chris Craft inboard, built in the 1920's for afternoon cruises on the lake. Looking at the slim jet-black hull, and the tea-colored mahogany planking of the deck, the red leather divan seats, the crystal bud vases and lemonwood cocktail holders that swung from the gunwales, Cobb had to acknowledge that, yes, it was very nice.

"Kenneth gave it to me for our anniversary," said Erica, glancing at him quickly. Her eyes were shining and her mouth, struggling to hold a smile, looked so uncharacteristically vulnerable that he felt a sudden relaxing sympathy for her. He stepped aboard.

"Oh, God," she said, looking around the cockpit, "we should have brought some bananas or something, shouldn't we have?"

When he threw off the lines she started the boat and idled it out of the slip. "I think you'll love this, actually," she said. "It takes less time than by car, and it's probably the last time I can take her out this year."

"Fine." Cobb's nervousness was dwindling. He resolved to be as gentle and helpful as possible.

"You know, she was a virgin until she was twenty-eight. And if it weren't for getting in her cups one night after a bird watch on Nantucket with Bo Pate, she still would be."

Somehow Cobb had the impression Erica was still talking about the boat. "*What?*" he asked.

"It's true, goddammit." Cobb looked at her and saw

that her face had gone cold as the gray lake water. She cocked her wrist and tapped angrily on the steering wheel with her fingernails. "You're all such bastards, really. I just hope she means something to you, is all." Just as it came to Cobb what she was talking about, Erica stomped on the gas pedal and the elegant old boat lunged for Colby Harbor.

When he thought about it later, he couldn't honestly blame the meeting with Foster Knapp on anything but himself.

He tried: telling himself that the combination of Erica's incipient hysteria and banging across a lake through foot-high waves in a fifty-year-old boat was enough to rattle anyone. But, in truth, he had enjoyed the boat ride. It was also true that the trip had seemed to calm Erica down; when he left her at the town dock, she was placid and cheerful. And finally, everything in the harbor—the marina, the supper-cruising paddleboat *Mt. Webster,* the boarded-up clam bar, the Quoddy moccasin store—was slumped between seasons, in need of paint, and walking up the homely little road that led to the center of town, dressed in a gabardine business suit and carrying his briefcase, it was most certainly true that Cobb had felt not so much rattled as luxuriously potent.

Thinking about it later at a booth in the Idlenot Café, he saw clearly that it was his own fault. He had stiffed himself, up here in the boondocks, by not even considering the possibility that Foster Knapp, chairman of the board of selectmen of Colby, New Hampshire, might be a crook.

The meeting took place at the Town Hall, in the basement of the Congregational Church. Knapp came in ten minutes late, squeezed Cobb's hand until it hurt, and told him again as he had over the phone that the entire town was "pleased as punch" about the camp. He was a burly man in a tight blue blazer with a florid face and mouthwash on his breath. The only desk in the room was occupied by a secretary, so Knapp seated himself and Cobb side by side in the middle of a row of little slatted wooden chairs facing a blackboard.

"Ayaa?" he said.

Turning awkwardly to face him, Cobb explained that

he was there about an obvious bookkeeping error in the property-tax bill recently received from Knapp's office by his client, Mr. Dangler. He took the bill from his briefcase and chuckled as he showed it to Knapp.

"As you can see, it's for six hundred thousand dollars. I suppose one of your girls just made a mistake . . ."

"Let me save you some time here, Mr. Cobb." Knapp shot his cuffs and looked at Cobb, his eyes bulging slightly. "Number one, we don't have any girls but her, and all she does is marriage and fishing licenses. I make out the tax bills myself. Number two, there isn't any mistake in that bill you're holding, except in that we rounded her off to the nearest dollar."

Cobb tried not to act surprised. "But the tax bill last year was fifteen thousand dollars."

"That was last year. We reassessed. Number one, we got a bad inflation up here. Number two, Mr. Dangler has made what we call capital improvements on that place. When you build a lift-served private ski area on your property, for instance, that's known as a capital improvement, and it'll run your taxes up."

Cobb thought he saw amusement in Knapp's face. He pictured him wheezing to someone at lunch: 'This fella came in thinking it was an *accident*.' He took out a legal pad, a calculator and his Cross pen.

"The tax rate here is thirty dollars per thousand?"

"That's right. You a family man, Mr. Cobb?"

"That means that Mr. Dangler's property was assessed this year at twenty million dollars."

"Ayaaup," said Knapp.

"Last year it was assessed at five hundred thousand. So in the opinion of the assessors the property has appreciated and/or been capitally improved by nineteen-point-five million dollars, or four thousand percent, in the course of one year. Is that correct?"

"Correct."

"Who were the assessors?"

"I am, and the other two selectmen—we don't believe in professional assessors; don't trust the ones from the state. You from New York, Mr. Cobb?"

"No," said Cobb. He knew already he was beaten in the conversation, but going with an old Bob Perch gambit, he tried to look as if he had won. He turned the silver sleeve of the pen, smiling enigmatically as he watched the point retract. "I will have to argue on behalf of my client that this assessment is wildly arbitrary and unrealistic. It seems clear that it has been made to provide general benefit to the town and to inflict specific and unconscionable injury on my client. We will appeal."

Knapp shot his cuffs again. "People think assessing is easy, Mr. Cobb. Well, it's not. According to the law, we have to come up with a figure that represents an arm's-length transaction between a willing buyer and a willing seller. Number one, it's hard to do that with a place like Mr. Dangler's. Number two, we tried. We were out there all one day. I'd say to old Melvin Bouchard, 'How much will you give me, Melvin, for my duck-shooting pond, four shooting couches and six hundred and twelve live and assorted ducks?' 'Well, I guess two hundred thousand dollars,' he'd say, 'arm's length.' Then Melvin would ask Francis Hebert what he wanted for his cresta run and polo field and two helicopter pads with subsurface heating combined. Enda the day, we'd spent over five million dollars apiece. I told the wife that night we might have to draw on the savings." Knapp smiled faintly, his face looking guarded and ruddy, and Cobb saw with clarity just how far behind he had been from the very beginning.

Knapp stood up. "The board of selectmen meets on Friday. You can bring in your appeal then if you want to. 'Course"—he smiled again—"we could deny it. Then you'd have to go look up the Tax Commission."

"I think I should inform you that I will run with this right to Superior Court if I have to. Also"—Cobb cleared his throat—"I won't hesitate to bring action against any malfeasance I might find."

"Fine," said Knapp. He took a tight hold high up on Cobb's left arm and led him toward the door.

"You know . . ."

"Excuse me," said Cobb, "you're hurting my arm."

"Sorry," said Knapp. They were at the door. He patted Cobb on the shoulder. "You know, you should think about settling in this area. We need a few nice young Jewish people like yourself."

Cobb had had a few minutes to kill before meeting

Erica back at the boat, so he went into the Idlenot Café on Fountain Square in the middle of town, sat at a booth, stirred three spoonfuls of sugar into a cup of bitter coffee, and wondered morosely whose fault it was that he had been flummoxed by a New Hampshire woodchuck in the basement of a church. Just as he figured it out, he realized that he was staring through his own reflection in the window at Hanspeter Gruenig. Gruenig was standing on the far side of the fountain talking heatedly to a slumped pear-shaped man in a stocking cap whom Cobb recognized immediately as the driver of the oil truck that had spoiled his view earlier this morning. He was being lectured, it appeared, by Gruenig, who was wearing a blue parka that said "Sun Valley Ski School" on the back.

Cobb had seen very little of Gruenig lately, even though their offices were next door to each other, and having him appear like a genie in the window unsettled him. A vision of the things in Gruenig's yard popped into his head —a plaster flamingo, a silver ball on a stand—and remembering his unaccountable dread that night with Divina, he felt his stomach clench.

The oil-truck driver was looking around, his face tight and dumb as a fist, trying to avoid Gruenig's harangue, and Cobb saw his eyes pass the street-front window of the Idlenot, and then back up, wide with recognition. Caught staring, Cobb continued to stare, even after the man pointed him out to Gruenig, but he added a little nod when Gruenig looked over. Gruenig listened to something the man told him, touched his skimpy mustache, and looked back at Cobb without expression; then the two men turned, crossed the street and entered a brick building on the corner.

On his way to the harbor Cobb walked past the building. A sign over the door said it was Curly Labeau's Sport Shop. Glancing inside, he saw neither Gruenig nor the truck driver; but he did see Selectman Foster Knapp, talking to a laughing white-haired man behind a counter.

Erica was on the boat when he got back to the dock, stretched out on the stern reading a paperback copy of *Anna Karenina*. The rear of the boat was full of packages.

"Poor Anna," she said, closing the book. "How was your meeting?"

She looked up at him and smiled, and Cobb was struck, as he occasionally was, by how beautiful she was. The question of physical beauty in women usually didn't interest him very much. Most of the undeniably beautiful women he knew seemed dulled prisoners of their faces—their personalities pacified and controlled by a jawline or the turn of a nose—but Erica appeared to charge around inside of hers, rearranging and inventing things there according to her mood. Her beauty was reckless and volatile. Something in it reminded him of hunger, and at times just noticing it felt like being slapped.

"Not so hot," he said. "How are you?"

"Much better." She motioned to the packages. "I went shopping. We should leave, there are scallops for lunch. But first I want to tell you a couple of things."

Cobb came aboard and loosened his tie. Looking over the harbor, he saw from the whitecaps on the lake that the wind had picked up. He felt tired and seriously discouraged with himself. "Shoot," he said, collapsing into one of the leather seats.

Erica came off the stern and knelt in front of him. She took his left hand in both of hers and put her face very close to his. He breathed slowly while she talked, and studied her sad full lower lip and the perfect curve of her cheek.

"First, I'm sorry I was so silly about Divina. You're the best thing that's happened to her in months. And that's really the second thing, Andy—there has simply never been a better friend than you've been to all of us over the past few weeks. Particularly to me. I love you for it and I want you to know that." She rubbed his hand against the cheek he was watching and stood up. "I *am* trying, I want you to know that too. I am trying to get through all of this, but it *is not* easy. He spends thirty minutes every night now under a freezing shower with a blindfold on, untying knots in pieces of rope. He comes out blue and won't speak for hours. There is nothing, God knows, easy about that."

"Why?" said Cobb. "Why on earth does he do that?"

"It's practice for climbing a mountain at night in a blizzard. It has to do with this Phase Two thing of his, and that has to do with making the campers really able to take care of themselves, and *that* has to do with . . . with the Arabs or something." She paused and bit her fist. "He just believes in things so hard."

"Yes."

"He just believes so hard in . . . possibilities."

"Don't you?"

"I believe in the body," she said. "That there are twenty thousand pores in a square inch of fingertip, I believe in that. We thought up this camp thing as a joke, sort of—as a place for people to have fun pretending they were doing things they weren't. Not something to get *beliefs* about. I thought it up just to get us out of Rye, to tell you the truth. We were not completely happy in Rye."

"I know," said Cobb.

"No you don't. Everybody in Rye had whole Orvis houses: Orvis mailboxes, Orvis wastebaskets, Orvis light switches, Orvis ice buckets. And in every single living room there was an English walnut table with little *things* on it— Aynsley birds, Fabergé eggs, lacquer boxes, little silver greyhounds. After we had been there two months I bought a walnut conference table the size of a soccer field and put seven hundred and four things on it—*that's* how unhappy we were." She raised her fist to her mouth again and looked at him over it. Her eyes, he was relieved to see, were still clear.

"I think it's about to rain," Cobb said. "Maybe we should go. We can talk more about this at the house if you want."

"It's all my fault. I made him do this."

"Listen, the season will be over in January and he'll be back to normal. He does everything this way."

"Just before we left Rye I said: 'You will do the big things now, won't you? You see, I want to see you at your biggest.' Do you know who said that?"

"You," said Cobb.

"Jean Story said that to Dink Stover in *Stover at Yale*." She stared at him for a minute, and Cobb thought she might cry, but she smiled instead and went to the bow and started the boat. "My father loved that book. Do you want some cheese?" she asked over the gargle of the engine. "I bought a Brie."

"I'll wait for the scallops."

"We'll have to hurry then," said Erica, and floored the boat out of the harbor, swamping as they passed it a sign on a post that said "No Wake." They hit the lake going wide open, running sideways to the whitecaps so that the boat rolled between them and Cobb had to clutch the gunwale to keep from coming off the seat. But it wasn't until Erica turned suddenly upwind, directly into the waves, giving the old hull over to an unbelievable twisting and slapping and throwing Cobb to the deck, that he realized their speed had nothing to do with lunch.

From there, on all fours, he looked up at Erica's profile. She seemed to be crying and talking to herself and laughing all at the same time.

"Stop!" he shouted.

"I might as well be living in *Fez* or someplace," she shouted back. "Oh, *ha, ha, ha.*"

Cobb lunged for her and grabbed her left arm, and the boat slewed violently in that direction. He heard something break behind him and felt a shock of wetness over his legs.

"For God's sake, stop!" he shouted, yanking at her arm.

"Let go of me, you bastard." Erica jerked her arm, lifting Cobb high enough to grab the back of the seat with his other hand.

As he pulled himself to his feet, trying to find a purchase on the bucking deck, he noticed two things: that it was raining, blindingly, in sheets, and that they were less than a hundred yards from the Wildwood dock and bearing straight for it.

He lurched over her for the wheel, and as he did, Erica turned and hit him in the face. He whipped the wheel as hard as he could to the right, feeling the drag of the screw as it caught, and at the same time flattened himself over her, trying to pin her to the seat. The boat made a screaming, fishtailing U in the water, throwing them both against the dashboard—and then stopped. It just stopped, and the only sound left was the rain and the small slap of waves against the hull. When Cobb looked up he saw that they were ten feet from the dock and drifting toward it. It occurred to him that they had very nearly died, and he stood up expecting to be furious. Instead, he felt like laughing. The stern of the boat was a shambles of broken ornaments, cushions and packages, floating in a couple of inches of water.

Erica handed him a key, and he realized that they had stopped because she turned off the ignition.

"Well," she said, brushing hair and the pelting rain out of her eyes. She grinned at him and he grinned back and grabbed a post on the dock. His whole body felt light with energy; he couldn't believe how good he felt. "Wasn't that wonderful?" said Erica.

She sat down on a gunwale and drew a leg up under her. Her face was clear and fresh-looking in the rain. She looked happy and spent as a tired child, and looking at her, Cobb wanted to kiss her eyes. He wanted to go back across the lake and do it again.

"Or did we have an argument?" she asked.

"No."

"Well, then . . . what the deuce?" she said, looking out over the lake. Cobb had the boat tied to the dock now, but she seemed in no hurry to get out. She yawned. "That's what they were always saying in *Stover at Yale:* 'What the deuce?' "

XI

———

Birch leaves, Dangler told them, are fine. Apple and poplar are OK, but bitter. Chokeberry, beechnut and willow will do in a pinch. But the best are elm leaves: the taste is neutral and they relieve hunger the fastest.

"Now, how about wintergreen?" he asked. "Did Hanspeter cover that?"

"Otherwise known as teaberry," volunteered Ruth Waterman brightly. "The sweet berries of this tiny plant are an excellent source of quick energy."

"Good. And how many calories are required per day for expedition activity?"

"Forty-five hundred is optimal," said Ames Cravens.

"And fat," added Peter Bigelow, "with its nine calories per gram, is your best source. From the arctic expeditions of Stefansson we know that human beings can thrive for many months at a time on nothing but the dried meat known as pemmican by the Plains Indians, because of its high fat content."

Dangler beamed at him. "Vilhjalmur Stefansson. In *The Fat of the Land.*"

"Forty-five hundred calories *is* optimal, isn't it, Kenny?" said Cravens. But Dangler, off into questions about finding water, ignored him.

Before survival eating he had covered navigation by the stars, and before that, tracking. Coincidentally, in the middle of tracking, someone back at the house had mistakenly put on the wolf howls—badly frightening the Fairfax sisters, who had not heard the record before, but no one else, including the packhorses. Everyone had stood toeing the trail while the wolves howled and yipped deafeningly throughout the woods and the Fairfax sisters looked hysterically from face to face.

When the record was over, Dangler said: "Apropos of our discussion, it might interest you to know that the weight of a wolf can be determined by multiplying the width of a forefoot track by its length and then multiplying that number by five. But of course," he added with a slight smile, "there are no wolves around here."

The people on the trail had looked at one another gravely. If there had been any doubt about it before, this unplanned renunciation of the wolf record now made it absolutely clear to everyone that Dangler meant what he had said in his speech last night—Phase Two was a brand new ballgame. And coming as it did just thirty minutes into their first expedition, that assurance had seemed more bracing than frightening: it had put almost everyone into excellent spirits.

They were twenty-five in all—the twelve campers, Dangler and Erica, Andrew Cobb, Divina Thayer, Hanspeter Gruenig, six recreation assistants, and a couple of men to handle the six packhorses that carried their tents and stoves and food, their sleeping bags and folding chairs and air mattresses and Coleman lamps, their down sweaters and balaclava hats and sheepskin camp booties. The hikers themselves carried only small blaze-orange day packs, "survival pokes" Dangler called them when they were issued after breakfast, each containing a flint for starting fires, strips of sinew for bowstrings, dogbane fibers for snares and fishing lines, a lump of pine pitch to boil out for glue, and a leather pouch full of dried corn.

Nearly an hour ago they had crossed the river west of the house, and they were now on a wide, gently tilted trail that switchbacked up the northwest ridge of Mount Webster to the summit, the expedition's goal. Boisterous and didactic, dressed in wool knickers, bloodred knee socks, Italian hiking boots and a Greek fisherman's sweater, Dangler led the way, with Erica beside him. Then came the campers, Cobb and Divina, a sullen Gruenig, and finally the horses and their handlers. The recreation assistants, all Nordic-looking teenagers, frisked up and down the line like cheerleaders, singing songs and passing around canteens of lemonade.

Next to Cobb, Divina was going strong, as she had been off and on for the past three days, on the subject of Dangler. "All this creation of fantasy around himself," she was saying, "I swear to God it's like Louis XIV or William Randolph Hearst, imposing their little-boy memories on the world."

Cobb sneezed.

"Are you feeling better, lovey? There's a rather good slate-colored junco," she said, looking through her spotting scope into the top of a fir tree. "You know, at San Simeon Hearst had a dining table that once belonged to the Knights Templars, and he kept Heinz *ketchup* bottles on it because it reminded him of when he camped in tents as a child. He told my mother that. . . . I'm simply concerned about him is all."

This was Saturday. Divina had been concerned about Dangler ever since Wednesday, the day after Cobb's trip across the lake. He was tired of hearing about it. Moreover, he knew that the source of the concern was Erica, and he was feeling short on sympathy for Erica.

After their boat ride he had gone first to his room to change and then to tell Dangler about the meeting with Knapp. He had found him in the library, ankle-deep in hundreds, maybe thousands of books which had been torn from the shelves. Neither of them mentioned the havoc in the room. Calmly they had discussed the best course of action to follow with the selectmen, and then Cobb had gone back to bed. The next morning he learned that after wrecking the library, Erica had gone to see Divina. They had talked for three hours, and at the end of that time Erica was back to normal and Divina was resolutely concerned about Dangler. For his part, Cobb had waked up the next morning sneezing, and tasting Erica at the back of his throat like too much whiskey from the night before. He remembered Dangler's stoic reasonableness in the library and was impressed. On the way to breakfast he decided that what Erica probably needed most was a good spanking. That decision had kept him feeling sentimental and protective toward Dangler all week, and it had made listening to Divina difficult.

"Did Erica tell you about his tying knots in the bathtub?" she asked him.

"It's *untying* them, in the shower," said Cobb, "and I'd rather talk about something else."

A few yards in front of them the campers and some of the recreation assistants had stopped and were forming a half-circle around Dangler at the side of the trail. Dangler lounged against a birch, at his feet a prostrate girl. Cobb saw that it was Pam, an assistant from Iowa, whose specialties were riding and golf. Pam was plump and had blond pigtails. She lay on her side facing the trail, her eyes closed and her lips pursed, looking like a snoozing cherub.

"Pam here," said Dangler when everyone had gathered around, "is in a bad way. She is not wearing wool clothing. The temperature is in the mid-thirties, it is windy, and an hour ago she fell into a stream, wetting approximately fifty percent of her body. Since then she has demonstrated increasingly impaired muscular performance as well as confusion and apathy. Now she has collapsed. Her present symptoms include severe muscular rigidity, dilation of pupils, and inapparent heartbeat and pulse." He looked around at the campers. "What is wrong with Pam?"

"Hypothermia," said several campers at the same time.

"Prognosis, Cabot?"

Cabot Waterman shook his head. "The prognosis is serious. According to the symptoms, her core body temperature has decreased to between eighty-two and eighty-six degrees Fahrenheit. Without immediate treatment she will die. Probably within an hour."

Dangler looked at his watch. "For Survival Situation Number Two you and Madelaine will have twenty minutes to save Pam's life."

Madelaine de Faurier looked up from whispering to Conny Ford. "Me?"

"Come on, Madelaine," snapped Cabot Waterman. "Get a sleeping bag and some dry clothes. I'll start the fire."

In Survival Situation Number One, staged just after they crossed the river, Norris Fish and Sithee Fairfax had been presented with a whole birch log, an ax, a pot of water, a tea bag and a single match, and given ten minutes to brew a pot of tea. Afterward, Fish had insisted on drinking the tea. Squatting by the trail and rolling the cup between his palms, he told Cobb, "When I was thirty I published *Solid State Engineering: An Overview*. All modesty aside, it revolutionized the industry. I haven't felt this good since then." He looked up at Cobb, his big face glowing. "Hell, man, we saved our *lives* back there."

During the second test the exhilaration was general. The campers stood across the trail from where Madelaine and Cabot were working on Pam and rooted them on. "Be sure to check for frostbite," shouted Weezy Bigelow. "Get in the bag with her, sweetie," coaxed Rocque de Faurier. "You have to be a *heat source*."

Cobb began to feel excited too, watching the chubby girl being brought around, not so much by the test itself as by a sense that something possibly more significant than peculiar was going on here, a burgeoning suspicion that this expedition was really some complex kind of experiment meant to allude to something larger than itself. It was exactly the same feeling he used to get reading Dangler's overseas letters and cables—a feeling that behind the zany, eccentric surfaces, something serious was being attempted.

"This is interesting," he told Dangler. "Also more fun than I thought it would be." Dangler was seated on a rock up the trail from the test, watching it, his face serene and organized. Erica was sitting beside him, looking thoughtful.

She said, "Tell him how you feel."

"I feel fine," said Dangler.

"Tell him what you told me."

"OK, I feel like Roald Amundsen in August 1905 when he saw another sail to the west and realized that after two winters of having his ship frozen in ice he was finally going to discover the Northwest Passage. That's approximately how I feel."

"Isn't that wonderful?" Erica leaned over and kissed Dangler on the neck. "Isn't that a wonderful way to feel?"

"I met with Knapp and the other selectmen last night," Cobb said. "They denied the appeal, just like we thought they would. We'll have to take it to the Tax Commission."

"Whatever you want," said Dangler.

"Well, it's clear they're trying to use you to lower the tax rate for the entire—"

"Done!" cried Cabot Waterman. "We're done."

"Yoo-hoo, we're finished," shouted Madelaine de Faurier. She and Pam were sitting up side by side in a green sleeping bag. Dangler yodeled at them. "Did they do everything on the list, Pammy?"

"Yes, Chief."

"First-rate, Cabot, Madelaine." Taking Erica's hand, he stood up and looked radiantly down on the campers. "Whether it's at work or play . . ."

"Find a challenge every day!" they boomed as one.

By eleven o'clock they were above three thousand feet and Divina pointed out to Cobb how the stands of maple and birch and beech were giving way to black spruce and balsam fir, and then, at around four thousand feet, an almost identifiable line where the hardwoods stopped completely and the pungent evergreen middle world of the mountain began. She showed him hobblebush, bunchberry and wood sorrel, a pile of fox scat, ravens, jays and flycatchers.

There were two more Survival Situations. Adrian Ford and Weezy Bigelow were given fifteen minutes to build a shelter from spruce boughs; and Ames Cravens, with only a jackknife and some animal sinew, had to construct a stretcher and drag Conny Ford a hundred yards up the trail to safety. Between the tests the campers strolled in one big merry group up the trail. Around noon the sun burned through a high skein of clouds, the temperature rose into the sixties and bright caps and wool shirts and cashmere sweaters began to fall by the side of the trail for the recreation assistants to pick up.

At one o'clock they stopped for lunch just off the trail,

where a small cliff tailed off into a stack of large flat granite slabs. Quickly and efficiently the assistants unpacked four of the horses, built a fire on the largest of the slabs, set up sixteen canvas camp chairs around it, and broke out the ice chests and a portable bar. Then they passed around cups of Senegalese soup, cracked Dungeness crab claws, iced cherrystone clams, a veal-and-truffle loaf, stuffed squash flowers, hearts of palm, a watercress salad, Brie and Stilton cheeses and five kinds of fruit. The campers, Cobb, Divina and Erica sat in a big circle around the fire on the bleached rock, taking lunch onto teak trenchers, drinking, and talking about the morning.

Dangler did not eat. He spent the break conferring with Gruenig, which visibly bothered Erica and put Divina into an irritable mood that was touched off toward the end of lunch by a conversation among the campers.

"Well, I don't mind admitting that I'm proud of us," said Madelaine de Faurier. She made a declamatory gesture with a crab claw. "All of us."

"Hear, hear," said Cabot Waterman, toasting her. "You know Kenneth is dead right—ordinary people couldn't handle this sort of thing. They're just not tough enough genetically."

"Common people, you mean," said Madelaine.

"Well, I don't like the phrase . . ." said Waterman.

"Neither do I," said Peter Bigelow.

"There are common people who are *not* ordinary," added Waterman.

"I can't help it," said Madelaine loudly. Looking over at her, Cobb saw that she was tipsy. Her sharp, pretty face was having trouble finding and holding an expression. "What Chief is talking about is *common* people. It's the common people who can't do any of this, because they're messy and have no moral imagination and throw beer bottles all over the place."

Divina looked at Erica and then at Cobb. "*What* did she say?"

Erica shrugged and said, "Maybe everyone talks like that in Texas."

"Oh, come on, Madelaine, this is America, for Christ's sake," said Waterman.

"Yes, but it's a different world, sweetie," his wife, Ruth, told him. "You and I grew up in a world where only good smells existed."

"Exactly," said Rocque de Faurier. "It's not so much the common people as their children. The whole country stinks of Coca-Cola and ketchup and plastic swimming pools."

"Not the children . . . insurance salesmen," Peter Bigelow said over a bite of veal loaf. He waved his fork at de Faurier and swallowed. "It's insurance salesmen who are ruining the country, with their damned bad manners. There's no respect out there anymore. Also no privacy, no order, no leadership . . ."

"We don't even *know* anyone in politics now," Weezy said. "Honest to God, I feel so . . . marginal nowadays. It's scary." She shuddered and drew her legs under her in the chair.

"We all do, I think," Conny Ford said quietly.

"Not here, though," said Adrian Ford.

"Of course not here," his wife agreed.

"You don't feel marginal here because things make sense here," Bigelow told them. "There's a point to things, and *values*. Values are what make this place what it is. Along with Kenneth, of course."

"A lot of the time at home I feel like I'm at a huge party where I only know two people and everyone is speaking a foreign language," Weezy continued. She was looking off toward the cliff, her bright doll's face distant and sad. "I mean, think: what good is money and taste and family and all that if all they do is make you into a minority?"

"And the only damn minority in America that no liberal group is trying to help," Cabot Waterman added with a laugh.

Conny Ford told Ames Cravens that personally she hoped that what they were doing at the camp might filter down, because she thought it was important for people who worked in factories to feel good about themselves and have fun too.

"Feeling good about themselves is fine," said Cravens, "but frankly, the most depressing thing in the *world* to me is poor people trying to have a good time."

But the last word on the subject came from Letitia "Tit" Fairfax, who, like her twin sister, Forsythe, was a rangy, fortyish woman with frosted hair, a leathery face and a small mouth that barely moved when she spoke. "*Egg*-zactly," she said two or three times, fumbling through her pack. "I *hate* the Bryn Mawr Fair and department stores and all those things . . . Now, listen to this." She pulled a compact from her pack, opened it and took out a folded piece of paper.

"Shhhh," said her sister, Sithee.

"This is from Vita Sackville-West, one of the great writers of our century. 'My manifesto,' " she read. " 'I hate democracy. I don't like tyranny, but I like an intelligent oligarchy. I wish *la populace* had never been encouraged to emerge from its rightful place. I should like to see them as well fed and well housed as T. T. cows, but no more articulate than that.' "

Tit looked up expectantly but was met with nothing but silence.

"Hmmm," said Cabot Waterman finally. "Well, that's a little bald, isn't it? I don't think that's exactly what we were getting at."

"Not at all," said Peter Bigelow.

Weezy Bigelow laughed self-consciously. "What in the world is a T. T. cow?"

Divina stood up, pale with anger, swiping at her backside. "You know, Tit," she said, "I saw Forrest Way Billings last month at the Myopia Hunt Club, and he was telling me that your cousin George has discovered he's a pederast, of all things."

Just then Dangler strode smiling into the center of the group. "Everyone get enough?" he asked.

"Quite," said Divina, turning on him. "As for you, Mr. Neo-Nazi . . ."

"We'd better move on up the trail then," he said.

"What are you telling these people?" Divina demanded.

"It's almost three. We're a good hour and a half from the top."

"What are you *telling them?*"

"That's enough, Divina," said Erica quietly. "He has a lot on his mind and he doesn't need you harassing him."

She looked at Divina, and Divina looked back at her, and Cobb saw something fine and bright as an electrical spark pass between them. The campers seemed to be holding their breaths.

"All right," said Divina.

"We'll leave Hanspeter and the assistants here to pack up, and meet them later at the campsite," Dangler went on. "Is everyone ready? What are we on?"

"An expedition," said the campers tentatively.

"Better than that," Erica shouted at them. "You'll have to do better than that. What's the good word?"

"Better to raise our skills than lower the climb," they roared.

The next half-hour was a long one for Cobb. He began it hiking with Ames Cravens, who had drunk too much Campari at lunch and talked disjointedly about the automatic sprinkler system outside his new house at John's Island. Then he dropped back to walk with Divina, who at first wouldn't talk at all and then looked at him pityingly and asked why it was that ninety out of a hundred Southerners were conversational cowards.

"I don't know," said Cobb.

"Did you or did you not *detest* that tacky little discussion at lunch? And do you or do you not find it immoral for Kenneth to be stirring up these people with half-assed social ideas?"

Cobb stopped in his tracks. "Why is it that ninety out of a hundred women overreact to everything? The fact is, I don't find it necessary to shoot my mouth off every time I disagree with someone, particularly when that person is simply being ridiculous. If you want to call that cowardice, fine. As for Kenneth, it's his camp and he can run it however he wants. It seems to me he's doing a pretty good job."

"Wrong," said Divina, striding away. "It's *their* camp."

The campers too appeared to take less pleasure in the hike after lunch. A boozy, digestive torpor had settled on them, and they responded stiffly and grumpily to the faster pace Dangler was setting and to the steeper, rockier terrain. Then, about forty minutes from the lunch site, the expedition passed the last stunted evergreens and was suddenly above tree line, into the alpine region of the mountain.

It was a transition Cobb had made a number of times

before on other mountains, and it always affected him in the same way. On Mount Washington, the state's highest mountain, there was a yellow sign at tree line on the main trail informing hikers in definite language that as of that moment they were sitting ducks to the environment. The first time Cobb climbed Mount Washington he had taken one step beyond the sign and hung there, realizing that his downhill foot was still in the abundant temperate zone of the hemisphere, while his uphill foot was in its arctic zone, a place where the only life under the brief summer sun was a few stone-bound plants with names like dwarf cinquefoil, where winds were frequently over one hundred miles per hour and temperature drops of thirty degrees in as many minutes were not uncommon. Getting the downhill foot to join the other one had been an act of will that took him nearly a minute to complete. Since then he had been able to make the transition without getting stuck, but never without his mouth going dry, and not without feeling a pressing need to urinate.

The climbing up the steep stone rubble of the summit cone was strenuous for the first time all day, and though it was warm for early November and relatively calm for the altitude, there was some wind and it was sharp. But no one complained. The grouchiness of the campers had ended with the trees. Surrounded by the lunar barrens of the upper mountain, each of them seemed to shift into a nervous and conscientious high gear.

Shortly before four they reached the cairn of rocks that marked the six-thousand-foot summit. In celebration, Dangler opened a bottle of pear brandy and wedged into the base of the cairn a bronze plaque engraved with the names of the expedition members. The campers hugged each other and laughed and took long drafts on the brandy straight from the bottle, and toasted the blue-gray peaks stretching below them into Quebec. But after five minutes of looking around, everyone was ready to leave for tree line and the campsite where Gruenig and the assistants would have the tents up and a fire going.

No one was more ready than Cobb. "Teach them 'Men of Dartmouth,' " Dangler suggested as they started down, and even with a dry mouth and a full bladder, he was more than happy to lead the campers in shouting off-key at the desolate mountaintop:

> *"They have the still North in their hearts,*
> *The hill-winds in their veins,*
> *And the granite of New Hampshire*
> *In their muscles and their brains . . ."*

In half an hour they were back among the comforting evergreens, picking their way along a narrow secondary trail that ran east from the main trail along a brow of the mountain.

"God, am I tired," said Ruth Waterman.

"*Tired,* tired," said Conny Ford. "I wonder if they brought some way to bathe."

Peter Bigelow offered Cobb his hip flask. "Wonderful day, wasn't it? I used to climb Katahdin before all the tourists ruined it. It was . . ."

"I have some rather bad news," announced Dangler loudly. He was standing with Erica and Divina at the end of the trail, in the center of a picturesque oval clearing surrounded by fir trees and yellow tamaracks. Cobb and the campers filed into the clearing and stood before him, silent as sheep. "The bad news is that this is the campsite, and Hanspeter and the horses are not here. They must have had an accident or gotten lost. I'm afraid we are on our own."

"On our own?" said Rocque de Faurier. "What do you mean, *on our own?* This is the wilderness, goddammit. Is this another one of these cockamamy tests?"

"No," said Dangler solemnly. "This is not a test."

Though he wanted badly not to, Cobb believed him. He had never known Dangler to lie about something important, and he knew without doubt that the question of whether or not they were here in these high remote woods with night coming on and no warm clothes or shelter was important.

"Well," said Ruth Waterman in a small voice, "what do we do?"

"That's the question, all right," said Dangler.

"Hanspeter," shrieked Sithee Fairfax, "Hans*peter,* Hans*peter,* Hans*peter* . . ."

"That's no good," Norris Fish told her. "We have to go home."

"No," said Peter Bigelow. "It will be dark in half an hour, and we have no lights. Someone might get hurt or wander off the trail. Besides, most of us are too tired to make it."

"We have to act coolly, and in the interest of the weakest members of the party," volunteered Ames Cravens.

"Oh, come on, Cravens," said Cabot Waterman with disgust, "this isn't a bloody survival class."

Conny Ford began to cry.

"Cravens is right," said Bigelow. "We stay on the mountain."

"But how?" asked Fish.

"Shelter," said Weezy Bigelow, "is our first priority."

Cobb had sidled over to Dangler. "This is real, isn't it?" he whispered.

"Yep," said Dangler, looking serious. Behind him Erica and Divina were sitting on the ground, their curved backs to the group, talking as nonchalantly as if they were on the beach at Antibes.

"Then why don't you tell us what to *do*? It's going to be below freezing out here tonight. Some of these people . . ."

Peter Bigelow held up a big hand amid the mounting babble. "We will be all right if we can find shelter. We can build a fire and eat the corn we have in our packs, and there's water back up the trail. I suggest that we split into four groups of four. Each group will scout in a different direction from the clearing, blazing a trail as it goes and looking for a cave or a ledge or a cliff. At the end of fifteen minutes we meet back here and see what we've got." He looked around at the other campers. No one said anything. "Chief?"

"Get it moving," said Dangler.

Bigelow divided them into four groups and designated a leader and a direction of travel for each. "Are there any questions?" he asked when he was finished.

"I want to go with Kenny," said Ames Cravens, who had been put into Cobb's group.

"You'll stay with Andrew," said Bigelow. "Let's go."

In addition to Cravens, Cobb found himself in charge of Divina and Tit Fairfax. Blazing every third or fourth tree they came to, he led them stumbling and prying their way west for ten minutes through the thick woods below the trail; then he turned them around and they followed the blazes back to the clearing. Bigelow's group was already there. So was Cabot Waterman's. It was very nearly dark.

"Nothing," said Peter Bigelow.

"We found a blowdown," Cobb said. "We might be stuck with crawling under that."

Conny Ford began to cry again, quietly and inconsolably. No one else made a sound. They stood huddled together, bedraggled and exhausted.

"We'll just have to go out farther," said Peter Bigelow after a while. He took a long pull on his flask. "We'll just have to try it again."

Suddenly Ruth Waterman burst into the clearing, laughing and sobbing and slapping her arms against her sides in a curious birdlike way. "We did it!" she cried at the startled hikers. "Chief sent me to bring you back. We've found this perfectly gorgeous *cabin*."

XII

The cabin, it turned out, was less than two hundred yards north of the clearing. Situated beside a rocky brook in a little clearing of its own, it was built of peeled spruce logs and looked to Cobb to be new and expensively constructed.

"It's a hunting camp," Dangler answered the curiosity about the place when everyone was inside. He had allowed two friends from Rye to build it during the past summer, and this was the first time he had seen it.

"It was fifty percent luck, of course, coming on it like this," he said. "But the other fifty percent was your calm planning in the crunch. That big metal box over there would be their cache."

"How about some light?" asked Cabot Waterman.

"You might find something in the back room," Dangler suggested.

They did. In addition to kerosene lanterns, Waterman, Cravens and Peter Bigelow found sleeping bags and air mattresses, down jackets, mittens, wool shirts and pajamas, ten Port-a-Potties, an Ashley stove and two cords of firewood, a rifle, a chain saw, axes, a first-aid kit, a small library, board games, a battery-operated radio and a jigsaw puzzle.

Back in the main room the campers built a fire, lit the lanterns and discovered behind a partition a gas stove and refrigerator, a pump and soapstone sink, cooking utensils, dishes, silverware and glasses. Then they gathered near the fire around the cache while Dangler pulled out bottles of Laphroaig Scotch and Bombay gin, tinned chicken and hams, bags of rice and flour and beans, dried vegetables and beef, coffee, sugar, tea, cans of evaporated milk and a box of Montecristo cigars.

"Can you *believe* it, can you *believe* it?" said Ruth Waterman when the cache was finally empty. "God, I feel like Alice in Wonderland."

"They certainly are well set up for a hunting camp," said Peter Bigelow.

"They plan to bring clients up here," said Dangler. He poured himself a glass of Scotch and settled expansively into an armchair. "The flag is out," he said.

After a long, chatty cocktail hour, the campers divided into work units to blow up the air mattresses, lay out the sleeping bags and make dinner. Cobb wound up in the lantern-lit kitchen alcove, pleasantly tight, dicing ham with Peter Bigelow.

"You were very good this afternoon," he told Bigelow. He felt warm and brotherly, and physically better than he had in days.

Bigelow turned to him woozily, knocking pieces of ham off the counter with his knife. "You know what my great sin is, Cobb?" he asked, waving the knife. "My great sin is gin." His big, melancholy face broke into a grin. "This place . . . ahh, not *this* place right here, but the camp, this camp is Lourdes. It's as simple as that. I've decided I may stay until I die. Not here; I mean the camp."

After the dishes were washed, Norris Fish suggested they play "Who Am I?"

"I have a toast to make first," said Dangler, and put a foot on a stool. His flattering eyes seemed to single out each person in the room. "Today you met face to face what Kant and Schiller called the Sublime—the ambivalent motive force behind all life, the determined yet purposeless world of nature. You met it on its own terms, asking no quarter. What's more, you prevailed, and in prevailing renewed our most basic resource, faith in our superiority over the natural world. I won't get preachy here, but let me just add that man is put on this earth . . ."

Out of the corner of his eye Cobb saw Divina throw a sleeping bag over her shoulder and stalk out the front door.

"The most significant of those abilities," Dangler went on, "is to dominate his environment, to force it to conform to human ambitions, and *not* simply to exist in it like a chipmunk. We are all here learning to dominate, and today"—he raised his glass, tilted it to the campers—"today you proved yourselves strong in mind and limb. You proved that you are as dominant and capable as you believe yourselves to be. I drink to that, and to our growing stronger still together."

Cobb found Divina seated on the ground, wrapped in the sleeping bag, hugging her knees and smoking hungrily.

"I would leave tonight if I could," she said. "If it weren't for Erica, I'd leave tomorrow."

"Why?"

"Because what he's doing now isn't the same as the canoe and those other things. This is something more, and it's dishonest and dangerous. He's got them really *believing* they can do things they can't."

"But they are doing them. We all did more than we thought we could today. I believe that's the point."

Divina smiled ironically, jerking the cigarette away from her mouth in a downward arc.

"I didn't know you smoked," said Cobb.

"I don't. What exactly did we do besides climb a mountain that any ten-year-old could climb?"

Watching her angry face, Cobb felt a sudden sympathy for her. He remembered what Erica had said about her having little talent for fun, and he wanted to hug her, to make her smile—to cajole her into enjoying herself.

He knelt beside her and said, "Can't we just relax and have some fun up here? How about a walk?"

"What did we do? Tell me."

"Look, I don't want to argue, but what we did was stay together in an emergency when we might have come apart. As I understand what Kenneth is trying to do . . ."

"What emergency?"

"Being stranded overnight on this mountain," said Erica from behind them. "What the hell is wrong with you, Divina?"

"You really believe he *found* this place, just happened on it," said Divina with a snort. "He knew it was here—he probably had it built especially *for* this."

"That's impossible," Erica said. "He would have told me."

"There were *exactly* sixteen sleeping bags, sixteen air mattresses . . ."

"He wouldn't do something new without telling me," Erica said.

Divina stubbed out her cigarette and put the butt in the pocket of her shirt. "Lovey, he said it was a hunting camp. There are no animals to hunt this high on the mountain."

"Oh," said Erica after a moment. She turned and walked off toward the cabin.

Divina stood up. "Come on," she said to Cobb.

Erica swung open the door to the cabin like a gunfighter. Ames Cravens was playing "Who Am I?" before the seated campers, and she nearly knocked him down on her way to Dangler, who looked up with curiosity from his armchair.

"This place is not a hunting camp and you ordered Hanspeter not to come. You're doing something new," she told him.

From the door where he and Divina stood, Cobb could see only Erica's back. She had on a man's green-and-black-checked wool shirt, and through it she appeared almost to be ticking.

Dangler got to his feet and started toward her, arms outstretched. "Steady down, now, sweetheart."

"No! You don't respect me any more than you do these idiots," she said, backing away from him through the gaping campers. "You think I need bringing along *too*?" She snatched up a coffee cup and threw it at him. "This thing is *ours*," she shrieked, "and I have to know. I don't care what you do to them, but *I have to know.*"

She stopped and looked around frantically for something else to throw, and Dangler leaped for her. In a flash he turned her around and picked her up by the waist, pinning her arms.

"Nothing to worry about," he said to the campers, making for the door.

Cobb held the door for them and shut it when they were outside. He followed Divina, who was following Dangler, who was weaving into the woods tilted backward and holding the stiff and silent Erica like an uprooted tree.

Twenty yards from the cabin Dangler put her down, turned her to face him and hit her in the stomach with his fist. Cobb saw the punch in the weak light from the cabin: it was short and unemotional and it landed with a whump. Erica coughed and doubled over.

No one said anything. For moments the four of them stood as still as statues in a garden. Then Dangler took Erica by the shoulders and straightened her up.

"I'm working, do you understand? If you pull that crap again when I'm working, I'll send you back to Bermuda for the rest of the year."

Cobb felt himself pop into gear. "Now, wait just a goddamn minute here, Kenneth—"

"And if I were you, I'd make a real effort not to interfere," Dangler told him, and marched off.

Reluctantly Cobb turned back to Erica, only to find that she and Divina had disappeared into the dark woods.

A light snow fell during the night, but the morning was sunny and still and the snow was all but gone when the campers came outside to play in it after a breakfast of oatmeal and flapjacks.

"Oh, *shuckins,*" said Weezy Bigelow, "there's not even enough for a snowball."

"You'll see more of that stuff than you want to see by the end of the season," her husband told her.

Peter Bigelow looked grouchy, and puffy around the face, as if he, like Cobb, hadn't slept well, but the rest of the campers seemed well-rested and jolly. The night before, Dangler had explained away Erica's scene to them as having been caused by the altitude, and when, after less than a half-hour in the woods, she had returned with Divina, to all appearances recovered, there seemed to be no reason for anyone to think any more about it.

If her tirade had raised any doubts about how the expedition had come to be at the cabin in the first place, they were dispelled as soon as Gruenig and the assistants arrived around 9:30 that morning, looking trail-weary and missing a horse. The animal had fallen and broken a leg, Gruenig told them. By the time they had dispatched it and transferred the load, it had grown too dark to follow the trail, so they had made camp where they were. He had come to the campsite this morning and the smell of cooking had led him to the cabin; he was as surprised as anyone about its existence.

After a run on the chemical toilets, Dangler called the camp on Gruenig's two-way radio and ordered a helicopter for anyone who didn't want to hike out. Conny Ford said she had shin splints and would take it; Cabot Waterman said he wanted the opening on the Dow and would take it. And they were the only ones, except for Divina. Divina was taking it because she had decided to leave the camp.

"I don't want to talk about it," she told Cobb when he walked her to the helicopter.

"OK."

"Last night did it, is all. I can't really do any more."

"I'll come to see you in Boston."

Divina stared at him for a second. "People hitting their wives in the stomach seems perfectly all right to you, does it?"

"Of course not. But Erica's not the only one who needs a little understanding right now."

"Well," said Divina, "you'll have to stand up to him sooner or later, whether you want to or not. He's going bonkers, and you may be the only one he will listen to."

"When I have something to say, I'll say it," Cobb told her.

Divina smiled at him, her big eyes skeptical.

Dangler staged the final Survival Situation of the trip back at the cliff where they had eaten lunch the day before. Before leaving the cabin he had devised one for Ruth Waterman and Tit Fairfax, and that left only Peter Bigelow and Rocque de Faurier to be tested.

Bigelow was not happy about the pairing.

"I just hope the ghoulish son of a bitch pulls his oar,"

he whispered to Cobb, reflecting the general attitude among the campers toward de Faurier, who was a shirker, a whiner and a braggart, who referred repeatedly to his vast family holdings as "the piggy bank," and who, the night before, had badly upset most of the other campers by showing off a collection of photographs, acquired from all over the world, of mountaineering corpses.

They were standing at the base of the small cliff where Dangler had assembled them.

"I'd say it was a 5.6 or a 5.7," Dangler told de Faurier. "Not much of a climb for a man like yourself, but it might turn out to be interesting. The situation is this: Bigelow has suffered minor injuries in a fall. You'll climb the cliff, then help him up from above, using prusik or bilgeri technique." He turned to the campers. "The assistants are getting out the chairs. I want everyone to watch this."

Shading his eyes with his cowboy hat, de Faurier studied the cliff. "Why don't I go around it?"

"Swamps," said Dangler. "Wild animals. You just can't."

"Chief, she's a real widow-maker. She may not look like much from here, but . . ."

"You'll do fine," said Dangler.

De Faurier's long face went truculent. "Listen, mister, Royal Robbins wouldn't try that wall without a top rope. I get protection from the top or I don't go, period. I have four separate companies to think about."

"All right," said Dangler. "We will posit a third man who has already made the climb. You rope up and get Peter ready. I'll send Hanspeter up to belay you." He walked over to Gruenig, who was lounging near the horses, and spoke to him briefly. Gruenig glanced at the cliff, shrugged and began to untie his boots.

"Have you ever watched rock climbing?" Cobb asked Erica. Seeing her standing by herself, he had gone over to try for a second time that morning to start a conversation.

"No," she said, and turned away. His first effort had ended that way, on a monosyllable and a turned shoulder. This time Cobb forged ahead.

"That's a tricky piece of rock—I can understand Rocque wanting a top rope. You know, he climbs pretty well, really, when he doesn't get impatient and when he feels secure." He cleared his throat. "I guess . . . well, that *all* of us need to feel secure in order to function well at anything. . . ."

He looked up at her consolingly, but Erica wasn't listening. She was staring over his left shoulder at Gruenig—Cobb found when he turned around—who was standing at the base of the cliff, his hands on his hips, barefooted, stripped to the waist, and looking boldly back at her.

With his shirt off and from the neck down, Gruenig was something to stare at. His upper body was a pale geometry of muscles, all ridges and ornate little curves.

"He looks like a fox," whispered Erica. "He's as perfect as a fox."

Gruenig looped a climbing rope over his chest. *"Was mich nicht umbringt, macht mich stärker,"* he announced loudly. Then he saluted in Cobb's and Erica's direction and turned to the cliff.

" 'What does not kill me only makes me stronger,' " Erica said. "God."

"Pardon?"

"Be quiet," she told Cobb. "Look at what he's *doing*."

What Gruenig was doing was climbing the steep little cliff with no protection, and with such grace and boldness that Cobb, who had watched hours of expert solo climbing, felt he was seeing something brand-new. Gruenig seemed to course upward along the rock like liquid, in subtle, continuous contact, going from one unbroken move to the next without once pausing or straining for a hold.

"Please watch the layback maneuver along that expanding flake," instructed Dangler, "and pay attention to how he is avoiding the vegetable holds. How fast does a man fall, Ames?"

"Sixteen feet in one second and sixty-four in two," mumbled Cravens, hypnotized, it appeared, like everyone else but Dangler, by Gruenig's progress.

Some ten feet from the top along his route was a small ledge, above which a holdless slab of rock sloped outward in a slight overhang to the top. With a mixture of disappointment and satisfaction Cobb realized that the Austrian would have to traverse below the slab, breaking the continuity of the climb. But once on the ledge, Gruenig didn't even look around. Leaning backward from the waist, he reached above his head, got both hands over the slab and let his body swing outward, so that he was hanging free from the top of the cliff, 150 feet off the ground. For a moment he dangled there; then, with a complex meshing of the muscles across his back, he levered himself waist-high to the lip of the cliff and stepped onto it. The climb had taken him less than five minutes.

"Full mantle. A very difficult move," commented Dangler.

"Now, that," Cobb told Erica, "*that*, by God, was rock climbing." Again she appeared not to hear him. She was staring at the cliff, and her face and throat were pink.

De Faurier was ready. He had put on his red wool balaclava cap and a pair of rubber-soled climbing shoes; he had draped himself with slings holding a bag of chalk for his hands, pitons, carabiners, and chocks; and he had tied one end of a climbing rope to a nylon harness circling his waist and thighs and the other end to a similar harness on Peter Bigelow. Now he stepped to the cliff and tied himself in to the rope that came hissing down from Gruenig.

Grinning manfully, his forehead glistening, he told Bigelow, "We'll get you up there, pal. How do you feel?"

"Fine," said Bigelow. "Good luck."

"Take this thing in hand, sweetie," said Madelaine de Faurier.

"Of course," said de Faurier. "But I don't mind admitting I'm sweating like a nigger writing a letter."

"On belay," shouted Gruenig from above, and the rope snaking down the cliff jumped twice.

De Faurier faced the rock without looking up. "Climbing," he said in a small voice.

Erica had seated herself cross-legged on the ground and was playing idly with a pebble, her face still flushed, inaccessible as the bleached stone she was sitting on. Cobb was about to make one more effort at conversation when Dangler called him and led him off behind the campers to a spot from which they could see both de Faurier and Gruenig, who was sitting at the top of the cliff, his feet braced against a boulder, pulling in slack on the rope as de Faurier bellied cautiously up the wall.

"What we have there, on the whole," said Dangler, squinting at de Faurier, "is a loudmouth coward. I am doing my best to change that. What I would *really* like to do is to read books and father children, but we are born to work in this world, and work, as someone said, is the only dignity." He paused. "I trust you are not also thinking about jumping ship."

"No," said Cobb. "Did you know that cabin was there last night?"

"Why do you ask?"

"I understand it makes an unlikely hunting camp, since there are no animals up there to hunt."

"You understand wrong. There are fifty mouflon rams up there. I had them put there in June. Do you have even the slightest understanding of what I'm trying to do here?"

"The last I heard, you were returning people to their birthrights. Before that you were destroying *accidie* wherever you found it."

Cobb disliked the sound of this answer; he realized that he was being troubled subliminally by de Faurier, who, a quarter of the way up the cliff, was singing "The Yellow Rose of Texas" over and over in a high, unnatural voice.

Dangler shook his head. "It's all in a straight line, Andrew, though frankly I didn't see the end of it myself until recently. Let me ask you this: do you ever wonder what happened to the cream of our generation? All those people we knew at Andover with more money and better families than God—where *are* they? Why aren't they running the country instead of a bunch of bottom-feeders? Well, I'll tell you why—because they are all drunk and shut away on the thirty-ninth floor of office buildings. They are all as soft and inept as that fool there on the rock. They have lost the stomach for struggle, and they have handed the goddamn country over to the lower classes. That's just the tip of the iceberg, by the way," he concluded. "There are things I can't go into."

Cobb was reminded of something he had heard the night before. "Did you really tell Weezy that religion was invented by the rich to keep the poor from killing them?"

Dangler looked at him with his new military face, the thin features gripped, the keen blue eyes full of marauding righteousness. "Get this, Andrew: I'm trying to make these people fit to lead again. I'm creating small, efficient cadres of the right people here who can overcome anything they have to overcome, including certain oil-rich foreign interests. I'm making them into survivors, mister, and I'll say whatever I have to say to do it."

"*What?*" said Cobb, suddenly feeling Dangler's megalomania all over him like a swarm of ants, feeling eaten alive with irony. "*This is a summer camp for rich people, for God's sake.* I mean, sure you're doing some interesting things, but let's be *honest* about it. None of these people aside from Bigelow can come in out of the rain. You can't go around hitting your wife in the stomach just because . . ."

"Enough," said Dangler, holding up a hand. "I invite you to watch the following.

"Rocque," he shouted at the cliff. Some thirty feet from the top, de Faurier stopped singing and looked down at him. "Rocque, we are now going to posit one more thing. Your belayer has just had an epileptic seizure, Rocque." Dangler waved his arm. At the top, Gruenig stood up, dusted off his trousers, and threw his end of the rope off the cliff. "As you can see, in the course of the fit, he has dropped your rope. You are now on your own."

De Faurier looked upward, and then down at the rope now hanging limply beside the one connecting him to Peter Bigelow. Then he turned back to the rock and laid his face against it. He shifted a foothold slightly. " 'She's the sweetest little rosebud that Texas ever kneww,' " he sang, " 'her eyes are bright as diamonds, they sparkle like the dewww . . .' "

The other campers were twisted around in their yellow chairs, staring at Dangler. Cobb tried to look casual. "You're not really going to do this, are you?" he whispered to Dangler.

"What . . . *what?*" said Peter Bigelow vaguely, looking back and forth from the cliff to Dangler.

Madelaine de Faurier waved at her husband with a cigarette. "Rocque? Can you hear me, darling?"

"Use your head here, Kenneth," hissed Cobb. "Do you realize . . ."

"Rocque," said Dangler.

"Do you realize what they are going to *do to you?*"

"Rocque, as someone has said, it is possible, even probable, in this day and time that a man might live out his entire life without ever knowing whether or not he is a coward." Dangler's voice was calmly in the lower register, resonantly conversational.

" 'You can talk about your Clementine, or sing of Rosaleeeee . . .' " sang de Faurier.

"Roquefort? Rocque, honey, can't you hear Mummy?" Madelaine asked him.

"Well, we are saving you from that possibility, Rocque," Dangler went on. "You have twenty-five feet of easy rock to go, and a refreshingly simply choice: you can either climb it or fall off the cliff. Now, climb, Rocque. And the rest of you be quiet."

Instantly de Faurier stopped singing and began to move upward.

Turning his back to the cliff, Cobb made an effort to speak calmly: "I see what you're doing, but it won't work. You said yourself that's an inept fool you're playing around with up there. But he is also a *human being* . . ."

"Cobb."

"Maybe Divina was right—you have . . ."

"This is my work, Cobb," said Dangler softly, his eyes on the cliff. "Mellon had his banks, Carnegie had his steel. My great-grandfather had the state of Florida. This country was not built by quitters, but by men of faith and vision." Dangler opened his palms and gestured at the cliff.

At Cobb's back there was a howl from de Faurier and then another, savage and triumphant, and the campers broke into wild cheering and applause. Cobb didn't even turn around. He took a deep breath and forced a smile. "Right," he said. "Of course . . ."

"I am American," said Dangler, looking at him warmly. "There is no one more American than I am."

XIII

Spirit at the camp the following week was even higher than usual. All the campers seemed to take a collective pride in de Faurier's climb, even to view it as proof that any of them was capable of similar conduct if the situation demanded it. "Grace under pressure" was how Cabot Waterman referred to it in one of dozens of dinner toasts to de Faurier: "To Rocque, who has reminded us all how to spell it."

There was a lot of talk about foreign expeditions for the following year—to the Hebrides and Himalayas, the fjords of Greenland and the valleys of the Hindu Kush. For the first time, all of Dangler's plans for camel safaris and white-water trips and distant mountain climbs seemed actually possible. In the meantime, he promised them—on Monday night after dinner—a winter expedition in January to close out the season. If everyone could get ready for it in time, he said, they would go back up Mount Webster and spend the night in snow caves. He had Gruenig and the assistants begin instruction in snowshoe technique and ski-waxing, the use of crampons and ice axes, avalanche detection and ice climbing. On Tuesday night he brought in to lecture the first of a series of bearded Englishmen who had climbed Mount Everest.

Cobb felt almost psychotically out of synch with all this activity and excitement. He had experienced no exhilaration, only relief, when de Faurier reached the top of the cliff, and now he felt none of the gaiety generated by the climb. Instead he felt encumbered and mentally tired. He missed Divina and he was depressed by the camp itself, in something like the same way he was depressed by beaches in winter. The weather had turned cold and gray. Frequent snow flurries boiled out of the White Mountains, and the enormous old house seemed suddenly cut off and bleak, the camp activities attenuated and faded, stretched too far into the wrong season. Despite their jollity, even the campers seemed out of place now. As a group they were characterized for Cobb by their nonchalance and their leather Topsiders, their cared-for nails and teeth and small pointed features, their Belgian loafers and red linen pants and polo shirts, their restraint in wearing jewelry, the blond hair on their brown forearms, their Rolex watches and old leather belts and citrus perfumes —all of which seemed to him to belong to warm sunny places. What they had here was winter closing down in northern New Hampshire, and he couldn't help wondering if they might not all be like a bunch of chatty, semi-tame mallard ducks he had passed every day one fall on his way to work that waited one night too long to migrate and were frozen into the Contoocook River.

He wanted the camp season to finish out safely and calmly—without anyone else being mortally toyed with on a cliff, without further flower-shooting episodes, or destruction to libraries, or nearly fatal boat rides. And he wanted badly to get the releases signed and the ridiculous tax situation cleared up. In the middle of the week he called Bob Perch.

"I'm going to take it to the Tax Commission," he said, after he explained Dangler's tax problem.

"Uh-uh. Superior Court. The Commission will screw it up. Let's get this into court, and pronto. I'll get a master appointed down here, and we'll flush these bastards out. What's the name of that head selectman?"

Cobb recognized the relish in Perch's voice and was grateful for it. "Knapp. But I doubt if he'll go along with a master."

"He will if one of his woodchuck buddies suggests it," said Perch. "I've got a few friends up that way who can arrange it. We'll flush those sons of bitches out and put the wood to them. I'll file the petition for abatement this afternoon."

"Thanks. And tell Grace to get me insurance on these releases. That I don't care what she has to do."

"Check," said Perch.

The conversation made him feel better. He was cheered up considerably more that night when Divina called to say she was coming back to the camp—so much so that he decided his low spirits over the past few days had been due simply to the isolation of having to work while everyone around him celebrated. Then on Thursday night he learned, to his surprise, that he was not the only one feeling jittery.

The camp had seen very little of Dangler since the expedition, and even less of Erica, who no longer came to any meals. Dangler still made the announcements and led the blessing at breakfast, but then he left without eating and didn't appear again until dinner. So it was apparent that something unusual was going on when he showed up at lunch on Thursday, looking crisp and urgent in a World War II Air Force uniform.

"There will be a campfire tonight," he announced after dessert.

"A *campfire?*" said Weezy Bigelow. "For heaven's sake, why?"

The campers looked around at each other, all but Adrian and Conny Ford, who stared into their pudding cups.

"The Fords, I'm afraid, are leaving us." Dangler stood up. "If no one objects, I'd like to stick with tradition and hold the ceremony outside. Bring overcoats or blankets if you must," he added, and strode out of the room.

"But *why*, darling?" asked Ruth Waterman after a moment. She was staring with exaggerated incomprehension at Conny Ford, and the dining room was silent.

"Well, we have this reservation at the Mount Kenya Safari Club, and Mary will be coming home from Bennington for Thanksgiving . . ."

"We all have *children*," said Madelaine de Faurier coldly. "Don't you think we all have children?"

Conny bit her lower lip.

"Sorry," said Adrian Ford, straightening his back. "We just have to leave. It's as simple as that."

Ford was a clubby Midwesterner with a flattering bray for a laugh and a way of hanging eagerly on conversations, waiting for an opportunity to use it. Cobb had never heard him utter a single unique word, much less take a position that separated him from the other campers, and therefore he was surprised by Ford's decision, but no more than surprised. The campers were outraged.

From the conversations Cobb heard that afternoon it was clear that they felt the Fords were violating a tacit agreement that everyone presently at the camp would remain there "for the distance," as Norris Fish put it. Weeks ago Dangler had stopped letting new campers in, despite a waiting list of over two hundred applicants, and had made it clear that the present group was "it" for the rest of this season—and perhaps even (this was Peter Bigelow's hope) forever. Now, ran the feeling, these people from Michigan were throwing all that . . . trust and faith and privilege, back into his face and theirs.

"How *could* they do this to Chief and the rest of us," wondered Weezy Bigelow, "now that we're really getting someplace?"

"Detroit," said Ames Cravens. "It all has to do with the way people live out there."

The campfire ceremony that evening was brief and awkward. The traditional songs were sung and Dangler made a short speech with the presentation of the paddles, but no one's heart was really in it: the Fords were nervous, the other campers sullen and cold, and Cobb was badly distracted.

On the way to the campfire he had found in his mailbox a note from Erica asking him to meet her in the library at six. The invitation intrigued him. He wondered what she wanted to say. Also, he had not talked to her since the expedition, and he was curious about her state of mind. But remembering his last solo experience with her and what she had done thereafter to the very same room they were sup-

posed to meet in, he decided not to go. He reached this
decision just as the campfire was breaking up, and though
he knew it was a sensible one, he couldn't help feeling a
little ashamed of it as he draped a blanket over his shoulders and trudged back over the dark polo grounds toward
the house.

When, just short of the terrace, someone touched him
on the arm, he jumped.

"Sorry," said Adrian Ford. "But Conny and I are leaving in the morning, and we were wondering if we might
have a word with you."

Over Ford's shoulder Cobb could see the pale orb of
Conny's face; she was watching him anxiously. "Of course,"
he said.

The Fords led him around the west wing of the house
and into the huge fluorescently lit room that housed the
Olympic-size swimming pool, where they talked for about
fifteen minutes. When they left, Cobb made a drink at the
bar and walked around and around the yawning green
pool, feeling too moved and elated to want to leave.

Ford had been a different person during the talk. For
one thing, his usually beseeching eyes had been calm and
settled in his skull. For another, he had not jerked fashion-
ably around as he usually did when he talked—patting his
tie, pulling at his trousers, and slicking his thin hair with
the heel of his hand—but had stood quietly, his meaty
hands dangling at his side, looking stripped somehow, and
comfortable for the first time since Cobb had known him.

He had begun by saying that they had come to Cobb
partially because he was Dangler's best friend, but also because they liked and trusted him and considered him the
only person around objective enough to be able to understand what they had to say.

"*Mature* enough," said Conny.

They were not *really* due at the Mount Kenya Club
until February, Ford said. They were leaving the camp because, frankly, they were frightened by some of the things
Dangler was doing.

"We think he's going crazy," said Conny.

"Overboard," Ford corrected her.

The expedition had made them both a little nervous,

he went on; but what had cinched it for them was an experience they had had the day before. He asked Cobb if he knew anything about the runaway horses. Cobb shook his head.

"You walk them out about a mile on the trail to this big gray rock where they bolt and gallop back to the stable. They're trained, you know. Well, Conny and I enjoy that, and we were down there yesterday getting ready for a ride when Kenneth came up."

"Eating *sun*flower seeds," said Conny sadly.

"He said it would 'help his feelings about us'—those were his exact words—if we were to try it once without the harnesses."

"Harnesses?" asked Cobb.

"They hold you in the saddle," said Conny. "Can you *believe* someone saying something like that to Adrian Ford?"

That was it for them, Ford said. They didn't have any illusions about who or what they were, and they enjoyed living. Then he looked at Cobb gravely, a little muscle in his jaw popping with emotion. "I was not good in sports at St. Paul's and Yale, Andy. I am not now a good horseman or a good wingshot, as much as I'd like to be. I *loved* the things we did here, and so did Little Mother, but I'll be goddamned if I'll Walter Mitty either one of us into a hospital to help the chief's 'feelings about us.' "

"Right. You're exactly right," said Cobb, feeling a surge of admiration and empathy for this plump little man in checkered trousers with a Rolling Rock Club patch on his blazer.

Well, they just wanted him to know how they felt, Ford said—it was as simple as that. They were sure Cobb would know what to do.

"None of the others will listen," added Conny. "Ade has *tried* to tell them."

Ford patted his wife's arm; then he stuck out a big hand and Cobb shook it and promised he would do what he could.

That was the thing, he told himself as he started a fifth lap around the pool. He had promised to *do* something with Ford's confidence and concern, and he meant it. The conversation made him see that he was not invisible at the camp, as he had half-thought he was. That even without costume at a costume party, he was perceived and appreciated, and that at least some of these people were sensing in him the resources he himself had feared were drying up. The Fords had come to him because they believed him to be an honest broker, and so he was. Of *course* he would do what he could, Cobb told himself, and he would do it well and according to his own lights.

Feeling wonderful, he made another drink and started another lap. Then halfway around he noticed a wall clock and remembered Erica. Putting the drink down firmly on the bar, he strode off for the library.

She was reading, lying on a couch at the far end of the room, when he came in. She looked up at him and smiled and said, "Would you lock the doors, lovey?"

Cobb closed the heavy double doors, but after a second's hesitation did not throw the bolt between them. Then he turned and looked at Erica, and seeing her curled on the couch at the other end of the fifty-foot Aubusson carpet that occupied the center of the room, he suddenly recalled the night in September when she had hung like Greta Garbo on these doors, fiddling with his bourbon-clouded head on the subject of loyalty.

Erica closed her book and put it on the floor. "I knew you'd come," she said. "Let's get this part over with and then we can enjoy each other: Kenneth has moved out onto our porch. He's sleeping out there in a tent. We are no longer . . ." She paused theatrically. "Living together."

"Good God," said Cobb. "A *tent?* He also tried to get the Fords to commit suicide on horseback. That's the real reason they're leaving."

"Well," she said, "I don't care about the Fords, and let's not talk about this anymore."

"It seems to me we have to."

"Not now, then. Come over here."

This time it was Cobb who hung on the doors, hearing as he did so the vague subliminal hum he occasionally heard in perfectly ordered atmospheres. Feeling peculiarly alert, his senses open as a cat's, he looked around the room. The buff-and-green-glaze walls between the bookshelves seemed warmer than usual, the lacquered Queen Anne furniture more inviting. He realized that there was music playing somewhere and a fire blazing beneath the Georgian mantel, and he noticed that the air smelled of tea rose.

"Well," he said finally, rubbing his hands together. "What have you been doing with yourself?"

Erica curled her legs under her and patted the place beside her on the couch. "Come over here, I can hardly see you. Julia Sykes came up to see me today from Boston," she said as he crossed the room. "You know her, don't you? *Au fond c'est la femme la plus dépravée qui existe.* She's going to Ireland on the fifth, and I told her about Dromoland Castle."

Cobb sat down beside her, crossed his legs and examined his cuff. "Dromoland Castle?" he said.

"Oh, Andy, it's the most idyllic place you've ever *seen.*" She tossed her hair away from her neck and looked up at the ceiling with a half-gay, half-desperate expression whose abrupt drama startled Cobb. She was wearing a diaphanous green caftan and her lovely throat rose from it in a perfect fluted parabola to the point of her upturned chin. Cobb found himself staring at her dilated nostrils as she talked, and having some difficulty breathing.

"Kenneth and I stayed there for a week right before we were married. There are these greeeen hillsides everywhere that look like they've just been cleared for jousting. And little copses of trees . . . in one there's this tiny domed cupola with a statue of Mercury on top and you can just *see* Heloise running to Abelard there. The lawns are all like green cloth, and the sky in the afternoon"—she lifted a hand gracefully at the imagined sky—"is salmon-colored with gray streaks.of rain in it and the air is full of pigeons coming in to roost, clattering in to the stone walls."

"It sounds very nice," Cobb said nervously. He had never seen her quite like this before and he had no idea what to make of it.

Erica continued to gaze upward. "Mmm," she said remotely and, dropping her left arm to the back of the couch, she began playing with his hair. With the movement, a gust of warm tea-rose scent hit Cobb and he began to shiver subtly. He knew that he couldn't trust his voice, so he just sat there hoping that his shivering wasn't noticeable, and feeling her hand at the back of his neck raise in him a welter of indefinable emotions.

"There's a garden on the south lawn," said Erica, almost whispering now, "with a keyhole fountain. And there's a lake where you can be rowed around, sort of trailing a hand in the water and feeling like Guinevere. There are Martel towers on the hills . . . and the River Shannon." She gazed down at him along the exquisite line of her nose and went on playing with his hair.

"It certainly sounds wonderful," Cobb said after a long silence.

"Well, it's not stunning, like Ashford Castle. There's one big castellated tower, and black-and-white piping on the windows. And a big black door."

She was still watching him, but her eyes were cooler, less engaged, and Cobb was sick with the sense that he was doing this *all wrong*—that he didn't know these lines.

"Andy."

Erica dropped her head and bent intimately toward him. She brought her hand around to his cheek and turned his face to hers.

"I think you've gotten under my skin, Andy Cobb," she said throatily, and moved her beautiful mouth toward his.

And then she changed. In the second before she kissed him, he saw her whole face arrive at the place her eyes had been a moment ago, and Cobb went suddenly, totally calm. And when she had drawn back and was smiling at him, her eyes now only friendly, he was still calm. He had the weird, satisfying feeling that something had been put carefully and permanently exactly where it belonged.

"Well," she said. "That's that. Would you do me a lovely favor? Would you read to me for a little while? Just until dinner?"

"I'd love to," he said.

She gave him her book and stretched out, putting her head unselfconsciously in his lap and crossing her ankles over the arm of the couch.

"My father read to me like this," she said. "Doesn't Vronsky remind you of Kenneth? I adore this book because everyone's hearts are always blazing when they see someone they love. Read the part where Anna takes him away from Kitty at the ball. It starts on page ninety."

Cobb read that part. And when the bell rang for dinner he went on reading the part where Vronsky breaks the mare's back in the steeplechase. After that he started on Anna Karenina's nearly fatal childbirth.

" 'Vronsky went up to the side of the bed and, seeing Anna, buried his face in his hands again,' " he was reading when the library door suddenly swung open and someone walked into the room.

For a second Cobb couldn't make out who it was. Then she came into the light and he saw that it was Grace Hurd. She was wearing a wool coat and a pair of L. L. Bean rubber-bottom boots that he had given her for her birthday. Standing alone in the center of the magnificent rug, she looked pitifully like a charwoman come to check the coals.

Grace stared at them for a second without moving, and then she raised a fist to her mouth like a child. "Ohh, my *God,* Pooh," she said.

Erica jerked upright and looked at Cobb, her eyes, for some reason beyond him, full of tears. "Who is this person?" she asked, her voice breaking. Then she turned on Grace. "How *dare* you walk in here like that?" she demanded. "Can't you see we're doing something beautiful?"

"Erica," said Cobb quietly, "I'd like for you to meet my secretary, Grace Hurd. Grace, this is Mrs. Dangler."

"I came to tell you . . ." Grace began, but then her face came completely apart and she began to sob. "I *got* your crummy insurance, and Perch got a master appointed, and now that everyone has done all your work for you, you can just . . . you can just *go to hell,*" she cried, running for the door.

XIV

Lloyd's of London had agreed to cover the releases at an acceptable premium, and Bob Perch had managed somehow to get one of his best friends appointed to hear the tax appeal.

Grace had driven up to tell Cobb these things and to celebrate them with him: on the backseat of her Ford Pinto was a cooler, and in the cooler, on ice, was a bottle of champagne. Also back there was her overnight bag; she had planned on staying over for a couple of days.

Running through the house, Cobb caught up to her just as she reached her car, and after absorbing a few hysterical punches to the chest he pushed her into the passenger seat, took the keys from behind the visor where she always left them and drove off, shouting at her to listen to him.

After ten minutes of riding around, she calmed down enough to do that, and not knowing what else to do, Cobb drove to Interstate 93 and pulled the car into a rest area, its hood facing Canada. He left the motor running, opened the bottle of champagne and explained for the fourth time that Grace had simply misunderstood what she saw—that Mrs. Dangler was emotionally upset and that he had only been providing company and kindness.

"Quit calling her 'Mrs. Dangler,'" was all Grace said this time.

She was still snuffling, but she was coming around. In ten minutes they had finished the wine and were necking. At first the necking was conciliatory on Cobb's part, and not entirely to his taste. Though at this point he believed what he had just told Grace about what had gone on between himself and Erica, he couldn't help feeling a little like someone who had left a Cordon Bleu meal to stuff himself on pot roast. But as things progressed he found himself wanting desperately, and for the first time in months, to make love to her. "Here?" she panted against his neck. "Like this? Couldn't we get a motel room?" "No, *here*," he insisted, "*now*."

He sat on the back seat of the Pinto and she straddled him, still wearing the rubber-soled boots. "I *need* you, Pooh," she whispered as she lowered herself onto him. "And I need you to be sweet to me." Cobb took one of her small breasts in his mouth and felt a dizzying rush of something like homesickness: he felt unbearably tender toward her, full of a fine stored spray of nostalgia. "I know," he moaned, gripping Grace's working, muscular thighs. "I need you too." As soon as he said it he knew he was lying: that what he needed was only her on his lap right now. But he needed that badly, and when after bringing her to a quick shuddering climax he came himself, it was with relief so deep and total it felt like sleep.

On the drive back to the camp Grace was buoyant and patronizing. She told Cobb that it was as plain as the nose on his face that he was being taken advantage of by a bunch of rich loonies; that he was in way over his head; that he was running catch-up on a slick track. She said that if he knew what was good for him he would come home to Concord with her that night, before he got himself into some kind of trouble she couldn't help him out of.

"I appreciate the advice," Cobb said. They were parked on the gravel turn-around in front of the house, and he had opened his door. "Do you want to come in?"

"Are you kidding? Well?"

"Well nothing. I'm not in over my head and I'm not 'running catch-up on a slick track,' whatever that means.

I'm doing a job here, and I'm going to stay until it's finished. Period. I appreciate your coming, though."

Looking at her under the dome light, he noticed how pinched and harried her face was. And looking at the little hairs above her upper lip and at her tired eyes, he wondered if one of the reasons why people like the Watermans and the Bigelows and the de Fauriers stuck so tightly together—formed so closed if not always so congenial a society—might not have to do with the fact that they simply didn't like to look at people who had to earn a living. The thought depressed him and he got out of the car.

With the insurance arranged, all Cobb had to do was coax the campers into signing releases. He had help in this from the first big storm of the winter, a full-scale blizzard that came howling dramatically out of the northeast on Friday night and lasted throughout the weekend, dumping over two feet of snow and keeping the campers virtually housebound. By approaching them this time one by one in their enforced idleness, by starting with the easy ones first to build a precedent, and by mentioning casually to each of them how much it was going to help the chief's "feelings about things" to have this business over with, he managed by Saturday night to get everyone's signature except Tit and Sithee Fairfax's.

The sisters were adamant. Speaking for both of them, Sithee told Cobb that five divorces between the two of them had been quite enough to teach herself and her sister never to sign anything outside the presence of one Joseph Barstow, an attorney from Philadelphia now vacationing in the Canary Islands.

On Monday morning Divina came back to the camp and the weather turned sparkling and windless. Over the next week the camp came alive with new physical activity. The cresta and ski runs were opened. The campers curled on the pond, went dog sledding and ice skating, and trained with Gruenig for the Winter Expedition. Every afternoon Dangler could be seen carrying on his own private training, sprinting up hills and skiing for miles across country. Even Erica appeared to have gone into training. She began taking three long solitary runs every day, and between them she skied with Divina or galloped her horses through the snowy woods.

"She always does this when she's unhappy," Divina explained to Cobb. "Exercise is what Erica does instead of Valium."

Divina herself had returned from Boston resolutely cheerful. She would not discuss her return, or the Fords' departure or anything else concerning the camp, and she would not talk at all about Dangler. Like Cobb, she said, she had her loyalties, but who was she to cast stones? She was certain that everything between Erica and Kenneth would smooth out after the season was over. And in the meantime —well, a long face certainly wasn't going to help.

Cobb was prepared to agree. The beautiful weather, getting ten out of twelve of the releases, and knowing that the Knapp situation was in control combined with Divina's return to put him into a much better mood than he had been in the week before. On Monday morning when he woke, he opened his curtains and looked out on the dazzling day feeling freshly optimistic and unburdened. He was as active that week as anyone. He learned to snowshoe, he skied, and ankles wobbling, he followed Divina around the trout pond on skates. He played platform tennis and drove a dog sled. He went to Winter Expedition classes and enjoyed them. In one, held out at the awesomely ice-bearded Revelation Cliff, he learned to pick and claw his way up a twenty-foot icicle, and he even enjoyed that. He tried out all the winter equipment he had bought back in September, and he ate and slept like a lumberjack. While shaving one morning toward the end of the week he couldn't help noticing that he was looking fitter than he had in years.

On Thanksgiving afternoon Hanspeter Gruenig put on a one-man exhibition at the ski hill. Except for Dangler, everyone at the camp was there, and the two wide slopes separated by the double chair lift were vivid with multicolored parkas and skis and plastic boots. The snow had been groomed all morning by a Sno-Cat and was lumpless as baby powder, except for midway down the steeper of the two slopes, where Gruenig had had six large bumps built forty or fifty feet apart in a line down the hill.

Skiing—slowly and gravely, making long, finished, dignified turns with a minimum of movement—was one of the five or six things Cobb liked most to do in life. But even higher on the list was watching good female skiers, so he spent the time before Gruenig began his exhibition standing on his old Kneissel White Stars at the base of the lift watching Erica and Divina short-swing down the hill: their upper bodies quiet and bent slightly forward at the waist, wrists flicking out the poles, their hips and legs dropping, rising briefly across the fall line and dropping again—knees bent, hips forming a cupped tender angle to the waist— then rising again and swiveling, the skis crossing beneath them back and forth across the fall line as precisely as wiper blades.

As in everything she did, Divina moved coolly and efficiently, while Erica's skiing had a swooping operatic emotion about it. Skiing side by side, they complemented each other beautifully, and Cobb could have watched them all afternoon, but at three o'clock, Richie, the assistant in charge of downhill skiing, announced that Gruenig was ready to begin.

Wearing the parka that said "Sun Valley Ski School," he appeared presently at the top of the steeper slope and stood leaning forward on his ski poles and looking down at the crowd while a tape of country ballads was put on the PA system. As the first song began, Weezy Bigelow, who was standing with Divina, Erica and Cobb, stopped putting lip coat on her cupid's-bow mouth and said: "What a strange little person he is." Erica looked at her. "I mean, wouldn't you think he'd play Strauss or *Tannhäuser* or something? How does an Austrian know about these American folk songs?"

"Actually, I've wondered the same thing myself," Cobb told her.

"There's something very unappetizing about his eyes," said Divina. "What do you suppose he's waiting for?"

Gruenig was waiting, evidently, for a song called "In Your Lonely Mansion on the Hill." As soon as it began, he kicked the tails of his skis off the snow and came lashing down the slope.

Cobb had never seen anything like what the Austrian was doing; it looked more like a form of crazed escape than skiing. Stabbing the snow with his poles, his skis stomping and slicing and jetting out from under him, Gruenig careened over the hill, much of the time on one ski or flailing spread-eagle through the air.

"I saw this sort of thing once up at Waterville Valley," Divina said delightedly. "They call it hot-dogging."

"You certainly wouldn't call it skiing," said Erica. She was staring at the ground and making rapid little punches at the snow with her ski pole.

On his second run Gruenig skied the entire slope backward, carving long balletic turns without looking over his shoulder. On his third, he did five spectacular jumps off the first five bumps, describing in one of them a 360-degree turn in the air. He left the sixth bump going very fast and at the height of his jump he arched backward, arms extended, tucked his legs, and brought the skis over and under him just a second before he touched the ground. It was a back flip on skis, and Cobb could barely believe he had seen it done. Along with everyone else he was applauding when Gruenig skied up and stopped abruptly in front of them, spraying Erica's skis and ankles with snow.

"Show-off," she said.

Glancing at her, Cobb saw with surprise that her face was flushed and furious.

"*Danke*," said Gruenig pleasantly. He took off his blue stocking cap and tossed it to her. "*Guck' was ich dir gegeben habe, Weib.*"

The cap hit Erica on the chest and fell to the snow. She made no move to pick it up. She just stared at Gruenig while Hank Williams sang "Lovesick Blues." "*Esel,*" she hissed finally; then she turned and skied off for the chair lift.

"*Danke*," said Gruenig again, grinning coldly after her.

"What was that all about?" Cobb asked Divina as they drove back toward the house.

"She called him a donkey, or a jackass—I'm not sure."

"What did he say?"

"Something about giving her something. My German is lousy. It was very unusual, wasn't it? He called her '*Weib,*' a sort of trashy word for woman—can you *imagine?*" Divina was driving fast over the icy road and her voice was excited. "The whole thing was so *strange.* But God, can he ski."

"I suppose," said Cobb. "Would you mind slowing down?"

They were alone on the road; everyone else was still back at the ski hill. As they crossed the river and came in sight of the house, Divina suddenly hit the brakes, throwing her Morris into a heart-stopping little skid that ended with the nose of the car buried in a snowbank.

"Are you trying to kill us?" shouted Cobb.

"That truck is over there again." Divina pointed toward the west wing of the house. "Hurry up and push us out of here, I want you to see this."

After they freed the car, Divina drove to the front of the house and parked; then she led Cobb by the hand around the east wing and across the slippery patio to the west tower, where she flattened herself against the stone, pulling him to her.

"This is the second time this week," she said, her eyes bright with intrigue. "Look, but be careful."

Cobb peered around the tower and saw the rear end of an oil truck. There was a hose running from it to a pipe near the corner of the patio. "It's putting fuel in the house, Divina."

"We'll just wait, then. It's very peculiar what it does," she said over the ratchety noise of the pump. She pulled him back against the tower and grinned. "You know, you and I would make a wonderful espionage team. We're both born spies."

"I tend to sneeze when I spy," said Cobb.

"What I mean is that we both like to be behind things. I'm never as happy as when I'm behind a camera or a pair of binoculars. And you are always looking out from behind your manners or something."

"Because I'm tied-off," said Cobb with a smile.

"That's how you and I are so different from Erica and Kenneth. They're *never* behind anything. They just roll through life like a Panzer unit. . . . They don't really know anyone else exists. I'd give anything to feel like that for just one day."

"No you wouldn't."

"Yes I would, and so would you. I'm tired of always watching things and hiding. Once before I die I'd like to just be *reckless* and not even think about it." Divina blew a smoke ring with her breath and watched it expand and fade. "Just for one day, though, I think."

The sun was almost down, and Cobb was cold. He was just about to suggest that they continue spying some other time when the pump stopped and all they could hear was the idle of the truck's engine.

"Watch what it does now," whispered Divina.

Peeking around the tower again, his head just above Divina's, Cobb saw the man he had seen driving the truck before, and then in town with Gruenig, get out and look around. The man went to the pipe, drew out the hose, climbed a ladder on the side of the truck, opened a hatch on the roof and stuck the hose into it. Then he got back into the truck and the pump started up again.

"Now, is there or is there not," said Divina, "something distinctly funny about that?" Cobb had to concede that there might be.

They stood for another few minutes watching the truck fill itself, the meter at the back clicking off gallon after gallon.

"What should we do?" asked Divina.

"Go see Kenneth, I suppose."

"You go see him," she said. "You can tell me what he says at dinner."

Dangler was not in his rooms upstairs, nor was he in or around the powder-blue expedition tent pitched on the porch off the bedroom, and Cobb had started back downstairs when he noticed an open door down the second-floor hall. Rapping lightly, he looked into a room he had not seen before, a large upstairs study cluttered with books and maps. A reading lamp was on, and the room had an occupied look to it, so he stepped inside. Glancing over his left shoulder, he found himself face to face with Herbert "Bull" Dangler.

Though he had never seen the portrait before, he knew immediately who it was. In Florida the arrogant features were engraved into countless bronze plaques on the hotels, office buildings and banks that this Dangler had constructed out of sheer physical impatience while waiting for his railroad to be completed. The painting covered most of the wall. It showed a fat man dressed in a tweed suit and knee-high leather boots astride a horse at the top of a sandy rise with palmetto trees and the ocean in the background. The man was turned at the waist, his mouth slightly ajar above a full black beard, and was staring directly at Cobb with hard piglike eyes. One small gloved hand held the reins in the crossover English grip and the other pointed grandly southward. Cobb knew the direction was south. From grammar school onward he had known all about what was going on here: how Bull had traveled in a private car emblazoned with the Hapsburg crest to the end of each new five miles of track, then ridden the horse to the highest point of land, bellowed for his foreman, and pointed out where the next section should be laid, inching down the state this way through the wild palmetto scrub from Jacksonville to Miami, building like a fire-ant as he went; and how, when he ran out of land, he had just moved over and come back up the west coast; and finally, how he had left the state for New York and New Hampshire the day the last spike was hammered, saying to the press that met him in New York that he had always detested Florida and was deeply gratified to be done with it at last.

"'The central legend of our time,'" said his great-grandson from the doorway, "'is the active will mastering the environment.' That was his motto. Also his epitaph. He had it carved on his headstone up on Mount Webster, where he had himself buried on horseback."

Cobb had no idea how long Dangler had been watching him. "The door was open," he said.

"'Never look back'—he had that put on there too. I was running," said Dangler, coming in. He had on a pair of sweat pants, heavy climbing boots and a T-shirt. Cobb was struck with how thin he had grown. He looked ropy and tough as a guava tree. Even his face looked sinewy, and there was ice in his yellow mustache.

"In those clothes?"

Dangler grinned. "I've learned to control my liver. By slowing it down I can drop my metabolic rate, making me less susceptible to cold."

"Oh," said Cobb. "Happy Thanksgiving."

"I have also learned how to close my mouth when I yawn."

"Why would anyone want to learn that?"

Dangler sat down in a red leather armchair and put his feet up on a table, knocking snow from the lug soles of his boots onto the glass top. " 'Be systematically heroic in little unnecessary points; do every day or two something for no other reason than its difficulty, so that when the hour of dire need draws nigh, it may find you not unnerved and untrained to stand the test.' William James." He put his hands behind his head and grinned at Cobb again, looking cheerful and lusty. "How are things, *mon vieux?*"

"Some things are fine. Your tax appeal is being heard by a master in Concord, and I'm confident we'll win it. Also, I went ahead with the releases and everyone has signed them but the Fairfax sisters, who refuse to."

"It doesn't matter," said Dangler.

"I wish I could agree. Anyway, I came up here to tell you . . ."

"It couldn't matter less," said Dangler, his face going suddenly dark. "The Fairfaxes are culls, like Ford and his wife and the de Fauriers and that fool Fish. I'm getting rid of all of them. They won't even be here in two weeks."

Cobb stood silently for a moment, working something out in his mind. "You got rid of the Fords?" he said when he was finished.

"I helped them to realize this was the wrong environment for them," said Dangler. "I will help the others as well."

Cobb felt tricked, imaginatively bested. Up until seconds ago he had credited Ford with a singular victory— with having made a courageous decision, and with having stuck to it in spite of Dangler. Now he saw that Dangler, as usual, had been a step ahead of everyone.

"By threatening them, you mean? Like you did the Fords?"

"Listen," said Dangler, holding up a hand, "if this is

going to turn into a diatribe, I will have to curtail my pleasure in seeing you and ask you to leave. I have yoga to do, and I won't be whined at."

"I came up here," said Cobb stiffly, "to inform you that you are being robbed blind by the company you buy your heating oil from. After they fill your tank, they keep pumping oil back into the truck, thereby running up your bill as high as they please. Divina and I watched a man doing it less than half an hour ago, and she has seen it a number of times before."

"So have I," said Dangler. While Cobb was talking, he had slipped into his third mood in so many minutes: he now looked bored. "The world is full of petty thieves, Andrew. If it worries you, please tell Hanspeter, who is responsible for things like that." He checked his watch. "I have thirty minutes of yoga now."

"Fine," said Cobb. "Be my guest." As he left the room, he added: "No wonder you live in a tent."

After Thanksgiving dinner, he and Divina went out to Gruenig's trailer. It was Divina's idea. Cobb was more of a mind to write the Austrian a memo about the oil truck, particularly in light of the fact that he knew the driver and Gruenig to be acquainted.

"Memos are what's wrong with this place," Divina said, putting on her boots. "If you don't come, I'll go by myself."

Once outside, she decided they should walk. It was a still, clear night with a full moon, and Cobb could think of no reason not to agree. As they crunched down the snowy driveway, she told him about a birding trip she had made the past spring to Baffin Island in the Arctic Ocean, and another trip, just before that one, to Portugal, and then in the next breath about how tired she was of travel and aimlessness and that she might go back to school in the spring, or into teaching, or working with underprivileged children, or maybe to New York to edit books.

"I don't do enough with my life is the point." She looked up at him. "Do you know why I came back to the camp?"

"Because you were bored in Boston. Anything is boring

after a month with Kenneth and Erica. And because you were concerned about Erica."

Divina stopped in the road, her big eyes alight with the moon, unblinking and grave. "What else?"

"Because you missed me, and knew I missed you."

"Very much that." She took his hands and put them on her cheeks. Her face drifted up to his, and she kissed him lightly. "I have this feeling that we could hold hands and go anywhere together. Did I hurt your feelings this afternoon, calling you a spy?"

"You were right: a master spy. I don't like it."

She tossed her head and began walking again. "Do you like me?"

"Very much."

"I mean really. It's a little hard to tell with you. And nobody else has, really—not that way."

Cobb put his hands in the pockets of his parka and considered. "I should tell you that I live with a woman. I'm not sure for how much longer, but . . ."

"You don't have to say any more." Divina took his arm and snuggled as close to him as walking would allow. "I know you like me," she said happily. "And we have plenty of time, don't we? It's not *always* cocktail hour with us the way it is with Erica and Kenneth . . . We have plenty of time."

Adjusting to her small, neat stride—a stride that made him think of golf courses—feeling her against him and half-listening to her fine husky voice, Cobb couldn't remember in all his life ever feeling quite so at ease with another human being. He felt an urge to tell her that start and then stop in him. All the time in the world, he told himself comfortably.

Caught up in each other, neither of them noticed the oil truck until they were directly across from Gruenig's trailer, though it was right there in front, parked between the plaster flamingo and the birdbath.

"Isn't that . . . ?"

"I think we'd better go," Cobb said.

"But that's the same truck," said Divina. "What would it be doing here?"

Cobb didn't know. Nor did he care to. Seeing it there,

hulking among the objects in Gruenig's yard, brought up in him the unreasoning dread he had felt in that same place a few weeks before with Divina, and now, as then, he wanted to leave.

"Of *course*," said Divina, gripping his arm. "Gruenig is *in* with them, don't you see? He's in *cahoots*." Still holding his arm, she crouched and began stalking the dimly illuminated trailer, pulling Cobb along.

"No," he said. "Stop it."

"We have to see them together," said Divina, tightening her grip. There was more than a touch of impatience in her voice, and it caused Cobb to remember his behavior the last time they were here.

"All right, goddammit," he whispered. "We see them together and then we leave."

Stepping carefully into footprints already in the snow, they stole up to the front porch and then around it and down the length of the trailer to a window near the end.

Crouching there, Cobb could hear a small chattering noise coming from inside. It was a noise he knew from somewhere but couldn't place. "I'll do it," he whispered, and inched himself up the cold aluminum side of the trailer, his heart pounding in his ears, until his eyes were at window level. Then he sneezed.

In the instant before Gruenig turned and saw him, this is what Cobb saw: a bottle of whiskey and a glowing movie projector on a kitchen table, Gruenig, the oil-truck driver, and Dangler's helicopter pilot, Rip somebody—and down on the far wall of the trailer, their images blurred and distorted but hauntingly familiar, two people making hectic cinematic love on a black fur rug.

XV

Hanspeter Gruenig rarely thought, because he rarely needed to anymore. A miracle had happened to him in Vietnam during the battle of Hue, when, running for his life along a flare-illuminated dike near the Perfume River, his body seemed to grow a mind of its own. It told him to cut left off the end of the dike, even though the captain and six of the other seven men were running right, and he did that (followed as usual by the *real* Hanspeter Gruenig), and the rest of the patrol had run into an NVA .50-caliber gun and was turned into cat food. Gruenig had been letting his body tell him what to do ever since.

With the old projector chattering away, he didn't really hear Cobb's sneeze at the window. His body just told him to look there—and then to throw first the whiskey bottle at the pair of eyes, which he did, breaking the window, and then two loads of bird shot from his Remington 1100 off to either side of the figures running up the road.

He was laughing when he came back into the trailer, but his body was already telling him there had to be a *reason* for Cobb and the woman to be snooping around out there.

"You vill leaf now," he told Tom Clover and Rip Gurnsey.

"D'jew kill 'em?" asked Clover, stupid as ever.

Gruenig turned off the projector and fell onto his bed. "Now. And keep avay from here that truck. Until I tell you."

Alone, he was surprised to find that he felt good. Always before at this time of night, whether he had watched the film with other people or by himself, he felt bad—so bad that he only had one thing to compare it to. Once in Idaho he had shot a deer in the stomach at twenty yards. The animal had turned toward him, hunching forward, its back bowing, and shivered violently two or three times, its whole body rippling. Then it opened its mouth, vomited a bucketful of blood onto the snow and died. When he dressed out the deer, Gruenig found that the bullet had torn a track to the lungs, breaking ribs and opening the intestines as it went. He wondered if it was bone or gut that made the deer shiver like that; he had always heard bone was worse. Whichever was worse, he reckoned, that was pretty close to how he had felt every night before this one after watching the film.

Feeling fine now, and alert and sharp, he decided to think for a while just for the fun of it. Taking first things first, he thought about why Cobb and Divina had come out to his trailer. When he had that figured, he thought about his skiing that day; Ketchum, Idaho; avalanches; a boy he had known in grade school named Fate; and baling cotton. Finally, growing tired, he thought about the forty-thousand-dollar Revcon Camelot motor home he was going to buy soon and about how he and the big woman would drive around the country in it. Then, without taking off his boots, he rolled onto his side and went to sleep.

The next day was Friday, his day off, and he slept late and then went into town as he always did. On the way in he smoked a Natur-Perle Brazilian cigar, listened to a Willie Nelson tape and drove the Blazer fast and loose over the slick back roads.

He went first to Curly Labeau's Sport Shop and told Labeau he would like to talk to him in the back room. Labeau was a potbellied man with swirling white hair and a white beard. He wore loud flannel shirts and red suspenders and he reminded Gruenig unpleasantly of a wind-up doll he had seen once in Montreal called "Vic the Voyageur," though Labeau was in fact from Norman, Oklahoma, and had been in the North for only three years.

In the back room Labeau handed him an envelope containing six one-hundred-dollar bills and offered him a drink of brandy. Gruenig took the drink and sat down by the wood stove.

"How about them hundred ice axes?" asked Labeau. "I have to order from California."

"No. For a while, nothing."

"Clover told me you was raided," said Labeau, laughing deep in his chest like Santa Claus.

"It vas that hand-job lawyer. He knows something. Probably he has seen the truck, but he hass no proof, and who vould listen to him anyway?"

"Dangler, maybe. That's the same fella's giving Knapp trouble."

"Mr. Dankler is very busy. He has no time for hand-jobs. For a while ve vait, and then business as usual. Alvays this sort of guy hangs himself."

"Yeah," said Labeau, grinning at him affectionately. "You know what I always say, Hanspeter. What I say is, 'One peter in the Han's worth two in the bush.' " He laughed again.

"Yah," said Gruenig, yawning. "I know."

He ate lunch alone at the Idlenot Café, and afterward he drove out to where Simmons Creek flowed into Lake Webster. The lake was freezing up, and he knew there would be salmon and lake trout lying in the shallow oxygenated water near the mouth of the creek. Waiting until there were no cars in sight, Gruenig took a six-foot gig from the back of his Blazer, ran down the embankment and speared one of the finning salmon. Then he drove back into town, the fish gutted and hidden under a newspaper, and went to see the matinee showing of *Benjy* at the Colby Cinema.

After the movie he decided to go home, instead of drinking with Labeau as he usually did, because his body was urging him to, and on the drive to the camp he felt giddy and expectant in his bones without caring why.

It was 5:30 when he got back to his trailer. Lightheaded with anticipation, he turned on all the lights, tidied up a little, and prepared the salmon. He put Sammi Smith on the record player, brushed his teeth, and poured a drink to calm himself down. Then he sat down to wait, knowing now what he was waiting for.

In less than fifteen minutes she was there, knocking on his door. Gruenig held his right hand out in front of his face, the fingers spread, and stared at it until he could see no movement. Then he snapped it into a fist, got up quickly and opened the door.

Her face was haughty and mad. She was in a running suit, hatless, beads of sweat on her forehead—matching perfectly one of his favorite ways of imagining her.

She understood he had this film, she said, and she wanted it. She hadn't told her husband yet, but if he didn't give it to her she would, and her husband would certainly fire him and probably kill him.

No, said Gruenig, her husband would certainly not do either. And no, she could not have the film, though he would let her watch it with him whenever she liked.

"Criminal," she said, and hit him in the head with a closed fist like a man. Listening hard to his body, making an effort not to think at all, he hit her back, trying to duplicate exactly the force of her blow; then he grabbed her and pulled her to him. She was struggling, exactly as he had imagined it, and his stomach felt like it would drop right out of him. "I haff a big fish for you to eat," he said tenderly into her hair, and felt himself step up onto some high plane of perfect action.

His body told him to bite her lower lip when he kissed her; it even told him that she was going to bite him back, and where and how to place his hands, and even—this was the most thrilling thing of all—the exact instant when she would stop struggling and start to moan in her throat.

On Tuesday of the following week Cobb went down to Concord to represent Dangler at the tax-abatement hearing. He went fully expecting that when he returned to the camp, Gruenig would be at least fired and gone, and preferably deep in jail, where he belonged. With the exception of a mass murderer or two, Cobb had never known or heard of anyone he wanted to see behind bars more than he wanted to see Hanspeter Gruenig there. He so wanted it that for the first time in his life he longed to be a prosecutor —and even, in one glandular fantasy, the man who turned on the gas in the small green room where Gruenig should by rights wind up.

Being shot at and having a whiskey bottle thrown at his face had frightened and infuriated him, but what had provoked Cobb's juridical outrage was discovering on the following day that Gruenig was not only a homicidal maker of lewd films, but a vicious liar and a preposterously arrogant thief as well.

After the incident at the trailer he and Divina had run almost all the way back to the house; they were looking through it for Dangler when they met Erica coming downstairs.

"Gruenig has a film of you and Kenneth screwing," said Divina. Cobb's phrase to her—when they had finally stopped running and it came to him who the people on the black fur rug were—was "doing it"; he regretted it now. "And we think he's in cahoots with a crooked oil man."

Erica was standing on the stairs looking down at them. "I see," she said thoughtfully, almost as if she had been expecting this bizarre information and was now pondering what to do with it. "You saw the film?"

"Just a little piece of it," said Cobb.

"I told you I didn't like his eyes," Divina said.

"Let me just say, I didn't really *see* anything," Cobb added. "I mean . . . only generally what was going on."

"What about the oil man?" asked Erica, and Divina explained it to her. "So you don't have any proof?" She seemed almost relieved.

"Well, no, not courtroom proof," Cobb told her, "but enough to go to Kenneth with."

"We won't bother Kenneth with this. We can handle this ourselves."

"He shot a *gun* at us, Erica."

"We will not tell Kenneth, is that clear? This is my house. You two find out what you can about the oil business and leave the film to me," she had said then, gliding past them.

The following day he and Divina found out all they

needed to know about the oil business, and more. It was Gruenig's day off. Cobb knew that he never visited his office on Fridays, and with that information and a spare key obtained from one of the housekeepers, they simply walked in and looked through Gruenig's unlocked filing cabinet.

In the file labeled "Clover Oil" were invoices indicating that since August Dangler had been paying out over two thousand dollars a month for fuel, much of which, they knew, had never left the truck: an average of 1,100 gallons a *week* had been metered and charged to Camp Wildwood over that period. Recognizing the name on the next file in the drawer, Cobb pulled it and found a fat sheaf of paid invoices from Curly Labeau's Sport Shop. Among the more recent were these: $1,590 for three hundred unstrung Slazenger tennis rackets; $3,756 for fifty pairs of Trak waxless touring skis; $5,180 for twenty-five Motobecane ten-speed bicycles; $7,200 for one hundred and twelve Swiss cresta sleds; and $32,000 for ten Winchester Model-21 20-gauge shotguns.

"Look at this," he shouted, waving the shotgun invoice. "What is going *on* here? Who orders all these things?"

"Gruenig, you ninny," said Divina. "He makes the orders and pays the bills, and these companies give him back a percentage of their business. He's getting rich. He's also supporting the entire town of Colby." She handed him the files on more grotesquely ballooned accounts, with a feed-and-grain store, a lumber company, an electrical contractor.

"Twenty seven hundred dollars for wiring the *horses'* stall? How can he get away with this?"

"Apparently no one checks on him." Divina tapped her nails for a moment. "Why would he leave these files unlocked, though—just sitting here like this? That's what I don't understand."

Erica did not come to dinner that night, and after dinner Cobb and Divina were unable to find her. Just before eight they were playing chess in the cardroom off the central hall when they heard her come in, slamming the big front door and singing to herself. She was dressed in a running suit, and as Cobb approached her he marveled at what physical exertion did for her: she looked calmer and more radiant than he had seen her in weeks.

"Hello, lovey," she said happily, tossing her hair.

Cobb announced that he and Divina would like to have a word with her, and followed her into the cardroom.

"What have you been up to?" asked Divina, staring at her.

"Exercising. You two look like Bolshevik conspirators. All you need is a samovar."

Cobb glanced at Divina and closed the door. "Gruenig seems to be involved with a bunch of merchants in town who are stealing Kenneth blind."

"We have proof now," said Divina.

"We've seen his files," Cobb said.

"He orders thousands and thousands of dollars' worth of merchandise from these people in town, and they give him a cut of what he pays them for it. You ought to see the . . ."

"We don't actually have *proof* he's taking a cut, Divina," Cobb said.

"Yes we do."

"No we don't. We're making a logical inference here, but we . . ."

"That's enough." Erica gave them both a quick, awkward look. "That's fine. I'm delighted you found out what you did. Now, leave it to me. You *sound* like Bolsheviks as well, by the way."

"What about the film?" asked Divina.

"I had a long talk with Hanspeter. Andy was mistaken."

"*Mistaken*," said Cobb. "What do you mean, mistaken?"

"It's a Time-Life film, on primates, I think he said. Of course he understands how . . ."

"What? It's a *what*? It's a film of you and Kenneth . . . doing it."

"I'd rather not discuss the film anymore," Erica said frostily. "And as for the other, I'll take care of that myself."

"How? By *asking* Gruenig if he's guilty? As Kenneth's lawyer and friend . . ."

"Andy." Erica stepped up to him and looked down slightly into his face. "I will not have Kenneth disturbed with this, do you understand? If you mention one word of it to him, I will never speak to you again. I will take care of Hanspeter myself."

"All right," said Cobb, narrowing his eyes at her, "if that's what you want: fine."

On the following Tuesday he went to Concord for the abatement proceedings, which were heard gaily and summarily by Bob Perch's tennis partner, Leonard Fine. Knapp was there in forced good spirits, dressed in a 1950's business suit. He had brought Fine a gallon of maple syrup made on his farm, and it stood pathetically on the master's desk throughout the brief hearing, with as much chance of winning the action as Knapp himself. Perch had put together a shapely, lethal little case, based on the testimony of the most respected property evaluator in the state, and at another time Cobb might have enjoyed himself, but today his preoccupation with Gruenig kept him from that.

He had planned on spending the rest of the week in Concord, but he drove back to the camp that night, and though it was late when he arrived, he went directly to Divina's room.

"Well?" he said.

She was wearing a long flannel nightgown and she looked boyishly slight in it, and irritated. "Well what?"

"What's happened with Gruenig?"

Divina looked at him for a moment, her night-creamed face shifting between expressions. "Erica is going to tell Kenneth about it when the season is over. You said yourself we don't really have any proof he's involved. I was almost asleep."

"What's going on here?" Cobb yelled. "You were the one who started all this detective business, and now you just want to *drop* it?"

"It's not really our affair. Some things are just better left alone." She stood up on her tiptoes and kissed him on the cheek. "It seems you need some sleep. I'll see you at breakfast."

Slouching up to his room, Cobb had the sure feeling that he had missed something simple and important just a minute before at Divina's door; but he was too tired to try to figure out what it could be.

For days he agonized over whether or not to go to Dangler with what he and Divina had found in Gruenig's files. On the one hand it seemed unthinkable *not* to tell his best friend and employer that he was being robbed massively and regularly, and that it was extremely likely his own manager was masterminding the robbery. And yet, on the other, it was Erica's camp too. No one knew Dangler better than she, and somewhere at the back of Cobb's mind, influencing his non-action, was the discomfiting suspicion that Erica's fierce determination that Dangler not be told might be due to legitimate worries about how he would respond. Dangler was, assuredly, volatile just now, and more than anything else—more even than he wanted to see Gruenig in jail—Cobb wanted no further mayhem at the camp. Finally, though it pained him, he decided that a thorough investigation of Gruenig and the merchants could wait until after the camp closed in January.

Less than a week after the hearing in Concord, Bob Perch called and asked him if he had looked at his mail that morning. Cobb said that he had not.

"Well, it's in there, baby. Signed, sealed and delivered. Judge Douglas signed the report yesterday. Dangler got what you might call a deal."

"That's awfully quick, isn't it?"

"We're in business to please," said Perch, and hung up.

A few hours later Cobb was at his desk reading over the master's report when Foster Knapp walked in.

"Like to have a talk," he said, looking around the office. He took Cobb's parka from the coat rack and handed it to him in a wad. "Like to take a little walk while we talk."

"Sorry, I don't want to walk. I'm busy."

Knapp looked at the report on Cobb's desk. "You a poor winnah, Mr. Lawyer from New York?"

"I live in New Hampshire, Knapp, and this was not a matter of winning or losing but of correcting a blatant injustice. Attorney Fine fixed the assessment at a million and a half. That means you people were off by eighteen and a half million dollars."

"It's a matter of more than that, son. I'd like to take a walk, if you don't mind. It won't take long."

This time it was a request, and reluctantly Cobb took the parka and put it on.

Outside it was beginning to snow for the third time that week. Knapp angled away from the back of the house on the path that led to the trout pond, walking in a rapid, delicate shuffle.

"That master down in Concord—he related to you?"

"You can appeal to the Supreme Court, you know."

"Well, we listened to the wrong people, I guess. But that's not what I came out to talk about. Like to explain a few things to you about town government, Mr. Cobb. . . . Watch your step there." Cobb had slipped on the path and Knapp had kept him from falling by catching his arm. "Have to know how to walk on snow up here in the North Country," he said with relish.

"Why are we out walking in a goddamn snowstorm in the first place?" demanded Cobb. "Will you tell me that?"

"Number one," said Knapp, resuming his shuffle down the path, "we have a tax base here in Colby of forty million dollars. That means we can tax at the rate of thirty dollars per thousand and raise the one-million-two we need to send our little children to school and do the other things we have to do to run the town. You with me so far?" Cobb said nothing. "Number two, if some shyster Concord master with a funny name decides to cut that tax base in half the way one just did, well, that's going to do two things: number one, it's going to double the taxes for everybody in town next yeeah—which is something damn few of 'em are going to like—and number two, it's going to leave this little town almost six hundred thousand dollars short on its budget for *this yeeah*. Do you understand me?"

"Number one," snapped Cobb, "I already know all this. And number two: tough luck, buddy, you brought it on yourself. Go borrow the money."

Knapp smiled at him. It was the faint smile of control Cobb remembered from the basement of the church. "Well, that's exactly what I had in mind," he said. He turned Cobb gently by the elbow, facing him toward the fish hatchery fifty yards off the path to their left. Cobb saw that a yellow van was parked there, its motor running. "I wanted you to see this," said Knapp intimately, leading him toward the van. When they were some twenty feet away, he stopped and shouted, "All right, Mrs. Burke."

A woman got out of the van and opened the sliding door on the side. Little girls seemed to pop out from everywhere at Cobb, like bright seeds. Dressed in short yellow skirts, knobby-kneed and shivering, their little faces grinning crazily, they formed a quick line in the falling snow.

"R-O-W-D-I-E," they shrieked, going into a frantic series of claps and bobs, "that's the way we spell rowdeee . . . Rowd*eee*. Let's get . . . *Rowdeee*. Yaaaaaa*aay:* Colby *Cougars*." Then as quickly as they had popped out, the children popped back into the van and the woman slammed the door.

"Those are our little basketball cheerleaders," said Knapp. "Without that six hundred thousand dollars, they won't have a team to cheer for, of course. . . . Likely won't even have a school to go to."

"That was a cheap trick, Knapp," said Cobb, starting back down the path. "*God,* what a thing to do."

Knapp shuffled after him. "I want your man Dangler to loan the town six hundred thousand dollars for five years, interest-free."

"Right. Count on it."

"Listen, Mr. Finesteen lawyer from New York, do you know what the police powers of a town are?"

Knapp put his hand on Cobb's elbow again and Cobb shook it off. "Get away from me," he said, walking faster.

"They empowa the *selectmen* to abate any and all public nuisances, particularly if they constitute a hazard to the public health and welfare, and there're quite a few nuisances might need abating around heeah." Knapp stuck his hands in front of Cobb's face and began counting on his chubby fingers. "Number one, no more creation of noxious odors by the flying of helicopters within the town limits; number two, no discharging of firearms outside of state hunting season; number three, no keeping whatsoevahh, of any live bears . . ."

"*What?*" said Cobb, whirling on the selectman. "What are you talking about?"

"We can't have no tourists getting hurt in the towna Colby, so I'd maybe get an ordinance against the instruction or performance of any activity which might endanger the life and limb of any and all out of state persons staying at the camp. I'd just maybe get an ordinance against everything you freaks *do,* Mr. Jew lawyer, and have Chief Jenkins and his boys out heeah every fifteen minutes on complaints until I get it."

"*Do it,*" yelped Cobb. "And I am *not Jewish.*"

"Unless your man loans us the money."

"*Do it,* you chiseling lowlife goddamn drooling idiot, and I'll slap a civil-rights suit on that thieving little town that you won't ever see the end of."

"Ayaaup," said Knapp, grinning. He turned and shuffled off toward the van. "You've got one week, Babyfat. Watch your step in the snow."

Back in his office, searching through the *New Hampshire Revised Statutes, Annotated* to try to determine if Knapp could actually do any of what he threatened to do, Cobb wished to God he had been born with the personality of Genghis Khan. Why couldn't he have just *hit* Knapp, he wondered —one clean John Wayne haymaker to the selectman's jowly chops. He hated himself for politely watching the wretched little cheerleaders (smiling inanely, even, the whole time they screamed at him) instead of walking off as he had wanted to do, and he cursed out loud whatever perverse concoction of sociology and genes it was that had rendered him as incapable of direct unconsidered action as he was of carrying a tune.

It took him most of an hour to calm down, and when he finally did, it was into a languid, throbbing, hopeless state of mind that felt like a hangover and was not helped by learning from the *Statutes* that Knapp could indeed do some of what he said he would do and, even if he was not successful, tie the camp up in months of litigation. His head in his hands, he spent a few minutes looking over a vision of his next few years as a dim, endless filing in and out of court to do battle with Knapp; then he locked the office and headed upstairs, aiming intently for the bar.

Ames Cravens stopped him just short of it. He was turned out in knickers and a stylish orange wind jacket, and he looked mildly troubled, as if he had misplaced something.

"Divina sent me to *get* you," he said, his handsome forehead puckering. "There's been some trouble up on Revelation. The Fairfax sisters have been injured rather badly. The big one may be dead. Tit, is it?"

Cobb stared dreamily at Cravens, his mind refusing to open on what he had just heard, feeling jammed like a door.

"We were practicing our glissades in Winter Survival class, sliding down this steep pitch of snow on our duffs. They were roped together, coming down side by side for their second or third turn, and Hanspeter was up at the top holding a safety rope that was tied in to the middle of theirs. Paying it out, you know, while they slid down. He must have dropped it. The end was tied off to a tree, and I guess it came loose, or broke or something. Anyway, they got going faster and faster, tumbling, you know . . ."

"Dead?" asked Cobb. "You say she's *dead?*"

"*May*be, Rebel, *may*be dead. Weezy thought so. She hit a rock."

"Oh, God," said Cobb.

"Well, they *had* their ice axes, and we've all been taught how to self-arrest. They panicked, I'm afraid."

"Where are they now?"

"At the infirmary. Erica and Divina are down there with them, and a doctor from town. No one can find Kenny. Have you seen him?"

"No. You say Gruenig dropped the rope?"

"He had a sort of clamp thingy he was using to control the speed, and my theory is it came loose. Norris seems to think he meant to do it, and is quite upset about it."

Cobb excused himself then. He walked outside, got in his car and drove to the infirmary. Divina met him at the door.

"Is she . . . Tit, is she . . . ?"

"Hardly," said Divina. "She has a broken collarbone and a concussion. Sithee is just mad. They've asked to be taken to the hospital in Boston and they're both talking rather loudly about suing. Where is Kenneth? I think he'd better come down here."

"Ames is looking for him. They were the only ones," Cobb said bleakly. "The *only* ones."

"The only ones what?"

"Who didn't sign releases. Do you know how it happened? Ames said Gruenig dropped the rope."

"Actually, he never picked it up. Norris Fish and I saw

it, I'm afraid. Gruenig untied the end of the rope from the tree just before they started; then he just never picked it up." There was an angry upper-class cry from the rear of the infirmary. "I'd better get back, the doctor is trying to sedate them. I tried to keep Norris quiet until we could get things sorted out, but he told some of the others. A few of them are rather up in arms."

"Yeah? Well, so am I," said Cobb. "By God, so am I."

Acting on automatic pilot for the first time in his remembered life, Cobb spun away from the infirmary and drove at sixty miles an hour to Gruenig's trailer. His body left the car running, attacked the front porch, and threw open the door.

"Back again, yah?" said Gruenig before Cobb could open his mouth, and Cobb realized dimly that the Austrian had seen him coming, standing as he was behind his stove.

"I'll see you rot in jail, you bastard."

"Careful, Mr. Copp." Gruenig stuck a wooden spoon into a pot on the stove and stirred. He was wearing an apron.

"I know about the oil *deeeeal*," said Cobb, and felt himself go into an inexplicable crouch. "I know about your deals with the sport shop and the feed store and all the others—and I have two witnesses who saw you try to murder those two women this afternoon. I'm gonna put you away in Concord, you little scab-face Nazi, and I'm gonna come in every Saturday for ten to twenty just to *look* at your sorry ass."

Cobb *loved* what he had just said. Crouching in the doorway, fairly slobbering with pleasure over the way his voice had gone suddenly hoarse and mean and Southern on him, he was about to go on—anywhere, say anything—but something in Gruenig's face stopped him.

Gruenig was blinking at him, chewing on his lower lip, something growing visibly behind his silver eyes. He blinked some more, then he opened his mouth, and when he spoke it was as if some great ventriloquist had taken hold of him.

"Listen, Jack, I'm gettin' sicka you comin' aroun' here. I been givin' you a *lotta* room to make yo' mess in, an' now my ice is gettin' chilly. . . ."

"What's going on here?" whispered Cobb. "What are you doing?"

"What I'ma *mind* to do is stomp a mud hole in yo' ass, but they's a few things I'm 'onna clue you in on first."

Good God, thought Cobb, is he mimicking me? But as Gruenig continued to talk, his long jaw sliding around the words brought up in Cobb's mind the objects in front of the trailer again, and this time, horribly, and at once, he remembered where he knew them from—it was from the hardscrabble dirt yards of the trailer park, white-trash-country South that he had hated and feared more than hell itself as a pudgy private-school kid whose father owned a lake in the country—and going numb with panic, Cobb realized that Gruenig wasn't mimicking at all: Gruenig was a *Southern red-neck.*

". . . you read me, Jack?"

"I beg your pardon?"

"I said if you decide you got to tell the police about them accounts, I'd have to tell 'em how Mr. Dangler *tole* me to throw the rope on them women. Have to tell Knapp, too, since he's lookin' for a way to close this place down. Now, listen to me, Hand-Job. You know Mrs. Erica Dangler?"

"Uhh-huh," said Cobb, watching transfixed as Gruenig seemed to swell suddenly like a puff adder, the boiled-looking skin on his face going crimson.

"Well, me and her's gettin' *married.* So you don' have long on the dole. Now, get on outta here 'fore I put some hair onna wall."

XVI

Every morning when Cobb woke he said out loud, as his mother had taught him to do: "This is the day which the Lord hath made, I will rejoice and be glad in it."

He meant that. Locked into Cobb as securely as his bones were the beliefs that he inhabited a beneficent universe, that at the root of everything was some sweet, mysteriously shaping force, and that the only legitimate, the only *possible* responses to being alive were joy and gratitude. He believed those things; he didn't give a rat's ass how depressed the intellectuals were.

He did, however, have his weak moments, and the morning after his confrontation with Gruenig was one of his weakest ever. He woke with clogged sinuses and an aching head and lay blinking up at the high carved ceiling. From the quality of light in the room he could tell that it was either snowing again or about to. He lay motionless for a few minutes, prodding at the memory of the past day and night as if it were a sore tooth, and finding a short supply of either joy or gratitude.

"This is the day which the Lord hath made . . ." he began, and trailed off. It hurt to speak.

After leaving Gruenig's trailer he had driven to the Colby Valley Inn and worn out the bartender there before eating a meal he could not now remember. Later he had drunk quite a bit of Cointreau and then driven halfway down the state, intent on flying to Florida, before he sobered enough to realize there would be no planes leaving the Manchester airport at midnight. On the long drive back he had drifted in and out of sleep and had finally been forced to pull off the road for a nap. He had gotten back to the camp, still drunk, at three-thirty that morning.

For half an hour he lay in bed staring at the ceiling, wondering murkily how to proceed. Then he got up, shaved and took a bath. Still feeling terrible, he was beginning to dress, counting on that to restore him, when Divina knocked once and walked in.

"Well, where have you been?" she asked brightly.

"Why don't we just get married?" he barked, jerking on a pair of flannel trousers. "I mean, if you're going to walk in on me whenever I'm dressing, for God's sake."

"Do you know, that's my first proposal?" Divina sat down on the bed. "It has been awfully busy around here, I have some things to tell you. First of all, Kenneth announced at dinner last night that he *told* Gruenig to drop the rope—that after everyone knew how to stop themselves and had slid down twice on the rope, to let them do it on their own. Tit and Sithee were just the first ones. He told everyone he was terribly sorry Tit was hurt but that she wouldn't have been if she had reacted properly."

"Right," said Cobb bitterly. "Right." He selected a yellow J. Press shirt from his drawer and a pair of tan cashmere socks. Dressing was a small but significant pleasure for him, and he tried to concentrate on drawing the socks up over his calves in spite of Divina.

"And then he said that anyone who was offended or angry about what had happened was welcome to leave."

"Good, because *I'm* offended and angry, and *I'm* by God leaving, welcome or not." Cobb slipped on a pair of loafers and looked through the closet for a sweater. "And I'd feel much better if you came with me . . . left with me, I mean."

"I'd love to, but not until the end of the season. You're not leaving either."

"The hell I'm not. I'm going as soon as I can get packed and talk to Kenneth. I've had the course up here. I'm sick of dealing with crazy people. Did you know that little madman Gruenig isn't even Austrian? He's some kind of insane impostor from the South who thinks he's going to marry Erica."

"*Marry* . . . ," said Divina. "But that's ridiculous. Besides, that's all over now. It was beautiful how they rallied around each other last night."

"Who?"

"Erica and Kenneth. I've never seen them closer. Listen, sweetie, I know how you feel and I certainly don't approve of the way Kenneth is behaving, but you simply can't desert them right now. Now is when they need us most. The whole place is sort of coming apart—Norris and the Watermans are leaving tomorrow, Norris is threatening to go to the police, and Sithee swears that she and Tit are going to sue."

Tilting his head in the mirror, Cobb brushed his hair with an English brush. He patted some bay rum on his cheeks and slid his money clip into his pocket. "All right," he said, feeling better, "I'll stay around for another couple of days and do what I can. But then I'm leaving."

"You won't leave until it's over, and neither will I. You know, you really should buy some new clothes, lovey—all your things are so sort of fifties and frumpy."

"They *fit* me, Divina," said Cobb. "Besides, I don't have time to look for clothes." He shoved an arm into his favorite tweed jacket, one he had had since prep school, and as he did, his thumb caught in the lining of the sleeve, ripping it.

"I have one last piece of news," Divina said. "A rather rude woman who called herself Miss Hurd phoned for you last night. She said to tell you that your goat died."

If during his first few weeks there the camp had made Cobb think of a luxurious windjammer drifting brightly on a calm night current of unseen effort, it now seemed more like a crippled ocean liner caught in a storm with its captain asleep. Over the next three days he hardly had time to light his pipe for scurrying to hold down the damage.

He began by talking an irate Norris Fish out of visiting the local police with what Fish kept calling his "sordid little story." He commiserated with Cabot and Ruth Waterman over their "painful" decision to quit the camp because, as Waterman put it, shaking his head, fun was fun but people actually getting hurt was just too rich for their blood. He arranged to have the Fairfax sisters' things packed and shipped to Philadelphia, and he dealt discouragingly and at length over the phone with Mr. Barstow, their attorney.

On both days he took a call from Foster Knapp and, praying that the selectman had not yet heard about the accident, he was overly solicitous and even told Knapp that Dangler was considering his proposal. Finally, along with Gruenig (who was back to speaking with an Austrian accent and addressing Cobb formally, if insolently—as though the soup-stirring scene at his trailer had never happened) he took care of the dismissal of the camp hairdresser, three chore boys and two waitresses, two maids and four recreation assistants.

He was directed to do this last by note from Dangler, who never left his rooms while the camp yawed and pitched around him. He and Erica had locked themselves in after dinner on the night of the accident, and they did not come out for two and a half days. There was an old hotel sign hung on the door to their suite that read "Do Not Disturb Except in the Event of Fire," and the only person admitted in to see them was the head housekeeper, who took them their meals and delivered notes from Dangler to Cobb and Gruenig but would take none back to him.

Divina called this a second honeymoon.

By Thursday morning, the third after the Fairfax mishap, the camp had subsided, but ominously; it now felt to Cobb to be on a long, sinking glide. The house was dim and growing dusty, there were cigarette butts in ashtrays, and the flowers in the great china bowls were wilting. At breakfast the eggs were overcooked and there was only one waitress to serve them instead of the customary three, but the six remaining campers were as chipper and ardent as ever. The only complaint anyone had was that the new snow on the ski trails had not been packed.

Incomprehensibly to Cobb, none of the remaining campers appeared to be at all alarmed by what had happened to Tit, or concerned by the departure of Fish and the Watermans. ("I hate to see them go, of course," Peter Bigelow had told him the day before, as Cabot and Ruth

Waterman were driven off in the camp limousine, "but Kenneth *is* right, you know. It's better to leave if you have any doubts about how you might handle yourself in a pinch.") Nor were they bothered by the cutback in staff or the resulting inconveniences, or even by the Danglers' mysterious holing-up. They seemed perfectly content to go on with their daily schedules of activity and classes and preparation for the Winter Expedition as if nothing had happened, speculating only occasionally at meals about when the Chief and Erica might be "coming down."

Cobb, however, given a chance this morning to think for the first time in forty-eight hours, decided that he had waited on Dangler long enough. Poking at a cold kippered herring after the campers and Divina left the table, he told himself tentatively that he had done everything he could do, and the statement sounded true.

He left the house, got in his car and drove to a service-station phone a few miles down the road toward town.

"Well," said Dangler heartily, "how are things back in civilization?"

"What do you mean?" asked Cobb after a pause.

"How do you like getting back to traffic and nine-to-five?"

"What do you mean? I'm at the Shell station down the road."

"Oh," said Dangler. "I thought you had finally jumped ship. Why are you telephoning me if you're still here?"

"Because you have seen fit to lock yourself *up*, that's why. And hang *signs* on your door to keep people out, and have your *meals* sent up to you while other people clean up your various messes. I haven't left yet, but I'm about to, and there are a few things I have to tell you before . . ."

"Then come up here and do it like a man. I hate speaking on the phone," Dangler said.

He and Erica were finishing breakfast when Cobb walked in, and immediately Cobb noticed a new, almost visible intimacy between them: it hung on the sun-flooded air of the sitting room, reminding him of their impenetrable Victorian closeness after the flower-shooting episode on the porch.

"Hi," he said, feeling de-fused.

Erica smiled at him. "I understand you're leaving us.

What a pity." She stood up and kissed him on the forehead. "You two have a nice talk; I have a horrid little something to attend to, and I haven't seen any of our babies in days. Will you be at lunch?"

"Well . . ." said Cobb.

"Fine then." She blew a kiss at Dangler and left the room.

"Let's get going," Dangler said. He led Cobb down the hall to his study, where he sat at the desk and motioned with a jade letter opener to a chair beneath the portrait of his great-grandfather. Holding the point of the letter opener to his freshly shaven chin, redolent of witch hazel, dressed in plush wool knickers and an Eisenhower jacket, he observed Cobb for a moment. "I seek the company of exacting and durable people," he said finally. "Everything else is mush."

Cobb sighed. "I didn't come up here to be fooled with, Kenneth. I came to plead with you to quit, to close the camp down and send these people home and to do something else with your time."

Dangler leaned over the desk, cocking the letter opener at Cobb.

"Picture this in your mind," he said. "It is five o'clock on a Friday afternoon in June, two years ago. I am in New York. I have been there all week, trying halfheartedly to stir up interest in that hotel I had in Nepal. I take a cab to the University Club—reluctantly, I admit—to meet a friend, but the friend has already gone. Everyone else is in Connecticut for the weekend and the place is practically empty. I am massaged. Then I walk out to the pool room. The room is white marble with a turquoise ceiling. The pool is white marble also. Attendants stand around, dressed in white. I can see through the plate-glass windows into the sauna. There are a couple of stockbrokers in there lying on sheets, drinking Saratoga water. A few more are out by the pool stretched on cots and covered with towels. There are large ceramic urns. I walk into the water and breaststroke to the far end, where a copper lion's head is spewing a two-foot arc of water into the pool. It is absolutely silent except for this fountain . . . Are you following me?" Cobb nodded, though in fact he was confused. "I sense that I am on a mission, Andrew—somehow I know what to do. I put my face directly in the stream of water coming from the fountain, and then I open my eyes. I do not blink. For three minutes, maybe five, I stare without blinking through the water into the lion's mouth. And what do you think I see there?"

"I have no idea," Cobb said.

"I see salvation. I see for the first time that I can escape the morgue of our times, and that I can lead other people out as well. Not *how* to do it—not then—but that it *can* be done, if I can make myself implacable." Dangler leaned back in the chair and looked with a knitting brow over Cobb's head. "My great-grandfather used to say that to make hero in this world you don't necessarily have to do something good, but you do have to do *something,* and do it implacably. He also said . . ."

"Please, Kenneth."

". . . that the true aristocratic ability is steadiness in the face of adversity; that the only significant difference between people of quality and the rest of the world is the same as the difference between good and bad Persian rugs: the good ones wear better. He also . . ."

"Stop," said Cobb. "I don't *care* what he said. What in Christ's name does all this nonsense have to do . . ."

"He said that to quit, ever, at anything, is cowardice."

"All right, *don't* quit," Cobb shouted. "You and your great-grandfather just go right on seeing things in fountains, whatever that's supposed to mean, and living out obsessions and ordering innocent people killed, but you'll by God do it *without me.*"

Dangler studied him, his blue eyes amused. "I understand that we will have to, Andrew. And I am prepared to deal, however sadly, with that fact."

He had been determined not to get angry, but he had, and now Dangler was toying with him. It was an old story. With a hand cupped over his eyes, Cobb waited briefly for his energy to return; there was no sound in the room except for the ticking of an antique bracket clock. Finally he took the hand away, smiled wanly and started from scratch.

He said that personally he felt both Dangler and Gruenig should go to jail for what had happened to the

Fairfax sisters, but that he would continue to do his best from Concord to keep Dangler, and only Dangler, out. Gruenig was another story, he said, and then he told Dangler about the invoices he and Divina had found in Gruenig's files. He told him that Gruenig had as much as admitted that he was criminally involved with the merchants in town, that he owned a pornographic film starring Dangler and his wife, that he was somehow under the impression that Erica was supposed to marry him, and finally that he, Gruenig, was no more Austrian than he, Cobb, was, but was in fact a cracker.

Gaining momentum smoothly, he turned to Knapp: his threats, his blackmail proposal, the danger of his finding out about the Fairfaxes. And as for the Fairfaxes—those culls, whose refusal to sign the releases Dangler had dismissed with such cavalier indifference a couple of weeks ago—they of course would sue, he said; he knew that from their attorney, and Dangler could confidently expect the suit to be devastating. Given these exigencies, he went on, continued operation of the camp, even if possible, was in his judgment unwise; though, he hastened to add, the more important reasons for his plea that Dangler close down the camp were personal rather than practical. In his opinion, he said sonorously, Dangler was not presently in full possession of his faculties: it was clear to Cobb, as well as to others, that the severe pressures of running the camp had rendered his judgment temporarily unsound and his behavior abnormal. Normal people did not move into tents on porches, or untie knots blindfolded in the shower, or hit their wives in the stomach, he pointed out; nor did they abandon on a cliff in one case, invite to commit suicide by horse in another, and cause to be injured and very nearly killed in yet another, paying customers simply because they were considered to be the wrong sort of people. It was for his own sake and Erica's, for the sake of their happy and stable future together, said Cobb, that Dangler should direct his remarkable energies into something less taxing. He closed with the assurance that no matter what Dangler decided to do, he, Cobb, would continue to provide whatever support and assistance he could.

"I am now and always will be your friend," he said. "I want you to remember that."

His eyes were glistening when he finished but, despite his false start, he felt satisfyingly delivered of a calm, professional, untheatrical summing-up. He also felt wary. He suspected that it was now, in the softened context of sympathy and old allegiances, that Dangler, rocked by Cobb's disclosures, would pull out whatever tricks he was planning to use to get him to stay.

Dangler nodded gravely. "Well, what can I say, old friend—except that you're one hundred percent right: I *have* been working too hard, and I have been a bit off balance lately. I only realized it this past couple of days. I want you to know that Erica and I have decided to close the camp before Christmas, right after the expedition I promised everyone. That's why I asked you to let some of the staff go. And then we're leaving on a six-month trip. I've rented a boat in the Adriatic."

"Wonderful," said Cobb. "I'm very, very happy to hear that, Kenneth."

"And things will be different next year, I can promise you that. We know exactly where we're going now and exactly how to get there. There won't be any more fumblings like the Fairfax incident. We're over the hump now."

"How do you mean?" asked Cobb, beginning to feel expansive.

"Well, there's a bit of a story here; I'll try to keep it brief. As you know, when we started this place, all we were interested in doing was using the woods and a few harmless natural confrontations to calm people down and make them feel better about themselves. Along with luxury and exercise and all that business, we gave them illusions of struggle and victory in areas where most of us are no longer competent but want to be. And it worked, Andrew. I could have half of America beating down the door to get in here for that program. But somewhere along the line I realized that we could do much, much more—I saw *how* to do here what I had always wanted to do, but only defined for myself that day in the pool." Dangler leaned across the desk again, his eyes widening, holding the letter opener in his fist with a thumb near the tip. "I saw that I could turn things around from here, by going back to the basics and learning again how to survive—*really* survive, by domination and without tricks, the way our great-grandfathers did—and then by teaching these campers how to do it too, by making them *able* to do the things they were only pretending to do . . . and then more campers, and more, until there were enough of us to begin to *grip,* to have an *effect,* and finally enough of us to take back the leadership that is rightfully ours by birth and blood—enough of us, I won't beat around the bush here, to stop the common people from selling this country down the river to the *goddamn Arabs,*" he said, snapping off a two-inch piece of jade with his thumb.

He studied the broken letter opener, his eyes contracting. "Of course, there had to be real consequences once in a while. On that hunt with Cravens and Fish, Gruenig and I did *not* shoot those boar. I fibbed to you because you were looking dangerously pale around the gills. Ames and Norris shot them. Had they missed, or failed to shoot, the survival consequences would have been quite real."

"Jesus Christ, Kenneth," whispered Cobb.

"It was Hanspeter's idea. So was letting Rocque climb the rock on his own, though it was my decision to let him know he *had* to do it. Getting lost on the mountain was my idea, and so was the glissade. I told Hanspeter to tell the campers they were on their own for the last slide, but he neglected to. That was the problem, you see, there was no continuity; it was all too haphazard, too . . . hit-and-miss. But don't misunderstand the *intent,* Andrew. I never put anyone into a situation with real consequences *because* they were the wrong sort of people, but to give them a chance to prove they weren't. You saw yourself what shooting that boar did for Ames, and how well Peter reacted when he thought we were lost. Making it up that little cliff even did something for de Faurier, though frankly not enough: the worse thing about the Fairfax blunder was that it cost me the Watermans instead of Rocque."

Dangler stood up and began pacing the room in front of Cobb. "I have learned from our mistakes. We tried to do too much too soon, with too little system and too much secrecy. I realize now that it's better if these people know exactly what they're doing and why, from the beginning. Which brings me back to next year. Next year there will be two camps, this place for the games and frills, to pay the rent, and another place for serious survival and expeditionary work. I've bought a resort in the Caribbean for that.

Gruenig will manage it, and Erica and I will fly back and forth between the two. Take our time, build slowly . . ."

"Gruenig?" said Cobb.

"Of course. He's the best possible man for it." Dangler stopped in front of him and looked down fondly. "Old Andy. You've certainly kept your thumb in the dike, my friend—looking after Erica, handling all that ugly business with the town . . ."

"Wait a minute," said Cobb, jumping to his feet. "Weren't you *listening* to me? Didn't you hear what I told you about Gruenig?"

"I heard you. The film, of course, is in bad taste, but the entertainment and social outlets up here for someone like him are limited. As for marrying Erica, Hanspeter has an active imagination—it's one of his great assets."

"But he's a thief and an *impostor,* Kenneth, for Christ's sake . . ."

Dangler held up a finger. "Not precisely an impostor. It happens he *bought* a new life from some Austrian he was in the Army with. His real name is Erpe and he's originally from Alabama. I had him checked out when he first came to work for me, though he doesn't know it. My feeling was that someone with a purchased life was likely to work reasonably hard at it. I was sure he would be a good man, and he has been. As for his arrangements in town, I've known about them from the beginning. They simply weren't worth doing anything about. I'm accustomed to being overcharged, and I'll find a way to use all the extra things he ordered. Also, I suspected I might want something on some of those people in town, and now I have it. I considered whatever money Hanspeter made under the table to be a sort of bonus, and since he knows that I know about his dealings, I rather think he considers it that as well—which no doubt accounts for why he is so relaxed about his files. And by the way, Andrew, if he had been shooting at you, he would have hit you."

Dangler walked back to his desk and looked down at his notes. "Let's seeee . . . The Fairfax sisters are not going to sue, I talked to them both this morning. And as for Selectman Knapp . . ." He turned to Cobb, grinning broadly. "I am delighted to report that we have that gentleman by the short hairs. It happens that his sister is married to Tom Clover, the oil man, whose illegal business practices here at the camp I took the trouble to record on videotape a few weeks ago. I'm sure that with that film even a less able attorney than yourself will have no trouble shutting Knapp's water off. Wouldn't you agree?"

Cobb said glumly that, yes, he would agree.

"That seems to be all," said Dangler. "You'll have to excuse me now. It's the bouillon hour, and I want to tell my people about the early closing. I'm sorry you'll miss our last little jaunt up the mountain."

Cobb made an effort to smile. "I have one question, Kenneth. Why aren't the Fairfax sisters suing, as they have every right and reason to?"

"Well, I made a small concession there: I told them they could come back next year. It appears that they were really more embarrassed than anything else." Dangler looked at him for a moment from the door. "I appreciate everything you've done up here more than I can say, and I'm very sorry you're leaving. You are the best of us, you know. . . . You would have been the best of my future leaders."

Back in his room, staring blankly into an open suitcase on the bed, Cobb knew for a fact that he would not fill it, and wondered if he had been manipulated somehow. After some reflection he concluded that, no, he had not been— that Dangler honestly didn't care anymore whether he stayed or not. Why, then, he asked himself, if Dangler had made no effort to change his mind, why in God's name did he now want to stay on—despite having been dismissed, despite Dangler's strange talk about epiphanies in fountains and turning rich people into guerrillas to save the country from Arabs, despite the galling embarrassment of learning that Dangler not only knew all about Gruenig and *didn't care,* but had out-thought him on Knapp and the Fairfax sisters as well? Asking himself that, Cobb couldn't resist marveling at his friend. *How* could he have talked Tit and Sithee out of a just suit simply by offering to let them come back here next year? How *could* he have gotten both Divina and himself, two grown people with lives of their own, up here and kept them here to do nothing but occupy his wife's manic attentions?

After more thinking, his head aching with effort, he had it, he thought. Ever since prep school Dangler had seemed to be in touch with a secret that eluded everyone else, some elemental, joyous knowledge that showed in his manner and even in his looks. He had always shared his joy with the countless people who were drawn to him, so that they felt uplifted and sparkling when they were around him, but he never revealed its source—so that when they were not around him, the same people, Cobb included, often felt an envious irritation toward him. What Cobb saw was that the source of that joy—the same thing that drew people to him and held them in thrall until he was done with them—was Dangler's awesome and total self-sufficiency, his gene-deep belief that he needed for himself nothing and no one. And with a surge of sympathy and affection, Cobb saw too how naturally that belief came to Dangler, how generations of assurances—of money and ability and power, of always being on the receiving end—had worked around the grain of his natural superiority to produce it in him like a pearl; and how not only easy but also inevitable for him it made his prodigal consumption of people and experiences, and the litter that consumption produced. Dangler didn't take, use and discard for himself, out of the traditional selfishness and carelessness of the rich; believing he needed nothing, he took in order to *give* —to do something for the world, however peculiar—using people to that end in the same way his great-grandfather had used rail. Cobb believed he saw that now, and if he himself felt used and discarded, the feeling was more than balanced out by the satisfaction of knowing that he had just inserted a crucial piece in a twenty-year-old jigsaw puzzle.

He stood up and closed the suitcase, knowing for the first time in months precisely what he was doing and why. Dangler had called him the best of the lot—let him show that he was. "He needs me, whether he knows it or not," he told the suitcase.

THREE

Cobb's Climb

XVII

———

Tuesday, the twelfth of December, the day Dangler had chosen to embark on the Winter Expedition, was perfect, just as he had promised it would be. There was light snow on Sunday and Monday, and a larger storm was predicted for later in the week, but Tuesday was a clarion day, a flawless patch of blue high pressure—and Wednesday, Dangler assured them, would be exactly like it.

Cobb woke that morning in a warm cast of sun that lay across his bed, feeling happy and eager for the trip. The brilliant morning seemed a good omen. Moreover, it seemed to reflect the bright spirits at the camp just now and the cheerfulness that everyone was carrying into the expedition. After making his mother's promise to do the best he could with the next twenty-four hours, he got out of bed, threw his curtains fully open and squinted out the window into the clear light. "Now," he felt like telling someone. "Now. This is what it's all about."

The feeling wasn't brand-new. It had grown on him over the past five days, beginning after lunch following his long talk with Dangler, when Kenneth and Erica had stood in front of the campers holding each other around the waist and announced the early closing of the camp with so much pleasure and warmth that the decision sounded as triumphant as their new relationship looked.

They were all on a new track, Dangler had said. Over the past months he had made mistakes, certainly, and he asked them all here and now for their forgiveness. The shortened season, however, should not be viewed as any sort of failure, but rather as a happy acknowledgment of challenging new directions for next year that would require time and care to plot. The remaining campers and staff— he said after a pause—along with Erica and Divina and Cobb, were his true and only family. He had nothing but the family's interests at heart, and the Winter Expedition, which would begin next week, should be considered a first, not a final, chapter.

"We are going away to Greece for an undetermined length of time," Erica had inserted oddly here.

A first and not a final chapter in their mutual adventure, Dangler went on. The capstone of their efforts for this year? Yes. A more exciting and rigorous challenge than any they had met before, and an opportunity for an ultimate victory over mindless nature and themselves? Surely. But also a beginning.

As was so often the case with Dangler, it was not so much what he said as some aloof, hypnotizing chemistry in his presentation that had stirred Cobb and everyone else at the table. After an absence of three days, with one short speech he had somehow welded them together and made them certain beyond doubt that everything was fine now and could only get better.

When he asked for criticisms or complaints, there were none. And after he had slipped his hand into the unruly hair at the back of Erica's neck, kissed her vividly and led her away, there had been no sound at the table for over two minutes. Finally, when Peter Bigelow spoke, he had seemed to speak for all of them.

"I would crawl to Juneau on my hands and knees for that man," he said.

Dangler was himself again—he was charming, attentive, engaged; the quality of arrogant, slightly crazed abstraction that had hung about him for the past months was gone as completely as if it had never existed—and that more than anything else was responsible for Cobb's blooming happiness. There were other things as well: Erica was sane and calm, Divina was untroubled, and the camp had a snug feel to it with the smaller group of campers, the looser schedule and the reduced staff. But what put the finishing touches to his sunny mood on Tuesday morning was the phone conversation he had had the day before with Foster Knapp.

"I'm about to start making life up there extremely ugly," Knapp had said. "Where is my six hundred thousand dollars?"

"Are you at all close to your younger sister, Mrs. Thomas W. Clover?" Cobb asked him. "Are you in any way whatever fond of her or concerned about her welfare?"

"I'm talking about *money*, here, mistah."

"Because if so, it might interest you to know that I am in possession of sufficient evidence to pack her husband off to jail for a number of years."

There had been silence from Knapp after Cobb explained in detail what evidence he had—a long, gratifying silence. Then the selectman sighed heavily. "Send me a copy of the film. I want to see it for myself."

"Not only do we want no harassment from the town; no one up here ever wants to hear your name again. Is that clear?"

"Aaya? Well, number one, that's too bad, because you will." Knapp's voice sounded tired. Even the threat Cobb knew was coming had a weary ring to it. "I don't quit quiet, Cobb. One way or another, I'll nail you people."

"Right," Cobb had told him with true delight. "That's the spirit, Foster. You hang in there, buddy."

After breakfast he spent a pleasant and painstaking hour rubbing Snow-Seal into his winter boots, adjusting his snowshoe bindings, and file-sharpening the twelve-clawed crampons that would strap to the bottoms of his boots for walking on the wind-scoured snow and ice near the summit of the mountain. The equipment, along with a two-foot wood-and-steel ice ax, was what Dangler had referred to last night in his briefing as "life-and-death gear"—things that each of them was personally to carry and care for. In the past month Cobb had learned the function and importance of the equipment, and attending to it now made him feel provident and expert. He hoped that he would measure up to the finely made tools, and hoping that made him realize that he wanted badly to do well on this last excursion —that as much as any of the campers he wanted to perform gracefully over the next two days. This, after all, was not a hike suitable for children, as the same trip had been in the fall. By way of emphasizing that fact, Dangler had promised them last night that he would impose no imaginary survival situations or invented hazards this time. This would be a *real* expedition, he had said. A winter summit attempt on one of the highest peaks in New England needed no embellishments: this would be an expedition without monkey business. They were ready for that, he had told them quietly; they had earned it.

Then he had gone on to how they would proceed. On Tuesday they would snowshoe up to the hunting cabin near tree line, where they would spend the night. On Wednesday they would climb, roped and in crampons, to the summit of the mountain, and be picked up by helicopter back at the cabin that afternoon. Thursday would be a rest day at the camp, and on Friday night they would celebrate the success of the expedition and the end of the season with a final campfire service. Finally, Dangler had passed out a checklist of the personal gear each of them should send ahead to the cabin the next morning with Gruenig in the helicopter and then wished them good night, sending them off to bed feeling briefed and confident.

Divina had toyed with the idea of not going. She had been having migraine headaches, she told Cobb, and she was afraid that one might ruin the trip for her. When she was not at breakfast, he figured that she had decided to stay behind, but at ten o'clock, when everyone met at the helicopter pad, she was there with her two packs of equipment.

"I'm glad you decided to come," Cobb said.

"It's just too beautiful not to." She smiled and looked around at the buzzing, gathering campers. "Isn't this fun? It reminds me of one of those wonderful ski-train weekends to Gray Rocks. Have you been?"

"I haven't been anywhere," said Cobb. "Is it nice?"

"Nice? It's heaven. It's against the law not to have wonderful fun in the Laurentians."

"Packs, please, everyone," shouted Dangler. Wearing knickers and a Navy greatcoat, he was loading things into the helicopter while Erica held open the door. "Andrew, will you and Divina please get your stuff over here *now?* Has anyone seen Hanspeter?"

"Frankly, I don't see all that much difference," said Divina, studying Dangler. "He's still behaving like a stormtrooper, if you ask me."

Cobb delivered their large packs to Dangler, and when he returned, Divina pushed her ski cap back off her broad forehead and said without looking at him, "If it wouldn't cause any problems with your lady friend in Concord, maybe we could go up to Gray Rocks in February? We could stay at the Ritz for a night and then take the train up with all those nice Montreal people."

"It won't cause any problems," said Cobb, "and I'd love to."

Divina wrinkled her nose at him. "Wasn't that cheeky —for a spy, I mean. Just to step out and ask you like that?"

"Downright reckless," Cobb said.

"And reckless of you to accept." She turned to him quickly and crossed her arms around his neck. "How about this? Not tonight, but when we get back—tomorrow night, say, do you suppose we could . . . ?" She brought her mouth to his cheek and whispered into his ear. "What?" said Cobb, looking at her with mock horror. He grinned. "You bet your ass we could."

"Well, *finally.*" Divina hugged his neck. "I thought you'd never ask."

Dangler had finished loading the helicopter and had paced around it four or five times by the time Gruenig arrived. Gruenig walked up with Rip Gurnsey, the pilot, and something about the way he stalked through the campers standing beside the helicopter made Cobb look away from Divina and Ames Cravens, with whom he was talking, and watch as Gruenig veered off from Gurnsey and the helicopter and headed for Erica. She was standing off from the others, listening regally to Madelaine de Faurier.

His face red and vehement, Gruenig caught her by the upper arm and whispered into her ear. Without looking at him, Erica jerked her arm free, as impersonally as if her coat were caught on something, and walked away. It was a cold, inexplicable transaction, and its inconsonance with the general tone of things bothered Cobb.

"Did you see that?" he asked Divina.

"See what?" she said, but she too was watching Erica.

"*Hanspeter,*" said Dangler. He was standing beside the helicopter, his hands on his hips. He was grinning, but his eyes were flat. "Are we going to stand around here socializing all morning? Or are we going to get to work?"

It was after eleven o'clock when the expedition finally got under way. Dangler had decided to take no recreation assistants along this time, so there were only the nine of them—himself and Erica, Divina and Cobb, the Bigelows, the de Fauriers and Ames Cravens. Carrying their snowshoes and ice axes and crampons strapped to their rucksacks, they hiked down the plowed road that led out toward the ski center on the northwest side of the mountain. As they crossed the river they had a full view of Revelation Cliff to the east; and its vast expanse of steep rock, creased from top to bottom with twisting silver and aquamarine gullies of ice, looked almost friendly in the sunny distance. Beyond the river they turned due north onto another road that brought them shortly to the base of the same trail they had hiked up six weeks earlier but which today, under three or four feet of snow, was impossible to recognize and only barely discernible as a threading white corridor between the trees.

Following it with his eyes into the sparkling woods, Cobb felt a knot of excitement in his chest, and he decided to forget the uneasiness he had been feeling about Gruenig and the expression on his face after Dangler shouted at him. Gruenig, he told himself, had nothing to do with this trip.

"OK," said Dangler, throwing down his rucksack. "Let's put on the snowshoes."

"Let me just try it once without them," suggested Rocque de Faurier. "The snow should be crusted up under that little accumulation we had yesterday and the day before." While he talked, de Faurier climbed the ridge of snow left by the plow at the end of the road. "After all, it would be a hell of a lot easier if . . ." Jumping from the ridge, he sank above his knees into the path and wallowed ahead for four or five steps, sinking deeper with each one, before he shrugged and turned around, panting.

"Sometimes, sweetie . . ." said Madelaine de Faurier slowly, gazing at the sky above him. She shook her head. "Well . . ."

Cobb couldn't get over how perfect everything was—the pungent brightness of the woods, the grip and crunch of his snowshoes on the new snow, and mostly, the developing feel of the expedition itself as they tramped upward in single and double file under the warming sun, precisely dressed and equipped, conditioned and comfortable with each other. It felt *real*, and deeply gratifying to be out here, walking into a season of nature that most people saw only from windows or ski lifts; it felt liberating and sharpening, to be moving upward with some technique and stamina toward a six-thousand-foot mountain summit in the dead of a Northern winter. At one point shortly after they began, he looked ahead on the trail to where Dangler was joyfully breaking trail fifty yards ahead and felt a sentimental affection for his friend's intractable fervor, his ornery vision. Watching him plow uphill, he remembered a comment Divina had made a month or so earlier during her bitter period. "Kenneth is really just an upper-class zealot," she had said loftily. "He believes that for all those missionaries running around in the jungles and the ghettos there ought to be at least one up here in the woods of New Hampshire attending to the wealthy."

The temperature was in the middle thirties, but with the rising sun and the exertion it seemed much warmer. Cobb began the trip dressed as they had been instructed to, in wool socks, long johns and knickers, with canvas gaiters covering his lower legs to keep the snow out of his boots. On his head he wore a balaclava cap that could be pulled down to cover all of his face except his eyes and nose, on his hands a pair of wool mittens over silk gloves, and on his upper body a fishnet undershirt, two wool shirts, a sweater and a down vest. By the third ten-minute rest stop he had shed the mittens, the cap, the vest, the sweater and one of the shirts, stuffing them into his rucksack along with his extra cap and mittens, his down parka and wind jacket and glacier glasses, and still he was sweating heavily when Dangler called the halt.

"Can you believe this weather?" Erica asked him, digging in her rucksack for a canteen. "The air is like iced tea."

She had stripped down to a T-shirt, and her two wool shirts were tied around her waist. As always when she was exercised, her vitality seemed a live thing, barely under the skin. Seated between her and Cravens on a large rock, it was all Cobb could do to keep his hand from wandering over to feel for it on her arms or neck. Instead he watched Weezy Bigelow paint red daisies on her boots with fingernail polish, and said, "Yes. It's beautiful."

"I feel like I could walk for weeks. My quadriceps muscles have never felt stronger, and my biceps femoris . . ."

"Your gluteus maximus has never *looked* better," said Cravens, and patted her on the hip.

"Oh, Ames."

"Oh, Ames," said Cravens.

"You're just so old-fashioned. It's touching, really. You remind me a little of madras."

"Impossible," said Cravens, his smile stiffening.

"The Kingston Trio," Cobb said.

"The fin-tail Cadillac," Peter Bigelow said, and chuckled.

"No, Nassau!" offered Madelaine de Faurier loudly. "Back when everyone used to go to *Nassau*."

"Actually," said Cravens, his blue eyes narrowing vengefully at Erica, "your gluteus maximus and surrounding areas *have* looked better. You're gaining weight."

Strangely, it seemed to Cobb, Erica blushed at this and looked away. She took a long swallow from the canteen and considered the plastic bottle. "Did you know, Ames," she said thoughtfully, "that you are two-thirds water? You are worth something less than ninety dollars on the hoof."

As they rose up the side of Mount Webster, the Presidential Range of the White Mountains seemed to sprout around them in the distance like white-capped mushrooms. Nearer, the surrounding hills were mauve and green, slashed white with gullies of snow and ice, and below them the bare tops of hardwood trees made the river valley look like a sea of gray-brown smoke. Around one-thirty they stopped for a simple lunch of cheese and sausage and raisins on the flat rocks where they had lunched before, and as they ate they looked across Pinkham notch into the bright triangular snowfield of Tuckerman's ravine on the south slope of Mount Washington. Though it was nearly thirty miles away, the mountain today looked close enough to leap to. It struck Cobb that he had hardly noticed it the last time he was here, and he wondered if Tit Fairfax and the boozy, unpleasant tenor of that first lunch were to blame, or if he might simply be growing more observant.

"Show me some things," he asked Divina when they started hiking again, and for the next hour and a half, all the way to the cabin, they lagged behind the others while she pointed out bird and animal tracks.

She called a chickadee onto her hand with a whistle and a chewed piece of gum. She showed him a grouse burrow in a snowbank, and tracing the blurred outline of its prints, told him that the bird grew feathers on its claws in winter for better flotation on snow. She showed him the intimate twin tracks of a pair of fisher cats, the zigzag tracks of a frightened snowshoe rabbit, and the perfectly registered prints of a stalking fox. It fascinated Cobb that she was able to speculate from the shape and depth and direction of a print on the mood of the creature at the moment it made it; that she could infer fright or hunger or curiosity from what seemed to him arbitrary marks in the snow seemed magical. By the time they neared the cabin, he was imagining a bird or animal at the end of each set of tracks, and he had developed a new sense of the woods as a populated place, teeming with emotional rabbits and foxes and burrowing feather-clawed birds, each of them following the clear tracks of instinct within a benevolent, harmonious society.

As they entered the clearing surrounding the cabin, he held back on an impulse, feeling emotional himself, and put his left hand on the curling skin of a white birch. The others were already inside; the snowshoes were stuck in the snow in front of the cabin. There was smoke rising in a straight line from the chimney, and he could hear laughter. Behind the cabin the sky was a depthless slate blue, just beginning to color with sunset. Cobb squeezed the tree, and for just a moment, for a matter of seconds, he felt in touch with every squirrel and vole, every rabbit and crow and deer and fox and bear on the mountain, and the natural world seemed to him so full and sweet that he wanted to stay in it forever.

"What's wrong?" Divina asked him.

"The woods are wonderful," he said unsteadily.

"I know."

"I was just thinking that maybe I'd change jobs. Get to be a warden, or one of those fire lookouts, maybe. I don't know . . ."

Smiling, Divina took his arm in both her hands and patted it. Then she laid her head against his shoulder and said, "Fine. That would be just fine, sweetie."

Gruenig and Rip Gurnsey had shoveled off the steps to the cabin, laid a fire in the fireplace, turned on the space heaters and rolled out nine sleeping bags on nine air mattresses. They had unpacked the big packs, hung up clothing, put ice in the ice buckets, laid charcoal in the indoor grill and cut limes. They had even unwrapped the nine Delmonico steaks and left a rich mushroom-and-lentil soup simmering on the stove. Their preparations were so complete that there was nothing left for the members of the expedition to do but drink and eat and talk about the day's hike and the next day's summit attempt—and after everyone had changed into clean clothes and down booties, that was exactly what they did. They sat beside the popping fire telling stories and eating macadamia nuts, refilling each other's drinks, holding each other's eyes when they talked, and seeming to Cobb very much like the family Dangler had called them. Thinking back on the last time they were here, it appeared miraculous to him that so much could have changed in less than two months. Warmed by the congeniality, the bourbon and the fire, the tender mood he had brought inside from the woods expanded in him, filling him with uncontainable affection. He gave Madelaine de

Faurier a fifteen-minute foot rub, talking to her the whole time with interest and feeling about Angora cats, an animal he hated. He told Weezy Bigelow that if he ever fathered a child, he would accept no godmother for it but her. And just before dinner, watching Erica's broad back while she washed lettuce alone in the kitchen, he felt a surge of love —for her and for everyone there—so strong that it almost knocked him down.

Walking up behind her, he wrapped his arms around her waist and buried his face in her hair. "God, I'm going to miss you," he told her. "And Kenneth. And . . . everyone."

"Do you feel that?" she asked, pressing his hands suddenly against her abdomen. "That warmth? It's like I've had a Duch oven inside me for the past week—I've never been so warm and happy in my body. Oh, Andy!" She tossed her head and turned around inside his arms, her face radiant with pleasure. "We're going *away,* and things will be the way they used to be, and God I'm going to try to make certain we never come back to New Hampshire." She pulled him to her and hugged him hard, swinging him from side to side. "But I'm going to miss you too. Sweet, sweet Andrew."

With all his lush feelings and luxurious tiredness, the right amount of bourbon, the fire, and after a fine dinner, Cobb's day had every chance of ending as perfectly as it had begun, and would have if he had not decided to drink a few brandies with Peter Bigelow and Rocque de Faurier after everyone else had gone to bed. The two men were as sentimentally liquored up as he was, and the conversation was nostalgic and slurred. After an hour they seemed simultaneously to run out of camp stories to rehash, and the three of them sank into a long silence.

"Never cared for you," said Peter Bigelow finally. He squinted up at de Faurier woozily. "Never cared for you at all, in fact."

"Sure you did, Peter," said Cobb.

"Thought you were a part of what went wrong with this country. Die for you now, though."

"Die for you too," said de Faurier. "Never cared for your wife, personally. Squirrelly woman, I told Madelaine. Seaboard snob. Die for her too now."

The two campers agreed that they would cheerfully die for anyone in the cabin at that moment. Then de Faurier sighed and said that he wished them all luck next year, that he would miss them.

"What do you mean?" demanded Peter Bigelow. "Where the hell will you be?"

"Oh, I know. I know," said de Faurier. He clenched his long jaw and shook his head. "I've known for some time that Madelaine and I are D's. We won't be back." He looked around abruptly for someplace to put his snifter. "Be here with all of you in spirit, though."

"Of *course* you'll be back," said Cobb.

"If I have anything to do with it, you'll be back," said Bigelow firmly. "I can promise you that, old Rocque."

De Faurier shook his head again. "I don't know. You do the best you can . . ."

"Have to see a fella about a dog," said Bigelow after another silence. "You guys want to join me? It's a beautiful night out there, and there won't be many more when we can walk outside together and take a leak."

The night was cold and unusually still. There was a high three-quarter moon with a ring around it, and it was bright enough for them to see where they were going even without the flashlight that de Faurier brought along. They strapped on their snowshoes and, led by Bigelow, followed a sort of path already packed by snowshoes toward a group of birch trees thirty yards behind the cabin.

"No yellow snow in the front yard, am I right, Andrew?" said Bigelow loudly.

"Wait a minute, what's that?" said de Faurier. He had been bouncing the flashlight over the snow in front of them, and now he had it focused on what looked like a large heap of torn black cloth between them and the trees.

It was not cloth. It was a pile of dead ducks inside a circle stamped in the snow. It was difficult to tell how many ducks there were; some of them were completely pulled apart, others were eyeless, decapitated, eviscerated. The pile was a bloody mayhem of feathers and entrails, bills and claws, surreal and horrible in the moonlight.

"Foxes?" asked Peter Bigelow nervously.

De Faurier snorted. "Foxes would have eaten them.

This has to be teenage vandals or something. What are they, crows?"

"Why would kids come all the way up here to tear up a bunch of birds?" asked Bigelow. "Use your head, for Christ's sake."

"Listen here, Bigelow . . ." de Faurier began.

"Ducks," said Cobb quietly. "They're black ducks." He thought now that he could make out how many birds were in the pile. He wondered what Dangler would want him to do. "I'm going to get some shovels. There's no point in having the others see this. And we won't mention it in the morning."

"Right. No point in upsetting the ladies," agreed de Faurier.

"What do you think it means, Andy?" asked Peter Bigelow.

"Nothing," said Cobb, turning toward the cabin and trying to hold his voice steady. "It doesn't mean a damn thing. It's just nine dead ducks in the snow."

XVIII

———

Cobb did not sleep well that night. He dreamed stormily and for hours, it seemed, about a white dog he had watched put away by a farmer when he was a child. The dog had been shot in the head with a .22 rifle and had died immediately with no sound. But in the dream the dog made horrible noises and refused to fall down in the dirt yard. Cobb woke a little before five—with the animal still grotesquely alive in his mind—exhausted and fearing he had talked in his sleep. For an hour he lay wide-awake in the down sleeping bag, afraid to go back to sleep. But he did, and when he woke again it was after eight o'clock. Everyone else was up. He heard conversation in the main room, smelled coffee and sausage frying and he felt better.

The morning was sunny, but different from the day before. After breakfast Cobb carried a mug of coffee out to the cabin steps and noticed that the air had a heavy, late-summer feel to it. The breeze out of the southwest was almost balmy. To the west the sky was white, but above the mountain and as far north and east as he could see, it was blue and streaked with only a few long thin clouds that were curled at their ends.

"Mares' tails," said Dangler, joining him loudly on the

steps. He nodded at the hooked clouds. "It looks like we might get that weather a little early. I talked to Hanspeter on the radio an hour ago and he said the station on Mount Washington is still calling for it tomorrow, but I wouldn't be surprised if we saw some of the white stuff before we get back here this afternoon."

"Snow, you mean?" asked Cobb irritably. "You're going to take us up to the top of this mountain in a snowstorm?"

Dangler looked him over. "If it starts today at all, it won't be until after we're off the summit. What's wrong with you? You look a little rabbity around the mouth."

"I didn't sleep well."

"Oh?"

"And last night after you went to bed . . ."

Cobb felt as though he had sprung a leak. He had had no intention of telling Dangler about the bunch of dead ducks now buried under a foot of snow. What is this? he wondered. He shook his head, hoping to stir up his blood, to get himself going a little more robustly this morning. "Rocque and Peter and I got into the brandy last night after you went to bed. I must have had too much to drink."

"The cure for that, my boy, is sweat," said Dangler. "Come with me."

For the next half-hour the two of them opened a trail from the cabin to just above tree line where the mountain steepened and the snow hardened, so that the expedition could proceed without snowshoes this morning. When they finished Cobb was red-faced and sweating.

Dangler looked at him analytically again before they went inside. "As William James reminds us, 'The noble things taste better.' Now you look like a mountaineer."

"At last," Cobb said, and cuffed him on the shoulder. "My ambition since childhood."

The expedition got off for the summit a little after ten o'clock. The temperature was already in the forties so they took their down parkas out of their rucksacks and left them in the cabin along with the snowshoes, giving everyone a lighter load than the day before, except Dangler, who transferred all the things in his rucksack including his parka into one of the large frame packs and added a gasoline stove and a battery-operated radio, a medical kit and a sleeping bag for emergencies, and a bottle of cognac for celebration. On top of the pack he strapped one of the three 165-foot climbing ropes. Cobb carried another one, looped over his shoulder and across his chest, and Peter Bigelow carried the third. Despite the fact that they did not expect to need any of it, Rocque de Faurier brought along a full complement of climbing hardware—dozens of pitons and ice screws and the oval metal clips called carabiners, a "deadman" snow anchor and two pairs of mechanical rope ascenders, all of which he attached to nylon slings and draped over himself and Ames Cravens.

Though the path that Cobb and Dangler had cleared followed an easy incline, without snowshoes they sank often up to their ankles in the snow and occasionally above their knees, so that by the time Dangler called the first rest stop at the small plateau where the path ended with the trees and the snow hardened into wind-pack, everyone was ready for it. Above them a steep open snowfield reared five hundred feet to a ridge. They would kick steps up to the ridge, Dangler told them, then follow it to the northeast col of the mountain, from which they would make the final push up the summit cone to the top. The going would be steep and there would be patches of ice and ice-covered rock, so from here on they would climb roped and in crampons. As he strapped the fanged steel plates onto his boots he reminded them to walk *en canard,* like a duck, to keep from goring themselves with the two-inch spikes. Then he instructed everyone to eat a candy bar and to drink four swallows of sweetened tea. While they did that he climbed fifty feet up the snowfield, giving a refresher demonstration in kicking steps and using the ice ax. On the way down he demonstrated again how to arrest a fall by digging the pick of the ax into the snow and throwing the body diagonally across the shaft.

They were all silent as they roped up. Dangler tied in to the lead on one rope, with Madelaine de Faurier in the middle and Erica at the end. Peter Bigelow would take first position on the second rope, followed by Weezy and Ames Cravens; and Rocque de Faurier would begin the lead on the third, with Cobb at the other end and Divina tied between them.

Cobb wrapped his end of the heavy Perlon rope three times around his waist and knotted it off in a careful bowline; then he examined and yanked at Divina's and de Faurier's knots, and had de Faurier check his. Finally, when every knot had been inspected, and the straps on every crampon and the wrist loop on every ice ax, Dangler looked up at the ridge above them and said, "Fifteen hundred vertical feet above us, ladies and gentlemen, is the summit of Mount Webster. Those fifteen hundred feet are composed of nothing but inanimate rock and frozen water. We are human beings. We prevailed in the fall; we shall now proceed to prevail again."

"Whether it's at work or play . . ." sang Weezy Bigelow.

"None of that today, Weezy," Dangler said, starting upward. "Today is something different."

The snowfield went slowly. Though all of them had practiced climbing in snow, roped and in crampons, they had practiced only on the short and gentle talus slope at the base of Revelation Cliff, where the Fairfax sisters had had their accident. The slope they were on now was more than five times as long as that and pitched at between thirty-five and forty degrees, so that, walking almost upright, they had only to reach out with their hands a few inches from their chests to touch it. Dangler's rope led off, and the other two followed at intervals of about fifty feet, staying slightly to one side and out of the fall-line of the people above. They ascended by traverses, climbing thirty or forty yards in one direction off the center line of the slope, and then switching back, making the pivotal step with the outside foot as they had been taught, holding their axes diagonally across their bodies with the picks pointed downward in the arrest position, and using the spike ends to catch the snow for a third point of balance.

They all knew exactly what to do—how to use the ax, how to swing the entire leg instead of just the foot to kick a level platform for each step, how to breathe properly and rest-step—but doing it here and now was much more difficult than Cobb, for one, had anticipated. His rucksack shifted from side to side, putting him off balance, and the thin straps bit at his shoulders; sweat ran into his eyes, and he was afraid to take a hand off his ax to wipe it out. After only fifty yards he was puffing heavily and his calves and the backs of his legs ached from reaching for the steps that the long-legged de Faurier was kicking. He wondered how the hell Divina was keeping up, or Weezy or Madelaine—and the fact that none of the eight people on the shimmering slope above him seemed to be having trouble irritated him. After another hundred feet the irritation turned into a small whiny anger: the snowfield was too goddamned bright and he couldn't get at his glacier glasses, the rope between himself and Divina kept getting in his way, loose snow from her kicking was hitting him in the face and he was *hot*.

"Stop," he shouted at Divina. "Tell Rocque to hold it a minute . . . I need to check something." He let himself fall against the slope and leaned there on his shoulder, panting like a dog and feeling completely taken over by a sniveling, rock-kicking rage.

"What's going on?" yelled de Faurier after a moment.

"*Shut up,*" Cobb bellowed uphill. "You're just showing off again with those long goddamned steps!"

De Faurier didn't answer, and in a few seconds Cobb had himself back in control.

"Sorry," he said abstractly.

He drove the ax into the snow, and using the pick as a handle, turned to face the slope again. Then he looked down. It was the first time he had done so, and the view of his exposure, two hundred and fifty precipitous feet from level ground, shocked more than frightened him. His chest and throat suddenly full of adrenaline, he looked upward again and began climbing. "I'm coming," he shouted.

Dangler gave them a fifteen-minute rest on the ridge, and Cobb was gratified to find that everyone seemed to need it.

"I didn't think we'd *ever* get up that thing," said Madelaine de Faurier.

"All of us had our problems," said Divina, and smiled at Cobb.

"Climbing," said de Faurier around a mouthful of nuts and raisins, "is all in the mind. The problem most people have is that they just aren't tough enough mentally."

"Or that they don't have legs like a chimpanzee," said Cobb.

De Faurier considered him sternly. "I saw you looking down. You should never look down."

"I don't know," said Cravens. "It seems to me it's pretty good motivation to keep going up. Isn't that right, Kenny?"

"How many mountains have you climbed, son?" de Faurier asked him.

"I'd like for everyone to put on their wind parkas, please," said Dangler. He was looking off to the north and appeared distracted. "Then we're moving out."

The wind was, in fact, coming up. It had shifted out of the south into the northeast, so that it was blowing directly down on them as they climbed the ridge toward the high notch or col just below the summit cone. A veil of cirrus clouds covered the sky completely now except for a bar of blue in the east, but it was still warm despite the wind and the cloud cover.

They remained roped, having switched leads after the rest stop, because the ridge, though less steep than the snowfield, was icy and narrow, falling abruptly on the right to tree line, and sloping off on their left to the floor of a wide bowl. The far wall of the bowl was a huge triangular snowfield that tapered upward into a gully leading to the summit, and Cobb wondered why they were not following that shorter, more direct route. He wished very much that they were—for though he wanted to be enjoying himself, he was not; though he wanted badly to feel confident and able, particularly after his recent fit of bad temper, he did not. On the ridge he was able to look around as he had not been able to on the snowfield, and what he saw was edging his usual nervousness above tree line toward panic. An occasional gnarled and stunted tree, some gargoylish cousin to a fir, told him what it meant to be stuck up here in this wasteland of wind and snow, glinting ice and granite, whose every surface was abrasive and cold, and he yearned to be back down in the populous, sociable woods.

Ames Cravens had asked to lead the ridge, and Dangler was letting him. Since the other two ropes had changed leads as well, putting Erica and Cobb at the front, Cobb had wound up climbing just behind Dangler. For a few minutes he tried whistling "Men of Dartmouth," but it didn't help.

"Why are we going way the hell around like this?" he asked finally. "Why don't we just scoot up over there?"

Dangler looked where he was pointing. "Don't you see the sunball tracks in the couloir?"

"The what? I don't see anything but snow, and neither do you, Hawkeye. It's too far away."

Dangler shrugged. "That's a convex leeward slope, and I can see sunballing. It's an avalanche track."

Ten minutes later, just as they were entering the col, a section of snow in the couloir let loose with a loud sigh. As they turned toward it, they could feel as much as hear the rumble and hiss of the avalanche as it poured down the gully and out into the snowfield, smoking and boiling, and gathering on itself like a wave. They watched the leading edge of the slide carry halfway across the floor of the bowl, and when it finally stopped, a white mist of snow hung over the bowl like a cloud.

Divina said that if it had gone on for ten seconds longer she could have had a picture.

"Jesus Christ," whispered Cobb, who had never in his life seen anything so headlong and massively wanton.

Dangler smiled at him, looking pleased.

"How could you . . . have *known* that? How many of those things have you seen?"

"That's the first, actually. But I've read everything there is about them."

After a quick lunch at the col, of meat bars and dried fruit, they climbed the summit cone, which was less than a hundred yards high but so steep and icy that they had to move with agonizing care, testing each step and purchase of the ice ax before they could put weight on it. Dangler took the lead again, and Cobb, again at the end of the last rope, could hear him above cutting the steps that got them over the worst places. Cobb concentrated on the sound of Dangler's ax and did not look down, and at twenty minutes after one o'clock he stepped onto the summit plateau, as exultant as everyone else there, but quite positive that it was the last winter mountaintop he would ever see.

"Weren't we all splendid?" asked Weezy Bigelow. Her little hands were balled into fists, and she was shaking them at Madelaine de Faurier.

Divina hugged Cobb around the neck and congratulated him. "You made it look too damned easy," he told her wearily.

Rocque de Faurier said that in the absence of a plaque to sign, he would announce to the mountain that they were there by urinating off its top, the way it was done in the Cordillera Blanca.

Cobb was pleased to join him. The wind was sharp on the summit, and it seemed to him that it was growing colder. Low pearl-gray clouds had moved in and were packed around the mountain on three sides, cutting off a view of anything except a few small hills to the south. The summit plateau itself was in and out of clouds, and ghostly —a jumble of granite boulders surrounding a dishlike depression of hard snow, with humped ribbons of dull yellow and aqua ice streaming from the sides. Cobb's whole body knew it was no place for human beings, and he felt a great gush of relief when Dangler said they would have to leave momentarily in order to meet the helicopter back at the cabin by three o'clock.

After a short toast by Dangler they each took a couple of swallows of the brandy he had brought along, and Cobb was putting the bottle back into the frame pack when Divina said, "Wait a minute, keep it out. I want to get a picture of everyone celebrating."

"We really ought to get moving," said Dangler, looking to the north again.

Divina was untying herself. "It won't take but a second. I only have three exposures left on the roll." She looked around quickly for a place to stand. "When I get these, I'll have two whole rolls on the camp, and you can all blow them up and frame them for your summer cottages or something."

As the group positioned itself, she scrambled up a large boulder below them, using her ice ax to help pull herself up. She was already on top and focusing the camera when Dangler noticed where she was.

"You ought not to be up there in crampons," he shouted to her over the wind.

"Smile!" she shouted back.

She took the three photographs and began backing off the boulder, holding the camera and ax in her left hand.

"Wait," yelled Dangler, trotting toward her over the snow.

When he got to the bottom of the boulder she stood up

in a crouch and tossed him the camera. The motion threw her a little off balance, and when she stood farther up to correct it, her crampons began to slide; she swiped once futilely at the rock with her ax, and fell, facing the ground, in a curving dive off the far side.

Erica leaped for the boulder, followed by Cobb and then the others. When they reached Divina, Dangler had her stretched out on her back and was probing underneath her sweater with both hands. She looked pale and uncomfortable, but she smiled when Erica dropped to her knees on the rocks beside her. "Lamb," said Erica. "What a dumb thing to do."

"She landed on a rock on her chest and abdomen," Dangler said. "There is some contusion, but no ribs are broken. I think she's all right." He gave Erica the camera.

Cobb realized that he had been holding his breath. He let it out slowly, and asked God to please get them all back to the cabin safely and as soon as possible.

"Of course I'm all right," said Divina, sitting up. But she was looking directly at Cobb when she said it, and he could see fear, like flecks of ice, in her eyes.

It began to snow just before they reached the col. It began as a small snow that danced and slanted on the wind, but by the time they were halfway down the ridge it was heavier, and they were having some difficulty seeing. They moved as quickly as they could and did not stop until they got to the place where they had first come out onto the ridge. The snowfield, Dangler said after climbing a few feet down it, was too steep to descend with poor visibility, so they would have to follow the ridge to the trees and then bushwhack back to the cabin.

He asked Divina how she felt and she told him she was a little cold but otherwise fine. Walking down behind her from the summit, Cobb had watched her whenever he had been able and had seen that she was moving well—much better, in fact, than he was. The climb down the glazed summit cone had been a nightmare of worry and hesitation for him. And now, staring dully through the blowing snow on the ridge, fidgeting with the knot at his waist and

munching the Cadbury chocolate that Dangler had just instructed everyone to eat, all he could think about was how
badly he had let himself down on this trip, how much less
gracefully he had performed than even the weakest of the
campers; and though he was sure he had never wanted
anything as much as he wanted now to be back at the cabin
with fresh clothes on and a drink in his hand, he wished
tentatively for one more chance—some small, easily met
challenge between here and the camp, something to make
his next few days with himself less humiliating.

Still hatless and gloveless as he had been all day, his
hair and mustache hoary with snow, Dangler checked
everyone's face for signs of frostbite before they started
down again. It was almost two o'clock. They could not stop
again, he told them, and they would have to hurry to make
the cabin by three. Peter Bigelow asked if the helicopter
would be able to land in this weather, and Dangler said that
as long as the wind didn't get much higher there would be
no problem—that Gurnsey and Gruenig could bring it
down in a blizzard if they had to.

They followed the ridge to tree line, then swung southeast on a compass bearing Dangler seemed to pull out of
the snowy air. The walking was all downhill, but in the
unpacked accumulating snow among the trees they wallowed like deer, sinking to mid-thigh with almost every step,
and for the first time on the expedition some of the campers
began to complain.

"I'm going to stop," announced Madelaine de Faurier
finally, and did just that. She had just pulled herself out of
a crater of drifted snow and she sat on the edge of it,
crossed her legs, and commenced jiggling her foot angrily.
The others made a circle around her.

"I'm going to sit here and smoke a cigarette. If no one
else wants to stay, fine. The helicopter can just pick me up
later."

"The helicopter can't land here, Madelaine. There are
too many trees," Dangler told her.

"Frankly, I don't care. It will just have to. I'm not taking
another step."

"Get up, Madelaine," said Rocque. He poked his wife
with his ice ax.

Weezy sat down on the snow beside her. "I think I'll stay too. To keep her company."

"Listen," said Dangler gently. "Let me make this clear to both of you. The helicopter can't possibly land here. You may stay if you want, that is your option, and if you do, you will die. Probably before midnight, and certainly before morning." He turned and walked off, drawing out the rope between himself and Madelaine. She watched it uncoil between them for a moment and then stood up and followed him.

Though it did not help appreciably with his feeling about himself, Cobb did not open his mouth or feel sorry for himself once on the exhausting forty-minute slog to the clearing. Nor, when they entered it—holding the sections of rope between them in coils and walking abreast, so that the sight hit them all at once—did he gasp or swear or moan along with most of the others, or feel sorry for himself even then. He just stood there shaking his head, looking at the brick chimney and, beneath it, the smoldering remains of the cabin, and feeling that something he didn't know the name of had finally caught up with all of them. I take it back, he thought, just in case this was the challenge he had wished for back on the ridge.

"The cabin burned down," Dangler said. He said it tentatively, as if trying out the observation in his mind.

"You've gone too far this time," bawled Rocque de Faurier, whirling on him. "I had three thousand dollars' worth of equipment in that cabin, you maniac."

Dangler walked in front of them and raised his arms like a band leader. "I swear that I had nothing to do with this. Someone must have dropped a cigarette, or left the stove on. It doesn't matter . . . it's a fact now, and we will deal with it. The helicopter should be here in five or ten minutes; we will salvage what we can until then. Now, unrope and cheer up."

There was very little that could be salvaged—a few aluminum shovels, some metal cups and pots, a coffee percolator, a rifle with a charred stock, and some metal climbing hardware. Everything else—snowshoes, clothes, bedding, ropes, bottles of water and liquor—had been incinerated, broken or ruined, and they could find no sign of the metal cache box of food. The campers picked for a while among the ashes and then quit. Erica and Divina sat on their packs talking, their backs to the burned cabin. Dangler paced, staring at the ground, and Cobb just stood, arms folded on his chest, watching snow fall on the charcoal.

At 3:15 Dangler called Gruenig on the radio.

"Yah," said Gruenig to the call numbers.

"Why aren't you here? It's sixteen after three. Over."

"You said four o'clock."

"I said three. Over."

". . ."

"The cabin has burned and we have an injured woman. Get Gurnsey and come immediately. Over."

"How iss the storm up there, Mr. Dankler?"

"It's getting worse. Wind out of the northeast at twenty to twenty-five, I'd say. You'll make it all right, but leave immediately. Over."

"Mount Washington says twenty-five to thirty. Barometric pressure of twenty-eight-point-five-oh of mercury. Do you know futt that means?"

"It means we're in for a big storm. Get up here, Hanspeter. Over."

"Yah. Two shakes," said Gruenig.

"How long?" asked Ames Cravens.

Dangler looked at the radio for a long moment before he answered. "We'll have to wait and see."

"I swear to Christ," said de Faurier, "if this is another one of your pranks, Kenneth, I'll sue your ears off for it."

"You signed a release," Cobb reminded him reflexively.

"I'll be *god*damned if—"

"Listen to me," Dangler said sharply. "We need something to do until the chopper gets here. Peter, you and Ames go get those shovels. We're going to practice snow-cave construction. And you, Rocque, will work hard and not open your mouth again on the subject of the cabin."

At 3:30 Dangler left the planning of the snow cave and called Gruenig again. There was no answer. At 3:45 he left the initial excavation and called again, without an answer. Both times he walked a long way off from the others to call, and when he left the digging at four to call a third time, he took Cobb with him.

"They should have been here thirty minutes ago," he

said when they were well away from the others. "I'm afraid we have a problem."

Cobb had been trying not to think, but he knew Dangler was right about that. It was growing dark, the wind was rising and the snow was heavier than it had been even ten minutes ago. "How could you let this happen?" he asked.

"I had nothing to do with it. Now buck up; I'm going to need you."

"K49270 mobile to K49270 base," Dangler said into the radio. "Come back."

"Yeah?" said a voice thickly.

Dangler shook the radio. "Hanspeter, is that you? Over."

"Thassa Rog, my man." The voice was distant and faint, but the Southern accent—burred, it sounded like, with whiskey—hit Cobb in the head like an ax and was followed momentarily by a dreadful intimation of what was going on.

"Why aren't you here, Hanspeter? Over," said Dangler calmly.

"I forgot, I reckon. I had some errands to run." Gruenig chuckled. "Too late now, though—too dark . . . too bad."

"The batteries are beginning to go from the cold," Dangler told Cobb. He shook the radio again. "I didn't copy that, Hanspeter, come back."

"What's *wrong* with him?" asked Cobb.

"I said iss *stormin'* too bad now, you asshole," said Gruenig.

"Hanspeter? Listen to me. Did you burn the cabin, Hanspeter?"

Gruenig laughed again faintly. "You're on your own now, sport . . . and out."

"Use your head, Hanspeter," said Dangler. He released the transmit button and chewed for a second on his mustache.

"What is he doing?" asked Cobb. "Why is he *doing* this?"

"I think I know what your problem is, Hanspeter," Dangler went on. "But this is an idiotic mistake you're making."

"*Don't* tell him that, Kenneth."

"There are plenty of fish in the sea, Hanspeter. Keep that in mind."

"*What?*" shouted Cobb. "What are you *telling* him?"

Dangler looked at the radio and pressed the transmit button a couple of times. "Nothing, I'm afraid. The batteries are dead." He looked up at Cobb, grinning. "He's right about one thing, though. We are on our own now. Back to back."

"Kenneth," said Cobb. "Why is he doing this to us? I want to know that."

Dangler told him. When he was through, he put his arm over Cobb's shoulder and in the closing dark they walked back toward the snow cave, leaning together into the wind and the horizontal sheets of snow it carried.

Peter Bigelow met them fifty feet from the cave. His big sad face under the hood of his parka was cracked with weariness and worry.

" 'Nature red in tooth and claw,' eh, Peter my boy?" said Dangler heartily.

"The helicopter isn't coming, is it, Chief?"

"I'm afraid not."

"Then we're in trouble. We have Divina inside the cave, and I believe she's going into shock."

XIX

The first time she called him beautiful, Gruenig had wanted to spit. He wanted to say, "You know what I think is beautiful? New snow and Mac Wiseman singing 'They'll Never Take Her Love from Me.' "

"You are beautiful like a fox. Or a wolverine."

Gruenig did not like foxes, and he had never seen a wolverine, but after the first few times he had gotten tolerant of being told he was beautiful and had even come to like it and, finally, to believe it.

He looked at his left hand. It was curled around the neck of his Gibson guitar, but he saw it lying in the valley of her lower back—strong and callused, humped against the white slope of buttocks. He thought of her thinking it beautiful like the rough paw of an animal, and it made him shiver. Moving the hand away from the neck of the guitar, he watched it pour out another drink from the bottle of Canadian Club. Then, bored with the hand, he looked at what he had written. It was three stanzas of a song, written on a pad that was propped against the FM base console over which he had just talked to Dangler for the last time.

"You lost a good thing, Baby, when you let me go," went the song. "I may be the best thing, Baby, that you'll ever know."

You lost a good man, Mama, when you lost me
The only real man, Mama, that you'll ever see.

I remember the first time, Baby, that I saw you.
It was a hot day, Baby, you were in a canoe.

He had been fooling with the song on his guitar for the last couple of hours while he drank and turned the radio off and on and listened to the storm come up. He was not happy with the last line, but he knew the correct version would come to him—just as the final details of what he would do that night and the following day would come to him—after a while. He was in no hurry for either.

Looking up from the pad to the radio, he wondered how long it would take a bunch of fools led by a madman to die in weather like this. Not long, he reckoned, even without a hurt one; the hurt one was gravy. He wondered who it was. He hoped it was Erica, then he hoped it was not; then he hoped again that it was. If it was, he could make a raid, he thought. He put down the guitar and asked himself if it would make any difference if he saved her—if he came whirling out of the storm in the chopper with Gurnsey, went down on a rope with the M 16 he had smuggled out of Nam . . . and *saved* her, say, would *that* . . . ? In a rush he thought about her hair, her long legs, her breasts. They were thoughts he had not allowed himself all day, and he could feel them confusing him now, so he cut them off and determined to go over in his mind once again, before he got too drunk, what she had done—not to try to understand it, he had given that up; but to stiffen himself, and to clear his head for the next twenty-four hours.

She had *come to him,* hadn't she? The answer was: like a sow to slop. And not once, but every day for ten days, coming late in the afternoons after her run, *every* afternoon until the one when he threw the rope on the two tall sisters, doing what Dangler had told him to do. And when she came she had *flat* come: Gruenig had not believed a woman in real life capable of such passion. Outside of magazines, he had never encountered anything like it before—all the moaning and fingernail-raking. At first all of that had startled, even frightened him—he had felt at times as if he were riding an SRX-440 Yamaha snowmobile with its throttle stuck, white-hot and tearing, ready to wreck. But then he had realized that it was probably only natural behavior for a woman who had never been with a real man before. He had realized that, finally, and it only followed that once she had, it would be impossible for her ever to be without him again. So that first afternoon when she didn't come (when the idiot lawyer instead had burst into his trailer while he was making a mushroom soup, so enraging him that for the first time in two years he had let his accent drop), he believed that Dangler had locked her up. The next day, when neither of them was around, he was sure of it. And by Thursday morning he had begun to plan how he would storm their rooms upstairs with the M 16 and liberate her. Then at noon she had walked into his office, looking snotty, and said she wanted a word with him. In the greenhouse, please. Following her there, Gruenig had been so excited over seeing her that his body told him nothing. He had only wondered—and he hated himself for this now—what balling in a greenhouse would be like.

"You," she had said, turning toward him in a pale rage, "are nothing but a tease-horse, Mr. Gruenig." She was holding a pruning shears at her waist. It was pointed at him, and her face was cold and white.

This was after she had announced in her uppity voice while snipping at a tomato plant that she would be unable to see him again, ever, except in a supervisory capacity, that he was to wipe out of his mind what had happened between them, and that she rather hoped he could continue on at the camp, but that if he felt he could not, she would understand; after Gruenig, totally bewildered, had asked if what she was trying to say here was that they were not getting married, and she had answered yes, that was most certainly what she was saying; after he had then called her a dumb cunt, pulled up by the roots and shredded four tomato plants, smashed a large potted geranium on the brick floor, and shouted to her that her husband was nothing but a fokking loony, and that she was just as crazy as he was if she thought she could go back to some nut-case after having had a taste of him.

"Do you know what a tease-horse is?" she asked him loudly and with precise enunciation.

"Hoor!" yelled Gruenig.

"Do you?"

"*No.* And I *dun't care.*"

"It is a common male horse, a plug, brought in to stimulate a thoroughbred mare, so that when the stallion comes in from racing or whatever important thing he is doing, he won't have to waste his time. Do you understand?"

Gruenig did not. He had stared at her, his eyes bulging, trying to penetrate this thing she had just said. Was this like being compared to a fox?

"If you ever mention my husband again to me, I will have you shot," she said then, and stalked out, leaving the scent of her perfume, and Gruenig standing there, rooted and dumb as one of the tomato plants.

He couldn't believe it. For two days he simply couldn't believe it. He put notes in her mailbox and searched morosely for her in the corridors of the house. He stomped things, got drunk, and, on the second afternoon, raged into the shed where the game birds were kept and shot twenty-five black ducks without even knowing he was doing it. He came to himself while pulling apart with his hands the fourteenth duck, and for a second couldn't understand why he was covered with blood and feathers. That night he accepted it—he told himself that he would never go away with Erica Dangler, and the statement registered as fact—and once it was accepted, Gruenig became furious, angrier than he had ever been before in his life: at her, at Dangler, at the campers, and particularly at Cobb, the lawyer, whom he suspected of wanting her for himself. The anger was so sharp that night that it took a Quaalude and nearly a fifth of rum to put it to sleep, but the next day it was cold and focused. He knew what he would do, if not yet how to do it; and when he saw her again at the helicopter—weakening at the sight of her, even whispering into her ear, "You haff a chance. Get in the chopper and Gurnsey flies us both avay" —when he gave her an opportunity to save herself and she didn't even *look* at him, but shrugged off his hand as if it were a horsefly, that had sealed it.

Since then it had just been a question of details, and those were filling in fast. Just after he and Gurnsey returned from preparing the cabin, he had learned from Mount Washington the new estimated size and position of the storm, and he had known then that he had it. Even if some of the details were missing, he had it, and he was so excited that he made Gurnsey fly him back up the mountain to leave them a sign, a message, that he had it.

He had spent most of this day lazily, waiting for further details. Shortly before noon his body told him to give the next three days off to everyone still working at the camp. After he and Gurnsey burned the cabin and carried off the food (Dangler had ordered them to do it, he told Gurnsey), he had instructed the half-wit pilot to gas the chopper, then fly it home and wait there for a call. He had passed the rest of the afternoon with the song and the bottle of Canadian Club. He knew there were other things to be done—something with Knapp; there was a new life to buy—but all that would come.

When he finished thinking about Erica, Gruenig realized he was hungry. He decided to go over to the big house and cook himself a chicken. And then an idea came up in him. It was a detail, and it rose in him like a bubble and broke in his head. He would *move* to the big house. Everything he wanted from the trailer was already packed and ready to go—he would carry it over to the big house, take her bedroom and sleep in her bed.

He poured a drink and looked at the song again. He picked up the pen, crossed out the last lines he had written, and wrote this:

> *I remember the last time, Baby, that I saw you.*
> *You were leaving for the mountain and the Devil too.*

As he walked toward the snow cave with Dangler's arm over his shoulder, it occurred to Cobb in a malign little vision that a particular red chair was very possibly at the root of their predicament.

He had just been told that they were in this mortal fix because Erica had dismissed Hanspeter Gruenig as a lover. That information had been so unnerving that it took him a moment or two to comprehend an even more horrible fact.

"You *knew* they were having a relationship?"

"From the beginning," Dangler said. "And I knew when she finally got around to ending it—it was while you and I were having that chat in my study last week. What I didn't know was that Gruenig was going to lose his head over it. Of course if *you* had only followed through, none of this would have happened."

Cobb was afraid he knew what that meant, but he chose not to think about it just then. "Didn't you *realize* he might get upset, you conniving son of a bitch? A murderous little maniac like that?"

"One doesn't go about being intimidated by servants, Andrew. No one has time for that. We'll have a night in a snow cave is what it amounts to. Everyone is trained for it. I suspect he'll change his mind by tomorrow and come for us, and if not, well, fair enough."

"Fair *enough?* What do you *mean,* 'fair enough'? This is a *real storm,* Kenneth." Cobb scooped up a handful of snow and showed it to Dangler. "Real snow. Real wind. How are we going to get off this mountain?"

"We'll manage." Dangler's eyes were bright; he threw his arm around Cobb. "You are exactly right: this is a real situation, and my people are ready for it."

Trudging bent into the driving snow toward the indistinct figure of Peter Bigelow, Cobb thought of the chair. It was a red leather armchair positioned beneath a mirror on the second floor of Porcellian, Dangler's club at Harvard. The mirror was aimed down through a window at the street below, so that someone sitting in the chair could lay his head back and observe the pedestrian life of Cambridge all day long if he wanted to, without ever being seen. The chair had been Dangler's favorite place at Harvard. He had once told Cobb that he would be pleased to die in it, and thinking of him in it now—an unseen seer with his feet up, dispassionately surveying a hubbub of crooked oil men, murderous hillbillies with acquired lives, affairs involving his own wife—Cobb came very close to wishing that he had.

The cave had been dug into a hillside snowdrift near the edge of the clearing. Bigelow and the others had tunneled upward into the center of the drift and hollowed out a rectangular chamber there about twelve feet long and six feet across. The ceiling of the cave had been scooped into a

dome that was less than three feet off the floor at its highest
point, so that the six people in the cave when Dangler, Cobb
and Bigelow wormed into it were sitting hunched over with
their backs against the two long walls. Someone had opened
a ventilation shaft in the ceiling with an ice ax and there
were snowflakes in the weak gray light falling through it.
The cave was full of a confusing variety of human noises,
and it smelled of vomit.

Divina was sitting up, supported by Ames Cravens on
one side and Erica on the other. She was moaning.

"Lay her out flat," said Dangler, tearing through his
pack.

"She wants to sit up," snapped Erica. "She doesn't get
sick that way."

"Lay her out. Andrew, spread out the sleeping bag and
get her on top of it. Peter, cut a ledge for this candle and
get it going and open up the medical kit. I have to warm my
hands."

"See what you've done," wailed Madelaine de Faurier,
and Cobb realized then that she had been talking loudly to
herself ever since he crawled in. "See what you've done
now? We're all going to freeze to death in this pit."

"Now's the time, you cur," Rocque shouted. "Now's the
time to goddammit call this thing off, or I swear to Christ
you'll pay."

Ames Cravens, who was helping Cobb spread out Dangler's sleeping bag on the floor of the cave, reached out and
slapped de Faurier on the knee. "Shut up, Rocque. Just
shut up."

Dangler laughed. He was hunched around his hands,
warming them on his stomach. It was a quiet, honest laugh,
and it ended all the other sounds in the cave. He drew his
hands out from beneath his coat and blew on them; then he
turned to Divina. "Candle, please, Peter," he said.

In the orange reflected light of the candle, Dangler
stripped Divina to the waist and pulled her wool knickers
down to her hips. Pale and silent now, she lay on her back
staring up at the ceiling, clutching and unclutching the red
down sleeping bag with her right hand and restlessly moving her legs while Dangler examined her. He took her pulse
and probed around her stomach, gently pressing and re-
leasing the flesh and watching her face for pain; then he

put his ear to her abdomen and listened for a minute or two. When he was finished he kissed her on the forehead.

"You've hurt something inside, the spleen probably, and it's bleeding. It will stop if you concentrate. I'm going to give you codeine and an anti-nauseant, and then we'll get you in the bag and warmed up. Look at me." Divina had been tossing her head back and forth; now she stopped and looked at Dangler, and the set to her mouth, a pained, childlike, confused set to her mouth, nearly broke Cobb's heart. "You're going to have to concentrate," Dangler told her. "No one has a stronger mind than you do. Concentrate on feeling better. And in the morning the helicopter will be here and everything will be fine."

"Could you make it come now, Kenneth? Do you suppose?" she asked him.

"I would like to do that, but I can't," said Dangler. "You will have to concentrate on feeling better." He held her head while she swallowed the pills, and then he finished undressing her and worked her into the sleeping bag. "We'll need someone in here with her for heat."

"Yes," said Erica, and immediately began taking off her clothes. "He's not coming because of me, isn't that right, Kenneth? This is my fault, isn't it?"

"It is no one's fault." Dangler stood up and straightened his blue Navy jacket. "I'm going out for a breath of fresh air now. I'd like it if the rest of you joined me."

It was practically dark outside the cave, and the storm was growing. It was snowing so hard that even in the partial lee of the hillside Cobb could not see his hands as he and Cravens, the Bigelows and the de Fauriers huddled miserably around Dangler, who had to shout to make himself heard over the steady freezing roar of the wind.

"Divina has a ruptured spleen and peritonitis. She is in shock and showing signs of hypothermia. Only two things could possibly save her—an immediate operation or spontaneous blood clot. None of us can operate, so we have to pray that the spleen stops bleeding. . . . Next to my wife I love Divina Thayer more than any other woman alive. I would happily die myself in order to save her life, but there is nothing I or any of us can do beyond hoping and making her comfortable.

"Item number two: for reasons I can't go into, Hanspeter Gruenig has deserted us here. He and Gurnsey may come for us tomorrow, but that is not something we can count on. We have a long uncomfortable night ahead of us. We have only one bag, little clothing and less food, but no one will freeze or starve in the cave tonight, and tomorrow we will find a way to get down. Item number three: I did not plan these circumstances, though if it helps or toughens any of you in any way to think that I did, please feel free to do so. You have been taught how to survive, and you *will,* all of you, if you control your minds."

"What if we don't, Chief?" said Weezy Bigelow in a loud, calm voice. "Tell everyone what will happen if we don't control our minds."

Dangler looked at her and then at each of the others, searching, Cobb imagined bitterly, for durability among the faces.

"It's not necessary, Weezy," he said. "Everyone knows the answer to that. You are as strong as you think you are —remember that. You can do whatever you have to do. Are there any other questions? I don't want any disturbing talk in the cave."

"How will we get down?" asked Ames Cravens. "I mean, I know we *will,* Kenny, I was just wondering how."

"I don't know."

"What if she dies?" sobbed Madelaine de Faurier. "Oh, God, what if she dies?"

"Come on, Madelaine," Peter Bigelow told her. "We can't have any of that."

"Good question," said Dangler. "If she dies, it will be entirely my responsibility. . . ."

"You'd better believe it will," said de Faurier.

"I will very likely lose my wife if she dies, and I will certainly lose what little regard I presently have for myself. But I'll be damned if I'll lose any of the rest of you because of it. You will not let down if she dies. Survival is a job you know how to do, and you will continue to work at it until I tell you to stop." He put one arm around Weezy Bigelow and the other around Rocque de Faurier's snowy shoulders. He looked around the circle, meeting every pair of eyes with his own. "You are my people," he said. "And we have come a long way together. I love each and every one of you very much, and I am *proud* of you. This country of ours was founded on the spirit of adventure and a willingness to pit oneself against the hardship that nature and the land impose. Our forebears met an unimaginable savageness of wild when they first came here—a fifty-percent death rate the first winter, having to put up houses along the one climbing street from the waterfront at Plymouth, their backs to the antagonistic land, their faces to the cold sea between themselves and England—and yet they survived and they prevailed. . . ."

As he went on, haranguing against the blizzard at the shivering little herd of campers, Cobb wondered how in the *name of God* he could have been so blind for so long, how he could possibly have failed to see before now the evil in this man. He hated Dangler. With Divina bleeding internally in a pit of snow, here he was, Cobb's best and oldest friend, manipulating a crowd like a carnival barker. The fact that it worked, that by the time they crawled back into the cave Dangler seemed to have united the campers and erased most of their anger and suspicion, only made Cobb hate him more.

Outside, and for a short while back in the cave, the hatred clarified things for him. Dangler and his wife seemed solely, malevolently responsible for everything that was wrong with their situation, including the storm, and if someone had handed him a gun during that period he probably could have used it on both of them. But then pity for Divina overtook him, and a choking fear for her and the rest of them, and the seeping cold. And within a couple of hours—by the time the candle stub burned out, leaving them in the deepest blackness he had ever known—nothing but his misery was clear to him, least of all whom to blame.

Erica was inside the sleeping bag with Divina when they came back in. Part of her bare back was exposed, and she was propped over Divina on her elbows, stroking her hair and crooning to her. The sight of the two women was so harrowingly intimate that Cobb could hardly bear to look at them. Everyone else seemed similarly affected: though their sleeping bag took up half the floor space in the cave, no one appeared to notice them, including Dangler, who, once back in the cave, became terse and businesslike. He disallowed smoking. He took an inventory of their clothing and gear and divided up what little food they had into four piles, three of which he stowed in his pack. The fourth, a collection of peanuts, meat bars, raisins, cheese and hard candy, he mixed into snow melted over the little gasoline stove for their supper.

By the time the stew was ready everyone had begun to feel the cold. With nothing but their rucksacks to sit on, it creeped into them through their backs and buttocks, and though the food took the edge off of it for a while, it was not long before it was back. Cobb sat on one flank and then the other. He took off his gloves and sat on them until his hands got cold, and then he sat on his hat. The high point of his hatred for Dangler came shortly after they had eaten, when, slapping his hands on his thighs and stomping the snow floor to warm his feet, he looked up toward the head of the cave and saw Dangler digging in the snow with his bare hands. Phony, he thought, you stinking phony bastard.

Dangler looked up at him as if he had heard, and grinned. "I'm going to add a room or two to our accommodations. We need a bathroom, among other things. Peter, grab a shovel and give me a hand. Why don't the rest of you play a game or sing a song?"

Around seven o'clock the candle burned out, and in the first few minutes of darkness Cobb was sure that he would go crazy before dawn. Staying sane began to feel like holding his breath, and he saw no way he could continue to do it for eleven hours. The wind outside the cave whined on two or three frequencies at once, a complex, maddening noise that seemed to be trying to communicate. He needed to urinate, but he had no idea how or where to do it. The campers were singing "Soldiers of the Cross" for the fourth or fifth time. Having worn out Peter Bigelow some time ago, Dangler could be heard farther back in the drift, still scooping corridors and anterooms out of the snow. And right in front of him, so close that his boots touched the bottom of the sleeping bag they occupied, Erica and Divina were carrying on a communication whose shape and movement, rising entangled out of the dark, were so fiercely exclusive, so rhythmic and insistent that just listening to it made Cobb feel hideously like a voyeur—and yet, try as he might, he could not ignore it. It ate at him like the cold, touching him in places where he had never been touched before, and—as it kept up and he could find no way to escape it, nothing to put in his mind to distract him from it —nearly suffocating him with pity and guilt.

Erica crooned over things they had done together, and places they had been; she described roads and houses and beaches and gardens and parties and college boys. She told jokes and narrated a field-hockey game in which Divina scored four goals. She quoted what sounded like a long poem in Italian and sang "The Marseillaise," and she named paintings and made Divina identify the artists who had painted them. At first she had to force Divina to talk, but after the codeine took effect Divina murmured along on her own, adding descriptions and details, humming, asking questions.

"What's that line from Crane?" Divina asked just after the candle went out. "Trow used to say it . . . 'the seal's wide spindrift gaze toward paradise'?"

"At the Ritz. He used to throw his arms up and say it at the Ritz."

"Trow's glasses . . . she stepped on them that night, that girl from Squam Lake with the red hair—what's her name? And he spent *hours* on the floor picking them up."

" 'With how sad steps, O Moon, thou climbst the skies. How silently, and with how wan a face.' Remember that? How no one ever knew that but you and Trow? And the other one, the 'evening air' one."

" 'Oh thou art fairer than the evening air, clad in the beauty of a thousand stars . . .' because it was *you*, Erica, when I heard it. . . ."

"Remember going to Abercrombie with Kenneth and Trow to visit Mr. Estey in the gun department and taking the limousine to Coney Island for hot dogs at Will's, and Trow wouldn't eat one because he said he couldn't get his mouth around it like Queen Elizabeth?"

"Yes," Divina said in a tone of voice that made Cobb know she was smiling. He imagined her smiling. "I remember that."

After about an hour of darkness she talked less. At one point Cobb imagined the cold leaking into her, filling her like gas, choking off her voice—and the image made him want to scream. He thought of how quick and controlled and fine she was. He saw her walking economically on a golf course in a pair of white golf shoes, her lovely legs flashing, and he thought of how she never seemed to sweat or tire or think of herself.

"There are twenty-five joints in your hand there, darling. Think of that. It's capable of over fifty separate motions. You have two hundred and six bones and over six hundred muscles. From here"—Erica paused, and there was a shifting in the bag—"to here, there are sixty thousand *miles* of blood vessels. And here . . . did you know there are over a half-million egg cells in an ovary, each one protected by jelly and surrounded by fluid, packed in there like little Waterford goblets? Isn't that wonderful, Divina? . . . Darling, isn't it?"

Cobb felt Erica's hand on Divina's stomach and he envied the feel of her flesh. He wanted to be in the bag with her himself.

Hours ago, still in his clear, blame-fixing state of mind, he had looked around the orange walls of the cave, recalled Dangler's declaration to Erica that their situation was no one's fault, and thought: Wrong, buddy; it is yours, as surely as it is dark outside, for your damned Porcellian aloofness, for always carrying things too far; and hers too, for learning from you, if she didn't already believe it, that it is perfectly OK to suit people up for your purposes, in the same way you do the woods, and then use them however the hell the two of you see fit, and for the dumbness of choosing to use the wrong one after I fell through as designated sexual distraction or whatever it is I was—for the unbelievable aristocratic dumbness of not knowing better than to fool around with Gruenig. Yours and hers, he had thought; that's whose fault it is.

Later, in his pooling confusion and fear, it seemed that it also had to be Gruenig's, didn't it? Despite his having written off the manager a long time ago as a result, not a cause, a motiveless malignancy no more responsible for where he struck than cancer or the storm outside. And the campers? Didn't it have to be at least partially the campers' fault for allowing Dangler to experiment with them like laboratory mice? Now, yearning to touch Divina, Cobb saw as clearly as if a lighted cue card had popped up in the blackness that he was at least as much to blame as anyone. With a sickening sense of not having recognized something important and right under his nose until too late, he saw that he might have prevented this night from happening— by insisting that Gruenig be prosecuted, or that Dangler close down the camp after the Fairfax sisters were injured . . . by standing up at some point along the curve of Dangler's messianic obsession over the past three months and saying, making himself heard: "This is far enough; no farther."

But he had not done that. Not done it, he knew, for fear of impact, a fear he had had all his life. And what he realized now—the strange realization that opened his mind to his own responsibility—was that that fear was for him the same as the fear of touching. As much as he wanted to be in the sleeping bag with Divina, to be touching her creatively and analgesically as Erica was, and to have spent the last few weeks touching her—holding her, touching her face—he knew that he was now, and had been, afraid to do so. Cobb saw clearly in the darkness how he had lived his whole life holding back, avoiding the responsibility of contact. Afraid from birth, it appeared, to take a moment and act on it, he had staged a long delaying action, not of effort but of touch. Seeing how he had waited and waited, uselessly saving himself, seeing his life as hopelessly discreet and small, Cobb felt—though he was surrounded by breathing, moving, whispering bodies—utterly alone and locked within his own dark.

" 'The beauty of the world . . . a paragon of animals,' " Erica was saying as he got to his knees, faced the snow wall, and after some blind fumbling, urinated onto it. Some of the campers were massaging each other's feet and backs; Peter Bigelow was reciting a prayer. "That's what we are, darling. Men produce two hundred million sperm cells a day, and there are sixty trillion cells in a single zygote. *Think* of that. There are exactly twenty-three chromosomes in each egg and twenty-three in each sperm to make up a baby. . . . Ohh, Divina, we are going to have babies, and name them Melissa and Georgia and Sam . . ."

"Erica," said Divina. It was the first word she had spoken in a long time, and she said it distinctly. "I want you to promise that you'll take Andy some places. Take him up to Gray Rocks, sweetie, will you do that for me? I want so much to take him and see the expression on his sweet face when he sees the fun everyone has there."

"We'll take him. All of us will take him."

"And please, Erica . . . try to stay calm."

"I am calm, darling. I *am* calm, and you're going to be fine, and . . ."

"Would you not talk for just a minute now? I think I'll take a nap."

"Yes. Put your head here and I'll hum to you. Wouldn't you like it if I hummed to you?"

After about ten minutes there was no sound at all from the bag and for a while the cave was quiet except for people shifting positions.

"We should do some more isometric exercises," said Rocque de Faurier. "How are everyone's feet?"

"They are cold, Rocque," said Madelaine, "everyone's feet are cold. Where do you suppose Kenneth is? Why don't we hear him anymore?" No one answered her. "I had a dog —isn't this funny, I just remembered this—when I was a little girl. Named Muffin. She was a golden cocker spaniel, and when I was stepping out of the house one morning to go to school, the chauffeur ran over her head. When I got home that afternoon my father had buried her and put up a granite headstone that said: 'To Muffin, Madelaine's beloved little friend. A pause to rest, A rest for paws, A place to moor my bark.' "

Peter Bigelow cleared his throat.

"It's still there, in Shaker Heights . . . it's my brother's house now."

There was another silence; then someone stomped his feet. Someone, Ames Cravens, Cobb thought, began whistling "Bye Bye Blackbird." After a rustling, someone at the far end of the cave started massaging someone else, and Cobb imagined that he could see them touching. He imagined he could see the faces of everyone in the cave, including Divina's sleeping face, and when Weezy Bigelow turned next to him and whispered to him, he imagined he could see her face.

"You know, Andy, isn't it funny how your mind works?" She was smiling, he thought, her eyes a little vague and vulnerable as they often were when she wanted someone to listen to her. "But I was just thinking, you know, about Corey. He's nine; he's our baby. And, you know, I was just remembering the funniest thing . . ." Here he saw her toss her head and look upward, a conversational gesture she had taken from Erica that said: Things are light, things are charming. "Just before we left to come here, we had a big party and I was upstairs lying on the bed feeling sort of woozy, and Corey came up. One of the maids sent him up because he had broken a Steuben rabbit, and he stood there in the door and told me about it. And I . . . I don't know, I guess I had had too much to drink, and I wasn't feeling well, and I shouted at him about the silly rabbit. He had on . . . he had on blue short pants and his little legs were so skinny, and his eyes were so big, Andy. He said, 'Yes, ma'am,' and he . . ." Weezy began crying then, and without any hesitation at all Cobb put his arms around her and drew her to him. "He just *meant* it so hard, you know?"

"I know," Cobb told her, rocking her in his arms.

After a while he slept, holding Weezy, and when he woke the wind outside the cave was louder and Peter Bigelow was saying the Lord's Prayer. Weezy sat up when he finished and asked him to say another one.

" 'O Lord,' " said Peter in his husky, alcoholic's voice, " 'support us all the day long, until the shadows lengthen and the evening comes, and the busy world is hushed, and the fever of life is over, and our work is done. Then in thy mercy grant us a safe lodging, and a holy rest, and peace at the last. Amen.' "

"Would you do one more, Pete?" asked Rocque de Faurier after a moment.

"I'll do them all night long if you want me to. 'O God of peace, who hast taught us that in returning and rest we shall be saved, in quietness and in confidence shall be our strength; by the might of thy spirit lift us, we pray thee, to thy presence, where we may be still and know that thou art God; through Jesus Christ our Lord. Amen.' Weezy?" he said. "Listen, honey, here's the one I was trying to remember. 'In particular, we beseech thee to continue thy gracious protection to us this night. Defend us from all dangers and mischiefs, and from the fear of them; that we may enjoy such refreshing sleep as may fit us for the duties of the coming day. And grant us grace always to live in such a state that we may never be afraid to die. . . .' " There was a pause. "I'm sorry," Peter said, his voice breaking, "just give me a second here."

"That's fine, Peter," said Weezy. "Darling? That's just fine."

As Bigelow went on, Cobb thought of Easter. He ached for Easter—for the sweet pastels, the hymns and new hats, the warm blue sky over the Episcopal Church in Contoocook, and crocuses and the smell of children—and reaching a hand above his head, he carved into the cold slick wall of the cave what he knew to be the perfect outline of a lily.

He fell asleep in the middle of a later prayer, and when he woke again he knew that it was much later. The hour felt deep in the night, and there was no movement or noise in the cave except for Erica, who was talking again, her voice barely audible over the hum of the wind.

"I know we're supposed to be happy, Divina, that we're God's chosen work and meant to be happy. But . . . ahh, God, darling, the way the moon sometimes is in the sky, and the way a fly folds up its legs when it dies . . . those things just break your *heart*."

Stiff and cold as he was, Cobb felt a great surge of happiness hearing her voice. It meant Divina was alive, and if she had stayed alive this long, the bleeding had to have stopped.

"And that day my father took us in to New York with him when we were eleven, and took us to the Plaza for tea. *That's* what I mean . . . the way he sat there in the Palm Court with his beautiful gabardine leg crossed and those beautiful black-and-white summer oxfords he wore, tapping his penknife on the table. And the violinist and pianist began playing Strauss. There were the marble-topped tables, the four marble columns and the potted palms. The green chairs . . . let's see . . . those big fluted chandeliers, eight of them, I think. Is that right? Someone says, 'Well, it's all personal, anyway.' And you draw this picture of a big pair of lips that say, 'Smack!' on a napkin and shove it over to me. And then those three Italian women and a man with a Southern accent walk in and sit by us. One of the women is pushing a flat stroller with a beautiful little girl in it. There is something wrong with the little girl's back, do you remember that? The woman rolls her up to the table and says, 'Shut up or I pusha your face in. Lie there and rock yourself to sleep.' And later one of the other women tells the man to go ask the violinist if he knows 'Oh, My Papa,' and the violinist is playing Liszt. . . ."

The next time Cobb woke, the cave was gray with light and it was much colder. It was 6:15. Peter Bigelow was up at the front of the cave, on his knees, working the pressure plunger on the stove.

"Any sign of Kenneth?" Cobb asked him, flexing his hands. He could no longer feel his feet.

"He's not here, not anywhere. He's dug out three or four more rooms back there, and he's not in any of them."

"How are your feet?"

Peter Bigelow looked up and grinned, and Cobb was struck by how old and plain he looked. He looked like an old sad-faced clerk. "Bad, I'm afraid. I can't feel them. How about you?"

"Neither can I. Maybe it's better that way for walking. Do you think I should wake the others?"

"Might as well wait until I get some snow melted. You know, I was thinking, if it weren't for Divina this wouldn't be all that bad. Rough on the butt and the feet, but not all that bad. Sort of like a final exam. How is she, do you have any idea?"

"I think she's better. I heard them talking early this morning. The bleeding must have stopped."

"How will we get down, Andy?"

"Walk. We'll have to walk, though I don't know how, in this new snow. Is it still coming down?"

"I haven't looked," said Bigelow. He lit the stove, and its steady hissing filled the cave. "We're almost out of fuel. Really, I don't see how we can walk down, do you?"

Cobb pulled himself up. With his first step a lance of pain shot through his foot up his shin to his knee. He took one more step and then got down on all fours and crawled past Peter Bigelow into the tunnel. At the mouth of the tunnel was a block of snow. He pushed it out of the way and looked outside. The clouds were gone but it was so cold that he could feel the air freezing the mucus in his nostrils. The storm had brought in an arctic cold front, a glittering sea of frozen air, and feeling it on his face and in his nose, Cobb felt what little hope he had for their getting down that day go out of him like the vapor of his breath. There were tracks in the snow outside the cave, but no other sign of Dangler. He pulled the snow block in place and crawled back inside.

"The storm is over, but it's damned cold," he told Bigelow. "It's below zero, I think."

"We'll get down," said Weezy Bigelow. "Chief will get us down."

She was sitting in the same position she had been in all night, massaging her boots, and Cobb was startled when he glanced up at her. She had always looked to him like an old-fashioned doll, oddly refined, a little unreal, with her large eyes and small pert features, her pale skin and vivid makeup. This morning her face was haggard and swollen and cramped with concentration, as if she had labored all night over figures. As the rest of the campers stirred and woke, each of their faces appeared to Cobb similarly transformed, almost unrecognizably deglamorized during the night, reduced—even Ames Cravens' arch and lineless beauty—to common human faces.

While Peter Bigelow made breakfast from one of the remaining food packages in Dangler's pack, the others used the latrine Dangler had dug, crawling to it in twos and threes. When the stew was ready they sat around the stove and ate it with their fingers, and a sort of tentative good humor set in.

Ames Cravens said, "The only thing you could *add* to this to make it more awful is onions."

"Maraschino cherries would help," said Weezy.

"Erica and Divina should have some anyway," said Madelaine de Faurier. "Neither of them ate last night."

Carrying a cup of the stew, Cobb pulled himself over to the sleeping bag, put his hand on Erica's tousled head and scratched her neck. "Chow time, ladies," he said, feeling strangely emotional, almost happy, and very close to everyone in the cave, particularly to the two women in the bag.

Erica turned over and looked at him, her eyes distant and soft. Cobb smiled at her and moved his hand to Divina's shoulder.

As soon as he touched her he knew she was dead. For a moment his mind went blank. Then he saw his mother's face, and then Erica's, and he realized that he was still staring at her and she at him. This is the day . . . which the Lord hath made, he thought.

Just as Dangler crawled into the cave, Erica screamed. Still on his knees, he had just said, "Good morning, everyone. I jury-rigged some snowshoes from branches," his voice hearty and pleased, when it came flashing out of her and hit Cobb in the face like a fist.

XX

It took Dangler thirty minutes to calm Erica down. What went on between the two of them during most of that time was totally unfathomable to Cobb. It was also painful to witness, but there was nothing for him and the campers to do but sit, numbly watching, as Dangler wrestled her into her wind parka—after she leaped naked and screaming from the bag—threw her to the floor of the cave and rolled around with her, fighting and consoling her at the same time. For minutes the cave was full of their scuffling and shouting, and then suddenly Erica went stiff and quiet. Dangler lay on top of her, pulling over the rest of her clothes with his feet, telling her over and over that Divina was all right now, no longer cold and sick, but in heaven where she deserved to be.

He dressed her as if she were a doll. Then he sat her up in the rear of the cave and smoothed her hair.

"Now where am I?" she asked him. "Where in God's name am *I* now, Kenneth? I don't have her and I don't have you . . . I certainly don't have you anymore. So where am *I* now?"

Dangler told her that she would always have him. She said, "No I won't. Just look at you—you've gone off too."

She was calm now, and though she was talking out of

pain as palpable to Cobb as the snow he sat on, he realized as soon as Dangler turned away from her and began to address the rest of them that she had seen something real. Dangler was turgid with energy, seething with it. It was a grizzled, sleepless energy, but there was authority to it, and a strange new distance. He appeared to have shifted gears somehow overnight, and now to be mysteriously beyond them all—beyond Erica's hysterics and Divina's death, even beyond the four and a half miles of steep snow and cold between them and survival. It was clear to Cobb, even through the confusion and horror of knowing Divina was dead, that Dangler *had* gone off somewhere—or rather, it seemed after a while, arrived.

"Divina is dead. There is nothing to be done about that," he began, and helped himself to a cup of the stew. "You don't have to die too. You *can,* easily, but you don't have to. It's up to you."

"But Jesus Christ, Kenny . . ." said Ames Cravens, his voice breaking, "I mean, is she really . . . ?"

"It will be difficult, but we can do it. We can get down if everyone works together."

"Wait a minute," said Rocque de Faurier. "I demand to know what's going on with Gruenig. I mean, *is* he coming today or what?"

"Not today, not ever." There was a long silence in the cave. "Hanspeter and I had a disagreement," said Dangler between spoonfuls of the stew. "I had to fire him, and now he seems bent on a moronic revenge." There was another silence.

"But what . . . do *we* have to do with all that?" Madelaine de Faurier asked in a small voice.

"Circumstance," said Dangler. "Pure and simple: you are victims of it."

"Can't we just stay here?" said de Faurier. "Why don't we just stay in the cave and wait for someone to find us?"

"Because no one would until long after we were stacked up in here like trout in a freezer." Dangler rolled the metal cup between his palms and looked up briskly, his eyebrows arched. "I don't want to overplay any of this, folks, but this is a private mountain. Hanspeter will make certain our absence is accounted for. We have enough fuel to melt one more pot of snow; after that there is nothing to drink. After two more small meals there is nothing to eat. With the clothing we have, frostbite . . ."

"All right, then, how?" demanded de Faurier. "How do we do it?"

"We go down Revelation Cliff."

"We do what?" de Faurier said quietly.

"All *rüght*," said Cravens. "Now you're talking."

"I have made some snowshoes that might get us to the cliff. They would never last all the way down the trail, and without them we couldn't possibly get off the mountain by dark. If we don't make it off by dark, we won't survive. The cliff is less than two miles east of here. We can't leave until the sun gets higher, but if we start at nine, and even if the snowshoes don't hold up all the way, we should be there by eleven. That will leave us time to get down the cliff by nightfall. Thanks to old Rocque, we have the technical equipment to do it."

"I don't know," said de Faurier.

"We have it." Dangler rubbed his hands together and blew on them. It was not to warm them. It was, Cobb knew, one of his ways of showing excitement. "Just enough. Everything is very fine here, very slim—time, equipment and so on. But it *can* be done if everybody humps. And if everybody controls his mind," he said, looking up at Cobb.

"What about Divina?" Cravens asked him.

"We have to leave her here. We will come back with a helicopter tomorrow."

"How about . . . her?" whispered Madelaine de Faurier, inclining her head toward Erica at the rear of the cave.

Dangler grinned. "Don't worry about her. She's stronger than any of us."

"Chief? said Weezy Bigelow. "I have one question." It was the first thing either she or Peter had said since breakfast. They were leaning against each other, their legs drawn up to their chests, looking collected and unfrightened. "What if we can't do it? None of us *really* knows how to climb except for you and Rocque. What if we just can't do it, no matter how hard we try?"

Dangler swallowed the last of his stew. "Then, Weezy," he said, "we will be operating on the principle of Michel Innerkofler, the great Dolomite guide, that it is better to fall off a mountain than to freeze on it. At least we will die trying, and together."

For the next two hours Dangler kept them so occupied that Cobb had practically no chance to think, and he was grateful for that. So far as the cliff was concerned, he believed that Dangler was right, that getting down it was their only chance, and though he doubted they could do it, he was up to trying it, he supposed, if only he didn't have to imagine it.

As for Divina, he knew that he could not think about her at all and continue to function. Every time he caught sight of the sleeping bag he felt a paralyzing sorrow begin in him, and he would force himself to turn his eyes away.

Dangler led them in thirty minutes of exercises. Then he had them examine everything they were wearing, checking zippers and snaps and Velcro tabs, any place where the cold could get in, and he told them repeatedly how important it was, once they were outside the cave, to keep moving. He questioned de Faurier about the best route down the cliff and then went over in detail how they would proceed once they reached it. He demonstrated the function of each piece of equipment they had with them, planting a "deadman" snow anchor in the floor of the cave, setting and resetting ice screws in the wall, clipping in carabiners and turning them so their gates faced inward, making sure that everyone knew how to arrange the six-carabiner brake for rappeling.

If everything went well, he said, they should have little to do but rappel, just walk down backward off the cliff on the ropes that he and de Faurier would anchor to the ice: they all knew how to rappel, there should be no problems there. And if for some reason they should have to go up, they had the Jumar ascenders, which would allow them to climb the rope mechanically.

When he finished with the technical equipment, he brought the snowshoes inside the cave. They were made of partially stripped fir branches laced and whipped together with parachute cord. They were crudely but painstakingly built, and it struck Cobb that it must have taken him most of the night to make them. He noticed too that there were nine pairs. Dangler had made a pair for Divina.

Erica sat cross-legged for the entire two hours beside the sleeping bag with her right hand resting on Divina's body. When Dangler was ready to go he told her to get up and to put on her hat and mittens. When she didn't move or look at him, he went over to her, knelt beside her and whispered to her for a minute or two, holding her face between his hands. Then she drew on the mittens, looking impassive and distant, and put on her hat.

"Well, what the deuce," she said mildly, and crawled through the campers to the tunnel and into it without looking back.

After the muted gray light of the cave the brightness outside was blinding. Cobb had to squint to tie his boots into the parachute-cord bindings of his snowshoes. The wind was blowing at a steady fifteen to twenty miles an hour out of the east, the direction they had to travel, and when he stood up and opened his eyes the freezing wind and brightness almost knocked him over. The sky was a searing blue wall that seemed to crash in on him, full of blown spindrift and shreds of clouds. When he turned into it, the wind whipped the breath out of him and the cold hit him with terrifying weight across the entire front of his body at once. As he followed Dangler, Cravens and Bigelow across the clearing, trying to put his snowshoes into the prints they had made, a panic as sharp as the wind took hold of him: they could never do this, he told himself, they would never even make it to Revelation Cliff in this savage cold, much less get down it.

Once they reached the trees on the far side of the clearing, the wind was blunted somewhat, but the new snow was unpacked and they sank in it above their knees with every step. Less than two hundred yards from the cave one of Weezy Bigelow's snowshoes broke and as they stood huddled and stomping while Dangler repaired it, Cobb's eyelids froze together. From then until they stopped again, he lost all sense of time passing. The agony of the cold in his hands and feet, his snowshoes coming off and having to be dug out, the falling over, the spindrift blinding him and filling within seconds the tracks ahead, the pain in his eyes from the glare, and the exhaustion—the spirit-killing weariness that began in his legs and worked upward, making each knee-deep, floundering step an individual nightmare of effort and self-pity—it all seemed immeasurable, uncontained by time; and he would experience it later, in dreams that lasted for months, as a constantly receding white horizon of tormenting noise.

At one point, watching Dangler break trail, wallowing waist-deep through the snow, it seemed to Cobb that it was his courage and will alone that was pulling them along: Dangler's idea of himself as savior, like a rope tied to all of them, dragging them forward after they had run out of themselves. But when Dangler stopped them again, Cobb fell onto the snow beside Bigelow and Cravens, believing that he could go no farther, not with any amount of help.

Dangler gave him a handful of nuts and chocolate and examined his face, as he had Bigelow's and Cravens', for frostbite. His own face was flushed but still eager and fresh. "Eat some snow along with it," he told them, and then each of the others as they came staggering up and fell in to the lee of the corniced boulder he had stopped beneath. Both Madelaine de Faurier and Ames Cravens were weeping with exhaustion. There were lines of ice on their cheeks, and frozen tears had built up into rime on their wool balaclavas.

"I can't *do* this anymore," sobbed Madelaine, and hurled her handful of food into the snow.

"Yes you can, Madelaine," said Erica, who had followed Weezy Bigelow in. "Kenneth . . ." Erica stopped to get her breath. She was sweating. There seemed to be an aura of heat coming off her. "Rocque has been yelling about his hand. I think . . ."

Just then de Faurier lurched up and bumped into her from behind without looking up. He was bent over, the rope he was carrying humped over his neck, and he appeared to be studying his waist.

"It's frozen," he said. He straightened up slowly and they could see that he was holding his left wrist. He held the left hand out to Dangler. It was absolutely white, as white as bone. "I lost a glove and now my hand is frozen," he said. "I've frozen my *hand,* Kenneth."

Dangler grabbed the hand and shoved it under his coat. "Get the pair of socks out of my pack, Andrew," he said, and Cobb got to his feet and did it.

Dangler kept the hand under his coat for nearly five minutes, massaging it through the material while de Faurier looked searchingly into his face. Then he wrapped the hand in both socks, cut a ragged square from Weezy's empty rucksack with his knife, and tied the piece of nylon over the socks with a length of parachute cord.

"We have to move," he said when he was done. "We can't wait any longer. We're no more than halfway there and it's almost eleven."

"I'm sorry, Chief," said Weezy, "but I can't." She had pulled her balaclava up to her forehead. Her face was pinched and livid and there were bright cords of frozen spittle around her mouth. "I tried . . . but I just can't."

"Neither can I, Kenny," said Ames Cravens. He pounded the snow several times with his fist. "I swear to Christ I can't *walk* anymore."

"And neither can I," said Madelaine flatly.

"The hell you can't!" Peter Bigelow shouted, and heaved himself to his feet. "*Get up,* all of you. We've been taking and taking and taking from this man—well, now we're not going to quit on him, or on ourselves. There are not many things in this world worth anything anymore, but one of them is not quitting on each other. Chief has taken us this far, now we'll go the rest of the way. By God, you *will* get up." He kicked at Cobb, grazing his leg, and then, stumbling, he kicked at Cravens and Weezy. "By *God,* you will."

Cobb didn't need the kick. It was not what Bigelow said, nor the fact that Cobb had never before heard him raise his voice; it was something in the big man's face that already had him getting to his feet. Some last-ditch, joyful-looking frenzy in Bigelow's face seemed to cut a cord in him, and he stood up along with the others and brushed himself off. He would move until he couldn't move anymore, he decided, and then he would die. But he would not die yet.

"Well done, Peter," said Dangler. "Let's move it along."

As Cobb stepped off after Cravens, he noticed without caring about it that he couldn't bend his feet or ankles anymore.

Gruenig had gotten a world of drunk after he moved over to the big house, and the evidence of what he had done while that way lay strewn all around the Danglers' bedroom when he woke the next morning. It was just after nine o'clock. He lay diagonally across the big bed, tangled in the satin sheets, surveying the mess and recollecting with a sore head and some guilt how he had made it.

He had put on their clothes.

After eating a whole baked chicken and half a pound of Iranian caviar, he had carried a bottle of something called Amaretto up here to the bedroom thinking to find a Bruins game on television and have another drink or two from the bottle of amber liquor that he had started with his meal, believing it to be some kind of wine. But before turning on the TV he went to the bathroom, and on the way back he had seen hanging in one of Dangler's closets the white military jacket with gold buttons that "the Chief" wore around the house all the time. Gruenig had tried it on and looked at his fuzzy image in the mirror. It was too big for him. Then he put on a full-length raccoon coat, and it was much too big. Gruenig threw the coat onto the floor of the bedroom and stripped Dangler's closets and then his drawers, trying on his suits, his tuxedo, his shirts, his knickers, his shorts, his shoes, even the ridiculous Indian headdress he wore at the campfire services, throwing each piece of clothing onto the floor when he had seen himself in it and slugging back the Amaretto between changes.

He had worked himself up into a sort of fit, he reckoned, because when he finished with Dangler's wardrobe he started in on Erica's, which was larger and took him most of the night and the rest of the bottle to get through. He began with a wolf coat and the green-and-black-checked wool shirt she wore all the time, and they were too big for him also. In a spiraling giddiness he put on her riding clothes, her slacks, her fragrant sweaters, and all the different sweatshirts and warm-up pants she had come to him in. Then he went through her drawers—an entire wall of cedar drawers beside an eight-foot mirror—that were full of leotards and panties and nightgowns and sheer satin slips, and one, the next to last he opened, of cotton and chamois shirts, some of which almost fit him except that the sleeves were all too long.

The last drawer was stacked to the top with blouses, the bright slippery blouses she had worn on summer nights.

Gruenig examined these unsteadily for a while as they lay in the drawer, and then, one by one, he took them out and rubbed them across his face. It seemed that every color blouse in the world was in that drawer—some with sashes, some with tiny pearl buttons, one with knotted silk cords at the neck—and when he tossed them up at the high domed ceiling of the bedroom they spread and floated down like miniature parachutes and settled vividly on the floor, still full of air.

Pie-eyed, naked and crying, Gruenig had taken one of the blouses, a raw-silk green one, to bed with him. Now, picking it up to add it to the other clothes on the floor, he saw that he had chewed on it while he slept—the way he had chewed on his blankets at night in the Army.

He got up and put on one of Dangler's dressing robes. He went to the bathroom, where he took four aspirin; then he looked out the window. Squinting, he admired the bright windy morning and the whorled new snow lying between the house and the river. When the glare no longer bothered him, he looked upward, following with his eyes the southeastern ridge of Mount Webster as it broke from the summit cone and angled downward, pitching and flattening along the hard blue sky, to where it ended abruptly at Revelation Cliff. At the rim of the cliff he thought he saw something move; then he realized that it had to be spindrift, and he took a deep satisfying breath. On the back side of the ridge, a little more than halfway between the cliff and the summit, was where the cabin had been. He wondered if they had died there, or if they had tried to walk off during the storm and died along the trail or in the woods. Either way their bodies would be covered with snow, and if they had left the clearing, it could be weeks before anyone found them.

Operating on what his body had decided overnight, Gruenig went next to the telephone beside the bed and dialed Foster Knapp's roofing-business number. Knapp himself answered.

"Mista Knapp? Mista Knapp, thissa Rip Gurnsey," he said, trying to zone in on the pilot's breathless, rushing, dim-witted manner of speech. He tried a slightly higher inflection. "I workfa Mista Gruenig uphereatha camp."

"Yeah, I know," said Knapp. "You drive the chopper. What do you want?"

Mr. Gruenig, Gruenig told him, had left town on vacation, but he had wanted Mr. Knapp to know that he "gotchuwhatchuwant, and you don't even have to pay for it."

"And what might that be?" asked Knapp. His voice sounded suspicious.

Hesaidtellya, Gruenig said, that the camp was closing down. That Mr. Dangler and all his people had disappeared and that he, Mr. Gruenig, had fears for their lives. Also, he had wanted the selectman to know that there might be a fire up at the camp sometime soon, and that he shouldn't worry sending out the engine or endangering anybody, since Dangler himself had probably ordered the place torched for the insurance money—and that Knapp's fire inspector would probably be able to tell him that.

After a moment of silence Knapp asked Gruenig if he knew where Mr. Gruenig had gone on vacation. Gruenig said Miami Beach, he thought.

"You'll probably be going on vacation too, am I right?" Knapp's voice was comfortable now.

"Maybe. That chopper might burn up too, bythaway. No need to look for it."

"Well, you give Mr. Gruenig my regards if you see him. Tell him I took his information under advisement."

After he clicked off the connection, Gruenig left the phone off the hook and lay back on the bed grinning, feeling fine now, his head painless and clear. He wondered how much Gurnsey would want for his identity. Less, he suspected, than Hanspeter Gruenig had wanted for his. He would take Gurnsey around with him for a while, he thought: fool around with him in the Midwest or somewhere for a while to soften him up. He would go anywhere Gurnsey wanted to go until he got the identity—anywhere that wasn't hot.

Anywhere that wasn't Boaz, Alabama, or something like it.

He had left Alabama at sixteen, buying his first identity with money he had saved running a soybean combine from a nineteen-year-old service-station attendant named Howar Erpe. With Erpe's name and papers he joined the Army, intending to make it a career if only it would send him someplace cool. Instead, it sent him two years later, in 1967, to An Khe in the central highlands of Viet Nam, where—as Erpe's captain had been fond of saying—it was hotter than a fresh-fucked fox in a forest fire.

Erpe was a radio operator with the First Cavalry Division, an Army unit that spent the whole war bailing out marines. He had nothing against marines, but he had nothing for them either, and at Ia Drang and Hue and other places he had quickly tired of his work. So had Hanspeter Gruenig, a young Austrian in his company who had been in America only three years before being drafted. Gruenig and Erpe got to be friends. Gruenig had been a ski instructor in Sun Valley, Idaho, and he talked endlessly to Erpe about the mountains there, the skiing and the beautiful women. To Erpe, who could not remember ever being cool enough, working as a ski instructor came to sound like paradise. The only hitch was that he didn't know how to ski. How important was that? he would ask Gruenig, and Gruenig, who had been on skis for seventeen of his nineteen years, would say that that was nothing.

Erpe and Gruenig were together for eighteen months in Viet Nam. During that time Gruenig taught Erpe how to speak German, and Erpe taught the Austrian how to fight with his feet and cheat at cards. When they were finally discharged, after having been tricked by a master sergeant into a second tour, it was March of 1969. They took a bus together from the Army discharge center in Oakland to Sun Valley. When they got there everyone was wildly happy to see Gruenig and everyone ignored Erpe, who couldn't get over all the glistening snow and glamorous women, the bright parkas, the flashing skis, the winy air; who recognized immediately that he had found his home, but who nearly went crazy washing dishes in a restaurant while Gruenig whizzed around the spring slopes of Baldy and Dollar in his blue instructor's parka.

Finally, near the end of the season, Erpe indicated to Gruenig that he might just cut his throat like a sausage hog if Gruenig didn't get him onto skis. The area was preparing a promotional film featuring Gruenig doing spread-eagle jumps off moguls, and Gruenig talked the manager into hiring Erpe to ski in front of him, holding a camera. Then he spent every early morning of the next week teaching Erpe how to ski backward.

For the next two seasons Erpe took any kind of work he could find that left his days free, and he put every dollar he earned into skiing. He spent his first two summers learning to climb, and at the beginning of his third winter in Sun Valley he joined the mountain's avalanche squad. That December he married a tall, long-haired waitress named Marthe, the first of three women he would marry while he was in Idaho, and for the next few months Erpe felt like his life had finally come together: he had a beautiful wife, he was a 5.10 climber, and he could ski with anyone on the mountain. But in June Marthe left him, and it became clear to Erpe that he would have to make more money in order to hold on to the new wife he wanted to take as soon as his divorce came through.

So he went to work for a climbing-and-wilderness-skiing outfitter in Ketchum named Kyle Moody—at first as a guide and then on the road, selling the outdoor equipment that Moody designed and manufactured. In late 1975 Moody came up with a fanciful product for duck hunters called the Moody Shooting Couch and decided to go national with it. He offered to pay Erpe his same salary plus a thirty-percent commission on every couch he sold if he would become the eastern sales representative for Moody Outdoor Products. Erpe, shakily into his third marriage, agreed, with one provision: he would have to be somebody else.

"Who?" Moody had asked him.

"Guy namea Hanspeter Gruenig. Don't worry about nothing—I'll pay him for his papers. I want a new Airstream too, and a Blazer to tote it with."

Erpe had found by experimenting that he sold more climbing axes and touring skis and rock-climbing helmets with an Austrian accent than he did with his own. Besides that, he was tired of being Howar Erpe.

In February of 1976, shed by annulment of the third wife, in possession of the Blazer, the Airstream, and a new identity for which he had paid two thousand dollars cash money, the new Hanspeter Gruenig set off for the east coast with five Moody Shooting Couches packed into the trailer. He started selling in Charleston, South Carolina, as far south as he could stomach going, and worked his way northward, making a series of Z's inland up the coast. By the time he reached Guinan's Sport Shop in Plymouth, New Hampshire, at the end of what he had decided was his northernmost Z, he had not sold a single couch.

"This is April," said the manager of Guinan's. "Nobody up here wants to think about hunting ducks in April. Besides, I don't have room on my floor for a gizmo like that."

Gruenig had been on his way out of the store when he heard a man with curly blond hair ask one of the clerks where he could buy a chair lift for a private ski area. "A chair lift?" Gruenig whispered to himself. His body couldn't tell him what to do fast enough.

"Yah, I know," he told the man, who then turned to him with a dazzling smile and a strange light in his eyes. "Something else you need?"

As the man reeled off the list—a bubble tennis court, sailboats, a ski jump, crestas, a helicopter—Gruenig, who prided himself on his control, could hardly hold his pad and pencil for trembling.

"How about a shooting couch?" he asked when the man finished.

"Sure, what is it?" The man held out his hand and smiled brightly again. "My name is Kenneth Dangler, by the way. I'm starting an adventure camp."

"Fut you need, Mr. Dankler," Gruenig had said, "is a goot manager."

It didn't really matter, Gruenig decided finally, how much Gurnsey wanted for his identity. He didn't want to spend time with the pilot to work him down. And besides, he could afford it whatever it was. In one of his suitcases downstairs was over sixty thousand dollars cash; add to that half of whatever they could get for the helicopter, and he wasn't in half bad shape to go to Alaska.

There were only a few things left to do, and at 9:30 Gruenig got out of bed, shaved with Dangler's razor, dressed and set about doing them.

He called Gurnsey and told him to get his birth certificate, his driver's license, his social-security card, his discharge papers and anything else that had his name on it, together in an envelope and to pick him up in the chopper in front of the house at exactly eleven o'clock. Then he went downstairs, taking Erica's wolf coat with him, and made himself a six-egg omelet with fried ham. As he ate, he checked over everything one last time in his mind and was forced to admire how perfectly all of it had come together.

After breakfast he moved his suitcases and the guitar case out into the snow near the fountain in front of the house to indicate to Gurnsey where to land. Wearing the wolf coat and whistling, enjoying the sparkling, frigid morning, he walked to the service garage, attached a sled to one of the Yamaha snowmobiles, and put six full ten-gallon gas cans onto the sled. He drove the snowmobile up to the front of the house, left it standing in the driveway, and carried the cans of gasoline into the entrance hall two at a time.

He used two of the cans upstairs, concentrating on the central rooms and Dangler's suite. It took all of the forty gallons left to cover the downstairs. He started in the west wing with the pool room and poured a zigzag trail of gasoline from it through the study, the gun room, the library, the card room, the dining room, the kitchen, and into the east wing, circling in the game room at the far end of that wing and retracing his route, splashing gasoline over the walls and furniture this time. He ran out of gas exactly at the front door at exactly eleven o'clock.

While he worked, Gruenig had thought about Alaska, and now, as he put on the wolf coat and pulled a Natur-Perle cigar from his shirt pocket, he realized that he was excited about going there. Alaska was the last frontier: a whole new world lay before him in Alaska.

The chopper came in at two minutes after eleven, and as Gruenig stood in the door, his hands on his hips, watching it settle, he felt savage and happy, exact in his instincts as an animal, free as a pioneer. He struck a kitchen match with his thumb and lit the cigar. Then he stepped outside, threw the match into the pool of gasoline on the floor of the entrance hall and closed the door.

XXI

―――――

D angler was standing above them at the top of a small ridge, buried to his hips in snow. Beyond him the sky was full of billowing gray smoke.

"We made it," he shouted down the creek bed, where Cobb and the others were batting through a stand of fir trees. "The top of the cliff is right over here."

Cobb cleared the trees behind Ames Cravens, who was stumbling badly, and followed him up the bank toward Dangler, willing one foot in front of the other, too mindless in his exhaustion to care that they had done what he had despaired of doing over an hour ago. He did not even wonder about the smoke.

"Congratulations," said Dangler when they were all on the ridge. "Very likely that was as hard a thing as any of you will ever have to do."

"Human being couldn't do much more," wheezed Peter Bigelow, who had fallen beside Cobb in the snow and was coughing violently. The other campers sat or sprawled around Dangler, their eyebrows and hair matted with ice, looking strangely pacified, quietly nursing their hands and faces. In addition to his feet and ankles, Cobb could no longer feel his hands, his cheeks or his nose. His eyes watered every time he opened them fully, and for the last half-hour of dreamlike falling and rising, of people dragging each other up and rolling downhill in plumes of snow, he had seemed to hear rather than feel a grating in his feet just above the toes. He had visualized it as ice crystals in the frozen flesh working deeper and deeper toward the bone.

"The rest will be easy," Dangler said, and began passing out the last of their food. "You've almost whipped it now. We're in a lee here, so we can rest for a minute or two."

"What's the smoke from, Kenneth?" asked Erica. She was standing. She looked warmer than the rest of them, and only mildly exerted.

" 'Have we vanquished an enemy?' asked Mallory after he whipped Mont Blanc. 'None but ourselves. Have we gained success? That word means nothing here.' "

"Kenneth? Is that a forest fire?" Erica asked.

" 'To struggle and to understand—never this last without the other; such is the law.' " Dangler tossed a handful of raisins and nuts in his mouth and chewed them. "Smoke's the wrong color. It has to be the house."

The campers looked up at him. Cobb looked up at him. "The camp?" said Peter Bigelow. "The *camp* is burning?"

"Oh, my God, what else can happen to us?" Weezy moaned.

"It's quarter past noon," said Dangler. "We're over an hour behind schedule, so we will have to hurry. Hurry without rushing is the ticket here."

Erica walked to Dangler and placed her arms over his shoulders. She looked at him for a moment without speaking, her face inches from his; then she kissed him on the mouth and said, "I have only had three people ever, and now two of them are dead. Please don't leave me like this. I love you more than anything." She put her face onto his chest and began to sob. She shook her head. "Oh, Kenneth, I'm so sorry about our camp. I'm so, so sorry."

"House," said Dangler, pushing her back. "It's only the house, and houses can be rebuilt."

From the ridge they followed him over a hundred yards of flat, wind-packed snow to the top of the cliff. Erica walked with him, her arm linked in his. When they reached the edge of the cliff she looked down for a moment, hugged Dangler tightly and walked off to sit in the snow by herself.

Cobb felt like hugging him too after he looked into the valley—not for his loss of the house, but because the ruin seemed to expose Dangler somehow, to make him freshly vulnerable, and Cobb felt his old protective feelings for his friend rise up in him as strongly as ever. But he didn't hug him. He looked at Dangler, who was staring down at the house, his face aloof and unaffected, and all he did was touch his arm and say, "I'm sorry, Kenneth."

The house was still burning, the flames rearing and settling fitfully in the wind. The roof was gone, and the cedar walls, leaving only the stone north wall, the sections of stone wall at the front of the house and the castellated towers at either end, one of which was partially crumbled. From this distance, what was left of Wildwood did not look grand, or even real. It looked as puny and insignificant as a destroyed stage set, and the east wind rampaging through the valley howled around it like wardrobe Indians.

Peter Bigelow wept at the edge of the cliff, and so did Weezy. The de Fauriers looked out briefly and turned away. Wild-eyed with weariness and anger, Ames Cravens asked Dangler if he thought Gruenig had done it, and when Dangler said yes, Cravens clenched his jaw and vowed to cut the Austrian's heart out. Dangler let things go on for a minute or two; then he blew into his gloved hands, rubbed them together and turned his back on the valley.

"Well," he said. "Here we go, then."

Rocque de Faurier led them along the edge of the cliff for two hundred yards to a group of four small spruce trees that marked the beginning of the route they would follow down. Dangler had them stomp out a platform of snow in the lee of the trees, and they sat on it, fumbling into their crampons, as de Faurier described the route. He had climbed it only a couple of times, he said, but he remembered it well enough. They should have a gully of good blue ice all the way down. Four rappels from the top was a cave where they could rest, and after the cave were two long rappels, the last exiting onto a wide switchback ramp—wide enough, he said, to drive a Volkswagen down—which they could walk on to the bottom. Each of the rappels was between a hundred and a hundred and fifty feet long, and each had a wide-enough ledge at its base for all of them to stand on, he thought. He wasn't sure. He had climbed the goddamned thing only once or twice, he told Dangler.

"Fine," said Dangler. "I'll go down first on each rappel

and chop out the ledges if they need it. We will use two ropes to rappel and the third to bring up the carabiners after each of you has made the ledge. Erica will come down after me, then Peter, Weezy, Andrew, Ames and Madelaine. Rocque will come last so he can check out the brake for each of you. I'll carry an ax, and so will Rocque. We'll leave the rest of them here."

"I don't like it, Chief," said de Faurier, shaking his head violently. "My hand is frozen and I can't feel my feet. There are too many people and too little equipment and not enough time. *We're all too* . . ."

"You had better like it, sweetie," said Madelaine. "I believe that's the picture."

"Let me just say this," said Dangler. "This cliff is our only chance. There is no other way to get off the mountain by dark. If we can do that, we will survive; if we can't, we won't. Is that clear enough?"

"But there's no place to go, Chief. Where do we *go* when we get down?" asked Weezy Bigelow. She appeared to be in the worst shape of anyone in the group. Her speech was slurred and she seemed unable to focus her eyes.

"We will walk out the road to the servants' quarters, Weezy, and call an ambulance from Plymouth. Now, remember, everyone, to lean back on the rappels and trust the rope. Watch where you put your feet, and keep your hands and clothing away from the brake bar. We are a little pressed for time, so don't stop to look at the view on the way down. Let's get to work, Rocque."

They placed a sling of two-inch nylon around one of the spruce trees, tied two of the 165-foot ropes together and ran it through the sling until the two ends were even, leaving the knot just to the right of the sling so that the rope could be pulled down from that side when all of them were on the first ledge. Dangler threw the loose ends of rope off the cliff. Then, working quickly and barehanded, he tied a swami belt of nylon webbing around everyone's waist and attached it with a carabiner to a figure-eight leg loop, making a sort of seat harness for each of them—and finally, with the last of the webbing, one for himself. He clipped the carabiner at his waist onto the rope, and by clipping six more of the large metal rings onto the first, formed a mechanical brake for the rope to run through.

Throwing off his pack, he took one of the two bandoliers of ice screws, pitons and carabiners from de Faurier, slung it over his chest along with some slings and looped the ice ax into it at his shoulder. He pulled the loose ends of double rope around his hip, held them in his left hand, tested the section connecting him to the tree with his right and walked backward to the edge of the cliff. Then he looked up at Erica, at each of the campers and at Cobb, checking their faces.

"Loosen up. We might as well have some fun here," he said, and backed off the cliff.

It was 12:50. Cobb looked at his watch, took a deep breath, and began methodically beating his hands against his legs to try to get some feeling into them.

"He's crazy," said de Faurier, hunkering over his hand. "Don't any of you *understand that?* This is suicide . . . you don't know what this cliff is like."

"That's enough, Rocque," Erica told him. "Just keep your crybaby comments to yourself." She was sucking on a lump of snow, and she looked perfectly capable of killing de Faurier.

"We have to work together here," said Ames Cravens. "We *have* to control our minds and work together, and Kenny will get us down."

"*We* will get us down," Madelaine de Faurier said, "because we are survivors. We are strong and we are capable and we will survive."

"That's right," agreed Bigelow. He was massaging Weezy's hands, looking old and very tired. "We will *all* get us down. And that, by Jesus, will be worth something money can't buy."

Erica made the first rappel almost as quickly as Dangler had, but Peter Bigelow was slow and Weezy even slower. It was five after one when Cobb clipped in to the rope, and he began to wonder how, at this rate, they could possibly make the bottom by nightfall.

He had rappeled before; he had even rappeled on ice in survival classes at the camp. But he had never before rappeled from this height or with senseless hands and feet, and as soon as he stepped off the edge of the cliff he could feel fear turn over and start up in him like a small motor.

He began to pant. Trying to turn off the fear, he concentrated on leaning well back, keeping his legs at a sixty- or seventy-degree angle to the wall, on paying the rope out smoothly through the carabiners, and on looking neither down nor up but only at where his crampons bit into the ice. It was a gully he was in, a flume of stilled water surrounded by rock. The shaft of ice was five to six feet wide, blue-green and candled. There was no wind on the face and the air felt much warmer to Cobb than on top of the cliff, though the ice itself gave off a chill damp breath. Halfway down the pitch his hands started to thaw, and by the time his feet touched the ledge they were hurting so badly that he could hardly bear to touch the rope.

"Good work," said Dangler. He held Cobb against the ice while he clipped him in to a large loop of nylon. Then he unclipped the carabiner brake, tied it to the end of the single rope and jerked the rope a couple of times. He and Cobb watched it being pulled up, the carabiners banging off chips of ice as it went.

"Back to back, huh?" he said, and clapped Cobb on the neck.

The ledge they were on was no more than twenty inches wide. Dangler had chopped the ice flat with his ax for five or six feet down the ledge on either side of the ropes. Now he went back to chopping, and Cobb noticed that he wasn't anchored. Attached to nothing, and whistling, he was hacking his way down an icy ledge eight hundred and fifty feet above the ground. Still facing the cliff, Cobb looked at his own protection. He, Erica—who was farthest down the ledge—and the Bigelows were all clipped to the same big sling. The sling was attached by carabiners to the heads of three hollow nine-inch bolts of metal screwed into the ice. The arrangement looked ludicrously insubstantial to Cobb even before he turned around. When he turned around, the nylon and metal holding him and the others to the cliff seemed simply to disappear; it could have been all the nylon and metal in New England and it wouldn't have existed in Cobb's mind. His vertigo was so immediate that it made him grunt, and he spread his arms against the ice, groping for holds.

"It will get better in a minute," said Bigelow. "Just look at the sky."

"And pray, Andy," said Weezy faintly. "We must all try to pray."

Cobb prayed. He also looked at the sky and listened to Ames Cravens coming down the rope. Before Cravens reached the ledge Cobb was able to look into the valley again, and this time he felt detached and strangely calm.

He found himself envying the trees. There was a sea of them out there between the river and the distant rolling hills to the south—dark troughs of evergreens and mauve swells of birches—each of them rooted in the ground, on flat earth where he would have given everything he would ever own to be. The distance separating him from the trees was only eight hundred and fifty feet, but it might as well have been eight million, so inadequate did his resources feel for ever getting down there again alive. As he looked out over the valley, over the river and the still-burning house into the unbroken stretch of wildness beyond it, feeling his own insignificance more poignantly than he ever had before, these Northern woods which only a couple of days ago had seemed so knowable, so invitingly ordered and sociable, now appeared remote and inhospitable as the moon—not hostile, but chaotic and inaccessible. Dangler was wrong, he told himself: learning how to operate here meant nothing anymore, because it couldn't be done. These woods were too far out of reach—they could only be toyed with now, or cut down. And maybe, he thought, that had been the case ever since the first white men laid eyes on them.

Just as Rocque de Faurier reached the ledge, complaining loudly and forcing them all to turn sideways to make room for him, the sound of a distant engine drifted up the wall from the valley. It was a chain saw or a snowmobile, Cobb figured, and its small chattering noise was the loneliest sound he had ever heard.

"Great guns," said Dangler. "We're going great guns."

"How the hell do you expect me to do all this work with one hand?" demanded de Faurier. "I can hardly hold the rope, and you've got me pulling up the goddamned carabiners and everything else."

Dangler clipped him in to the sling. "You're doing fine,

Rocque. When you come down this time, bring the protection with you."

"I *can't*," shouted de Faurier. "How can I get the screws out with one hand?"

"You'll find a way. Watch your heads." Dangler had been pulling on the right end of the rappel rope, and now, clear of the sling above, it came whistling down and landed heavily on the ledge. He had already set up the next rappel, a triangle of ice screws connected by a sling, and while he ran the rope through this new anchor he chatted about rebuilding Wildwood. He would spend the next three months establishing his place in the Bahamas, he said, and begin to rebuild up here as soon as the ground thawed. The camp would be back in operation and better than ever by autumn, and then maybe he and Erica would take a vacation. As he backed off the second pitch, he was still talking happily, and his lean face was glowing and gay.

At the top of the cliff Cobb had found this joviality of Dangler's disconcerting and irritating—it almost seemed designed to prod at his misery. On the first ledge—with the eight of them crowded front to rump nearly a thousand feet off the ground, listening to him discuss his building plans—it seemed grotesque and demented. But somewhere between the second and third, or the third and fourth pitches, standing on one of the absurdly narrow ledges or picking his way down the vertical ice between them, he realized that Dangler's cheerfulness was saving them—that it and the confidence it implied were supporting each of them on this descent as surely as the rope. He wondered where Dangler could have acquired all the climbing knowledge he was now putting into practice, and then, remembering how he had learned about avalanches, Cobb decided he didn't really want to know. It was enough that he seemed to know what to do; and by the time they reached the cave at the bottom of the fourth rappel, the fact that he was doing it all so expertly and with such obvious relish had Cobb believing for the first time in nearly twenty-four hours that they might have at least an even chance of getting off the mountain alive. In his growing optimism he even felt a familiar combination of affection and pride as he sat in the cave with Erica and the campers and watched Dangler bring down the rappel rope.

It was ten after three. They had made good time on the last three pitches; there were only three hundred feet now between them and the wide switchback ramp down which they could walk—even in the dark if they had to—to the bottom; and the cave was large enough for all of them to sit for the first time in over two hours. As they waited for Dangler to set up the next-to-last rappel, there was a tentative hopefulness among the group. Ames Cravens took from his parka a bacon bar he had been hoarding and divided it up. Weezy Bigelow, who had been growing increasingly incoherent and awkward, regained some control of her speech and movement, and Rocque de Faurier said that he had known all along the route would "go." Only Erica appeared unaffected. Unlike the rest of them, she had no white patches of frostbite on her face, and her hands and feet were not frozen, but ever since the first rappel she had seemed to be dealing with more pain than any of them. Now she sat at the back of the cave, hugging her knees and saying nothing.

Outside the cave to their right, Dangler was working on a sloping platform of yellow ice which split some six feet from the mouth of the cave and tailed off the cliff in a Y. After he had anchored the next rappel, he set his crampons on the lip of the cliff, leaned out against the rope and looked down.

He asked de Faurier which way the route went.

"What do you mean?"

"There are two gullies here. Which one do we take?"

"I don't know," said de Faurier. "Can't you see?"

"There's an overhang . . . I can't see whether they both come in to the ramp or not."

On his knees, using the ax in his good hand to pull himself along, de Faurier crawled out to Dangler and looked over the edge. He said something that Cobb couldn't hear.

"You're sure?" Dangler asked him.

"*No,* I'm not sure," de Faurier shouted. "I told you I've only been on this route once before in my life, and that was in the summer. It looks right."

"Good enough," said Dangler. He clipped on the brake and moved the rope over to the larger of the two ice ridges.

"One more after this one and we've beaten it," he yelled to the cave. "We're almost home free."

The rappel was shorter by twenty or thirty feet than the others had been, and except for an overhanging belly-shaped bulge of ice near the top, it was less steep. But the shelf they had to stand on at the bottom was the narrowest yet, and Dangler had to hack away at it for minutes to make room for all of them. He was still chopping when de Faurier reached the ledge, yelled, "Heads!" and pulled down the rope.

Dangler looked up at him. "I wanted to check below before we brought the rope down. This pitch angles too far to the west. We may be in the wrong gully."

De Faurier stared at him, still holding one end of the rope in his right hand.

"Oh, God," said Cobb, mouthing but not speaking the words. "Please don't let it be wrong." But the minute he said it the prayer felt hopeless. The place was wrong, it had a wrong, narrow, final look to it; but though he felt it was wrong, it still came as a shock to hear it from Dangler right after he began the next rappel.

"The gully runs out," he shouted up to them. "There is nothing but blank rock down here—no ledges to rappel from."

"Oh, sweet Jesus Christ," said Peter Bigelow, and from down the ledge Madelaine de Faurier moaned.

"I didn't know . . ." said de Faurier. "I *told* him I didn't know."

"Listen to me," Dangler shouted. "I think I can get across to the other gully. Rocque? Rocque!"

"What?" said de Faurier.

"I'm going to free one end of the rope, and I want you to belay me, do you understand?"

"I'll do it!" yelled Cravens. "Let me do it, Kenny."

"Rocque."

"What?" said de Faurier.

"You have to do it, Rocque."

"All right," said de Faurier. His voice sounded tiny and exhausted.

"There's a horizontal crack a few feet above my head. I'm going to climb up to it and traverse over to the other gully. I can see it from here. I'll climb down to the next ledge when I get there and tie off the rope, and you can send everyone across on a diagonal rappel. Have you got that? Then we'll bring the single rope across and you can come across on it. Have you got all that, Rocque? Do you see it in your mind?"

"Yes," said de Faurier bleakly.

"I'll need tension on the rope, but not too much. Now, pick up the end of the rappel rope to your right. It's clear."

De Faurier picked up the rope, looped it around his waist and began to take up the slack, keeping the rope taut as Dangler climbed.

"He's going to die," said Erica in a matter-of-fact voice. "And then that will be that—that will be the end of it."

"He can't die," said Cobb without thinking. "He has all of us to save."

The shelf they were standing on, all anchored to a central sling, was no more than a foot wide, but by craning their heads to the left each of them could see Dangler leave the gully some fifteen feet below them and start across the crack. The rock band was slightly convex, and they could not see the other gully, but by looking upward at the angle it took from the top, Cobb figured that it had to be at least fifty feet away. With crampons on, Dangler could only occasionally get a foothold on the rock. He was doing the traverse almost entirely with his fingers, walking them along the two-inch horizontal crack and swinging his body beneath each new hold. Less than halfway across the part of the wall they could see, twenty feet out from the gully, he stopped and hung there, perfectly still, by his fingers.

"The crack is iced," he said calmly. "I can't . . ."

"Oh, God," said de Faurier, clutching the rope to his waist and turning in to the cliff.

In slow motion, it seemed to Cobb, Dangler's right hand slipped out of the crack, sending his body swinging to the left. He shouted, "Tension," and grabbed for the crack with his right hand. Then his left hand came free and he fell, arcing beneath them with his feet out, looking in the direction he was falling, and hit the ridge of ice below with a dry, cracking sound.

Just as he began to fall, Madelaine de Faurier screamed

and Weezy Bigelow slumped forward, almost pulling them all off the ledge before Peter hauled her back. Throwing out his right arm to support Bigelow, Cobb cried, "*Hold* it! Hold the rope, goddammit," and flinging his left arm across Madelaine, he grabbed de Faurier's wind parka. He could hear the rope hiss across the nylon parka for a moment and then stop.

"I have him," de Faurier said, looking crazily at Cobb. "I goddamn well have the son of a bitch."

"Weezy," said Bigelow, "sweetheart, please try to . . ."

"Ken-*neth,*" Erica shrieked out across the frozen valley, her voice cracking like a whip, so full of pain and fear that it sounded insane.

There was a long silence. Then they heard Dangler drive his ax into the ice.

"I'm all right," he said. "I've broken my ankles, but I'm all right. Rocque?"

"What do you want, you bastard?" panted de Faurier.

"I want you to tie off the belay, Rocque," Dangler said, and Cobb could have sworn he heard amusement in his voice. "I can hold on here while you do it. I want you to tie off the belay and then I want you and Andy to help pull me up."

When he was up, Dangler sat on the shelf, his useless lower legs hanging over it, and said the following: "You have to do it, buddy. You're the only one who can. We have to get back up to the cave and go down the other gully—and maybe we have just enough time to make it. The only way to get up there is for someone to climb it and fix the rope so the rest of us can come up on the Jumars." He was looking at Cobb when he said it.

"You can do it, Rebel," said Ames Cravens.

"You *have* to do it, Andy," said Peter Bigelow, staring at him mournfully. "Rocque can't because of his hand, and neither Ames nor I have ever . . ."

"I know," said Cobb, "I know."

He leaned back against the wall and looked at the sky, which was losing light quickly, feeling that his entire life had been a preparation for this moment. This moment had always been out there waiting for him, he thought: it was he who had come to it, not it to him.

Dangler was coiling the double rope, still sitting on the

ledge. Erica was sitting silently, expressionless, beside him, and neither of them was clipped in to the sling.

"It's about eighty feet long," Dangler said. "And a walk-up except for that bulge near the top. Now, let me go over the technique with you."

"No," said Cobb. "I know the technique. Just tell me what you want me to do."

"When you get to the cave, put in three ice screws and attach a sling to them with carabiners. Tie the rope off and toss it down, and we'll come up on the mechanical ascenders. Where are the Jumars, Rocque?"

De Faurier looked at him. "I left them on top."

"You *what?*" Dangler whirled around at the waist, and for the first time Cobb could see pain in his face.

"I didn't think we'd need them. We *wouldn't* need them if you . . ." De Faurier stopped, and Dangler turned his back to the cliff again.

"Then we will have to do it another way. We'll tie each person in to one end of the rope and pull on the other end from down here while Andrew pulls from above. The person on the rope can help by walking up with his feet."

"How about you?" asked Cravens. "Can you use your legs, Kenny?"

"You can lower me the axes and I can help pull myself up with them," Dangler said. "Andrew . . . you know you were a better lineman in prep school than you thought you were."

"It's not necessary," said Cobb, "I'm going."

"I know you're going. I just wanted to tell you something: I've always depended on you more than you know, and more than anyone else in my life. You'd better get started."

"Do I put in ice screws for protection?" asked Cobb.

"There isn't enough time. And you don't know how to do it."

"What if . . . ?"

"You're leading this climb, Andrew. The leader doesn't fall."

"Good luck, Andy," said Madelaine de Faurier.

"Go it, Rebel," said Cravens, and from down the ledge Peter Bigelow, pale as the gully ice and holding Weezy against him with his right arm, raised his fist and shook it.

De Faurier tied one end of the rope onto the back of Cobb's waist strap and handed him the axes. He held up his bandaged hand. "If it weren't for this mitt, fella . . ."

"Right," said Cobb.

Dangler had turned onto his side and clipped in to the sling so that he could lean away from the ledge to watch Cobb. His legs were in Erica's lap, and her left hand lay casually and intimately on top of his knees.

Cobb looked at the two of them and smiled. "I loved Divina. Did you know that?"

"Yes. Be careful, Andy," said Erica without turning around.

Cobb unclipped himself from the sling and faced the cliff. He looked up the column of ice, and a few high clouds racing toward him overhead made the cliff seem about to topple over on him. Dropping his eyes, he swung the ax in his right hand in an arc and set the toothed, down-curving pick into the ice as high as he could reach. It went in smoothly and had a solid feel when he pulled on the handle. He drove in the pick of the other ax a little lower and tested it; then he raised his right knee and looked down at the front points of the crampon. They were two clawlike spikes, sticking straight out from the toe of his boot, and they had never looked to Cobb even remotely capable of doing what they were supposed to do. He picked a small nubbin of ice a foot and a half above the shelf, kicked the spikes into it and stood up on them. Then he kicked in the front points of his left crampon and he was there, stuck to the wall.

"Good," said Dangler. "Keep your feet at right angles to the ice and don't move but one thing at a time. Climb with your legs."

Cobb relaxed his arm muscles a little and tested most of his weight on his front points. The shift felt tenuous and pulled at his calf muscles, but he knew from doing this in survival classes—belayed from the top of a twenty-foot manmade icicle—that he would never make it up using only his arms. He freed the right ax and set it again at the limit of his reach. Then he pulled at the left one, and nothing happened. He yanked at it. It didn't move, and Cobb felt his first rush of fear.

"Flick it out, don't jerk it," said Dangler gently.

Cobb flicked the hardwood shaft, and the pick came

free. He set it into the ice across from the other one and advanced his right foot, and then his left.

"A foot and *then* a hand, Andrew. A foot and then a hand. You're doing fine."

He had made twenty feet before the real terror came. He had been moving smoothly if slowly—one point at a time, a foot and then a hand, testing each purchase in the ice before putting weight on it, his mind focused tightly on the moves. He had just set the left ax and was taking a step with the opposite foot when he let his left heel ride up and the front claws of the crampon pulled free. Hanging by the straps of his axes, Cobb felt a flash of adrenaline, and then pure panic seized him. Squirming against the ice, he kicked frantically for holds with both feet. Dangler was shouting something to him, but he couldn't hear it, and when he finally got his front points back into the ice, he was so terrified that he could no longer think. His hands and feet were numb, the muscles in his arms and chest burned and his eyes were watering so badly he could hardly see. Hysterically he freed and swung the ax in his right hand, cracking his knuckles against the ice. Then he began to scramble, hacking madly at the gully as if he were out to kill it, gasping and moaning and cursing himself and the cliff. He wanted to chew up the ice; his mind felt poisoned, convulsed with fear and the peripheral frustrations of pain, his watering eyes, the awkward axes.

Wild with panic, seeing clearly in his mind the seven people below him and the abyss below them, it hit Cobb that he had been set up—that Dangler, Erica, the campers had sent him up here to kill him, and as he hacked and wormed his way upward, he began to sob for himself and for the pitiful life he was about to lose. "*Please* no . . ." he panted. "Oh, God, please . . . Please come out," he pleaded with one of the axes. "Oh, you pathetic idiot, couldn't you *see* it?" he sobbed.

Then he was at the bulge. He had climbed the last forty feet in an unseeing frenzy, and now he was directly beneath the overhanging hump. Squinting up at its shadowed underside, Cobb gave up. He hung in the straps of his axes, dropped his head onto his chest and gave up.

Dangler's voice sounded far away but pressing, and

Cobb realized that he had been hearing without listening to it for minutes.

"I said that was quite a show. . . . Can you hear me?"

Cobb nodded.

"All you can do is die or make it, Andrew. And it won't make a particle of difference to this cliff either way. We go back three and a half billion years, and part of everything that made us durable is in you. Any idiot can die. Dying is nothing."

Cobb imagined himself dying. He looked down the cliff for the first time and imagined himself falling and landing on the talus, or maybe on the ice of the river: the impact, the sudden void. Then his mind seemed to stop on a dime; he felt something heavy and old inside himself shift and fall away, and his body began climbing—purposefully again— toward the bulge.

For the first time, he noticed the ice as he climbed. He seemed to notice it, not with his usual perceptions but with an intense new affinity for what he was seeing, and at the same time a disregard. The ice was simply there—a distant, aqua, sea color, knobbed and waxy and indifferent—as he was there. It no longer played on his sense of transience, torturing him with the fear of slipping off it. He no longer felt antagonistic toward it, or even separate from it. He, the freezing air around him, the axes and the ice all seemed parts of the same illimitable moment, and Cobb experienced it whole and clear. He felt radically present, locked into the second, and he climbed the bulge as if he had done it a thousand times, as if he knew every frozen particle of it. When he was over it, he lay against its sloping top, breathing on the ice, feeling delivered and free, and happier than he could remember ever feeling.

"We can do it," he told the top of the bulge. "We are by God *going* to do it." He put his tongue on the ice, and it tasted salty.

He practically danced up the last ten feet of gully to the cave. When he was there he set up the anchor, pulled the rope through it and lowered it down the ice he had just climbed. Without clipping in to the anchor, he sat down and braced his feet, feeling wildly exhilarated but calm in his mind. "All right," he whooped down the gully.

The rope made a pulley, and with Cobb pulling at the top and the others from the ledge, Rocque de Faurier came up quickly.

"Good work," de Faurier said without looking at him. "I just hope to Christ we still have time after all this futzing around. I figure we have about an hour of light left."

"We have time," said Cobb. "How is everyone?"

"Cold. It dropped about ten degrees while you were fooling around in the gully. Weezy is hypothermic but she can operate. Kenneth is getting weaker."

"*Kenneth?* What do you mean he's getting weaker?"

De Faurier sat down beside Cobb, braced his feet and took hold of the rope, which was already being pulled from the bottom. "He has two broken ankles, Cobb. He *is* a human being, you know."

Weezy Bigelow came up next, then Madelaine de Faurier and Erica, and with each of them the hauling at the top grew more difficult. There was room for only two people at a time on the lip of the ledge, and de Faurier could pull with only one hand, so when Ames Cravens came up he took over for him and de Faurier crawled back into the cave with Weezy and Madelaine. Erica sat directly behind Cobb, saying nothing.

"Kenny says to send down the axes when Peter is up," said Cravens, pulling hand for hand with Cobb. His face was tight with exhaustion and pain. "Jesus, I think I've *lost* my feet, Rebel. I think they're gone."

"How is he?"

"Who?" said Cravens, looking at him. "Kenny, you mean? He's fine, of course."

They had a hard time with Bigelow at the bulge. The rope kept slipping to one side of the hump, where it was wearing a constricting groove in the ice. With Bigelow's cap just visible below the bulge, the rope stopped completely, caught in the crack, and no amount of pulling would free it.

"Get out here, Rocque," Cobb said over his shoulder. "See if you can get the rope under Ames's arms and help us pull."

"I can't," said de Faurier from the mouth of the cave. "I only have one hand."

"Goddammit, Rocque . . ."

"You'll have to kick out, Peter," Dangler shouted from below, his voice faint. "Can you hear me, Andrew?"

"Yes," yelled Cobb.

"Pull up on the rope when he swings out. And hurry —we're almost out of time. . . . Andrew?"

"I heard you," Cobb shouted.

"You're getting it done, buddy."

Bigelow kicked outward from the bulge, freeing the rope momentarily, and Cobb and Cravens hauled up on it, getting Bigelow's upper body just over the crest of the overhang. He lay there gasping. "It's getting dark," he said miserably. "How in the name of Christ can we do any more than what we've done?"

When Bigelow was up, Cobb sat him behind himself and told Cravens to sit behind Bigelow, and de Faurier behind Cravens, so that they could all pull in a single line. Quickly tying the two ice axes onto one end of the rope, he lowered them to Dangler and told Erica to throw the other end down the gully they would be rappeling down and to coil the loose rope in the cave as they pulled it in.

"I'm going to try to keep the rope in the center of the bulge, away from the groove," he said, "so everyone pull smoothly."

Almost as soon as they began to pull, Cobb knew that they wouldn't make it. With the rope hanging over the brow of the bulge, away from the wall, Dangler couldn't do much with the axes. Cobb could feel him clawing at the ice with the picks, and almost thought he could feel through the rope his frustration at being unable to help. He knew that Dangler's dead weight would be too much for them at the bulge—and his only reaction to knowing that was mild surprise that something had finally gone wrong that Dangler couldn't fix. He felt no fear; nor did he speculate on consequences. He would try with all he had, and if he couldn't pull Dangler up, he would lower him back to the shelf and join him there, and de Faurier could rappel the rest of the group off down the other gully. As he pulled, putting every muscle in his back and arms precisely to use, Cobb looked into the cobalt sky now speckling with stars and was perfectly content with that plan, and with not thinking beyond it.

When Dangler was about halfway up, there was a jerk on the rope and the pulling became suddenly easier. It was a moment or two before Cobb saw why. Something Dangler had done below had thrown the rope off the center of the bulge, bringing him closer to the wall, but the rope was now working its way toward the groove in the ice that had hung up Peter Bigelow.

"Pull smoothly," Cobb shouted behind him. But he could see that it was just a matter of seconds before the rope reached the groove, and with Dangler still some twenty feet below the bulge, it did, and froze there.

"Pull," he shouted, and wrenched at the rope. It moved an inch or two and stopped. He could hear Dangler clawing at the ice. "Pull!" he shouted again. "We'll do it, Kenneth. It's like fourth and goal, you remember? when you said, 'There's nothing fancy about fourth and goal . . .' "

"We're running out of time," shrieked Rocque de Faurier. "Do you want us *all* to die up here?"

"Pull, you miserable coward," yelled Cobb, "or I swear to God I'll . . ."

Suddenly de Faurier was beside him on the edge, panting and screaming, his long face jumping crazily. "*Coward?* You think I'm a coward?" he screamed, tearing at the nylon bandage on his left hand. "You think I don't count?" He thrust the bare hand, yellowed with frostbite, into Cobb's face, and then, as Cobb watched, he put his little finger in his mouth and bit down savagely into the top joint, gnashing at it like a dog at a bone. With a quick twist of his head, he severed the end of the finger and spat it out on the ice.

Cobb took his right hand off the rope and slapped de Faurier as hard as he could in the face. The Texan fell over on his side and lay there with his knees drawn up to his chest, holding his bleeding hand.

"Get inside the cave, Rocque," Cobb told him, and turned back to the rope.

"It won't move at all now, Andy," said Peter Bigelow. "It just won't move."

"I'm going to try to free it. Keep it tight."

Holding on to the rope, Cobb backed off the ledge, down a short pitch of steep ice and onto the roof of the bulge. Wrapping his left wrist around the rope above him, he leaned out and yanked at the section stuck in the groove directly beneath him.

The rope balked; then it gave and came up weightless.

XXII

The window at the foot of his bed looked out on a parking lot. On the far side of the lot was a small brick clinic, and beyond that was a hillside of birch and evergreen trees. Cobb noticed this view for the first time on his third day in the hospital. He woke at 5:30 that morning, feeling the necessity to ready himself for something, and watched dawn come up outside, revealing bit by bit the lot, the clinic and the trees. As they took shape in the gray light, they registered with him as real for the first time since he arrived here, and Cobb felt an odd, comforting assurance and fascination in their growing actuality.

At first he couldn't understand why everything was covered with ice. Then he remembered that there had been freezing rain the day before, lasting into the night. On the brick walls of the clinic and on the evergreen trees the ice looked at first like a heavy cracking coat of milky varnish. Then, just after six, the sun rose from behind the hospital, the piece of sky Cobb could see turned a soft blue, the ice on the trees burst into a brilliant crystal glitter as though millions of jewels were nestled in the boughs, and for about five minutes, as the evergreens sparkled, the tops of the birches were a tender, opalescent pink against the sky.

He had never seen such a new-looking morning, and

when the color faded from the birches he found that he had strained his eyes with looking. He closed them, and avoided thinking about the stirring pain in his bandaged hands and feet by trying to remember what it was he had to prepare for. He couldn't do it, though his mind felt as unclouded this morning as the sky outside the window. For two days his mind had not been at all clear, and Cobb felt an impulse to rest it now in order to avoid straining it as he had his eyes. He said his morning prayer, let the pain come up into his head and examined it. His right foot—where yesterday they had cut away parts of a toe along with the blistered skin there and on his other foot and hands—was still bad, but not as bad as it had been, and the pain in his hands was almost gone. On the whole, he felt much better this morning in both body and mind, and when the nurse brought his breakfast at 7:30 he was hungry for it.

He remembered that the nurse's name was Kemp.

"What day is this?" asked Cobb.

"You ask me that every morning," said the nurse. She put a bib with a picture of a lobster on it around Cobb's neck and tied it. "What day do you think it is?"

"Sunday."

"Very good," the nurse said, as if she were complimenting a child. She rolled up the top half of the bed, sitting Cobb up. "And what happens today, do you know that?"

Cobb knew. Grace Hurd was coming to pick him up and move him to the hospital in Concord. "I'm going to Concord," he said. He was very hungry. He was hungry particularly for rare lamb, but what was on the tray looked good enough.

While Kemp fed him, Cobb asked her about the others.

"I've told you all this a dozen times," she said. "Twice a day every day."

"I'd like to hear it again."

He and Ames Cravens were the only ones still in the hospital in Colby, she told him with exaggerated patience. The Bigelows had been moved to Boston, and the de Fauriers had been flown to Houston, along with one of the country's foremost frostbite specialists, by de Faurier's brother. Specialist or not, de Faurier would certainly lose most of his left hand, she said. Ames Cravens might have to give up a toe or two—it was still too early for the doctor to tell. She didn't know about the others. Mrs. Bigelow had been very sick, and cold at the core, when she got here, but she had warmed up quickly.

"And Mrs. Dangler?"

The nurse looked at him. "In Boston too, I believe."

"How is she?"

"None."

"None what?"

"No *frost*bite. I told you. Dr. Merton couldn't believe she had been on the same mountain as the rest of you. The poor woman, though—she has something worse than frostbite to get through. You know," said Kemp, shaking her head, "she never said a word while she was here. Never opened her mouth. Here." She cut and tined a piece of French toast and held it up to Cobb. He didn't want it now, thinking of Erica, but he ate it anyway.

He had expected screaming, every sort of mayhem, a suicide attempt—anything but silence. But silence was what Erica had met Dangler's death with, and everything after that. After he had wrenched the rope out of the crack and felt the terrible weightlessness at its end, Cobb's only clear thoughts were of Erica blowing up, coming loudly apart, throwing herself off the cliff. Images of what she might do filled his head as he climbed back up from the bulge, blocking out the actual fact of Dangler's death so thoroughly that when he reached the ledge, scrambled by the gaping, horrified faces of Peter Bigelow and Ames Cravens to where she was sitting and fell on her, pinning her beneath him, he couldn't even remember for a second what it was he had to tell her. When he did, she didn't make a sound. Bigelow was bellowing, "*No, no, no . . .*" at the lip of the ledge, and Cravens was crying out Dangler's name. There was screaming and hysteria on the ledge, then and for minutes afterward, but none of it was Erica's. Erica had only bitten her lower lip and looked up at Cobb silently.

And the silence had lasted. All the way down the next rappel and the next, set in the last seconds of sufficient light, as he drove the campers to hurry, hounded the now useless de Faurier, placed protection and worked the ropes, Cobb had waited for it to snap and for Erica to come hurtling out of herself, wailing like a banshee. But it hadn't happened. She had come silently, pacifically down the ropes with the rest of them. And during the steep dark walk off the ramp, and the awful stumbling down the talus boulders to the bridge, and the freezing tramp out the road to the deserted servants' quarters, she had been not only silent but had helped Cobb carry the all-but-unconscious Weezy Bigelow and keep the other campers going.

He couldn't be sure: he suspected it had happened only in the turmoil of his imagination, but if she had made a single sound during that last hour and a half, it had been to whisper something to him as she lay beside him on the hardwood floor waiting for the ambulance. Whether she had spoken them or not, the words had come into his mind —on a soft slant from above him, bordered by silence—and they had brought him some peace.

In a little while, when his head was cloudy again with medication, the nurse came back and changed the dressings on his hands and feet. And sometime later she brought Cravens into his room in a wheelchair and rolled up Cobb's bed. Cravens' legs were raised and his bandaged feet stuck straight out in front of him. He was wearing a hospital robe, and even in it he looked dapper. Cobb was happy to see him.

"You're looking good, Rebel," he said.

"So are you."

"I understand you're leaving. Too bad. We could have played some chess." He looked at Cobb's bandaged hands lying on the bed. "I suppose I *was* lucky with the hands. How are yours?"

"Just a few blisters. How about your feet?"

"Oh, I'll be here for a while, I imagine, but that doesn't bother me. I haven't any particular place to go, and I'd much rather be catered to in this little hospital than ignored in one of those big-city numbers. My ex-wife tried to get me to move down to Boston, but this suits me fine."

Cobb wondered what Cravens' ex-wife was like. He remembered hearing from someone, Dangler perhaps, that she had taken Cravens for quite a bit of his inherited money during their divorce.

"You never met Helen, did you?" said Cravens, as if he had read Cobb's mind. "She lives in Georgetown now. Remarried. The loveliest woman you ever saw, Rebel." He smiled at Cobb. It was a forced, wan little smile. "We're still quite good friends."

"Why don't you come down to Concord with me, Twist? Ames, I mean—sorry. My secretary can set it up. It's a very good hospital, and we would have each other's company."

Cravens looked at him seriously. "I appreciate that, Andy, but I'd just as soon keep an eye on things up here for a while. Maybe I could come for a visit this summer, though, if you're going to be around."

"I don't know," said Cobb. "I'm not sure yet where I'll be."

The conversation was beginning to feel awkward to him. Something seemed to be in their way, and Cobb was having to make an uncomfortable effort to think straight and to say the right things. He shifted in the bed, and a wave of drowsiness passed over him.

"You know they haven't found the body yet," said Cravens.

"Yes."

"The idiot police chief up here thinks now he fell through the ice into the river. He says it might be spring before they find him."

Cobb felt himself getting irritated. He decided to change the subject. "How about Divina? Do you know if . . . ?"

"She was buried yesterday in Boston. My cousins the Cryles said it was quite a beautiful service. Erica was there, apparently, and the Watermans."

"Buried . . ." said Cobb, testing the word as he had tested the pain in his hands and feet. The pain there, he discovered, was just beginning. "You're really up on everything, aren't you? And you want to stay around up here to make sure they find his body, is that it?"

"I just *don't* trust that chief of police, Rebel. He says

things like Gruenig might have died in the fire. Yesterday he implied to me over the phone that the fire *could* have been an accident."

Cobb threw his head back on the pillow and stared at the ceiling. "Who cares, Twist? Who cares what happened to Gruenig or the house? And Kenneth might very *well* have fallen into the river."

Cobb could feel Cravens staring at him.

"Then I want to *know* that he did," he said after a moment. "*I* care about the house—for Erica's sake mostly. I've put my lawyer on it. And I've put some acquaintances of mine on Gruenig. I care very much about *him*. I plan to see Gruenig rot in jail, or at the very least, killed."

"Good luck," said Cobb bitterly.

"Listen, Andy, you did what *you* could for Kenny on the cliff. You were wonderful up there, before and after the accident. I couldn't have done it. None of the rest of us could have, and we never would have made it down without you. You paid him back with that, and no one will ever forget it. I'm just trying to do what I can for him now—in my own small way. . . ."

"I didn't owe him anything, and neither do you. And it wasn't an accident. He *cut* himself off the goddamn rope."

"To save our lives."

"He took his knife while that bastard de Faurier was chewing on his hand and *cut himself off the rope*, Cravens. Let's get that straight anyway, for Christ's sake. I saw the rope. There was nothing accidental about it."

"He *did* it to save our lives."

"Or maybe because he couldn't save us," Cobb said. "Maybe because dying was better than admitting that anything was beyond him. He did it to make some *point*, can't you see that? And because he was bullheaded and selfish and egotistical and crazy . . ."

"*Stop it*," said Cravens.

"Because he thought he was God, and we all *let* him think it."

"*Stop it*," said Cravens, his voice edging toward hysteria. "I *demand* that you *stop* this at *once*."

Cobb raised his head and looked at Cravens. His handsome face was livid and quivering. Nurse Kemp was standing behind him in the open doorway, one hand raised to her throat.

"You poor sucker." Cobb sighed and dropped his head back onto the pillow. "Roll this bed down, will you, Kemp?"

His outrage had shocked him. Lying perfectly still and concentrating, Cobb tried to figure out what had caused it. Cravens' dumb loyalty and zealous appropriation of responsibility had been part of it, but after a while Cobb realized that it was Dangler, not Cravens, he had been railing at. With some difficulty he had kept Dangler submerged in his mind for two days, beneath his sense of dislocation, his pain and the drugs; now Cravens had pulled him up, and Cobb saw that he was furious at him. What he saw, when he thought of Dangler now, was an infuriating panorama of waste, stretching back as far as they had known each other.

He saw himself and Dangler at sixteen and seventeen, drinking sloe-gin fizzes in the Biltmore Hotel bar; "feeling up" two Emma Willard girls in a hot small room at the Roosevelt; sitting in the parlor of Gussie's and Sally's whorehouse in the Village, surrounded by prep-school pennants, while Dangler's father's chauffeured limousine idled outside. He saw the two of them throwing around a gin bottle with lacrosse sticks on some snowy train platform on their way to Larchmont to see a girl; and then, two or three years later, reeling arm in arm out of a French restaurant in the Eighties and onto the thrilling late-night Manhattan streets, and he heard Dangler saying, "At this point in time, Andrew, I happen to know every headwaiter in New York City." And Cobb remembered—the memory twisting in his chest like something alive—how magical each of those moments had seemed at the time, how luminous and vivid with significance they had seemed, and how privileged it had made him feel to share them with Dangler.

They looked desolate now, meaningless and desolate: a wasteful, glandular flopping around by affluent children with too many options. And so did Dangler's lazy, melancholic years at Harvard and the frantic years afterward—all the ambitious, quirky campaigns on life, the imaginary wars, the hunting down of legends, the exuberant adventures which Cobb had read about in letters and yearned to be involved with—and finally the Adventure Camp. It looked suspiciously like play to him now, staggeringly wasteful play. And Cobb felt cheated. He had always believed fervently that there was some purpose behind whatever Dangler did, some point to it, no matter how personal or elusive. If—Cobb had believed—Dangler was able in the eerie tradition of the over-rich to make important things seem insignificant and insignificant things seem important, it was because he was radically serious about his concerns, whatever they were—so serious that he could actually transform them with his own sense of their gravity and worth. Now it appeared to him that Dangler had been playing all the time, that nothing had ever been important to him but pursuing fantasies of himself, and Cobb felt as if after twenty years of paying to watch someone pull a quarter from behind his ear, he had finally seen the coin palmed. It was not only Dangler's waste he saw, spread out before him, but his own.

Around eleven o'clock Dr. Merton came in and heartily examined Cobb's feet and hands. "Ten days," the doctor told him. "Ten days and you should be up and around. Don't let them keep you in the sheets any longer than that down there. I knew a man in Canada who saved his feet by dancing on them for forty-eight hours straight."

"Right," said Cobb, trying to smile.

Kemp came in a little later with his pills and his lunch. Cobb swallowed the pills and left the lunch, which looked like mushroom soup poured onto a piece of white bread. He wouldn't have eaten it even if it had been rare lamb, because he was onto something. And just before the codeine hit him, washing him out completely, he realized what it was, and it felt like finding the knob to a door in the dark: Erica was the biggest waste of all. It was Erica who had brought Dangler to where he had been on the mountain the morning after Divina's death—who had somehow allowed him to find a final form, a true self. Then he had stripped her off like a bandage, and all he had been able to do with that raw new self was to lead a handful of people three-quarters of the way down a mountain.

With the knob in his hand, Cobb opened the door and saw the real source of his anger. It was simply that Dangler had died—that he had been mortal after all. Dangler's death was the palmed coin. He saw that, and then he went to sleep.

He slept for less than an hour before Kemp was in his room again, readying him to leave. And at two o'clock on the nose, Grace Hurd walked in, dressed in a yellow wool coat, looking bright and cheerful as a buttercup.

"I feel very woozy and very tired," Cobb told her. "Please don't talk too much."

"Your father is delighted that I'm bringing you back to Concord. He has decided to come up for Christmas, and we can all have dinner together in your room. By the way, I got you a room you won't even believe." She bustled over to his bed. "We'd better make it snappy. The traffic is going to be hideous with all the skiers up here this weekend." Leaning over, she kissed Cobb brusquely on the forehead. "How do you feel? You look much better than you did yesterday."

"I told you, I feel tired. And I feel very strongly that I don't want to eat Christmas dinner with you and my father in a hospital room," Cobb said.

After they had lowered him into a wheelchair and covered him with a blanket, Grace and the nurse wheeled Cobb outside to the station wagon Grace had borrowed from Bob Perch. Cobb had nothing to take back with him but the toothbrush and the books and magazines Grace had brought him yesterday and the day before; the station wagon was so that he could stretch out on the mattress she had placed in the back. She had put a copy of the *Christian Science Monitor* back there too, but Cobb knew he would not get a chance to look at it.

Kemp and Grace set him up on the mattress with his back propped on pillows against the tailgate. It felt very much like being in the hospital bed with the back rolled up. Grace drove slowly through Colby and out of it down the two-lane highway south, chattering about his insurance coverage, about the Christmas shopping she had done for him and a new divorce case the firm had taken on. It was a sunny, unseasonably warm afternoon, and at first Cobb enjoyed looking out of the back windows of the station wagon.

There were Christmas decorations and lights up in the towns they passed through. Everyone he saw seemed to be smiling and busy, and it felt good to look at ordinary life again.

But less than a half-hour from Colby, things turned suddenly sour on him. Grace had been talking about vacation possibilities. They both needed some time in the sun, she had said, and Bob Perch had cleared two weeks for them to go away somewhere as soon as Cobb got out of the hospital. Of course, they could always visit his father. But how about the Bahamas or the Virgin Islands instead? Or Key West? She had heard Key West was interesting.

Cobb wasn't listening. He was looking out the windows, wondering if he might be hallucinating.

They were on the main street of a town, and the street was chockablock with automobiles and people. Every automobile had on its roof a rack bristling with skis and poles, and every person Cobb saw, in the automobiles or on the street, seemed to be on the way to some fancy-dress party. The whole town, it appeared, was dressed in purple jumpsuits and orange down parkas and polka-dotted vests, in knee-high reindeer boots and cowboy hats and striped stretch pants. Moreover, everyone wore the same expression, or lack of one; all the faces Cobb saw looked torpid and a little stunned, as if every person in the town had just gotten up from eating too much.

"What's going on here?" he said, feeling panicky. "*Grace?* What is this place. What's happening here?"

Grace Hurd turned around and looked at him. They were stopped at a traffic light. From the window of the car next to them a vacant-looking teenage girl in wraparound mirrored sunglasses was languidly chewing gum and staring at Cobb.

"It's Washington. You've been here a hundred times. Do you feel all right?"

"What's . . . wrong with all these people?"

Grace looked out her window. "They're just skiers. Trying to beat the rush back to Boston, I imagine. Are you all right, Pooh?"

"Skiers," said Cobb, feeling relieved. Of course they were just skiers. "I'm fine, thank you. And please concentrate on the driving, Grace. We have plenty of time to talk."

The Mount Wilderness ski area, he remembered foggily, was just outside the town of Washington; he had skied there himself a number of times. At the town limits, where the main street became highway again, he saw the mountain over a stream of cars in the other lane, a couple of miles off to the east, its bald, snow-cone summit and winding trails gleaming and ghostly in the late sun. The mountain appeared to float out there on an ocean of evergreens, and for a moment it looked like some great dead sea animal to Cobb—a whale maybe, killed and stripped by sharks—and the remaining skiers whom he could see dotting the slopes might have been schools of colorful scavenger fish gliding between the ribs.

"Slow down," he snapped at Grace Hurd. "And drive this thing carefully or I swear to Christ I'll get out and call a cab."

Grace had been talking to him in the rearview mirror and had almost run up the back of another station wagon full of skis and pacified-looking children.

"Sorry," she said. Her face puckered in the mirror, the way it did whenever she had something important to say. "It's these goddamn Massachusetts people. Honest to God, Pooh, between the skiers in the winter and the hikers in the summer and the leafers in the fall, the people who *live* in the state can't even get around the north country anymore. These people from Massachusetts and New York are taking over up here."

They were past the ski area now, dropping out of the White Mountains and onto the long sloping peneplain that ended at the big lakes near Laconia, where they would pick up Interstate 93 leading to Concord and then Manchester and Boston, to bigger and bigger aggregations of people. And though Cobb knew positively that he would never again set eyes on the country north of where he was right now, he felt no urge to look back at the disappearing woods.

"They can have it," he told Grace Hurd. "And, Grace . . ."

"Yes?"

"You and I may work out and we may not, Grace. I'm willing to give it a few weeks to see if anything has changed . . . But the next time you call me 'Pooh,' one of us is moving out."

XXIII

―――――

On a windy Friday in late March a memorial service was
held for Kenneth Dangler at St. James Episcopal
Church on Madison Avenue and Seventy-second
Street in New York City.

Dangler's body had still not been found, and the state
Fish and Game Department had curtailed its search to a
daily surveillance at natural openings in the Monnussuc
River until the ice went out. Dangler's immediate family
had insisted finally on the memorial service, overruling
Erica, who had not wanted even an obituary printed in the
New York *Times* until there was definite proof Dangler was
dead.

"Life must go on," Dangler's sister had written in her
letter to Cobb asking him to act as an usher at the service.
"And it is unkind to all of us, as well as to his memory, to
allow Erica to continue to put this off."

The letter seemed to assume that Cobb had been in
touch with Erica, but in fact he had not heard from her
once in the past three and a half months.

His shuttle plane from Boston was late that morning,
and he did not get to the church until 10:45, fifteen minutes
before the service was due to begin. At first he thought he

had come to the wrong place. He had never been to a memorial service, but he had imagined them to be small, private affairs. There were hundreds of people here, going in through the blond oak doors and chatting to each other on the street, and it was not until he noticed Cravens standing with a cane near the entrance that Cobb paid the taxi driver and joined the flow of people.

Cravens embraced him at the top of the steps. When he stepped back and looked at Cobb, holding him at arm's length, his blue eyes were glistening. "There are almost a thousand people in there," he said. "He was a very beloved man, Rebel."

"I'm glad to see you, Ames. How's the foot?"

Cravens looked down and tapped his right foot with the cane. The cane was slender and black with a silver head, and it was very becoming to Cravens.

"I lost a couple of toes, but I'm right as rain now. De Faurier lost most of his hand, and I believe Madelaine lost a big toe."

"Are they here?" Cravens was waving to someone over Cobb's head.

"No, but the Bigelows are, and the Watermans and Norris Fish. And the Fairfax sisters. It's almost like a reunion. Peter and Weezy both lost a toe or two. And Weezy was in the hospital almost as long as I was."

"How is Erica doing?"

"Holding up like a soldier. You knew she sold the camp."

"No." Cobb was jostled by someone from behind. When he turned around he saw a tall gray-haired Army officer entering the church.

"That's General Weyland," said Cravens. "One of the Joint Chiefs of Staff. *Gave* it away, really. Apparently Kenny had it all in her name. She sold the buildings and a hundred acres for practically nothing to the YMCA to use as a summer camp, and gave the rest of the property to the Forest Society. It *infuriated* that man up there. What's his name—the selectman? Something about reducing his tax base."

"Knapp." Cobb smiled. "Have you had any luck finding Gruenig?"

Cravens scratched his forehead and looked away. "Not

much. We thought for a while we had him located in Argentina, but it turned out to be someone else. Actually, I've sort of given that up, to tell you the truth." He took Cobb's arm and led him into the crowded vestibule. "I'm keeping the guest book. Why don't you stand here with me until the service begins?"

"I was supposed to usher," Cobb said vaguely. "But my plane was late . . ."

Looking around the elegant red-tiled vestibule and through the leaded glass windows into the filling church, he saw quite a few people he knew. He saw many more whom he did not know, but he felt as if he knew them too. It was a big, familiar, but impersonal crowd that felt small: made up of men dressed in dark business suits and women in small pearls and tasteful black dresses, all of whom might have been the same age and all of whom knew each other or knew people who knew each other; who belonged to the same network of private clubs across the country, who had gone to the same schools, and worked—or did not work— at the same businesses, and summered in the same coastal or mountain compounds, together. They all looked and sounded the same; they even smelled the same. Watching them enter the church—nodding formally to each other, the women walking with small neat steps, their covered heads lowered, the men shooting their cuffs and fingering their ties—Cobb felt disappointed, and a little embarrassed for Dangler. He wanted an Indian or two for him, a trapper, a few models, a Greek shipowner, an emerald merchant, even a couple of portly, criminal-looking Italians with diamond rings—a few colorful people, who would testify to the eccentric range of Dangler's life. With the exception of the general, he noted, no one here had even bothered to put on a costume for Dangler.

"And finally I just ran out of patience," Cravens said. "You don't think I was wrong to quit, do you, Rebel?"

"Quit what?"

"Searching for Gruenig."

"No," said Cobb. "I don't think you were wrong. Gruenig will take care of himself. And all of us . . . most of us, anyway, quit things."

Ham Schultz, Dangler's roommate at Harvard, waved,

and Cobb waved back. Schultz was ushering into the chapel an elderly lady in a fur coat. Just beyond them Cobb saw a bony and fine old white head. It belonged to Dr. Noble Whitney Swann, whom he had seen last ecstatically defying the recorded wolves from the living room at Wildwood.

"This is quite a . . . quite a large crowd."

"Kenny had a lot of friends," said Cravens, who had gone back to signing people in.

"I think I'll wander on in now," Cobb said.

"The first five pews on either side are reserved for the family and close friends. Will you be at the River Club afterward?"

Before Cobb could answer, Cravens turned around to greet someone, smiling his brilliant white smile, his eyes thoughtlessly delighted, charmingly amused. Looking at him, Cobb felt very fond of Cravens—too fond of him to want to say anything else.

Halfway down the aisle he decided he did not want to sit in the reserved pews. He ducked into the nearest seat, bowed his head and sat for a few seconds staring at the floor, trying to work up some private, appropriate emotion. But nothing came. For the past fourteen weeks he had tried out and suffered through one Dangler-assessing emotion after another. He appeared to be out of them now, and it seemed unfair to expect himself to produce something just for the occasion. He tried to feel at least in touch with Dangler, but even that was difficult. Dangler seemed too far away.

Cobb raised his head and looked around—at the white stone pillars and the oak pews, the tall stained-glass windows along the length of the chapel on either side, and at the carved, gold-painted altarpiece with its central figure of a peaceful, open-palmed Christ in a white gown and gold cape, the Last Supper carved beneath him. He looked up at the inlaid wood Gothic arches of the ceiling, which along with the ruby and sapphire colors in the windows made the chapel feel like the inside of a jewel box. The light was pale and diffused; the chapel was silent except for an occasional stirring or cough, and it smelled of waxed wood and stone. Its dim, vaulted calm, its serene inertia and docile openness to anything that might happen in it, began to work a feeling in Cobb, and when the feeling crystallized he found himself, for the first time ever, pitying Dangler. He pitied the commotion of his life, the long noisy battle he had had to wage toward an idea of himself. He pitied his inability to accommodate quietness in himself; and most of all Cobb pitied him his ambition—the legacy that had kept him all his life in ceaseless competition with himself and the ghost of his great-grandfather.

In the front of the church, beneath the overhanging pulpit, Ham Schultz was ushering in Dangler's family. His mother and father came in quickly and sat down, followed by Dangler's sister—a thin, nervous Westchester matron in whose face Cobb had never been able to detect the slightest hint of Dangler—her husband, her son, and finally Erica. Erica was not dressed in black, but in a cream-colored suit and a wide-brimmed almost jaunty green hat. She looked back into the congregation, her face as startlingly beautiful as ever beneath the brim of the hat, and her eyes settled for a second on Cobb, making his heart race, before she swept a hand under the back of her skirt and sat down.

The rector, a young blond man with a soft eastern face, came in immediately after the family was seated, stood in front of the pulpit, raised his robed arms and said, "We have come together this morning to remember and give thanks for the spirit and life of Kenneth Austin Dangler, which is appropriate to do, for the Christian faith is that though the body is gone the spirit and influence live on forever in the Kingdom of God, and in our hearts . . ."

Cobb thought of a certain spring afternoon when Dangler had come running with him and a couple of other boys on the Andover cross-country team. Dangler did not run cross-country; he had come along only to see what it was that Cobb liked about it, and then proceeded to try to beat him at it. It was a ten-mile training run over moist, breathy spring trails. Dangler would sprint ahead of the rest of them and then drop back, sprint and drop back, until he had exhausted himself and had to walk. Cobb had stopped running and walked with him, letting the other two boys go on ahead. When they came in sight of the gymnasium, Dangler had bolted for it. Cobb could see him doing it now—his arms pumping, his yellow hair flying—and he could see the fierce happiness on Dangler's face as he stood by the gym, panting and yelling out to Cobb that he had beaten him.

"'In my Father's house are many mansions,'" the rector was saying. "'If it were not so, I would have told you. I go to prepare a place for you. And if I go and prepare a place for you, I will come again, and receive you unto myself; that where I am, there ye may be also. . . .'"

Something like a membrane seemed to let go in Cobb's chest, and he felt himself flood. For the first time since the hour of Dangler's death, he wept for his best friend. And for the first time in his life, he wished his own mildness on the rest of the world.

"'I am the way, the truth, and the life; no man cometh unto the Father, but by me,'" said the rector. "Let us pray."

He was almost to the door of the vestibule, following the crowd out of the chapel and looking at the carved words in the lintel beneath the choir loft—"The Lord Shall Preserve Thy Going Out and Thy Coming In"—when someone tapped him on the shoulder. It was Dangler's sister's son, a tall teenage boy with acne, wearing a blue blazer with the Andover crest.

"Excuse may, Mr. Cobb," said the boy, flashing Cobb a self-conscious prep-school grin. "I don't know whether you remember me or not. I'm . . ."

"Yes. Yes. I know who you are," said Cobb, shaking the boy's hand.

"Very nice, didn't you think? Mother didn't want any eulogies or hymns or that kind of thing."

The boy had a loud, adenoidal voice. They were holding up people behind them.

"Yes, it was very nice," said Cobb, and began to move forward again. "Please give your mother my regards."

"Actually, it was Aunt Erica who sent me over. She would like to see you in the reception rhum, if you have the time."

"All right," said Cobb. "Tell her I'll be right there."

The boy grinned unattractively and backed off with his hands in his gray flannel pockets, bumping into people behind him. Though he looked hard, Cobb could see nothing of Dangler in his face either.

The reception room was a comfortable place with armchairs, a green rug, and paintings on the walls of former St. James rectors holding prayer books. Erica was not there. Cobb walked around the room, looking into the sturdy faces of the rectors, until she came.

"Andy," she said from the door. Cobb turned around, suddenly dry-mouthed. "God, I'm so *glad* to see you."

It was as if nothing had happened. Hugging her in the middle of the room, his face buried in her neck and smelling her hair, his hands on her strong back, it felt to Cobb as though nothing in the last six months had happened; it was as if Dangler were right outside the door, full of some new plan to tell Cobb about over lunch at 21.

Erica was smiling at him. She looked healthy and calm, without a trace of tension in her eyes, and a bit heavier than the last time he had seen her.

"Are you coming to the River Club with us? Peter and Weezy will die if they miss you."

"I'd like to," said Cobb, "but I have to get back. I'm selling my house, and I have to meet the surveyor this afternoon. I did want to see you, though. You look wonderful."

"You're leaving Concord?"

"I'm moving back down South. I don't know exactly where yet—I suppose I'll stay with my sister for a while. I'm not even sure what I'm going to do. Only that it won't be divorce cases."

"Good for you," said Erica. She smiled again. "What about that pushy woman who's in love with you? Your secretary, isn't it?"

"Grace," Cobb said. "She'll be staying in Concord."

Erica looked at him, her green eyes bright and sane. Cobb couldn't get over how whole she looked, and fresh.

"*I* love you too, you know," she said.

"And I love you. Very much."

"Us. You love *us* very much."

Cobb thought she meant herself and Dangler, and the comment shocked him.

"I'm pregnant." She took his face in her hands, her eyes sparkling. "Over four months. Isn't that wonderful?"

"It certainly is," Cobb said. Without thinking, he added, "I hope it's a girl."

"A girl would be fine. If it's a girl I can name her Divina. A boy would be fine too, though—a Kenneth the fourth."

"What are you going to do? Ames told me you sold the camp."

"Stay in my mother's apartment in Boston until . . . well, for a while. And then we're going to Greece. I want to rent a big white place on the sea with bougainvillea and a sand beach, where all our friends can come and visit. Oh, by the way, I have something for you." She opened her purse and took out an envelope. "These are some of the pictures Divina took at the camp. I had them developed, and I wanted you to have them."

"Thank you," said Cobb. He put the envelope in his pocket and looked at the green rug. "I have a question. You don't have to answer if you don't want to. After we got down off the cliff, before the ambulance came, did you say something to me?"

"I said that no one had ever done anything for him half as important as what you had just done. Getting all of us down. It's true, you know—you gave him his first complete act."

"I just wondered," said Cobb.

They walked out of the empty church together arm in arm, and he kissed her good-bye at the top of the steps. Below them was a waiting limousine and a chauffeur standing beside it. In the back, Cobb could see Dangler's sister, her husband and her son.

"We made it, didn't we, Andy?" Erica said, her voice happy and strong. "I mean, we all came through onto the other side of things. Except for Divina, and she was already there. We really *are* sort of survivors, don't you think so?" She dropped her head and looked up at Cobb, tilting the brim of her hat against the sun. She smiled, looking perched at the top of some secret delight. "Keep in touch with us," she said, and ran down the steps.

Cobb watched her get into the limousine. He watched the limousine drive away, and after it was gone he looked up and down Madison Avenue, admiring the handsome buzz of the Upper East Side. He felt strangely buoyant now, and he wanted to do something before he flew back to Boston and drove to Concord to meet the surveyor, but he couldn't think of anything in particular to do. Across the street was a Mediterranean shop, and a drugstore advertising discounted vitamins. Farther up the block was a sandwich shop. And within walking distance, he knew, were dozens of art galleries. What he really wanted, when he thought about it, was to eat. He couldn't think of a good restaurant nearby, so he trotted down the steps, crossed the street and went into the sandwich shop.

He sat in a booth with a view of Madison Avenue and ordered a cheeseburger and a milk shake. Then he took the envelope of Divina's pictures from his pocket and opened it. They were three-by-five black-and-white prints, and when he spread them out on the table and looked at them, the pictures seemed to set into motion a whole parade for him, marching out of the early fall and into winter. He could hear the voices of the people, the loons on the lake, the wind whistling out of Canada. He could see the turning leaves and the V's of migrating geese. As he fooled with the photographs, trying them out in different relationships like pieces of a puzzle, he began to think he could see some direction to the parade, some shadow of the route that had led to the frozen top of Mount Webster. He couldn't be sure, but he knew that if it was there he would find it sooner or later.

It had been an expensive parade, and a doomed one, but Cobb felt no regret and no sense of waste now. Mostly, looking at the pictures, he felt glad to see himself in them —glad for some visual proof that he had bugled or drummed, at least once, in something larger than he could ever have mounted himself.

When his food came he stacked the pictures and put them away, knowing that it would be some time before he looked at them again. And then, simply because he felt like it, he decided to cancel his appointment with the surveyor and spend the night in New York. He would get a room— or better yet, a suite—at some first-rate hotel. And tomorrow, Cobb decided—he would start off tomorrow by buying himself some new clothes.

Divina Otis Thayer

Kenneth & Erica

Fords on "runaway" horses

The Watermans

Norris Fish's Boar

Rocque on Revelation

Divina, Erica, & I on the back terrace
the week D. came.

Dangler Island

Watermans

Weezy & Ames

Adrian Ford   weezy Bigelow

Fords campfire service

Watemans, Tit, Sithee

Beauchamp   Ford

Fish

Charlotte

Madeline

Ames   Rocque

David Tyndall

Bigelows

Erica's friend
from Boston

Fish & Cravens shooting "boxed birds."

Bigelows & Waterman's on track.

Si'Thee & Ames

The First Expedition

Hanspeter Gruenig

Erica with Major Black

Phase II

The Last Expedition

Revelation Cliff

Historic Dangler Mansion Burns:
Colby Selectman Suspects Arson

See Story P. 11